The Fifth Kingdom

The Fifth Kingdom

A NOVEL ABOUT THE SPANISH-PORTUGUESE JEWS

JANE FRANCES AMLER

iUniverse

The Fifth Kingdom
A Novel About The Spanish-Portuguese Jews

iUniverse books may be ordered through booksellers or by contacting:

iUniverse LLC
1663 Liberty Drive
Bloomington, IN 47403
www.iuniverse.com
1-800-Authors (1-800-288-4677)

ISBN: 978-1-4620-5297-4 (sc)
ISBN: 978-1-4620-5299-8 (hc)
ISBN: 978-1-4620-5298-1 (e)

Printed in the United States of America

iUniverse rev. date: 08/25/2014

Christopher Columbus's Jewish Roots (Aronson 1991); Haym Salomon: Patriot Banker of the American Revolution (PowerPlus Books 2004); The Color of His Blood, aka J.F. Lewis (iuniverse 2009)

Dedicated with much love to my family

Acknowledgements

I am indebted to my father, the late Alfred Benjamin Amler, a direct descendant of Don Isaac Abravanel, and to my mother, the late Annette Amler, both of whom instilled in me a love for history and pride in our family's ancestry. Larry, Scott and Jessica, Michael and Stacey, and my little ones, all my life's work is for you. I could not have written this novel without the guiding lights of Drs. Shelby and Martin A. Cohen. I also wish to acknowledge my cherished friend, the late Mary Cheever, for her editorial help and encouragement, and to Linsey Abrams for her inspirational advice. I want to thank Elizabeth Lewis, at Manhattanville College, and Michael Signorile for so carefully editing the manuscript. To my family and friends, thank you for your support. In loving memory, I wish to thank Pamela Adler Golden who never wavered in her enthusiasm for this novel.

Every effort has been made to represent historical events and historical characters accurately. All other characters, including Abravanel's wife, brother-in-law, female characters, and enemies within the royal courts and Church are fictitious.

Portugal
House of Avis

Manuel I-Isabella (Grandson of King Duarte-Isabella-Daughter of Spanish Catholic Monarchs) 1495-1521

João II 1481-1495

Isabel-**Afonso V** 1438-1481 Leonora Joanna Fernando
　　　　　　　　　　　Fernando Duke of Braganza (Son of
　　　　　　　　　　　Afonso, Duke of Braganza)

Lenora-**Duarte I** 1433-1438 **Pedro Henry João Fernando**
　　　　　　　　　　　Afonso-Duke of Braganza
　　　　　　　　　　　(Illegitimate son of João I)

　　　　　　　João I 1385-1433-Phillippa

Spain
House of Castile and Aragon

Juana-Philip　　　　**Isabella-Manuel I**　　Juan Maria **Catherine**
of Hapsburg　　　　　　　　　　　　　　　　　　　**of Aragon**

Isabella the Catholic—Ferdinand the Catholic
Queen of Castile 1474-1504 King of Aragon 1479-1516

Infanta Juana　　　　　　　　**King of Aragon-Juan II**
　　　　　　　　　　　　　　　　　1458-1479
King of Castile-Enríque 1454-1474

Modified from original: W.L.Langer, ed. *An Encyclopedia of World History.* Boston: Houghton Mifflin, 1972. 309. Highlighted historic characters are mentioned in the novel.

CHAPTER 1

Clutching his father's sweated hand, seven-year-old Isaac Abravanel was mesmerized by the enormous white sails of Prince Henry's caravels as they gracefully sank into themselves while bearded, barefooted sailors hurried to tie them down. Standing on his tiptoes at the wharf in Lisbon, Portugal, 1444, Isaac felt his stomach summersault when he saw for the first time King Afonso, who was so young he had no trace of beard. Astride a diamond and gold caparisoned white stallion, the young king passed them, smiled, and gave a slight nod of acknowledgment. Isaac beamed up at this father, so proud that the king had noticed them. However, as the regent, Don Pedro, trotted past them on an equally adorned creamy mare, he ignored the even deeper bows of Isaac, his father, his father's friend, Count Barcellas, and the count's son and grandson. When the trumpeters' horns blared, Isaac tried to pull his hands up to shield his ears from the hot, bellowing noise, but his father, Don Judah Abravanel, tightened his grip so that he could not. Now knights in armor, on sleek black and brown Arabian steeds, all equally covered in jewels, followed the king out to greet Captain Antão Gonçalves and valiant crew as they rowed skiffs in from the caravels. With his father's hand still clenched around his own, Isaac cringed when he saw black men, women, and children, their legs and wrists shackled in iron chains, blood crusted where iron met skin, prodded like sheep out of the skiffs. He also glimpsed gold shimmering within canvas bags that landed with heavy thuds onto the piers lining the wharf. Though they were close to the water, Count Barcellas's position, as a bastard prince of the royal House of Avis, placed them a hundred yards away from where the captain and sailors were coming ashore. While the spectators pushed and jostled for a better view, Isaac was buffeted about as he tried to see between the wool-stocking legs of men and women's skirts. He grew frustrated because the unfolding scene seemed like mismatched pieces in a puzzle.

"Let's get closer to the water," Jonathan Ben Ezra said. Though two years older than Isaac, Jonathan was his closest friend.

"May I, father?" Isaac pulled on his father's hand and begged.

Don Judah Abravanel bent down to hear him.

"May I go with Jonathan?" he repeated.

His father nodded yes, let go of his hand, and then turned back to his discussion with Count Barcellas and Jacob Ben Ezra, Jonathan's father.

Following Jonathan into the crowd, Isaac squeezed between noblemen and women dressed in fine linen, satin, velvet, and silk in a rainbow of colors. He passed Moors, other Jews, jesters, troubadours, and merchants selling bright copper pots, vibrant red, blue, and yellow pottery, silver and gold filigreed glass goblets and beads, mirrors, razor-sharp knives and swords. As they walked further away from the king's entourage, Isaac passed men and women in tattered clothes, dogs gnawing on old bones, horse dung, fish heads with grey eyes staring back at him. Elbowed by rough children with angry scars, cuts, and bruises on their faces, arms and legs, Jonathan led Isaac out onto the next pier and inched their way toward the end for a better view. Isaac looked down to see the thick pilings in the muddy water, gently lapping below, soaking the slimy wood. They finally found a space just behind a tall red-headed lad.

Standing on a wooden podium built for the majestic occasion, with the king and regent by his side, Prince Henry raised his arms to silence the crowd. In his black hat and cape, looking more like a sea captain than a prince, Isaac recognized Henry, often referred to as the Navigator, for Isaac had accompanied his father twice to the royal castle and had listened to the men discuss complex financial transactions. Isaac peered over the shoulder of the red-headed lad, who turned and stared at him, annoyed by his proximity.

"He's a court page," Jonathan whispered, pulling Isaac back. "I wonder why he's not with the royal party?"

Isaac was impressed with Jonathan's seemingly unlimited knowledge and stared reverently at the back of the page's beautiful blue and white satin tunic, and then up again at Prince Henry.

Henry began, "My liege, noblemen of Lisbon." He bowed to the king and then turned to the crowd. "Captain Antão Gonçalves and his crew have just dared to sail once again into dark and dangerous waters. With God's grace, the good captain eluded vile sea serpents, forged a path through perilous storms, and finally reached the golden lands of Africa!

We must praise Him who has guided our heroes safely and helped them achieve our first and foremost goal: to bring the true faith to the far reaches of the Earth. Let us give thanks to our Savior, the Lord Jesus Christ."

All assembled bowed their heads in grateful prayer, but the excited crowd could not be silenced for long. Isaac looked around him as people began to chant a frenzied "Long live King Afonso! Long live Prince Henry!"

The chanting swelled into a roar until Henry finally waved his arms for silence. When the noise had subsided, he continued.

"Our second goal is to find Prester John and his kingdom of treasures. Prester John was blessed by God and led to a land where miraculous fountains bring youth to the aged, where stones taken from the enchanted earth can restore sight to the blind, and where emeralds, rubies, diamonds, and gold are as plentiful as grains of sand. Our greatest quest is to find this kingdom and Prester John for he will teach us how to cure disease and to eliminate famine and war! Henceforth, I dedicate my ships, my fortunes, my life to finding the divine kingdom, and the holy man who dwells within it."

Isaac watched, fascinated as men and women in well worn capes and muddy boots clapped their hands, stamped their feet, and shouted over and over, "Long live King Afonso! Long live Prince Henry!" Their unrestrained shouting frightened him so that he inched closer to Jonathan. King Afonso's uncle and regent, Don Pedro, raised his arms and tried to silence the crowd, but his efforts were futile until he finally had trumpets sounded. Like water thrown on a roaring fire, the noise began to hiss, spurt, and then dissipate until, at last, Don Pedro nodded to his brother, and Henry continued.

"On this great occasion, I proudly present to King Afonso slaves and gold from Africa, and I vow to find Prester John and his kingdom!"

Pushed from behind, Isaac accidentally bumped into the red-headed page, causing him to fall into a puddle and splash muddy water across his fine tunic. A fat man began to laugh, as the page stood, trying to brush off the mud stains. The page turned. When he realized that it was Isaac, the Jewish treasurer's son who had pushed him, he was furious.

"What were you trying to do, boy, stab me?" the page cried. A ragged group of men gathered around the boys, staring with indignation at Isaac.

"We better go," Jonathan said, trying to pull Isaac back, but the page unsheathed his knife and waved it menacingly. Jonathan stepped between Isaac and the knife.

"Stand aside," the page said, pushing Jonathan away. "Look how scared he is!" Growing brazen as more men surrounded the boys, he turned back to Isaac and Jonathan. "Where's your knife, boy? You used it fast enough behind my back!"

"I have no knife!" Isaac cried.

"Leave him alone," Jonathan interrupted. "He's Don Judah's son, and you know very well Jews are not allowed to carry knives."

But when the men realized that a Jewish boy had pushed the page, they encouraged him to fight for his honor. The page pointed his knife close to Isaac's face.

"Down on your knees. Down!" He ordered, the men cheering him on.

"Do as he says," Jonathan whispered. "I'll find your father." Jonathan quickly disappeared into the crowd.

Isaac could feel the blood draining from his face as he fell to his knees.

"Please," he said softly, for his voice was failing, "I meant no harm . . . . I have no knife!"

"Ha! Do you hear that? He lies like the devil himself!" The page continued to threaten him, pointing the knife at his throat; Isaac watched as it came closer, touching his neck, and felt the heat of the page's breath as he shouted, "Down, Jew, down on your face, and rub it in the mud where it belongs!"

Desperately fighting to control his tears, Isaac could not understand the page's anger. He had only bumped into him by accident. He bent down, thinking, "Please hurry, father!" Then, in a stronger, louder voice, "Please, sir, please. I meant no harm." Where was Jonathan? His father? Peering between the legs of the men surrounded him, he searched the crowd, looking for his father, Jonathan, anybody who could help, but when he looked up, all he saw was hatred in the faces threatening to engulf him. He pressed his cheek to the ground.

"Now rub your face in it."

"No," he answered, tears streaming down his cheeks. His father had taught him to be proud of his Judaism. Why was this boy so enraged? He hadn't meant to hurt him.

"Do it!" the page cried, as the crowd closed in on the boys, fanning the page's wrath.

"No." He gritted his teeth. He wouldn't put his face in the mud.

The page lunged, but Isaac rolled onto his side, causing the older boy to slip on the slimy wood and drop the knife. Isaac picked it up, stood, and began to run when he felt a hand grab his leg, tripping him. He fell. The page was on him, reaching for the knife when in one desperate effort, Isaac struck out, catching the side of the page's face with the knife. The boy rolled over, screaming, holding his hand over his eye, blood oozing down his cheek. In disbelief, Isaac saw blood on the blade still in his fist.

As the page struggled to his feet, he dropped his hand for a moment. Isaac inched back, staring at the blood streaming from the corner of the page's eye. Shaking, sobbing, Isaac couldn't believe he had caused this, wished with all his heart and soul he hadn't, didn't understand how it had happened.

"Place the boy under arrest!" two huge men cried as they grabbed him.

Isaac could feel nothing but his heart thudding in his chest, neck, throat. The men were choking him. Then just as suddenly, they let go. Isaac fell back trying to catch his breath as the crowd parted for Count Barcellas, his father, and Jonathan.

Wailing uncontrollably, clutching his eye, the page sank back onto the pier. Still shaking, Isaac stood alone, a wave of nausea swept over him when he saw his father's face turn ashen.

"What's happened here?" The count stopped short, recognizing the wounded page, Carlos Málaga, a bastard of the royal house. Count Barcellas turned and saw Isaac holding the knife. "You, boy, aren't you Don Judah's son?"

Isaac stepped forward to speak, but he couldn't form words.

"Aren't you Don Judah's son? Answer me!"

Finally, "Yes, my lord," came out.

A man, in a long black velvet cloak, pushed his way forward to address the count.

"My lord," he bowed, "I am witness to the whole fight. This child maliciously stabbed the page."

"That's not so, my lord," piped a small voice in the crowd. Count Barcellas turned to see his grandson, Prince Fernando, making his way toward them.

"Did you see what happened, Fernando?"

"Yes, my lord. From where we were standing, I saw Isaac accidentally bump into Carlos. With no warning at all, Carlos began to argue with him and unsheathed his knife. He forced him to the ground, and then Isaac tried to defend himself."

"You lie!" screamed Carlos. "The boy had the knife. He's still holding it."

All eyes turned toward Isaac, who looked down, terrified to see the bloody knife in his hand.

"Isaac, is that your knife?"

"No, my lord." He couldn't stop the trembling that overwhelmed him and dropped the knife.

"He lies! He lies!" Carlos cried.

Fernando spoke up again.

"My lord, you know that Jews are not allowed to carry knives. Look!" he said as he pointed to Carlos's empty sheath. "There's no knife and look at Isaac; he's not even wearing a sheath. Carlos threatened him with his own knife."

There was a hush amongst the onlookers when the Count Barcellas turned his fury on Carlos who was still doubled over in pain.

"Normally, I'd have you rot in the dungeons, boy! You've insulted my grandson by saying that he lies. You've attacked an innocent child, Don Judah's son. It seems, however, you've earned a just reward for your actions. Someone see to it that his face is properly bandaged."

He had begun to usher Isaac, Don Judah, Jonathan, and Fernando away when Carlos Málaga cried, "If my father were alive, the lad would be put to death!"

Count Barcellas's face reddened as he stared at Carlos and then at the king's regent, Don Pedro, who was with the king, holding heavy ledgers, counting bags of gold. Don Pedro looked up to see that Málaga had been injured but showed no emotion and turned back to his ledgers.

"Take him away," Count Barcellas ordered, and Carlos was ushered off.

There was angry talk amongst the crowd. It was unprecedented for a member of the royal family to side with a Jew, but Count Barcellas's orders were followed.

Away from the motley crowd, back toward the king and his entourage, clutching his father's hand, Isaac heard him say in a low voice, "I'm eternally grateful to you, my lord, for saving my son from that mob."

"Nonsense, Judah," said Barcellas, waving his hand in a grand gesture. "It obviously wasn't Isaac's fault, but we must be very careful to be judicious, especially before hungry men looking for trouble. I'm afraid, my dear friend, that even though the Jews have been here for centuries, there are many in our kingdom who would bring harm to you and your people." His eyes were fixed on Don Pedro, his half-brother, whom he despised. Only Prince Henry kept an uneasy peace within the royal house. Don Pedro had won the regency from Count Barcellas and the Queen Mother, Leonora. This incident would only serve to heighten the tension between the two most powerful men in Portugal.

In hushed tones, Judah Abravanel continued, "I am well aware of our regent's new policies toward my people, my lord, and you can be sure that we were distraught when you and Queen Leonora lost the regency in the courts."

"Queen Leonora, yes," Count Barcellas said in a hushed tone. "Pedro will pay for Leonora. He will pay for her death."

He glanced over his shoulder and continued in an even quieter voice, just above a whisper to Judah, "Someday King Afonso will learn the truth about his mother's death. I will see to that. And this young Carlos Málaga, he must learn the truth about his parents. He thinks his father was the late King Duarte, poor boy. Someday he must learn the truth, Judah."

"That would not be wise for many reasons, my lord," Judah answered quietly. Count Barcellas and Judah stared at each other, no words passed between them for a long moment. Clearly, they knew something about Carlos Málaga that Isaac did not. Then the count sadly shook his head and patted Judah on the shoulder.

"My trusted treasurer, my trusted friend, Judah, it amazes me that you are so content with your life as a Jew. This incident with Isaac, for example, would never have happened if you were Christian," he said, trying to regain a normal tone. He turned to his son and grandson, Fernando senior and junior, who had followed them down to the water.

"Did you know that Judah's father was Don Juan Sanchez de Sevilla, high treasurer to the Castilian king, a direct descendant of the Biblical King David?" Turning back to Judah, he asked, "I can't understand why your father converted back to Judaism?"

Isaac stared up at his father, towering above him, and heard him reply, "My father could no longer face his life as it was in Castile. In his heart, he was always a Jew, and he could not live with the hypocrisy. It's true we live behind the gates of the Judería, but here, in Portugal, we are free to worship God as He has commanded us. We can honor the Sabbath, light the candles, and say the prayers that have been our sustenance for so many centuries. My father could not turn his back on who he was, on what his people had sacrificed for him, for me, for my sons." Don Judah gazed down at Isaac.

"A heretic . . . in Castile . . . I was unaware. But here in Portugal, you can't even come and go as you please. Is it worth giving up the life of a free man?" the Count queried, meaning no malice.

"Perhaps in our lifetime we will be free of the walls that separate us. You and I, my lord, can teach our people that we are not so very different, just good men trying to live decent lives," Judah answered.

At that moment, the trumpets sounded for King Afonso, Don Pedro, and Prince Henry to leave, and all paid homage to their young sovereign and his entourage as they mounted their jewel caparisoned horses: emeralds, sapphires, diamonds, opals, lapis lazuli, silver and gold winking in the sunlight. The royal party waved to the cheering crowd. Don Judah, Count Barcellas, his son and grandson, the Ben Ezras, Don Judah and Isaac, all bowed with the others before their king.

Following ceremonial protocol, Count Barcellas and Fernando senior and junior, who were all on foot, were next in line to leave. But as the young Prince Fernando passed before Isaac, he stopped. Isaac bowed, and when he looked up, his eyes met Fernando's.

"Thank you, my lord," Isaac whispered, for he was still shaking.

"I hope we shall be friends," Fernando answered.

"I hope so too," Isaac whispered.

Their eyes locked only for a moment, but a bond was formed that neither the political intrigues of the royal Portuguese House of Avis, nor the Royal Trustamaras of Castile could destroy. Fernando trailed behind his father and grandfather, mounted steeds waiting for them, and they followed the royal party into the heart of Lisbon.

"This child will never again accompany me to a royal ceremony!" Judah fumed as he entered their home. Holding the infant Miriam in her arms, Isaac's mother, Sarah, came forward to greet them, but Judah strode past her. Judah was so enraged that Isaac saw his older brother, Samuel, press his back to the wall, shivering. As Don Judah entered his library, Isaac tried to hide under the hood of his cape.

"What happened, Judah? You're frightening him!" Sarah cried.

"He should be frightened! He practically blinded Carlos Málaga!" Judah threw off his cape.

Sarah handed the infant to Samuel and knelt beside Isaac, pressing him close.

"How did this happen?" she whispered, stoking Isaac's hair. "Poor Carlos."

Holding his breath, his body rigid, he knew she could not help, could not change what had happened. He adored his father and would have done anything to please him. He had never seen him so furious and wanted to crawl deep into the earth, never to come out. But his mother's words, "Poor Carlos," sprang at him, striking him more painfully than his father's wrath.

"He attacked me."

"I'm not surprised," she muttered, rocking him in her arms.

"Isaac!" Judah called from the library. Isaac pulled away from his mother's embrace and marched into the room. Judah slammed the heavy oak door.

Surrounded by a costly collection of manuscripts, Judah strode to his intricately carved wooden chair, his eyes glaring down at Isaac, and when he spoke, the words seemed to reverberate around the room.

"Do you realize you could have been sent to the dungeons for what you did? You endangered the life of a member of the royal house!"

"Papa, I . . ."

"Silence!" Judah thundered from his wooden throne. "Sunlight would never strike your face again. It would be as if you were buried alive with nothing but molded bread and putrid water to eat and drink. Rats would gnaw at your flesh until there would be nothing left of you but bones."

His face reddened, Judah stood and lifted his arm as if to strike. Isaac shrank back, more afraid of his father than of rats, putrid water, cold, dark dungeons, or Carlos Málaga.

"No, Papa, don't!" Isaac cried, shielding himself. "I didn't mean to hurt him! He wanted me to rub my face in muck because I am a Jew." His voice broke, but gathering strength, he looked up and seeing his father's arm fall, he gained some courage and continued. "He was angry with me because I'm Jewish. Why, Papa, why? Why was he so angry?" Uncontrollable tears were streaming down his face. He didn't understand any of it, not Carlos' hatred, his father's anger, nor his mother's pity for Carlos.

"Isaac," his father said in a low but stern voice. He bent down, now, speaking to him face to face, his lengthy beard inches from Isaac's chin, his hands gripping Isaac's shoulders, his fingers pressing into Isaac's shoulder bone, hurting him. "You must learn to be very careful in the world outside our Judería. You were right not to bend to Carlos's hatred, but you must remember you are my son!"

Judah released him and stood up, towering over him. "As treasurer to the royal house, I represent not only my own family, but all the Jews of Portugal. Their safety and security are in my hands and the hands of only a few other Jewish men who have access to the royal house, like Jonathan's father, Jacob Ben Ezra. One incident like this can destroy years of gaining favor in the royal court. You will follow me as treasurer someday, Isaac. Not Samuel, but you, Isaac, you have the mind it takes to be a treasurer to the royal house. You will follow me just as I followed my father. That is why the Abravanels move freely between the Christian world and our own. The royal house depends on us to help them rule the kingdom. Someday you will become a great treasurer, and it will be your job, no, your duty, to work for the safety and security of our people. This is something you must learn, to hide your own feelings, and to always work for what is most important: the security of our people." Judah stood and retreated to his desk.

"I didn't mean to hurt him, Papa . . . ."

"But you did!" Judah answered, leaning across the great desk, growing angry again. "And with your actions you've jeopardized the security of the whole Judería!" He slammed his fist against the hard dark wood. "Now, go to your chambers!"

Weeping, Isaac ran past his mother, who was waiting to comfort him, past Samuel whose face was ashen, to his room. He could hear his mother shouting that his father was to blame, that he should never have let him go off alone. He could hear his father arguing with her, something he had never heard. Now his parents were angry with each other because of him, because he had hurt Carlos. Exhausted, his body tense, Isaac began to think about the wounded Carlos. When he closed his eyes, he saw Carlos's face, blood oozing from the corner of his eye. Isaac's throat felt tight, and it seemed as if the room were spinning. He ran to the open window. How could it have happened? He wondered, panic stricken.

"I didn't mean to hurt him. Why does he hate me? Papa, forgive me! Please, Papa!" he cried. He turned back to his bed and threw himself down.

After what seemed to be an eternity, Isaac fell asleep. At first, visions of Carlos standing over him, the knife next to his throat, appeared; then rousing, he shuddered. He tried to stay awake to keep the visions away, but his eyes would not stay open. He sank into a deep sleep and felt as if his soul were lifting from his body, floating over a peaceful ocean with one wave rolling gently after another, as if it were trying to wash clean his troubles. He continued to rise into the night sky and become lost in the heavens. From far away, he saw a black cloud emerge and move toward him, taking on different shapes as it came. One of the forms was grotesque—Carlos's bloodied face, then a stallion was rearing, a rider on his back. The nightrider drew closer, growing larger, looming over him. Slumped forward in his saddle, a black hood concealing his face, the rider seemed weary, but the horse continued to move forward, lifting one heavy hoof after the other, coming closer, closer, and then just as Isaac reached out to touch him, he vanished.

Isaac felt a cold wind sweep into the room from the open window, waking him. Shivering, he rose and walked to the narrow slit to stare out into the night sky, expecting to see the unknown figure riding away. The stars were brilliant, and as he stared at them, he felt as if they were swirling about him, catching him up into the universe itself. Feeling dizzy, lightheaded, he wondered if he had been dreaming or had actually seen a spirit of the night. As he watched and waited for the rider to return, his head began to nod, his legs collapse beneath him. Huddling against the stone wall, he fell asleep.

CHAPTER 2

Portugal had become a wealthy land in the five years since Captain Antão Gonçalves had returned from Africa with slaves and gold. Secure within the womb-like walls of the Judería, the twelve-year-old Isaac only ventured out when his father demanded his presence. He was content to walk down the narrow streets of the Judería and watch the merchants sell their wares: cloth in forest greens, yellows, blues and reds; cheeses, olives, lemons, oranges, figs, and dates, hanging in bunches straight from the orchards. The flies buzzed around the butcher shops where meat was drained of blood and then blessed. Friendly merchants gave Isaac honey-nut cakes to munch as he walked home from school. He enjoyed pretending not to hear the old wives whisper about his math wizardry. They all worried about how little he ate. Hannah, in her old brown patched cloak, always stuffed almonds in his pocket. Men and women loved to gossip about Sarah and Judah, criticizing them behind their backs.

"Isaac is much too thin. Don't they feed him at home? Now Jonathan, there is a handsome lad. He's so tall and filled out already! So gorgeous!" they chattered. And though he let the gossip slip down his back, Isaac had to admit that Jonathan Ben Ezra, his closest friend, was handsome indeed. With his beautiful, strong muscular body, golden hair, blue eyes, and clever mind, Jonathan was everything Isaac wasn't. Constantly stumbling over his own feet, uncomfortable with his growing body, Isaac felt awkward, incompetent next to Jonathan. He would be sitting next to Jonathan tonight at Count Barcellas' royal banquet. It was the first time he had been invited to such an affair, and he felt more secure facing the Portuguese nobility, knowing that Jonathan would be by his side. He hoped and prayed that he would not see the page, Carlos Málaga, whom he had hurt so long ago.

That evening, sitting upon his horse next to his father and brother, Samuel, outside the Barcellas castle, Isaac watched the nobility enter. Dressed in fine velvet cloaks, he saw ladies gracefully descend from their litters and escorted into the castle, which was glowing with the light of a thousand candles. He watched Don Pedro enter the castle as well, and then leaned forward in his saddle to ask his father, "Have Don Pedro and Count Barcellas settled their differences? Prince Fernando told me that Don Pedro has made the Count a Duke!"

Judah raised his eyebrows and stared at Isaac before he answered.

"It's true. Don Pedro has bestowed the title of Duke of Braganza upon Count Barcellas. However, I'm afraid their differences are far from settled. After King Afonso married Don Pedro's daughter, Isabel, they were forced to make peace with one another."

"But I don't understand, Father. If Don Pedro still doesn't like Count Barcellas, why would he have made him a duke?"

"Barcellas was prepared to declare war, son. It is hoped that the new title for Barcellas, along with the marriage of Don Pedro's daughter to the king, will ease the tension that has been building in the royal house. Remember to address Count Barcellas as the Duke of Braganza, when you see him."

Isaac and his brother nodded and patiently waited until the nobility had entered the castle. At last their names were called, and they were admitted. The guests were seated at tables which lined the great banquet hall, and Isaac's eyes feasted on silver and gold goblets and plates, on fowl simmering in orange sauces, on lobster, shrimp, mussels, clams, and chorizo bedded on saffron rice, food that were forbidden to Jews. The smoky scent of roasting pig also filled the great hall. The finest red and white wines were served. A tall thin man, wearing a brightly striped jacket and black hat, wove in and out of the tables, strumming his strange guitar, singing ballads about Portugal's past.

Isaac was relieved to see the Ben Ezra family already seated. Jacob Ben Ezra, Jonathan's father, was one of the most respected jewelers in Portugal. Jacob, Jonathan and his sister, Rebecca, were discreetly eating fruits, vegetables, and cheese from the great banquet table. Isaac slipped in between his brother and Jonathan. He nodded to Rebecca, his betrothed, but she cast her eyes down, too shy to acknowledge his greeting.

After King Afonso had finished eating, Isaac, Samuel and Jonathan were called to be presented. The Jewish boys stood and made their way to the king's table and bowed. Isaac had not seen the king in five years and was surprised to find him a grown man with silky black hair and inquisitive brown eyes. The king addressed him: "Aren't you the young lad who had a scuffle with my page a few years ago? I believe it was at the royal ceremony for Gonçalves."

"Yes, Your Majesty," Isaac answered staring at the tile floor, startled and frightened that the king had remembered the incident. What had his father said to him that night?-that one incident could jeopardize the Jews of Portugal.

"Málaga!" The king called. A tall red-headed young man with a black patch over his right eye stepped forward from the king's private guard. "I believe you owe this lad an apology."

Isaac's knees grew weak; the red-headed boy had grown into a man well over six feet tall. Towering over Isaac, Carlos spit out an apology, but before he had been properly dismissed, he eased his way behind Don Pedro and disappeared.

Isaac noticed Don Pedro's hand gripping the king's shoulder; nothing was said about Málaga's insolence.

Instead, the king continued, seemingly unperturbed, brushing Don Pedro's hand away. "I understand you have quite a way with numbers, and I hope that in the near future you will be of some service to my treasurers."

Isaac was about to answer when, looking up at the king, he was chilled by the hate in Don Pedro's eyes. He was unable to speak. Don Pedro glared a moment longer and then abruptly left the king's side. Relieved, Isaac took a deep breath and answered, "I would be most honored, Your Majesty." More relaxed with Don Pedro's absence, the king continued, "You are a very thin fellow. I think that even though your strength is in the mind, not body, it would be beneficial for you to study with a knightly master, perhaps with Prince Fernando's master. You should be trained in throwing the javelin, fighting with quarterstaff, sword and buckler. Alfonso!"

The Duke of Braganza stepped forward and bowed.

"I should like Isaac to spend more time with Prince Fernando."

"It shall be done, sire," the Duke of Braganza answered with a deep bow, winking at Isaac.

"Would you like that, Isaac, to be able to fight at my side should the need arise?"

"I should like to serve you in any way I can, your majesty," Isaac answered. He bowed and melted back into the crowded room.

The room seemed to reel. Ladies laughing, their white teeth shining, men holding their fat bellies as they drank and ate, all swam before him, circling him, engulfing him. The king had asked for his services! He wanted him to serve his treasurers, to learn to become a knight! But the hatred in Don Pedro's eyes also stunned him, making him wonder if he dared to serve the king. The news of the king's proposition to Isaac was whispered about, and as he listened to the lords and ladies gossiping, he smiled, for it was indeed a great honor! Judah managed to find him and embrace him. His brother, Samuel, and Jonathan pounced on him like exuberant pups, and the boys bounded out of the room. Prince Fernando, now a tall, dark lad of twelve, caught up with his friends in the courtyard as they pranced about, celebrating Isaac's good fortune. They stopped abruptly, however, when they saw Fernando's father and grandfather arguing in hushed tones in the far corner of the yard.

"I'll not go on with this plotting. I've had enough! You're talking like a madman, and I'll have no part in it," Fernando's father said. The boys ducked behind the lush greenery, afraid now of being seen.

"I tell you, Fernando, Pedro has to be stopped or he will destroy the kingdom. King Afonso is charmed by Isabel, and he listens to her as if she were court council. She is a mouthpiece for her father. Pedro has more power over the king than ever before," the duke said.

"He's just made you a duke! How can you say Pedro wants to crush the nobility when he has given you more power? I'll not spread lies! If you must continue this mischief, then leave me out. I want no part of it! Do you understand?"

"I'm doing this for you. Don't you see? With Pedro disgraced, we will become the most powerful house in Portugal. Your son might someday be king!"

Isaac didn't dare look at Fernando but could feel the blood surging to his ears, his friend, his Fernando, king!

"Now you're speaking of high treason! I will not listen to this anymore." Fernando's father abruptly left the courtyard and returned to the other guests.

The duke was following him when King Afonso wandered out of the great hall into the open air.

"Your Majesty." The duke bowed to the king. "I'm glad you've come out into the fresh air, away from the heat of the party."

"It's a lovely evening," King Afonso said, taking the duke's arm and strolling back toward a stone bench not four yards from where the boys were hiding. Isaac wanted to flee, to turn to stone, to die.

"You've truly outdone yourself as a host tonight." The king glanced up at the clear stars. "On nights like this I like to think my mother is with me." He turned to stare at the duke. "Tell me, Uncle, do you believe my mother really died of a fever? That's what they told me when I was a child, but I've often wondered. She was so gentle with me. I truly loved her."

He spoke in a quiet voice, but there was tension in it, as if he were searching for some hidden truth.

"Leonora, yes, she was an extraordinarily fine woman. You know, your father actually left the regency to her and to me as well. What difference can it make now?" The duke stood up with his back to the king.

"All the difference!" The king also stood and swung him around to face him. "Tell me, Uncle, why did she go to Castile? Why has the truth been hidden from me? I'm no longer a child. I am the king! I demand to know!"

"She's dead, my liege, let her lie in peace."

Grabbing the duke's cloak, practically strangling him, the king questioned, "Did my mother die a natural death or was she murdered?"

"There were rumors at the time, of course, no one could . . ."

"Tell me what you know!" He shook him. "You were her friend. Do you think I don't know that? How did she die?" still clutching his cloak, choking him.

"It was poison, yes, from the accounts I received at the time . . ."

"Who murdered my mother?" the king said, tightening his grip.

"Pedro," the duke spit the name out. The king let him go and staggered back a step as if he had been stabbed.

"No! My father-in-law? It's not possible!" he whispered, bending over in pain. Then he straightened and stared up at the sky. After a long while, he took a deep breath and looked back at the duke. "Why didn't you tell me this sooner, before I married his daughter? Why did you keep this from me?"

"It was only a rumor and news like that, coming from me," he said, trying to catch his breath. "You must remember Don Pedro won the regency to your throne in the courts. He has enjoyed great power."

"But why did my mother go to Castile?"

"Leonora was distraught when Pedro won the case against us. She went to Spain to have her brother, King Juan of Aragon, raise an army against Pedro, but she never returned. Some say she fell ill, others spoke of poison; only our Lord knows the truth. I never had proof that she was murdered. As I said before, leave it alone. It will only cause you misery."

King Afonso stared at his uncle for a long time before he spoke again. "And Henry? Did he know of this? Why didn't he tell me?"

"Don Pedro was in power, you were a child, and Prince Henry cared only for his ships; as long as they were sailing, he would not interfere. Only I cared, my liege, only I mourned your mother's death."

Staring up at the sky again, Afonso whispered, "She will be avenged! I swear; she will be avenged." Abruptly, he left the courtyard and returned to the great hall.

The duke was following the king when he caught several pairs of eyes staring at him. He pulled Fernando out of the greens. "What have you heard? Tell me!"

"Nothing, Grandfather. We hid ourselves here only so as not to disturb you and the king."

"Come out of the bushes, all of you," the duke ordered.

The boys marched out, hanging their heads low. Isaac dared not look up. "Did any of you hear what passed between the king and me?"

"No, my lord," the boys chimed.

"Well, if you did, and one syllable of it ever escapes from your lips, I'll see to it that your tongues never wag again. Is that understood?" The boys nodded. Brushing off his cloak and straightening his collar, the duke returned to the banquet hall.

Fernando turned to his friends. "My grandfather means what he says. We heard nothing."

The boys nodded and began heading back to the festivities when Jonathan's sister, Rebecca, came running out, colliding with Isaac, and fell on the hard stone of the courtyard. She started to cry for she had bruised her hand, but when she realized that she had bumped into Isaac, she composed herself. Isaac took her hand in his and held it just for an instant. Her hand was so thin that he could see the crisscrossing fine veins, and the red stain of her bruise. He gently dropped it and gave her a bittersweet look. How would this slender child ever grow up to become a woman? He wondered. With the heated conversations still gripping him, and he stared at Rebecca, his betrothed.

Rebecca was the wealthy jeweler's only daughter and had many necklaces of gold, rings of diamond, ruby, and emerald, silken clothes, but she hungered for her mother, Bathsheba, never hearing a warm word from her father. Rebecca had been told that her mother had died shortly after she was born and the cook's long cold stare after she told her this made Rebecca's heart shrink with the thought that her birth had caused her mother's death.

Rebecca had once dared to ask her father about her mother, but his eyes grew misty, and Jacob Ben Ezra walked away, leaving her alone, trembling. She never asked again. And so she watched from behind the crack in her door as Jonathan received all of their father's attention and lavish affection. There was always a fuss over his clothes, his education, and his friends. While Rebecca was left home to embroider cloth for her wedding chest, Jacob paraded Jonathan about. Tonight was the very first night her father had taken her out to be seen, and though her gown was sewn with gold threads, and her hair filled with pearls, she was afraid she might utter one wrong word that would send her back behind the closed doors of her father's house. Rebecca looked into Isaac's eyes for a moment and then withdrew her hand.

Isaac stared sheepishly at Jonathan who, in turn, seemed startled by their childish intimacy. As usual, Isaac felt small, inadequate next to Jonathan, everyone's favorite. Though Isaac sailed brilliantly through his school work, often assigned the same material as Jonathan, Jonathan's two-year age difference gave him the extra edge to beat Isaac in every lesson. Jonathan was always the first one done, with a perfect score; then he would hum and tap his fingers as the other boys struggled to finish. Isaac would always finish second. Jonathan was an excellent rider, able to jump upon a stallion and race off, leaving Isaac far behind as he struggled up on his mare, making a futile effort to catch him. Jonathan was not only Jacob Ben Ezra's pride, but the community's pride, and Isaac and Rebecca stood in his shadow.

Rebecca looked up at Jonathan and said, "Father is looking for you," and then ran back into the banquet hall. Isaac watched her slight, delicate form disappear. It did not occur to him that Rebecca would look different on their wedding day, and he wondered how this fragile little girl would make a suitable wife. He turned back to see Jonathan laughing.

"I really don't see the humor in holding a little girl's hand!" He felt furious, impotent before the golden-haired fourteen year old.

"I'm sorry, Isaac," Jonathan said, making small effort not to laugh, "but if you could have seen your face when she ran out of the courtyard . . . ."

"Jonathan, leave Isaac alone," Samuel interrupted.

"We'll all have to face our matches sooner or later," he added, hoping to appease his brother.

"Just because a match hasn't been made for you, doesn't mean you can torture those of us whose fates are sealed!" Isaac continued to fume.

"Isaac, my father will never settle on a girl for me. Don't you know that? None are pretty enough or rich enough-and I agree!"

"Jonathan, sometimes you are incorrigible!" Prince Fernando threw his arm protectively over Isaac's shoulder, and the boys started back to the banquet hall. Isaac turned, looked back, and was surprised to see Jonathan's head hung low; then almost as if he were aware of the gaze, Jonathan lifted his head, winked at him and followed.

When the evening drew to an end, Isaac mounted his mare and with his brother and father began the long ride home. The words that had been spoken between the duke, his son and the king were still before him. These men had such power, the power of life and death. Realizing the full weight of their power caused him to feel a chill, to shudder, but gazing up at the myriad of stars in the sky and letting the cool ocean breeze ease his tension, he followed his father and brother through the dark shadows of the night.

CHAPTER 3

Isaac and Jonathan had to hurry for school had already begun. Rabbi Joseph ibn Heyyien's favorites usually slipped in a few minutes late. Other lads who were a bit slower with their lessons were less fortunate; lashes were handed out generously for mistakes and daydreaming. Once Isaac and Jonathan entered the small room, the world changed for the rabbi. For them, biblical study was a joy. They discussed Maimonides and Aristotle for hours, when suddenly, they'd notice the sun was setting. Other sleepy boys packed their papers and left, but Isaac and Jonathan, still in a heated discussion, lingered with the old man and his wealth of knowledge. The rabbi hoped that as long as there were youths who could study and absorb knowledge the way they could, Judaism would survive.

As the boys arrived at their school, the sun was almost blotted out by the buildings. Instead of expanding outward, the Jewish section had been pushed upward, forced to grow taller inside the surrounding walls. Their classroom was on the third floor of an old cracked building. Mosaic tiles, the battered remnants of the past Moorish grandeur, graced each entranceway. They made their way up the steep, narrow stairway and entered the classroom.

"You're late! I will not stand for further tardiness in my school!" Rabbi Heyyien was not in a forgiving mood. The other students in the room were stunned into silence, as neither Isaac nor Jonathan had ever been reprimanded. "How could he do this?" Isaac thought as he and Jonathan stiffly walked over to their beloved teacher. Jonathan's face had flushed bright red. Isaac's vision was blurred, but he fought back tears lest one should slip before the others. They put out their hands and the lash came down three times. The boys walked back to their seats, ignoring the snickers in the room. Isaac sank onto his bench, wishing he could slide through the wooden floor.

The rabbi did not call on either of them for the rest of the morning; Isaac realized that he wanted them to know he expected more from them than from the other boys. He realized that the rabbi had been much too lenient.

"Isaac," the rabbi called sharply later that afternoon. Isaac jumped to attention, hoping this would be his chance to make amends for the unpleasant morning.

"Yes, sir."

"Explain Maimonides' concept of creation."

"Yes, sir," he answered respectfully, feeling relieved that this was something he could do. "Maimonides took his concept from Aristotle. He wrote that the stars and heavenly bodies are more perfect than man, and that they have souls. He reasoned that they are more important than man in God's creation."

"And what do you think of this, Isaac? Are we so unimportant?"

Isaac did not hesitate to answer. Though he was fascinated by Maimonides' teachings, he did not believe them to be true. How could Maimonides have questioned the prophets? It was heresy!

"I believe that since we on earth are at the very center of the universe and since God has given us the ability to reason, that man was the central purpose for creation."

The rabbi shook his head and pointed his bony finger at him, "Ah, but Isaac, Maimonides would disagree. He tries to show us our insignificance in the universe. You may be seated."

Isaac sat next to Jonathan but did not look at his friend. He couldn't believe he had answered incorrectly.

"Jonathan, how would you interpret this subject?"

Jonathan stood up straight and tall and commanded the respect of all the students in the room. Still recovering from the lashing, he was in no mood to make a mistake. He answered the rabbi in a strong, clear voice, confident that his answer was correct.

"I believe in Maimonides' point of view. Think of our weak mortal bodies. A plague can enter our city, and within a week hundreds of people die. How can we equate ourselves to the moon, the stars, the sun that God has given eternal life? If our bodies and our minds are of such great importance, why does He eliminate us so easily? I believe that our souls are insignificant compared to the souls of the heavenly spheres." The boys in the room looked up at Jonathan admiringly.

"Yes, he must have hit upon the truth," Isaac thought, but then he saw the frown on the rabbi's face and realized he had not. Terrified that they might be called next, the other students shriveled in their seats. Isaac knew each lad prayed he would not hear his own name called.

The rabbi coughed, cleared his throat, then said, "Your points are well taken, Jonathan, you may be seated." As the rabbi surveyed the room, Isaac could see a little smile creep across his lips. All the boys' faces were looking at the ground, their heads bent as if in prayer-all except for Isaac. Unable to believe that Jonathan had made a mistake, he stared at the rabbi, waiting for him to challenge him. The rabbi sighed, nodded his head and said, "Isaac, can you answer this argument?"

Isaac stood, his foot tapping the floor, his fingers rubbing his tunic. "What is he after? How shall I answer him?" he wondered. A seagull called to him from the blue sky, and Isaac felt himself soar with the bird. He closed his eyes and spoke from his heart. "I believe that a bird is more important to God than the tallest trees because it is a living being, it is sensitive. How can you compare the rational thinking of man to spheres floating in the heavens? It is true they may endure while our earthly life will not, but this is no proof that they are alive or have souls. How do we know that the spheres will not just spin away from their places? The soul of man needs no earth, no planet to last. It is eternal, and it was for this reason that God created our universe."

The rabbi's eyes were misty as he beckoned Isaac to come near to him.

"I can see you have reached a level of spiritual understanding that the others in this room have not." He watched Jonathan, whose face was red, eyes welling with tears, as he stared out the window. "Yes, you are ready now. I can see that you are. Tonight, you will begin to study with the wise men." He turned to the others and said, "The rest of you will work on the next portion of Torah. Class is dismissed."

Jonathan was the first one out the door as the students left the room. He didn't want to walk home with Isaac-not today! He had never been lashed before the others; the whole day had been a disaster for him, humiliating! He had studied for a whole year, waiting for the rabbi to choose him to study with the wise men. He was older than Isaac, already called to the Torah for his Bar Mitzvah reading! Isaac was a child and though he had to admit he was a good student, it wasn't fair! What would his father say when he heard that it was Isaac who was chosen this year to read with the wise men and not him? It was wrong! He should be taught before Isaac. Jonathan envied Isaac's genius, for it was not just his knowledge of the Bible, the Talmud, philosophy, but the way he could evaluate a situation and quickly come up with the correct solution. Jonathan could have taken the traditional philosophy instead of supporting Maimonides' ideas. He had not understood, as Isaac had, that the rabbi did not support those views. He rejected the idea of spirits and souls, but he could see that Isaac deeply believed in a direct translation of the Torah, as did the rabbi. Jonathan knew that the rabbi would never let him study and prepare for the mystic teachings of the Kabbalah, and this rejection seared.

Isaac was at once exhilarated and hurt, for it was a great honor to study with the wise men, but Jonathan was not there to congratulate him. No one Isaac's age had ever been invited to do so before, but as he gathered his papers to leave, he watched Jonathan run from the room without looking back. Isaac brushed past the other boys and ran to Jonathan who was already turning the street corner.

"Wait!" Isaac called as he caught up to him. "Jonathan, wait!"

Jonathan stopped but did not turn around. "What?" he asked.

The smile on Isaac's face faded, and all his excitement at the great honor drained away. "Well, aren't you going to congratulate me?"

"Congratulate you?" Jonathan was incredulous. "Very well, Isaac, Mazel Bueno!" he answered sarcastically. "Mazel Bueno for winning my honors!"

"Your honors! If you had deserved them, you would have received them."

"Ha!" Jonathan shouted, ignoring the passersby who turned to stare at them. He began to march off with Isaac trailing behind. "Don't play the fool, Isaac. You answered the way the rabbi wanted you to. Mazel Bueno, your judgment was better than mine."

Isaac grabbed his arm and spun him around. "I said what I felt, Jonathan, not what I thought the rabbi wanted to hear. It's what I feel, here." He pointed to his heart.

Jonathan crossed his arms and looked at him. "Well then, you deserve the honor. I also answered from my heart and for that I will not be allowed to study Kabbalah. Now if you'll excuse me, I have to get home." He turned and hurried off. Isaac watched him grow smaller as the distance between them lengthened. He walked home alone feeling hurt instead of honored.

One warm summer evening Isaac sat with his head bent over the ancient scriptures. The rabbi's cloudy blue eyes and wrinkled hands rested on him. The old man looked up to see Judah standing in the doorway patiently waiting for them to finish. With his fine gray beard and his elegant blue robes, Judah Abravanel reminded Isaac of King David. It seemed as if David himself were standing before him.

"Don Judah," the rabbi whispered, "it is a great honor to have you here in my school. Your son is like an angel to study with. He has tremendous insight for such a young lad, not even a Bar Mitzvah! He has a fantastic knowledge of the Bible. It's incredible in one so young."

Judah answered respectfully, "My dear Rabbi Heyyien, with you as his guide how could he not achieve a deep understanding? I've allowed him this time to study at great cost to his other work. The boy needs to be taught how to run the finances of kings, and yet I wanted him to have this experience. I want the Bible to seep into his mind, and let this knowledge become a part of his soul. Without respect for God, he will be useless to his fellow man."

"But you underestimate him, Don Judah. The boy was meant for high Talmudic study. I would like to send him to a school . . . ."

"No," Judah interrupted. "He will finish his study with you, and then he will become my apprentice."

"You would be making a grave mistake. The boy was meant for the rabbinate. Our people need men with minds like Isaac's to explain the ways of God. Let me have him for a few more years. Please, Don Judah," the rabbi pleaded.

"Isaac will study with you until his Bar Mitzvah, and then he will concentrate on running the affairs of kings."

Judah was firm.

Isaac wanted to stay here in the school where it was safe and continue to study with the rabbi, leaving the outside world and all its treachery to his father.

"Please, Father, if I may say a word on my own behalf. I want to study further. I feel as though I'm near the end of a forest. I've made my way so far. Please let me continue."

"Enough has already been said! Now come along with me." Judah was annoyed by the boy's insolence. Isaac had already spent too much time with his studies.

Isaac carefully put his papers away, kissed his teacher's knotted hand, and left quietly with his father.

He admired Judah more than anyone else in the world. There was something in the way he carried himself when he walked, the way he spoke and dressed that suggested royal blood.

Isaac held himself erect and tried to match Judah's stride.

He found it always took several minutes of exposure to cold air to clear his mind. It seemed as if he had to travel from the world of the past, the world of Abraham, Isaac, and Jacob, back to his world.

"Isaac," Judah explained, "I know that you are excited with all that you're learning, but you must pull your head out of those books and come up for air, son. People are talking abut the way you look. You are too thin, and your mother is worried about you. You're pale, you don't get any exercise. It's got to stop! You've got to put the books down for a while."

"Since when have you cared what people say about me? They've talked like that for years. Please let me continue, Father, please!"

"You've spent too much time studying! I want you to spend more time with Fernando and Jonathan. Now is the time for you to have some fun. You will have your work and family to keep you occupied soon enough."

"Father, how can you talk to me like this? I've been chosen to study with the greatest rabbis of our time. I'm so close to understanding our creation, our universe . . . ."

"That's enough talk about the universe," Judah interrupted angrily. "Isaac, listen to me. This is a real world, here and now, in which we have to live. Our people are caged like animals behind stone walls. Only influential families like ours can convince the world that we don't need walls. We must show them that we can all live in harmony. Why do you think I've taken so much trouble to cultivate my friendship with the duke? He has the ability to influence the king, and we need him if we are going to better the conditions for our people."

Judah walked rapidly as he spoke, with Isaac trailing behind. He ran now to catch up with him.

"Is that what friendship is for you, Father? You are using them."

"No, Isaac," Judah turned and faced his son. "They are using us. We are using each other for mutual benefit. How else are we to survive? I'll tell you, it's not by keeping our heads in books!"

"I'm studying the Bible, and you tell me to take my head out of books!" Isaac felt indignant. "Father, listen to me, I believe that I can make a great contribution to the explanations of the prophecies. I'm so close to understanding so much. I think the wise men will let me study the Kabbalah after my Bar Mitzvah reading! No one my age has ever done that before! We need this kind of work too if we are to help our people. Think of the disputations . . . ."

"You think you can make a greater contribution than Saddia, Bar-Hiyya, and Nahmanides! Your young mind is bright, maybe brilliant, but it would take years to build up arguments like theirs. Isaac, listen to me, your studies are important, perhaps more important than anything else you will ever do, but we live in a precarious world.

One word from our king and our whole community can be obliterated. It is our family's responsibility to keep a warm relationship with noblemen of this kingdom. Perhaps when you serve the king, you will bring even more security for our people, as I have been explaining to you." They had reached home, and Isaac ran in ahead of his father.

The Abravanel house was an old, elegant structure built by Moors. Huge arches graced the courtyard, and the large central room had a blue tile floor which seemed to undulate like the sea. The main room opened into a small inner courtyard with well-tended shrubs. Each season saw another bush in flower. The almond, lemon, and orange trees scented the yard for the delight of all who entered. Isaac loved to sit by the fountain in the corner and listen to the water trickle down the cool stone. He often slowed his pace when he walked into the courtyard. Tonight, though, he hurried to his room. His head was spinning from his father's stern lecture.

He gazed out at the sea far below and thought to himself, "Why, dear God? Why can't I study with the wise men forever?"

As the sun bled into the ocean, Carlos Málaga, cloaked in black, bent down to Don Pedro.

"The duke is gaining power over the king with lies," Carlos said.

Don Pedro's face darkened. "What lies have been spoken about me?" He grabbed Carlos' cloak which had been flapping in a brisk sea breeze.

"While you were gorging yourself with food at his party, the duke was whispering to His Majesty that you had poisoned Queen Leonora." His laugh was quickly squelched by Pedro's darkening eyes.

"Keep your voice down! I don't want anyone to hear us! I'll deal with my bastard brother, but he has friends in Lisbon who have grown too powerful. The Jews have filled his coffers to overflowing, and I'm sure this Judah Abravanel is an alchemist. With the king far away in his castle in Evora, I want the infidels humbled!"

Carlos laughed.

"A group of drunken peasants tried to storm the Judería yesterday. We can finish what they began."

Forgetting himself, Don Pedro yelled above the sea breeze which was quickly growing stronger, "I'm not talking about stones and drunken men! I want blood to flow in the streets! The Dominican friars are behind us, and you'll have no trouble finding men."

"The Jews have made their enemies. We will strike tomorrow-let them cry to their God for mercy!" Carlos turned and rode away.

Don Pedro watched the muscular young man disappear into the city streets, and a vicious smile crept across his face.

"I'll have my revenge, Bathsheba!" he whispered to the wind which nearly threw him to the ground.

CHAPTER 4

Rice, cork, olive oil, and grain were being loaded onto waiting ships, and from the Lisbon port, they would be distributed to England, Flanders, and the Netherlands. Isaac ran to keep up with his father as he tallied exports for the House of Braganza.

"Where does the rice come from, Father?" He was astonished to see rice as an export.

"From the southern portion of our country," Judah answered, closing one ledger and opening another. "We have many paddies. The cork and olive oil come from the *Alentejo* lands. Some of the cork also comes from the forests in the lands of *Beja*. We also export oranges, figs and almonds." He counted the crates waiting to be loaded—"Fifty-one, fifty-two, fifty-three, four, five—" marked the ledger and closed it, then turned back to Isaac. "Captain Gonçalves says that the southern half of our country reminds him of Africa!" Judah's servant carried the heavy ledger away, and a captain patiently waited for him to sign an important document. While Judah chatted with the captain, the twelve-year-old Isaac watched the sailors, with their red and white striped caps, carry sacks of grain, crates of oranges and figs up the gang planks. They swaggered back and forth as if the land beneath them were swaying like the ocean waves.

Pink melted into deeper orange with streaks of violet ever changing shape as the sun set over the water. Judah and Isaac mounted their horses and turned home. Isaac felt elated by the day, for the easy game of numbers was now being translated into so many bags of grain, rice, and cork that were to be shipped to foreign ports, laying the foundation of the kingdom's economy.

His elation was dampened as they rode toward the Judería, for they were caught in a current of angry men shouting obscenities. With the horses giving them some protection from the men on foot, Isaac and Judah pushed forward toward the gates. The closer they got the more violent the men were becoming, throwing rocks, brandishing swords, knives and clubs. As the smell of smoke drifted over him, Isaac beheld the Judería shrouded in black, fires leaping out of control, the gatekeeper clubbed to death, a massacre erupting. Riding close to his father, he saw fires raging, hungry for wooden structures, and fierce men swinging blades, gleaming silver against the fire as they were lowered, dripping blood when raised. Isaac made way next to his father through the crowded, smoky streets. He saw an old man pleading for mercy, his arms opened wide, and then watched as a man standing above him plunged a knife into the old man's chest. The old man's arms dropped, his body collapsed, his head struck the dirt. Bile rose to Isaac's throat as anger replaced his fear. Why were these men butchering his people? They were men he recognized, men who worked on the wharf, men who bowed to his father earlier in the day—why had they gone mad?

Suddenly he thought of his mother, and as if his father could read his mind, Judah yelled, "Go home, Isaac," and then he galloped off toward the burning synagogue.

Isaac turned his stallion toward home. He saw a wounded woman crawling in the filthy street. She muffled a cry as she crept along, her arm bleeding, and brushed back tears from her muddy face. A group of men began to surround her, so Isaac galloped toward them. His horse reared, forcing the madmen to turn aside and look for easier prey. Isaac dismounted, helped her up, and led her into an old building. She sank to the floor, looked up at Isaac and started pulling her hair, shrieking. Isaac shrank away from the woman, terrified, now for the welfare of his own family-his mother, brothers and sister alone in the house. He mounted his horse and raced toward home, but when he rounded the corner of the narrow street where he lived, a black-cloaked horseman reared before him. Isaac detoured down an alleyway to lead him away through the winding streets he knew well, but the horseman was an excellent rider, and Isaac could not lose him. Catching up to him, he brandished his sword crying, "Death to you, Jew!" Isaac, turning, saw the rider's hood fall back and recognized Carlos Málaga. He ducked and kicked his horse as he had never done before and raced, at full gallop now, around the battered old buildings until his horse skidded and threw him off. Málaga dismounted, sweat, dripping down his face, the black patch askew, and walked toward him with his sword drawn.

"Too bad you didn't fall five years ago, Jew boy. No one mocks me before the king."

"I didn't mean to hurt you, Carlos," Isaac said as he backed up against the wall of an old building. His fingers pressed into the cracks, he continued in a high tight voice as Carlos advanced, "I wasn't carrying a knife that day nor do I have one now. I'm unarmed, Carlos . . . I have no weapon." He opened his arms to show him. Málaga laughed and swung his heavy sword toward Isaac, who jumped to a window ledge and hung by his finger tips. Again Carlos swung his sword, and this time Isaac kicked him in the face. Carlos flew back, his mouth bleeding, and hit his head on a stone. Isaac dropped down from the ledge. He fled, running around the corner into a group of men. Without the protection of his horse, he was easy prey. One man carried a whip, and the others quickly stripped his tunic off his back and threw him on the ground. His face cracked against the dirt, his ribs ached, then a pain ripped through his body as the whip tore at his skin. He jerked, but he could not free himself-men held each arm and leg, their fingernails cutting into him. Again the pain ripped through him; he tried to scream, but as he lifted his head, the whip came down again and again until an enormous black pain engulfed him.

The men were so bent on killing the helpless boy that they fell easily, one by one, as Jonathan and two other young men, Saul and Benjamin, plunged daggers into them.

Like skilled hunters, they overpowered the four men holding Isaac, stabbing them. When the killing was done, Jonathan, sickened by the blood on his dagger, bent down over the inert form. "Oh God!" he cried when he realized the boy was Isaac. He picked him up in his arms. "Oh Isaac, don't do this to me. Oh God, Isaac, don't die," he whispered. Saul and Benjamin helped Jonathan carry Isaac's lifeless body toward Isaac's home. As he rounded a corner, Jonathan caught a glimpse of Carlos limping away.

The boys had to pound on the front door of Isaac's house, for the servants would not come while the attack on the Judería continued. Isaac's mother, Sarah, finally opened the door.

"Isaac!" she screamed when she saw the young men holding him, blood dripping. "Oh! My boy! Is he alive?

Please, bring him in here." The boys carried him into the library and laid him down. Sarah ran to Isaac's side and held his head close to her as Jonathan bent over him. He lifted his arm and felt for a pulse.

"He's alive, Sarah . . . . I pray he'll be all right," he said in a hoarse voice.

"Oh! My God! Oh, please, dear God! Someone quick call Samuel! Samuel!" she shrieked for her eldest son.

Samuel came running into the room, and then stopped short when he saw Isaac.

"Quickly, get me some hot water and bandages, Mother," he said as he approached his unconscious brother. He bent over Isaac and wiped a blood stain from his face. Isaac moaned. Sarah ran for soap, water and towels, and when she returned she gently washed him while Samuel, who was studying medicine, cleaned and bandaged his wounds.

"He'll have scars, but otherwise, he'll be all right," he said, trying to reassure her. Sarah turned as Jonathan left the room with Saul and Benjamin, and ran to them before they got to the door.

"You can't go back out there. If they see blood on you like this, they'll kill you." Hanging their heads, Saul and Benjamin fell back. "Come, clean up, and wait here until this is over, please." Sarah started to lead the boys away, but Jonathan walked to the door. She ran to him. "Jonathan, you can't go out!" She tried to hold him back.

He pushed her away.

"I must find my father. He and Judah were trying to put out the fires in the synagogue. I have to help them." He pushed past her and slammed the door. There was anger in Jonathan, a fierce temper that she had never seen before, and she realized for the first time that at fifteen, he was no longer a child.

Dagger in hand, Jonathan ran back into the chaotic streets. The heavy smoke from the fires had collected between the close buildings. His nose and eyes burned, his lungs filled with smoke. The smoke had chased most of the madmen from this section. He squinted as he made his way toward the synagogue and could make out one man carrying another. He inched his way forward until he recognized Judah carrying his father, whose face was so blackened he barely recognized him. Jonathan took his father from Judah and carried him back to the Abravanel home.

"What happened?" Jonathan stammered.

"A fiery beam fell on him. Just get him into the house!" Judah cried.

Stumbling over burning timbers and through smoke, they carried Jacob into the house and laid him down. Removing his smoking clothes, they were horrified to see that in some places he was burned to the bone.

"Samuel!" Judah called. The young man came running from his brother's side. Again he stopped short, and then forced himself to pick up Jacob's good arm to feel for a pulse. He swallowed hard and turned to look at Jonathan.

"No! Don't die!" Jonathan cried, shaking the dead man, and then falling on him sobbing. Samuel tried to pull him away, but he clung to his father's body. Judah stood over him.

"Jonathan, please, son, please, you must come away."

Jonathan let go, but everything was blurred, indistinct, and nightmarish as he fled the home into the roiling Judería before anyone could stop him.

Blood flowed for days as men, women, and children were butchered. King Afonso ordered his own troops to squelch the attack. The king was severe with the leaders of the mob, and death came swiftly to those who had taken part in the bloodshed. Rumors flew that the attack had roots in the king's own castle, and he was determined to find out who had organized it. As King Afonso walked into a small chapel in his castle, he contemplated the very grave matter. If his father-in-law Don Pedro had caused the uprising, it put his own power and authority in question.

He was beginning to understand that Don Pedro was not satisfied with having his daughter sitting as queen on the throne, but was determined to keep the power in his own hands. Afonso knelt in prayer for some sign from God as to his course of action.

The Duke of Braganza waited patiently, and when Afonso had finished his prayers, he started the king with his presence.

"Excuse me, Your Majesty," the duke said, bowing, "but I'm afraid there is serious news concerning the attacks on the Jewish section."

"Yes, what is it, Uncle? Please feel free to speak to me."

"Jacob Ben Ezra died of burns while trying to save the synagogue, and Don Judah Abravanel's son, Isaac, was seriously beaten." The duke spoke with as much indignation as if they were members of his own family.

"Uncle, the time has come. It's clear to me now. Don Pedro must be stopped before he tears apart the kingdom with his treason."

Jonathan grieved for his father. He shredded his clothes and washed himself in ashes. He would neither eat nor receive visitors. Rebecca mourned, and in a strange way, she felt she had lost Jonathan as well. She was almost eleven and now had only Jonathan and Isaac to care for her. She wandered about the rooms of her home alone, she ate alone. Servants tried to amuse her, and her tutor tried to interest her in her studies, but as long as Jonathan locked himself away, she could not concentrate.

She begged him to eat, but he ordered her away. After several weeks of mourning, Rabbi Heyyien came to talk to him.

"Jonathan, this is not natural. We weep for our dead, we bury them, we say prayers, but life must go on. You cannot lock yourself up in this room forever. You have a sister to look after, business to attend to."

Jonathan didn't answer but stood looking out of the narrow window at the ocean below.

"She jumped from this window," he whispered.

"What? I'm sorry, I don't know what you mean," the rabbi questioned.

Jonathan turned his cold blue eyes from the rabbi and continued to stare at the ocean and rocky cliffs far below.

Isaac recovered slowly from his ordeal. From nightmares of whips slashing and men on horseback chasing him, he would wake to find himself in the security of his own room, though he lay in a pool of sweat. The wounds were healing well, but he would be scarred forever. After two weeks in bed, he struggled to his feet, Samuel holding him up on one side and Sarah on the other. His younger brothers, Jacob and Joseph, cheered as he made his way across the room and back. Gently they helped him back into bed; the walk was a major accomplishment. As soon as Don Judah permitted, Prince Fernando came to visit. He found Isaac in his bed clothes resting in the warm sunlight of his beloved courtyard. Isaac tried to get up, but Fernando stopped him and embraced him, though gingerly.

"I'm glad to see that you are up. I hear that you're healing well and will be about in no time at all." He tried to sound cheerful.

Isaac managed to smile as if he felt no pain, though he still had trouble turning his neck. He sat stiffly and said, "It's good to see you, my prince. How is Jonathan? No one will tell me why he hasn't come." Isaac was annoyed with his family for their silence on the subject. Why wouldn't they speak of Jonathan? He didn't feel so sick that he had to be kept in the dark concerning his friend in mourning! "It seems to be a great mystery."

Fernando hesitated for a moment, and then answered, "No one has seen him since his father's funeral. He has shut himself up in his room and won't speak to anyone. Rebecca can't even get him to eat. Your rabbi has tried to bring him out of mourning but he did not succeed."

"Haven't you gone? I'm sure he would talk to you." Isaac suddenly felt deeply anxious about Jonathan.

"I've gone three times to his door, but he won't open it. I even told him I had a message from you, but that didn't make a difference." He stopped then bent forward and continued in a whisper, "I think Jonathan has gone mad." He stood up and turned away. Isaac could see him shudder. Leaning heavily on a cane, Isaac stood and walked over to Fernando, gently placing his hand on his shoulder.

"It's all right, Fernando. Once I'm well enough, I'll ride over there and talk to him. Please don't upset yourself."

Fernando turned around quickly to face him, nearly knocking him over. "I'm not; it's just that . . . ."

"What?" Isaac couldn't understand his friend's pain. "Why are you so distraught? You're not the one who was whipped," he said a little more sharply than he meant.

"How do you think I feel? I'm Christian, and look what my people have done to you, to Jacob Ben Ezra, to Jonathan. I feel your pain in my heart. I will always carry this shame with me."

"You know I don't blame you for what happened. Your father helped put the rebellion down. We owe you our lives, Fernando, you, your father, and your grandfather."

"My grandfather! Do you know what he's plotting this very moment? The death of Don Pedro!"

"Do you think I'd weep over Don Pedro's death?"

"No, I don't think you would, but my father will have nothing to do with this plotting. It's between grandfather and the king. My father says one death will only lead to revenge and more death. If Don Pedro is killed, my grandfather's life will be in jeopardy. What I've just said-it must be kept in strictest confidence. You are the only friend I trust. The others are all bootlicking sycophants." He kicked a stone across the courtyard.

Isaac felt a gulf rise between himself and Fernando that had never existed. Feeling very weak and tired, he collapsed back into his chair. Growing up in the Judería, he could not grasp all the power and treachery that existed in the kingdom. Realizing that brother could rise up against brother, he no longer envied the prince.

Fernando walked back to him. "Please, Isaac, never repeat what I've said, never!"

Isaac stood again, with some difficulty, and the boys clasped each other. "Never, you have my word."

After they had drunk cool glasses of the sweet juice of Valencia oranges, Fernando left. Isaac resolved to see Jonathan soon. He was sure that if he could spend some time with him, he could shake him loose from his deep sadness.

Within the week, Isaac chose a time of day when his father was not home to mount his horse and ride to Jonathan. Samuel, however, caught him as he was leaving and held onto the reins.

"Are you mad, Isaac? You can open those wounds; they are not properly healed yet."

"Will you keep your voice down or Mother will hear you!" Isaac answered. He had hoped to sneak out unnoticed for just an hour.

"You'll answer to Father if those wounds don't heal. I'm not treating you all these weeks for you to end up an invalid!" Samuel called after him as he rode off.

"I'm fine, Samuel; I'll take the blame if I hurt myself." He trotted off to show his brother he was not in any pain and perfectly capable of riding, but after he was out of his brother's view, he slowed his horse to a walk. Every time the horse's hooves hit the road a streak of pain ran down his back. The slow walk was just bearable as he carefully made his way through the winding streets of the Judería to the largest home near the sea, which now belonged to Jonathan.

Three servants had to help Isaac dismount when he arrived. He staggered a little, a terrible pain stabbing at his back as he tried using his legs again. Rebecca ran out to him, and as she reached him, he fell against her.

"Isaac, are you all right?" She hadn't known how badly he had been hurt. "You shouldn't have been out riding so soon."

"Rebecca, just help me up to Jonathan's room. I must talk to him." His voice was breathless from the throbbing pain.

"I'm afraid you've come for nothing, Isaac. He won't talk to anyone. Prince Fernando has been here three times . . . ."

"I know. Just help me upstairs." Isaac was in so much pain he could barely speak. He was growing apprehensive because of Rebecca's appearance; she had become so thin and pale; she, too, was suffering, he realized.

"I'm so sorry, Rebecca, about your father. It must be a terrible loss for you."

She leaned her head on his shoulder even though she was holding him up. Isaac was the only important person left in her world.

35

"Do you miss him too?" she whispered.

"Yes, of course. It's a terrible loss for all of us."

"No, I don't mean Father, I mean Jonathan."

Isaac felt a shiver run through his body. What had happened to Jonathan that everyone felt as if he were gone as well? At the top of the stairs, Rebecca retired to her chambers, and Isaac watched her sit down by the fireplace and attend to her embroidery. He limped to Jonathan's room by himself.

Knocking on the door, Isaac waited for Jonathan to answer. He knocked again, but still there was no response.

He turned the doorknob, surprised to find it unlocked, and silently entered the room. He stood there and stared at Jonathan. His skin was white, his blue eyes gray, his golden hair was matted, and he was slumped over in his chair, staring out at the sea below, completely unaware of Isaac's presence. Isaac sat down next to him. He didn't know what to say; he had never seen anyone in such a state of despair. He loved his friend, and he grieved to see him this way, so lifeless, so broken.

Jonathan looked up at Isaac. He hadn't spoken to anyone since his father's death except to order them away, but the sight of Isaac, hunched over in the chair next to him, thin and bruised, trying to bring him some comfort, was too much to bear. He began to laugh. Looking at him as if he were mad, Isaac made him laugh even harder until he fell off the chair and onto the floor. He laughed until he cried, and he cried now as though his soul had been ripped from his body. Isaac gingerly knelt down beside his friend and held him. Jonathan's body shook so much that Isaac was afraid he'd never gain control. They held each other for a long while, until finally Jonathan's tears subsided, and he began to catch his breath. He stood and walked back to the window, then turned to see Isaac struggling to get up, came back, and gave him a hand.

"And I'm going to give you to my sister?" was all he could manage to say. "Isaac, you can't understand. No one can."

"Jonathan, it's a tragedy, but life goes on. You have responsibilities. You can't stay locked up here forever."

Isaac didn't grasp the problem.

Jonathan turned on Isaac in a rage.

"You don't understand! He was my last connection. I'm cut off . . . . I don't belong anymore!"

"What are you talking about?" Isaac was afraid that Fernando was right, that his friend had really lost his mind.

"It's over, Isaac," Jonathan said with finality.

"Don't be ridiculous! You're a young man. You've inherited a tremendous fortune. Nothing is over; your life is just beginning."

"Don't talk to me about beginnings; it's over. I don't want to live here anymore." He was frustrated by Isaac's perplexed look. "Don't you see? No, you can't, you never will. You, you are the light, the one they will turn to. You, Isaac, not me! It will be you who will stand before the king for our people."

"Jonathan, have you lost your mind? You've had a great shock. You need some food, some rest, and then things will make more sense to you."

"Nothing will ever make more sense than it does now. I love you like a brother, Isaac. I'll not stand in your way."

"You're not standing in my way!"

"You know what I'm saying," Jonathan's voice had grown ugly. "You just don't want to understand."

"Don't I?" Isaac was losing patience. His back was aching.

"You took my place before the rabbi, and you'll take my place before the king."

"Your place! The rabbi chose me because I had the ability to understand. Your mind was closed . . . ."

"I said I won't stand in your way."

"Jonathan, you're not making sense. No one man represents our people. If I have a voice with the king someday, I'll need you beside me." He was beginning to realize what Jonathan meant, that he wanted to leave the Judería. "I need you, Jonathan," he said, his voice failing, the full weight of Jonathan's intentions hitting him.

"After you and my sister are married, I'm leaving. I won't be second to you or to any man. I'm not going to live my whole life behind these walls like an animal. I'm going out into the world. I'm going to have what I want!"

"What do you want, Jonathan? What's out there that is so much better than what we have?"

"There's got to be more than this!"

"Yes, but not for Jews!"

"That's the point!"

"What are you saying?" But he knew. Ever since the rabbi had chosen him over Jonathan, ever since he had begun to study with the wise men, he knew Jonathan had lost his love for their studies, the synagogue, in God.

"Don't be so shocked, so innocent! I'm not going to spend my whole life wondering when they are coming for me. I'm not going to die in flames the way my father did! To save a burning synagogue!"

Isaac struck Jonathan.

"Take that back! You've gone mad—you don't know what you are saying." He reached for his friend's hand.

Jonathan pushed him away.

"With my blond hair and blue eyes, they will never know I'm a Jew. I'm a man, just as good as any of them, and I'm going to be one of them."

Isaac stared into eyes he didn't recognize. Jonathan was mad. He felt he no longer knew the young man standing before him. His thought now was to save Rebecca from his madness. He couldn't let him take her with him. "When are you leaving?" he asked, coldly, steadily.

"I said I'd stay until you marry her," he answered as if he could read Isaac's mind. "And don't think that I'll leave without regret. If she weren't so in love with you, I'd take her with me. I'd never want her to live behind these walls for the rest of her life. If you breathe a word of this to anyone, I swear I'll kill you, Isaac. No one is going to stop me."

Isaac felt as if his heart had cracked. His body trembled as he made his way to the door which he opened and closed without looking back. Rebecca was standing there but evidently had not heard the words spoken.

"Isaac, do you think he will eat something? I'm so grateful you've come. Will he come out now?" she asked.

Isaac couldn't talk, words, a thousand words, stuck in his throat. He wanted to scream, to cry, "Traitor!" to pull her away from Jonathan right now, but she was still just a little girl, only ten, and he was not quite thirteen. Instead, he embraced her, fled the house, struggled onto his horse, and rode home.

After Isaac's visit, Jonathan's recovery was swift.

He took great care in his grooming and had rich new wardrobes made for him and Rebecca, of the finest silks and brocades imported from the East. He threw himself into his father's work and quickly saw profits greater than his father had ever realized. He had a sharp eye for fine stones, and his skill in working gold, incomparable with the work of other goldsmiths, turned out one dazzling piece after another. Even the king ordered several pieces for his queen. Everyone except Isaac was relieved that Jacob Ben Ezra's son had shed his mourning clothes and come to life again. Only Isaac knew that every jewel, every coin dropped into Jonathan's black coffer brought him closer to his goal. To the world, he and Jonathan seemed as close as they had always been. Prince Fernando sensed an estrangement between them, but Fernando had worries of his own.

One clear spring morning, the wind blew fresh air across the land, bringing with it a touch of green to the grass and a pink blush to the buds on the trees. The king and the Duke of Braganza sat on horseback ready to cross Don Pedro's land at the Alfarrobeira River. Don Pedro was pacing back and forth on the other bank, waiting for Prince Henry to arrive and help settle the dispute between himself and the king. The count of Avranches and others who had participated in the attack on the Judería were with Pedro and swore to him that they would stand by his side in battle should the need arise, but of course, they were sure Henry would keep the peace as he had always done. As they waited for Prince Henry, one of Don Pedro's soldiers accidentally let go an arrow which landed close to the king's tent. Within moments, the king's army descended on the noblemen and their few soldiers. After a quick clash of swords and the drawing of blood, the king seized the power that was due him. His regent, Don Pedro, fell with an arrow in his chest, and the nobility who had supported him lay dead by his side. Wearing a commoner's hood, Carlos Málaga ran to Don Pedro and lifted the dying man.

Don Pedro opened his eyes and whispered, "My son."

King Afonso had finally put down the rebellion, threatening to take his throne from the time he was a boy.

And with his rise, rose the House of Braganza, now the most powerful in Portugal, save the king's. Just before King Afonso and the Duke of Braganza rode over to view the dead Don Pedro, Carlos Málaga mounted his horse and galloped off to bring the grievous news of her father's death to Afonso's Queen Isabel. As the wind whipped through his hair, he thought over and over again, "No! No! No! My father was King Duarte! How could my father have been Pedro? Why didn't he acknowledge me! Why does the truth come now—now that he is dead?"

CHAPTER 5

The day Isaac was to be called to read the Torah as a bar mitzvah arrived with all the tumult of a great occasion. The most honored members of the community had been invited to the synagogue for the morning Sabbath service. Isaac looked up at his mother in the balcony and felt her warm, proud smile caress him. As he chanted the story of David, he gazed at Rebecca, who was sitting next to his mother and little sister, Miriam, and the warm glow turned into a nervous sensation. Rebecca's hair was the same golden shade as Jonathan's, but her large brown eyes had a depth that her brother's blue eyes never revealed. Her slender nose and full pink lips formed a beautiful profile. Suddenly the warm glow that he was feeling inside turned into a nervous sensation and he quickly looked away.

His gaze then fell upon Jonathan, who was sitting in the center of a bench surrounded by elder members of the congregation. His elegant velvet cape, his rings with precious stones on his fingers, seemed out of place next to older men whose finest garments were the Prayer shawls draped over their shoulders. Isaac stood straighter, trying to make himself a little taller as Jonathan returned his steady gaze. From Jonathan's expression, Isaac guessed that Jonathan felt as if he was being forced to sit there, forced to listen to him read the Torah. He could see that the biblical story of David and his friendship with Jonathan was making him uncomfortable as if the biblical friendship had something to do with theirs. Staring at Jonathan, Isaac recited Samuel 20:16:

> So Jonathan made a covenant with the house of David . . . .
> for he loved him as he loved his own soul.

Their eyes met and Isaac felt as close to Jonathan as they had been in childhood, but Jonathan then looked away. They were no longer children; his father was dead, and their paths would be divided.

Isaac looked like a prince of the past with his white prayer shawl, embroidered in gold and blue draped over his shoulders. He was growing into a lanky young man. His straight brown hair had turned almost black and his dark eyebrows gave depth to the rich brown of his eyes. His nose was straight and fine, and his thin red lips spoke of ancient deeds with a freshness that made them seem as if they had just happened. His voice was growing deep and resonant, though to his dismay, it squeaked from time to time. When he finished his reading, the rabbi blessed him and the congregation. The service was over. The elders of the congregation shook his hand and offered their blessings. Isaac felt important, respected, and ready to take his place before the congregation as a man. Jonathan was not in line to shake his hand.

The afternoon of singing, eating and rejoicing commenced at the Abravanel home. The wine made Isaac's head feel light, and he found himself wandering away from his guests, searching for Jonathan, wondering why he hadn't congratulated him after the service. He made his way up to his chambers and, surprised to find the door closed, quietly pushed it open and peered in. Jonathan was on his bed with a giggling someone—a woman! Jonathan was on his, Isaac's bed, with a voluptuous young woman! Isaac felt trapped; if he stirred, they would catch him watching. He was ashamed to watch, and yet he was magnetized by the scene before him.

Jonathan had taken off her clothes from the waist up and was caressing her full white breasts, kissing her neck and now her mouth. Isaac could not tear himself away. Jonathan pulled off all the clothes from her creamy white body. Now Jonathan's fine velvets fell to the floor as well. It was fascinating to see the woman's body wrapped around the lean, muscular young man. Jonathan's hand was caressing her most private part, while his tongue roamed over her flesh as if to devour her. He mounted her and Isaac watched them unite.

"What's so fascinating, Isaac?"

Isaac slammed the door and turned to face his father. "It's nothing, Father, really. We should be getting back to our guests."

"Isaac, I want to know what's going on in there."

"Nothing, Father, nothing important." Isaac blushed red.

"Something had your undivided attention. You didn't even know I was here until I spoke to you!"

"Oh!" Isaac laughed, "Its just Jonathan. He-ah-he had to change, and he was using my room."

Judah went to open the door. "Please don't do that, Father."

Judah looked at Isaac angrily. "You tell Jonathan that I would like to speak with him now!"

At that moment, the door flung open, and Jonathan walked out.

"You wanted to see me, Don Judah?" he asked.

"Yes," was all Judah could say.

"Well, shall we go downstairs and join your guests?"

"Yes, yes that's why I came up here. The guests are waiting. There is someone I want to introduce you to, Jonathan."

Isaac stole one last glance at the closed door, drew a long sigh of relief as he followed Jonathan and his father back downstairs. Jonathan turned and gave him an unnerving wink.

Jonathan had been fairly sure that Isaac would come looking for him after his bar mitzvah, and though he never said so, he felt that the experience he had given Isaac was his own extremely personal gift. Jonathan wanted to prepare Isaac for manhood before he left. The next step in Jonathan's plan for Isaac's education would be the bullfight. How could any man reach maturity without a complete understanding the brute force of the bull, the ultimate test of man against nature? Jonathan wondered.

Throngs of people had gathered at the Plaza de Toro. The streets had been boarded and boxes built for the privileged spectators. Prince Fernando's box had an excellent view, and the boys were in high spirits as they made their way to it. Though the fights were always scheduled for Christian holidays, the Moors were always the most enthusiastic spectators. Some said that the bullfight originated with them, but the Christians believed it had started with the Phoenicians, and scholars recalled the Greek King Minos and his royal bull court.

Today's bull had been fathered by a prize stud, and Isaac was amazed by its massive size as it sat in the wooden cart which labored into the plaza. The trumpets blew, King Afonso and Queen Isabel arrived, and the parade began with each participant bowing to them.

"I can't believe you've never been to a bullfight before, Isaac!" Prince Fernando yelled above the roar of the crowd.

"Why should that shock you, Fernando? He's only just learning about the important things in life!" Jonathan's face broke into a big smile when he saw Isaac blush. "Fortunately, he has us for friends."

"I don't know how I'd manage to grow up without you," Isaac retorted. "I'm sure I'd remain a child forever if it weren't for my dear friends." He gave Jonathan a shove. He had had enough of his teasing. Jonathan abruptly sat down and stared out at the plaza turned bull ring.

"What's the matter with you two lately? Jonathan, apologize to Isaac." Fernando had only an intimation of what deeply divided them.

Jonathan solemnly looked at Isaac. "I'm sure, my friend, you will grow up with or without me. It just wouldn't be as much fun. So you see, Fernando, I've nothing to apologize." Quickly changing the subject, he continued, "It's important to understand the fight: man lording it over the beast." He had swung his arm around Isaac's shoulder.

"Must you put your arm around me?" Isaac pulled away still annoyed. As if he didn't understand, as if he were a child who didn't know about these things!

"Isaac, please listen to me." Again Jonathan swung his arm around him. "This is the highest form of control, of grace that a man can achieve. His mind and body are so finely tuned that he can control the beast with style, with finesse. I want you to watch the *cavalieros* control his body and his horse with fantastic precision."

"Do you think they will jump the bull today?" Fernando asked.

"Jump the bull? What is that?" Isaac was mystified.

"They haven't in the last few fights, but maybe today. The pega! There is the true test of a man's courage!" Jonathan answered.

"It sounds as if you wish you were fighting the bull yourself!" Fernando was amazed at Jonathan.

Jonathan's eyes grew moist.

"Were I not a Jew, there would be many things I'd like to do."

Isaac extricated himself from Jonathan and seated himself closer to Fernando.

"It seems to me, Jonathan, that you are the one who has a lot to learn, not me!"

Feeling uneasy with the conversation, Fernando spotted a beautiful *Señorita* a few seats away. He stood up and blew kisses to her.

"My beauty, I'd give you my life, I'd die for you, for one kiss."

"It seems I'm the only sane member of this group." Isaac pulled Fernando down into his seat as the young girl drew a fan across her face.

"Isaac, my friend, my brother, when are you going to learn how to live? Life is always so serious for you. Here, drink this-then maybe you won't be so gloomy!" Fernando produced a flask of dark red wine and the boys each took a long drink.

Isaac tried to maintain his indifference, but the scene passing before him was intoxicating. A parade of men, the first group dressed in scarlet, the second in sliver and gold, passed before the king, each bowing and then moving on. There was a pause in the flow of color and the *cavalieros* dressed majestically in black satin embroidered with gold rode toward the King on a magnificent stallion, the horse's plumed headpiece and ribbons matched the rider's colors. The *cavalieros* was the firstborn son of a nobleman. Even the horse's trot had an aristocratic air as the rider made his way toward the king's box. When all had taken their positions in the plaza, the bull stormed forward. Isaac watched the beast's muscles rippling as it circled the plaza, and he felt exhilarated by the animal's strong, oily scent of hide, hoof, and dung. He could feel the animal's weight as its hooves thudded against the hard earth, shaking their box. He sensed its confusion, its frustration, its desire to meet all challenge. This bull was an animal trained to kill. The gaily-dressed men now moved in to prod the animal to enrage him. Other men were yelling, waving their arms to confuse the animal, goading him in different directions while the *cavalieros* quietly studied his foe. By now quite intoxicated, Jonathan whispered to Isaac, "Watch the *cavalieros*, he is preparing his mind and body!" He took a long drink, emptying the flask.

The prodding had stopped, and now the *cavalieros* spoke to the bull, who, sensing his enemy closing in on him at last, charged at full speed toward the man who rode to meet the bull until at the last possible moment, he curved his body and horse away, leaving darts in the bull's hide. Isaac jumped as though he had been hit.

"Don't worry, Isaac, they only prick the hide; no damage is done. It heightens his anger. Makes the sport just a little more dangerous, more exciting!" Fernando explained. Jonathan was yelling at the top of his lungs with the rest of the crowd.

Now the *cavalieros* challenged the bull and again both charged. The bull, fully roused, was thundering for his pride, his life. He sped forward, powerful grace, but again the skillful rider cleared the charge and left more darts in the animal's side. The bull, now wild, ran directly toward Fernando's box. Isaac stood, his eyes riveted to the black eyes of the beast and then watched, almost dazed, as several men with their long prods, steered the beast away. Isaac fell back into his seat as the *cavalieros* and the bull began a third charge at full speed. Like the devil himself, the beast with his thick head bent for destruction, horns in deadly aim, nostrils snorting the heat and sweat of his body, charged the *cavalieros*, whose taut body and that of his horse once again swerved clear of the beast. Just as the rider was coming out of his curve, the bull quickly turned and charged him again, though fortunately the armed men in the plaza moved in and headed the bull away. The *cavalieros*, slightly shaken by the unexpected charge, rode to the royal box, bowed to King Afonso and Queen Isabel, and then, slowly around the plaza to the wild cheering of the crowd.

"What an animal!" Jonathan roared. "What horsemanship! I'm sure they won't jump the bull today, not with that beast!"

"Fantastic!" yelled Fernando. "Did you see him hold onto the horse with his knees? I was sure he was going to fall on that last turn!"

Isaac said nothing, but his face turned white, as a young man, dressed in a brown velvet cape trimmed with gold, entered the plaza.

Fernando stood and whispered, "That's the *cavaleiro's* older, more experienced brother. I know him! Is he mad?" The drama was to continue; the young man was going to jump the bull.

There was a great hush as the *matador* strutted to the king's box and bowed. Then he made his way to the center of the plaza and danced for the king, for the crowd, for the bull. The animal was let loose and charged while the lad had his back turned to the thundering hooves and breath of the outraged beast. The *matador* turned at the last moment, took the animal by the horns, and tried to hurl himself over the bull's back. The enraged bull violently twisted his head as the young man rolled over its back. Isaac froze. Men went running into the plaza to hail the young lad, the crowd was cheering, Fernando and Jonathan were standing, stamping their feet and screaming with the crowd—but Isaac saw the blood. It was slowly dripping down the beast's side. The lad slid off the animal and onto the ground. As quickly as the cheering had swelled, the hushed murmurs fell. Holding his side, the young man collapsed on the cold earth, his dance floor only moments before. A priest ran out and was bending over him as others lifted his body and carried him away. King Afonso was assured that it was only a surface wound, and that the young man would survive. The crowd cheered for their new hero, the noise so deafening that Isaac couldn't hear what Jonathan and Fernando were saying, adding their voices to the crowd.

"Wasn't that incredible! What courage! What timing!"

Jonathan cried, flushed from the wine.

"What a fool," thought Isaac to himself, but said nothing.

Fernando seemed to read Isaac's thoughts.

"This was very unusual, Isaac. I've been to a lot of bullfights, and it's rare to see anyone hurt. That bull was wild; the *pega* is usually not that dangerous."

"I thought it was magnificent!" Jonathan continued, scarcely hearing them.

"What was magnificent? A young nobleman was nearly gored to death, and you think that was magnificent!" Isaac was incredulous.

"You've missed the whole point. He could hear the hooves pounding dangerously close, feel the animal breathing down his back, and yet his timing, his graceful movements were perfect. Only a coward would not appreciate what we saw today," Jonathan said.

Isaac was raging.

"There's more to life than throwing yourself before a charging bull. There's more to being a man, a hero, than proving you're not a coward."

"What more is there? You tell me what!" Jonathan exclaimed.

"There's duty, there's love, there's God," Isaac answered in a strained voice.

"Your God, Isaac, not mine! For me there is only this, and I'm going to have it all—the excitement. This is my life, my life, Isaac. I'll not follow laws that were made thousands of years ago in a world that had nothing to do with our world, today! I'm going to be part of this . . . . I promise you." He turned, abruptly left his friends, grabbed the arm of a blond woman with painted red lips, and danced off with her.

"He is still suffering the loss of his father, Isaac. I can see that now," Fernando said trying to soothe things over, but not at all convinced that Jonathan was still in mourning. "Of course, there's more to life than bullfights and loose women. He'll figure that out someday; maybe I will too," Fernando joked to lighten Isaac's scowl. "But he is right about one thing."

"What's that?"

"Fine wine and pretty women should never be ignored." Fernando jumped on his stallion, catching the reins of Isaac's mare, waiting for him to gingerly mount. Just before the boys left the Plaza de Toro, Isaac caught a glimpse of Jonathan, now with three women, two dark beauties and the blond one, bending over him, severing him tapas and red wine, as if he were a king.

CHAPTER 6

In the year 1455 Isaac and Prince Fernando rode on horseback along a rocky road out of Lisbon, and then raced through the countryside. Isaac loved to feel the animal move, carrying him across the dry arid land. They raced so quickly that he did not at first notice the ringing of the bells. Then Fernando abruptly brought his horse to a halt.

"Do you hear bells?"

Isaac brought his horse up next to Fernando, his cheeks flushed, invigorated from the ride.

"Yes, I wonder what it's for. Do you think someone has died?"

"They ring church bells out here only for very important occasions. I hope nothing's happened to the king!"

Fernando directed his horse towards the nearby small town. Some villagers were coming in from the fields while others were making their way toward the church. Fernando bent down to a farmer.

"What's happened, old man? Why are they ringing the bells?"

The grizzled man looked up at the prince dressed in his fine silk clothes.

"Haven't you heard, my lord?" He bowed to Fernando as he spoke. "There's an heir to the throne! The queen has given birth to a boy, a healthy one at that." He laughed heartily and fell in with a crowd shuffling toward the church.

"Isabel has given birth to a boy. Shall we be the first to tell my father the news?" Fernando asked.

"I'm sure he already knows. I just hope she doesn't name him Pedro!" Isaac joked, though it wasn't funny.

The young men took off, their horses moving easily though the late afternoon. Isaac's heart was beating wildly, thrilled for King Afonso; imagine-his firstborn, a son! It seemed a good omen. As they galloped toward Fernando's castle, the setting sun cast a golden light on its stone walls and turrets. Isaac felt as though he had dreamed all of this only a week or two before, almost as if he were riding toward the castle with this same knowledge for a second time. On the surface all seemed good, and yet a premonition hung over him; something from the dream was lurking in the shadows of his mind. Something he sensed but could not remember.

Had Isaac been at the cradle of the sweetly sleeping new babe, the nature of the danger to him would have been clear, for a tall red-haired man guarded the sleeping prince. King Afonso didn't know that Málaga had been on the field that bloody day when Don Pedro died, and felt quite sure all of Pedro's men had perished. However, Afonso didn't trust Málaga to a state position. Having learned the truth about Málaga's father, Don Pedro, from the Duke of Braganza, Afonso knew enough not to trust him with his army, but to guard a sleeping prince, that seemed fitting for a bastard of the royal house. His Queen Isabel was fond of Málaga, though she didn't know he was her half-brother. Málaga's mother was a mystery, even to the king.

Carlos Málaga stood erect beside the cradle. His fist was so tightly clenched around his halberd that his knuckles had turned white as he silently suffered his new post. He would guard the king's son well, oh yes, very well. They would be friends, he and the prince, great friends, for this prince would grow to be a king—Málaga could wait. Carefully nurturing his hate for the Braganzas as they wormed their way to becoming the King's confidants, he watched the Abravanels help them grow rich from their estates. The Braganzas treated the Abravanels like royalty, privileged members of society. Málaga would have to wait, but he had learned to be a patient man.

The wind blew cold off the Atlantic Ocean, its chill breath rolling over the Portuguese Mountains down, down, down into Castile. It gathered strength as it shrieked and gusted over the bare countryside of Castile. A queen heard the howling night wind and ran to her sleeping princess. It was not unusual for Princess Isabella to wake with her mother standing over her in only a nightdress. Tonight the queen was crying.

"Mama, Mama, please don't cry. It's only the night wind you hear calling you." The child cradled her mother in her arms. "Sleep, Mama, sleep," she whispered.

"My beauty, my precious beauty," the queen murmured as she looked at Isabella with her wild eyes. "They want to take you away." She cried like a baby into the child's lap. Isabella could not control her mother, and finally the servants had to gently usher her mother back into her own bed. Awake now, Isabella climbed out of bed and gazed into the black night. She was lost between the stars when a noise startled her. She turned to see her little brother standing in the doorway rubbing his eyes.

"Alfonso . . . ." She ran to the prince. "It's all right, my love. Come and I'll tell you a story, and then you must go back to bed." She helped the child into her own bed and pulled the covers against the cold night air. With the candlelight flickering and the warmth of her brother's body next to hers, Isabella felt less afraid of the wind and the night spirits her mother feared.

"Please tell me the story of El Cid before I go back to bed." Alfonso was delighted to have been invited to stay.

"How many times have I told you the story of El Cid," she said smiling. She really wanted to tell him her favorite story of her heroine, Joan of Arc.

He knew what she was thinking.

"Please, please tell me the story of El Cid." He looked at her with his large blue eyes, so innocent, so pure; she could not refuse.

"Very well." She sighed and began the story. "El Cid was born in 1043 to the noble family of Diaz. He was a tall man with black eyes as fierce as fire, and when he looked at someone it was as if he could see right into the center of his soul." She made her eyes as fierce as she could, and her brother laughed. "You're not supposed to laugh," she scolded. "Roder Ruez Diaz Cid was his full name. When he rode for the glory of Spain, he wore a silver suit of arms that caught the sunlight and sent terror into the hearts of the heathen. He rode with the cross, and town after town bowed down to him, Valencia, Curate and Bairen. He cut down the hated heathen and brought the teaching of our Savior, the Lord Jesus Christ, to our people."

"Please tell me about the scorpion's sting," Alfonso interrupted.

"The scorpion's sting isn't important to the story of El Cid." Isabella laughed then stared out into the night sky.

"Please, Isabella," he pleaded as he tugged on her nightdress. "I want that story." His whining voice betrayed his fatigue.

"Very well," she said realizing he'd stay awake for only a few more minutes. "The infidels rose up against El Cid in a bloody battle in Valencia. With a mighty slash of his sword, El Cid hacked off their heads so that their eyes rolled and their clothes were stained red. He left their bodies for the vultures to pick apart. At last their general, Ibn Yehaf, came crawling to El Cid pleading for mercy. He groveled at his feet squealing, 'I will give you the scorpion's sting,' and handed it to El Cid. It was heavy gold scorpion, elaborately jeweled, and carried an evil curse. 'Spare my life' the simpering general pleaded. But there was no mercy, and El Cid had him burned at the stake in a bloodless death, the auto-de-fé. Ibn Yehaf entered hell from earth's fires, and his soul still burns to this day."

Isabella watched Alfonso's head nod, and she whispered into his ear, "God rewarded El Cid with the scorpion's sting, for he wore the pendant into one heroic battle after another and broke its curse. God rewards those who carry the cross and the sword."

The prince was asleep, and Isabella carried him back to his own room and tucked him in to his bed. She placed a tender kiss on his cheek and on her way back to her apartments saw a figure standing in the doorway to her bedchamber.

"Oh, Father, you startled me."

"I didn't mean to frighten you, my child; I just wanted to make sure that you and your brother were all right. I heard your mother was up again tonight."

Father Tomas Torquemada, a friar of the Dominican Order and Isabella's confessor, stood blocking the entrance.

"Yes, Father, we are fine."

She was embarrassed to find the friar staring at her in her nightdress. As he stood there, tall and gaunt, candlelight threw strange shadows on his face. The wax from the candle dripped over his fingers as he made way for the girl to pass into her chamber. Isabella saw him blow out the light of the single flame, but she wasn't sure he had left her apartments. She had the feeling he was standing there, watching her, but she drifted back to sleep, feeling comforted; her confessor was protecting her and her little brother from the spirits of the night wind.

CHAPTER 7

Five years had passed since the massacre in the Lisbon Judería, and though Isaac was often at the wharf with his father carrying heavy ledgers and tallying numbers for the House of Braganza and occasionally for the King, at the age of seventeen he still felt uneasy around men he recognized as having taken a part in that ugly day. Most of the bearded sailors loading the ships, however, had not been involved, and he loved to listen to their stories of foreign ports. He admired these men who dared to sail the rough dark waters, often to uncharted lands. Sometimes Fernando rode by to try to convince him to joust, telling him that unless he kept up, his skills as a knight would be useless in battle. But Isaac, more often than not, waved his friend on, content to work by his father's side.

However, the evenings were his, and these few precious hours of peace were devoted to his studies. He was now a *Maskil* or Understanding One. He met with the wise old men and was allowed to study the Kabbalah. He believed that the prophets' visions and interpretations were messages from God. Every night he searched the Bible for hidden meanings, for truth-knowledge men needed in order to lead better lives. The old men steered his mind around the secret paths of the *Sefirot*, the numbers from which God created the earth, the sun, the moon, the stars, the whole universe and even man. He learned that the first four *Sefirot* represent the four elements of the entire world: the spirit of God, ether (the spirit that is the world's atmosphere), water and fire. Isaac was amazed at how close this was to Aristotle's four basic elements: air, fire, earth, and water. He had written an essay called "The Forms of the Elements," based on Aristotle's work, when he was fourteen; and now again these elements became the basis of his studies. He also learned that six other Sefirot represent the six dimensions of space. These in combination with the spirit of God caused the whole of creation.

Tonight as he waited for the old men to arrive, he watched their shadows dance in the candlelight. The air seemed to be alive with spirits, dancing, haunting, beseeching.

"Tonight we will discuss Daniel 2," the rabbi said and then began to chant the ancient story in Hebrew. They took turns reading portions of the story of Daniel's revelation of Nebuchadnezzar's dream. Now it was Isaac's turn to read. His voice seemed to echo Daniel's as he read from the Book of Daniel:

> God of heaven hath given the kingdom, the power, and the strength, and the glory . . . . thou art the head of gold. And after thee shall arise . . . . another third kingdom of brass, which shall bear rule over all the earth . . . . And the fourth kingdom shall be strong as iron . . . . And in the days of those kings shall the God of heaven set up a kingdom, which shall never be destroyed . . . .

The rabbi held up his hand to stop Isaac at this point. "Isaac, which kingdoms are represented in this vision of Nebuchadnezzar?"

"They are Babylon, Persia, Greece and Rome."

"And the fifth kingdom, Isaac, what do the Christians believe the fifth kingdom to be?"

"The establishment of Christianity."

One of the older men stood.

"Excuse me, rabbi, but it is a difficult point to refute; after all, Christianity was established with the fall of Rome."

"Isaac, how would you answer this?"

"Perhaps it is not the establishment of Christianity but rather the second coming of Christ which Daniel foresaw, so close to what we ourselves are waiting for."

"You mean the Messiah?" the rabbi questioned.

"Yes, the Messiah." Isaac answered. As the evening settled in upon them, Isaac felt the darkness creeping into every nook the candlelight couldn't reach. He was sure that the prophet's words would come to pass. It was only a matter of time.

After the evening of study, he left the synagogue and in his own home where night's blackness was broken only by his single candle, illuminating great ideas, he forged ahead by himself. He was writing his own commentary on the prophets. He would call his work *The Crown of the Elders*. As he poured over the scriptures, he'd return to the passages of

Daniel, passages that always left him feeling so disturbed; they seemed so dark, as if to say beware! Here lies the truth, the destiny of man.

The world as he knew it would be destroyed, the earth consumed by fires, to be followed by the judgment and the promise of the final peace, the kingdom that is never to be destroyed, the Fifth Kingdom. Isaac closed the holy book and walked over to his narrow window. The world was to be consumed by fire, the element unleashed with all its force in one final moment of destruction. He shuddered, and then closed his eyes in prayer. "Help me, God, to understand; must we go though this destruction? Who am I to ask these questions? Dear Lord, forgive me, forgive me for asking. Only let me be strong for You; I will carry Your commandments with me unto my death." He closed his eyes for a moment and visions of burning buildings, of burning people, of the earth melting, haunted him. He remembered the Judería as it crumbled under flames and wondered what would be left of Lisbon, of Portugal, of the world with the coming of the Messiah and the fifth kingdom. He wanted to cry for man. What would be left of civilization, of all that kings and queens fought over? Nothing. He wanted to scream; his body shook with fear at the words written so long ago. Why couldn't men see that their wealth, their power, their schemes for control were meaningless?

He opened his eyes and thought about the dark churning waters of the ocean. The world, so solid with wood, rock and earth, was also so fluid, with the vast oceans, rushing rivers and bubbling streams. How could it all be consumed in flame? How could one element devour all the others and completely destroy the world? It seemed incomprehensible, yet there had been the flood; the world had nearly been destroyed once before by one of its elements. If it was written in the Bible, it was a prophecy to be reckoned with. Someday the Earth would be destroyed by fire, of that there was no question; it was only a matter of time. Would it be in his lifetime? He thought of Rebecca, soon to be his wife, and of his unborn children. One must go on living; he still had to balance the ledgers of the Braganzas. Perhaps he had not yet discovered why he had been placed on this Earth. He would have to go on searching until this business of living made more sense.

Rebecca woke with a start. How strange that she should have such an unsettling dream before her wedding! She couldn't remember the details, but only a raging, consuming fire, the memory of which left beads of sweat on her forehead. Perhaps the dream was a result of the lecture and prayers the rabbi had said the day before. Having been washed with holy waters, she felt cleansed. Rebecca was startled to see the brilliant sunshine pour into her room. How could she have slept so late, today of all days! She jumped up and poured cool water from her white china pitcher into its matching bowl and began to wash her face and neck. As she washed, she thought of Jonathan, of leaving him for Isaac. Ever since her father's death, he had paid little attention to her, as he was so absorbed with his jewelry business. She sighed when she realized he'd do very well without her. The servants were scurrying about getting her bridal gown ready. She had worked for months embroidering gold threads into the red velvet material of her dress. As they laced the gown and brushed her hair, she could hear the guests arriving to form the procession to Isaac's house where she would be married. She heard Jonathan giving orders as if he were about to lead an army into battle. When someone tried to calm him down, he yelled that this was his only sister, and that it was his right to be as nervous as the bridegroom! Rebecca glowed when she heard him; she had never imagined that he cared so much about her. Maybe he would miss her after all.

There was a knock on the door, and Jonathan poked his head into the room.

"May I come in for a moment?"

"Yes, of course," Rebecca answered.

Jonathan stared at her, unable to speak. Her golden hair glistened, her brown eyes sparkled, her cheeks were flushed, and she reminded him of their mother.

"You look like an angel from heaven," he whispered. He came over and kissed her forehead. "I want to speak to you alone." Rebecca nodded to her servants, and they left. Jonathan took her hands and led her over to the window to watch the ocean stretch out before them. He turned to her; his eyes seemed so full of sadness.

"You are happy, aren't you?" he asked in a very low voice.

"Oh yes, I love Isaac."

Jonathan looked out at the ocean again. "You know you look just like Mother, except for the color of your eyes."

Rebecca glanced down at the reference to her mother but said nothing. She knew it was a subject closed to her and painful for Jonathan.

"I loved her so," he choked on his words, "and I love you, Rebecca. I want you to be happy."

"Oh Jonathan, I will be!" she said, but then when he turned away. She felt confused; had she hurt him?

"Yes, I know," he whispered. He patted her hand and then abruptly said, "Well, we must not keep the guests waiting." He seemed forlorn when he left, and feeling guilty, she wondered if she was doing the right thing.

The servants returned to finish dressing her. They placed the veil over her head and led her downstairs. Twenty guests, dressed in velvet, satin and silk, were waiting. Musicians began to play on lutes and pipes and led the wedding party out of the Ben Ezra home and down the winding narrow streets to the Abravanels'. Others joined in the procession so that when they arrived, there were over one hundred guests. Rebecca looked up to see Isaac standing on the steps of his father's home, throwing rice and coins at her as she passed before him. She came into the central room of the house where Isaac's brothers, Samuel, Jacob and Joseph, and his father, Judah, held up a blue velvet and gold wedding canopy. Her hands were cold. Isaac stood so close to her that she could feel the warmth of his body, but she was too nervous to look up at him. She looked up to see his mother and sister, Miriam, beaming. The rabbi was chanting in Hebrew the benediction over the wine for now they both must drink from the same "Cup of Life." Isaac drank and then the rabbi lifted her veil just enough for her to drink. She could see the moisture left by Isaac's lips, and she sipped from the same spot. The rabbi continued his chanting, and though Rebecca could not understand the Hebrew, she knew he was reciting their *Ketubah,* marriage contract. Then Isaac was commanded to repeat after the rabbi, "Be thou with this ring consecrated to me, according to the law of Moses and of Israel." The wedding ring had been made by Jonathan and was a beautiful gold band with no stones. Her hand shook as the rabbi slipped it on her index finger. She was led seven times around Isaac. Now Jonathan brought forth a silver tray with a glass on it, and Isaac smashed the glass, making a popping sound. Isaac lifted her veil and brushed his lips against hers.

Never had she looked more beautiful to him. Wisps of golden hair framed her face. Her soft brown eyes glowed with an inner radiance. Her delicate pink lips were slightly parted. Reluctantly he drew back. He hadn't realized how soft and moist her lips were. Everyone was shouting, "Mazel Bueno!" But as they were swept away by the exuberant guests, Isaac could think only of her soft, moist lips. A great feast of lamb and rice dressed with steamed fruits was being served, and the musicians played Romanceiro ballads.

Isaac could feel the blood returning to his face. Before the ceremony, he had suddenly felt nauseous and wondered what he was doing. He didn't know this girl who was to share his bed and his life forever! The whole ceremony seemed like a blur. He managed to speak at the appropriate time and to kiss her. Yes, yes it had all happened. He had taken her for his wife. It had been decided so long ago, by his father, her father. At least the match had been made before Jacob died. He was glad of that, for he would have felt he was stealing her away from Jonathan if it had not been decided so many years ago. Jonathan looked sad as if he had lost his best friend, instead of gaining a brother-in-law.

Isaac sat down next to Rebecca at the large banquet table. He had glanced at her only once since the ceremony and the kiss. He wondered what the rabbi had said to her last night before the wedding. The rabbi was supposed to instruct her on her responsibilities as a wife, and he, in turn, had listened to a similar lecture. He gazed at her now. Her veil was off and her hair glistened in the light. She had the same delicate face he knew so well, but the rest of her had changed! He blushed, as he thought of her body. "Rebecca, delicate Rebecca had grown into womanhood! Her breasts swelled under her bridal gown, and he noticed how her waist curved, the material of the fine gown clinging to her. Imagine Rebecca with such a body!" he thought. He pictured her lying next to him in bed. Unfortunately, or fortunately, depending on how he looked at it, that would not come for a few hours. He had been lectured, had watched Jonathan, once, but he was still a virgin.

His brother, Samuel, was making a toast: "Isaac, I remember a night long ago, at the Duke of Braganza's castle; I doubt you remember, when we teased you about this match. You ran off in a rage and knocked this lovely young woman over; then she was just a slight child. We laughed at the attention you gave her, but I will never forget the look you had on your face when you held her bruised hand and stared into her eyes. It was a look of caring, of love. I hope that you both will grow to love each other until you know not where one soul begins and the other ends. L'Chaim! To life! May you both have a long and happy one!"

"With many children!" Jonathan added, and everyone laughed. Jonathan was just a little drunk. He stood and gathered his wits about him, as best he could. "Fortunately, I didn't memorize a speech for this moment, because in my present state I'd not remember it, but after all it's only once that I'll marry my sister to my dearest friend. However, since we have no father to speak for her, it behooves me to say a few words. Isaac . . . ." He bowed and continued, "if I must lose her to any man, then it could only have been to you, my friend, and now my brother. May you live long happy lives together and when troubled times come, and they will come, I hope that you will be a source of comfort to each other as your parents are, Isaac, and my own parents once were. And I hope that in the end, come what may, the love that you have for one another will carry you through those turbulent times. You two are very lucky to have found each other, to have found true love. It is a rare flower indeed. To each and everyone I say, L' Chaim!"

He bent down and kissed his sister. It was a gentle, sad kiss. Isaac stood moist-eyed, and they embraced. Jonathan then gave Isaac a heavy gold chain that he had been working on for weeks. The center of the chain twisted and wound about itself into the form of a scorpion. The scorpion's eyes were made of rubies, and diamonds sparkled about the gold as if it held sunlight. Then with tears in his eyes, Jonathan left the room.

Isaac's parents were busy seeing to their guests, making sure that wine glasses were full and plates piled high with lamb. A harvest of fruits filled bowls, and bouquets of flowers perfumed the air.

The guests ushered the shy couple to the stairs with song and dance. Isaac and Rebecca would stay in the house for seven days to guard against evil spirits that might try to harm their marriage. But even after they retired, the merrymaking continued.

Isaac gently closed out the noise of the wedding celebration and retired to his chamber to change. Rebecca's quarters were already arranged for her. She undressed rapidly, lest he come in before she was safely under the covers, and then she lay for what seemed like hours until he came.

He inched into the bed, a fraction away. Her body was so stiff next to his that he was afraid to touch her, not daring to even look at her to see if she was completely undressed. Finally, he gently took her in his arms and held her as if she would break. Amazed at the softness of her skin, he softly kissed her forehead and eyes.

"Please don't be afraid. I'll try not to hurt you."

"Isaac, I want to be a good wife . . . . I want to make you happy. It's just that I don't know what to do. I won't cry; I never cry."

"Shh . . . it won't hurt that much. Try to relax just a little," he said as he fumbled with her nightdress, in an effort to remove it. She pulled a string and the dress seemed to fall away. He was taken aback by her soft white curves. Her breasts were full, much fuller than he had guessed, so firm and incredibly smooth. As his hands caressed them, he kissed her lips, gently at first, and then he demanded more.

Exquisite sensations had been rippling through her with his touch and his kisses. She wanted him and was ashamed of her desire. He had pulled off his nightshirt and as she ran her fingers over his back she felt the angry scars of his old wound.

"Isaac, oh Isaac, I never realized how badly you were hurt!"

"Hush, it was long ago, please; don't let old memories spoil this moment." His head was spinning with desire and his old scars were the last thing he wanted to think about, as he caressed her.

"I love you, Isaac, I've always loved you," she whispered.

His body ached with her honeyed words. He hungrily explored her. She was so warm—he was beginning to understand how men could find comfort in their wives. His heart pounding, he kissed her, forgetting everything but her body. When he took her sharp and hard, she moaned. He knew he had hurt her, but he couldn't stop, his mind was lost in waves, oceans crashing over him until he was thrown upon a sandy shore. His body felt as though warm sunshine had reached his inner being for the first time. He was born anew, as if he had never taken a breath. He breathed deep, long sighs, unsure of where his body stopped and hers began.

"Isaac please." She tried to pull away.

"I love you, my wife, my love," he whispered as he swelled again. He couldn't pull away, not yet; again the ocean devoured him, throwing him helplessly from wave to wave until at last he lay once again in the sunshine on the warm breathing sand.

"Isaac, please." She was in tears now. She had tried not to cry, but she was in pain. He had hurt her. "Please, Isaac,"

He pulled away and began to kiss her again.

"Rebecca, I'm sorry; it will be better next time. They say it only hurts the first time. I'm sorry I made you cry; please don't cry." He rocked her in his arms, trying to make the pain go away. All the exquisite joy he had felt was washed away by her pain. Still, he knew it could not be helped. When she finally fell asleep in his arms, his fingers followed the lines the tears head made on her cheeks, and then began to kiss her. He couldn't believe he wanted her again, but he didn't wake her. The glow he felt was fading, but as he drifted off to sleep, he felt a well-being he had never experienced before. He was a man!

When she woke, she was alone in bed. She could hear him rustling around the room. Then the door to the balcony opened and shut. She was so grateful to be alone for a moment. It had not been at all as she had expected it to be. She knew there would be pain, but she had been enjoying it all so much just before he came to her. She felt shame, shame that she had enjoyed it, shame that she had cried. She got up, quickly put on her sleeping gown and robe, and went out onto the balcony. He was startled to see her.

"Rebecca, are you all right?"

But from the way she tensed when they embraced, he could see that she was still in pain.

"I should have had some experience; then I wouldn't have hurt you," he chided himself.

She clung to him—that was exactly what she had dreaded.

"No! It couldn't be helped. I'm fine, and I'll do better next time," she said as cheerfully as possible, but she thought, "Please, Dear God, let him wait a few days."

Isaac did wait, though his new-found power was hard to suppress whenever he gazed at her, whenever he touched her. Five days later, she felt she was ready again. He kissed her face, her neck, her arms, her breasts until he felt as if he were spinning, as if his whole body were about to explode. How he loved her, her warm body reaching up for him; she wanted him, and he took her, this time with more control, gently, but Rebecca felt an exquisite throbbing, a rippling that made her shudder over and over until, at last, panting, she lay still in his arms, his hands cradling her head. Falling asleep, there were entwined, had become one.

Simon, Isaac's servant, knocked gently on their door. Isaac rose to meet the man whose face was unusually pale; it was a very serious matter to disturb a newly-wed couple.

"What is it, Simon? What brings you here like this?"

The man bowed to him.

"My lord, I'm greatly distressed to intrude on you, but it's my lady's brother, sir; no one has seen him since your wedding night."

"No! Isaac, it can't be true!" Rebecca ran to his side.

"Let him finish. Speak up!"

"No one knows what to fear; he has just disappeared, my lord. He's gone. All his jewels, his tools, his clothes are all gone. Last night a man on his way back from Castile saw a well-dressed gentleman crossing into Castile, and from his description it sounded very much like Señor Ben Ezra. I felt I couldn't wait any longer to tell you."

"Get my cloak, Simon." Isaac was afraid Jonathan had indeed carried out his mad plan.

"Isaac, you can't leave the house! Our marriage—you'll bring bad luck!"

"Jonathan is gone! Can't you understand what Simon just said? Perhaps I can catch up with him; perhaps I can bring him back. I have to try!"

Isaac quickly dressed and then rode with Simon to the Ben Ezra home. Except for a few servants, it was empty. Isaac went to the back courtyard to the workshop. The room was neat and clean—all of Jonathan's tools were gone. Isaac was about to ride to Fernando when his eye caught a piece of paper with his name on it. He broke the seal and read:

My dearest brother,

Do not grieve for me. I am fine and not so very far away. It brings me sorrow when I think of leaving you, but you must not search for me. I am gone from your lives, never to return. Take care of Rebecca. She is precious to me. I told you once before I would have taken her with me, had she not been so in love with you. I love you too, Isaac, and this parting is like a tearing of the flesh, but you have set me free from my obligations to my sister and to the Jews within our Judería.

I will be forever grateful. May you always walk in peace. If you cannot forgive me, at least please try to understand that I cannot live within the confines of the Judería, our way of life here in Portugal.

Your loving brother, Jonathan

Isaac ripped the paper into shreds. A cold chill swept over him as he cried, "Jonathan! Why? Why is life so very difficult for you? Why can't you accept who you are?"

Isaac wept as he had never done before. What would he tell Rebecca? She would never understand this. Jonathan was dead, yes, for all of them, he was dead. It would be less painful for her to think this than to know the truth; only Isaac would know the truth, that he was not dead but alive and well somewhere in Castile.

CHAPTER 8

The Braganzas gave Isaac a castle near Lisbon for a wedding gift, and no one dared to challenge the breach of law. Leaving the walls of the Judería was the fulfillment of a lifelong dream for Isaac's father Judah, when he and Sarah joined the young couple. Isaac beamed as Fernando handed him the key to the gates of his new home. But remembering the violence of men who lived outside her protective walls, the men who had brought about her father's death, Rebecca could not rejoice. She did not want to leave the Judería, the place where she had been raised, where she knew everyone, and they knew her, Jonathan's sister, Isaac's wife. But she bravely faced her jubilant family as they celebrated their good fortune with Fernando and his brothers at a breakfast feast in the castle's banquet hall. Dressed in a fashionable low cut crimson silk gown, she caught the roving eyes of all the young men in the room. With her long golden hair and her soft brown eyes, she brought a sigh to the lips of more than one. Isaac's brothers, Jacob and Joseph, were to live within the castle walls with the family, but Samuel would stay in the Judería and continue his practice of medicine. Rebecca was grateful that two of her brothers-in-law would be with them, for it meant men would be around to keep intruders away. She worried about the peasants who worked their new lands. How would they take to a Jewish lord? Her fears, however, were unfounded for when the Braganzas issued an order, their word was law; only the king could challenge them. When he heard about the Braganza gift to the Abravanels, King Afonso thought it a splendid idea and gave Isaac another charming villa near one of his own castles in Evora.

After the dishes of smoked fish and vegetables were cleared and the delicate desserts all enjoyed, the lord of the castle excused himself and his precious bride, and guided her down a stone path to the ocean far below. The sea was calm as gentle aquamarine wave after wave washed the rocky shore, the water stretching before them until it merged with the clear blue sky. The sun's rays shattered against the water sending splinters of light skimming across its surface. As Isaac pressed her close and began to kiss her, Rebecca could feel his body tense with his need. She pulled herself away and chided him, "Isaac, if you want to make love to me, then we must go back."

He pulled her close to him again and smiled.

"No, Rebecca, I want to take you here by the sea." He tried to remove her gown.

"Isaac! Please, don't!" Trying to stop him, she held his head close to her breast. She whispered in his ear, "Please, Isaac, not here, I don't want anyone to see us." Isaac pulled away from her embrace and drew her to the ground. Heady from the sun and the wine, she let herself sink into the warm sand, and she wrapped her arms around him. He began to unfasten her gown again.

"Isaac don't! You're pulling off my gown! Don't!" she continued to plead.

He held her close and whispered, "Rebecca, my love, no one will see us, and even if they do, I don't care! This is my land; I am the master." He kissed her again and again until she gave in to him. As she relaxed, Isaac slipped the crimson silk off her body, and then rapidly undressed himself before she could change her mind. In the warm sunshine, they lay on her gown. He wanted this—to take her at the water's edge. Her breasts were so white, so soft to touch. He kissed her lips, her neck, while his hands caressed her body. He swelled and united with her, lost to the rhythm of the sea. Their souls soared meeting again and again, sparks setting fire to fire above the blue water. Then slowly, very slowly, they sank back into themselves until they rested locked in their love.

Isaac pulled away, kissing her arms and hands as Rebecca reached up for him to come back. He turned and plunged into the cold, clear water. Rebecca let the sun melt like warm butter over her body; it seemed to caress her as Isaac had done. She sat up and searched for him in the waves, where he was moving swiftly. His muscular arms, the same arms that had held her so tightly moments before, pulled him forward. She was amazed to see him swim so well and was fascinated to watch his long lean body, flashes of white flesh, moving in the sea. Gingerly, she made her way to the water's edge and sat down. She let the waves lick her toes, icy cold compared to the warm stones and the heat of her own body. She was surprised by an overpowering wave which threw her back against the shore. She struggle up and promptly dressed, feeling she was not meant to be in that enchanting but dangerous element.

When Isaac finally swam back and emerged from the water, he was disappointed to see her dressed. He laid his head on her lap and let the sun dry him. She tickled his ear.

"I didn't know you could swim so well!"

He laughed, his eyes sparkling.

"There is a lot I do well that you don't know about." He tried to undress her again.

"Isaac, don't." She shied away. He pressed her no further and contented himself with his head on her lap.

"Tell me, where did you learn to swim like that?" she asked.

"Fernando taught me a long time ago, but it was Jonathan who . . . ." When Rebecca tensed at her brother's name, Isaac did not continue. He had told her that Jonathan was dead, but she didn't believe it—not for a moment. She had heard their servant say that someone fitting Jonathan's description had been seen heading into the Spanish countryside. This made more sense to her; she knew he was dissatisfied with his life, and she also understood why Isaac could not accept what he had done. But for her, he was not dead; he was alive and, she hoped, happy in another land. Maybe someday she would see him again, but for now, she let Isaac believe that she accepted his death. In a way it was true, for he was gone from their lives. She gave a little sigh; he was gone.

They drifted off into a deep sleep. The sun had begun its descent by the time they awoke, and Isaac got up to dress. They sat on the stones and watched the fiery sun sizzle into the ocean, throwing streaks of red and blue, then violent purple and brilliant pink, across the western sky in a special display for their delight; as if to say God was pleased with their love.

Kneeling before an altar of gold, with Christ on the cross high above him, Jonathan was baptized Juan Sanchez de Sevilla, Isaac's grandfather's Christian name.

"Very fitting," he thought, as he rose and smiled at Prince Fernando who had accompanied him into Castile for the great occasion. They walked out to bright sunshine, but Jonathan did not feel the elation, the release of pressure, he had hoped. After walking to Toledo's Plaza Mayor, they drank red wine, and Fernando ordered a plate of shrimp, giving Jonathan his first taste of the previously forbidden shellfish.

"Sweet tasting," he said, smiling, but after trying a few, his stomach felt slightly queasy, so he decided not to have any more.

Sensing the tension in his friend, Fernando put his hand on Jonathan's shoulder.

"It will be hard at first, I know, to accept your new world. But you will be happy, Jonathan, I mean Juan. You will find an inner peace you have never known before. It was the right thing to do. I pray that someday Isaac will follow in your footsteps."

Jonathan looked at him in surprise. Surely he didn't think Isaac would ever convert! Isaac! The precious lamb of the Judería!

"That will never happen, Fernando," he answered. "If you expect your friendship with Isaac to flourish, you must never expect that of him. He and I are very different."

"But why? Why shouldn't he see the light as you have?"

"Because his light comes from within. His faith, his hope is so strong I fear it might someday consume him," Jonathan said bitterly, then took a long swallow of wine.

"I've bestowed upon him a castle outside the Judería."

Jonathan choked, sputtering on the wine.

"What! You did what?"

"I didn't want him buried behind the walls of the Judería, so I've moved him and his family out." He patted Jonathan on the back.

Jonathan carefully wiped his face and tried to wash away a small wine spot from his white satin shirt.

"Well, that was very generous of you," he said, trying to remain calm, his red face betraying his voice. "I must say, I can't imagine Rebecca moving out of the Judería."

Fernando, absorbed in his own thoughts, didn't seem to notice Jonathan's agitated state.

"She wasn't pleased, but I'm sure she'll quickly get use to the idea."

"Yes, I'm sure she will," Jonathan answered, closing his eyes for a moment, the sun striking his face. As he let the idea sink in, the idea of Isaac living in one of Fernando's many castles, he felt heavy, weighted, for it seemed that in this one strikingly generous move, Fernando had given Isaac everything Jonathan wanted, to be free of those walls, that ghetto, that prison.

"I love her you know," Fernando whispered.

"Who?" Jonathan asked, coming out of his reverie.

"Your sister."

Jonathan sank back deep into his seat, so uncomfortable with the idea that he didn't know how to answer.

"You must never, never let Isaac know."

"I don't intend to. Have no fear; I love them both too much to ever hurt them."

Jonathan smiled back, and they toasted one another, but as he drank his wine he wondered if he'd ever find the happiness Isaac always seemed to enjoy.

Fernando's horse thudded to a halt while the gates of the castle were opened for him. Kicking up the dust, he galloped into the main courtyard and dismounted. Isaac hurried out to meet him; he had never seen him charge into the castle like that before.

"What's wrong? Is it something serious?" Isaac's worry eased when he saw Fernando's grin.

"King Afonso has made a match! His sister, the Princess Juana, will wed King Enríque of Castile!"

"Well! This is something to celebrate, though I've heard he's an odd man."

Fernando roared with laughter.

"Odd is putting it nicely!" He threw his arm around Isaac and said superciliously, "Isaac, don't you know about the good king of Castile! You know, of course, why his marriage to Queen Blanche was annulled. Some say it was because there was no heir. However, I have it from the finest authority that he couldn't . . . you know" He broke into a boisterous laugh.

"What are you insinuating?" Isaac asked, though he clearly understood.

"His impotence is only one of his problems."

"Who told you that? Besides, I thought there is an heir to the throne."

"Oh yes, there's an heir to the throne, but he's no threat. He's Enríque's half brother, a frail child, Prince Alfonso; the king doesn't expect him to reach his manhood. The boy has an older sister as well, the Princess Isabella, but Enríque keeps both of them locked away in a lonely castle in Segovia with their mad mother."

"I'd like to know where you get all this gossip. I've often wondered about you and your Spanish information!" Isaac was joking, but Fernando reddened, cast his eyes down and said nothing. Uneasy with the strained silence, suddenly wondering if his source could be Jonathan, Isaac said, "Come, let's go inside and tell Rebecca this latest news."

"A grand idea!" Fernando perked up again.

Fernando had been hoping Isaac would suggest that. As he had confessed to Jonathan, he desired Rebecca though she was the one woman he could never possess. He felt nothing for his own wife. Most women, in fact, he found insensitive to the world around them. Rebecca's deep brown eyes could see the pain, the loneliness in others. Perhaps it was the glint of gold in her hair or the way her eyes sparkled—he was never quite sure—but she definitely resembled Jonathan. How could he tell Isaac that he and Jonathan still communicated with each other? He loved Isaac and would never do anything to hurt him, but he loved Jonathan as well and was proud that he had converted to Christianity.

The men entered the courtyard where Rebecca was standing. Fernando had wanted her to live in this castle. He wasn't sure whether he had given it to Isaac because he wanted him out of the Judería or because of her. He knew she wasn't pleased, that she felt isolated here, but when he saw her standing among the blooming roses and jasmine, her hair glistening in the sun, a warm blush on her cheeks, he felt he had done the right thing. Rebecca belonged here, surrounded by this serene beauty. Beside a cool fountain, they sipped sweetened lemon juice and ate small almond cakes. He watched with desire as Rebecca licked the sweets with her quick tongue and bit the cake with childlike delight. How he loved her! Isaac interrupted his thoughts.

"So, you were saying, this royal match is a most unusual one. Knowing what he does about Enríque, why has King Afonso consented?"

"My dear friend, can't you see the grand opportunity this is for Portugal? With the Turks in control of Constantinople, the Saracens are tightening the noose around the neck of Christian lands. They are swinging their scimitars in our direction! We need all the alliances we can get. We must unite the Christian world to show the Moslems we are invincible." He continued in a hushed tone after he had quickly looked over his shoulder, "King Afonso is going to raise another crusade. He wants to push into Africa!"

"What can he accomplish? Does he think he can conquer Africa?" Isaac was incredulous.

"There is power in the cross, Isaac. Though it may be difficult for you to believe, God will help us accomplish the impossible, if our faith is strong. Or would you rather see the Moslems multiply and have us open our gates to them as your ancestors once did?"

This remark stung Isaac; he had thought Fernando incapable of hurting him.

Fernando quickly realized he had insulted him.

"Isaac, I'm sorry. I was only joking. Were there ever trouble in our land, you know I'd count on you before all others for aid."

Isaac decided to ignore the remark; Fernando was too good a friend. He continued the conversation as if there had been no slight.

"Where would he begin such a campaign?" he asked.

"After his father's terrible defeat in Morocco, he'd start there. His brother, my uncle, Prince Fernando, died in prison there, and the shame of it still smarts. He wants to take Alcacer Seguir and then move on to Tangier."

"So you're saying King Afonso is willing to trade his sister's happiness for support for this campaign?"

"Yes. King Enríque will pressure the Moors in Granada while King Afonso leads the crusade in Africa. Juana was prepared for this. A princess is raised knowing her marriage will suit the political needs of her kingdom. Besides, she won't suffer; after all, she will become Queen of Castile! And there are always handsome knights about to please a queen, whatever her needs may be!" He laughed.

"Fernando!" Rebecca had gotten up to serve more lemonade and hadn't heard the beginning of the conversation, but she got the gist of it.

"I'm sure Princess Juana will perform her duties as a wife and produce an heir to the throne who will be worthy of the titles bestowed upon him!"

"Spoken from the ruby lips of a satisfied bride, Rebecca." Fernando teased and she blushed.

"I'm afraid marriage is not always a blissful state of affairs, but your delicate ears should not have to listen to rumors that have spread about the King of Castile."

Isaac didn't want Fernando to reveal any sordid details to his wife and was about to interrupt the conversation when Rebecca said, "Women can take much more pain and suffering than men; I'm sure Princess Juana will overcome whatever fate has in store for her and make the best of it!"

Isaac quickly changed the topic to taxes and balancing Fernando's ledgers, topics that excluded Rebecca from the conversation, but he watched Fernando's eyes devouring his wife. He knew Fernando was in love with her, and he wondered just how deeply she cared for him.

The moment Princess Juana met King Enríque she realized her brother had traded her for his own political purposes. None of the fabulous jousts held in her honor, nor the bullfights, the parties, the magnificent jewels lavished upon her, could make her happy. The Spanish attempt at pageantry seemed pathetic to her, for she had been raised in wealthy Portugal. The gold could not compare; it didn't have the same luster. The silks and satins, though they came from the same foreign ports, didn't have the same sheen. Even the fruits and fowl tasted sour to her well-trained palate. Castile was a poor kingdom compared to Portugal, and the king, the king had as much sexual allure for her as her chambermaid.

These thoughts crossed her mind as she was traveling back to Madrid with the royal hunting party. The horses and riders were prancing down the road with King Enríque in the lead, followed by the Marquis de Villena, Juana in her litter, five knights and their ladies, and twenty men at arms, when a fully suited warrior, his visor down and lance tilted to do battle, stopped them along the way. The king quickly called for one of his men at arms to see who this menacing figure was. The guard galloped back to report that the warrior challenged all who passed to fight for the superior beauty of Queen Juana. She, in turn, was annoyed to have their trip delayed, for the litter was most uncomfortable, but Enríque was delighted with this display of chivalry, and they pulled their entourage off the path to watch the mysterious man display his talents. Shortly after they stopped, the king's own guards began to challenge the warrior.

"What is it that you want?" the king lisped.

"To prove my worthiness to your lady."

"Oh, this is grand, don't you think?" He asked Juana, who stared out the other side of litter, unimpressed.

However, when one by one the warrior pitched the knights off their horses, the knight finally caught her attention. The call went out across the land, and many men left their sheep and oxen in the fields to watch the *caballeros* challenge the mysterious knight. All day long men took their turns trying to unhorse him without success, for he was by far the strongest and most skillful with a lance. Several young men broke their arms and legs; and one poor fellow broke his collarbone and had to be carried away by his father and brothers. Annoying mosquitoes and flies buzzed about Juana as she watched the man pitch armored knights and young squires off their horses to hit the ground with a thud, but she grew more interested, perhaps even a bit quizzical about the man behind the metal visor. The sun was blazing, and she was sure that after a few strenuous hours any man would give in to the heat, if not the competition, but he did not. The metal suit shone in the sun as he met challenge after challenge in his tribute to her. So far he had not identified himself.

The champion finally dismounted when no one else came forward at the end of the eventful day. He pulled off his helmet and let his black curly hair fall across his face. His skin dripped with sweat, and he had suffered burns from the hot metal armor, but he bowed to his king with great dignity.

"Your Majesty, Beltrán de la Cueva, your servant."

"Cueva, Cueva," he answered in his high, thin voice, "Yes, I know your father. You may rise, Beltrán." He stood before his king.

"You have shown yourself to be a true champion today and deserve to be given a title!" His voice grated above the noisy crowd that had gathered.

"It is my most fervent wish, Your Majesty!" Beltrán bowed once again to King Enríque. The royal procession took up where it had left off, and they continued now with one more in their company. Beltrán bowed to Queen Juana as her litter passed. Pulling aside her curtain to see him, she held her head high and though she was fascinated, she tried to seem untouched by his curly black hair, shining black eyes and muscular body. However, she felt naked under his piercing stare and took her time closing the curtain, letting a smile cross her lips for him to see just as the curtain was drawn.

A great feast was set for the new champion in King Enríque's court. The king was ecstatic with the day's unprecedented performance, having never seen such prowess in a man! When Beltrán entered the hall, the women buzzed with excitement. Juana was annoyed that they all found him so attractive, for even though it bothered her a great deal, she was attracted to him. Rumors flew. He was the son of a wealthy *caballero* and had been trained for combat from infancy. No, he was not married and had taken vows never to marry. Could it be that he was in love with the queen?

After the feast, Enríque stood, placed his naked sword on the young man's shoulders, and bestowed upon him a knighthood, the new Count of Ledesma. The king decided that a monastery, dedicated to St. Jerome, was to be erected on the spot where Cueva had fought for the honor of his queen. Don Beltrán bowed to the king and queen, brazenly kissing her hand before the entire court.

"Pity," Juana thought as she gazed at herself in a clear pool of water in her private courtyard one week after the feast.

"I'd rather die than go to bed with Enríque again." She stroked her long black hair and tears slid down her cheeks, as she thought about her wedding night. Intoxicated, Enríque had come to her after she had fallen asleep. She didn't know how long he had been standing there staring at her, but she woke, frightened by his figure. He had roughly pulled back her covers, lifted her gown and then laid on top of her. Though he was not a fat man, the weight of his body hurt her, and she felt revulsion as his icy fingers crept up and down her body. She felt no pain that night and wasn't even sure she had been taken.

"How could my brother have done this to me? I am King Duarte's daughter, granddaughter of King João I! How could Afonso have matched me with this poor excuse for a man!" she fumed. At that moment, another image appeared in the pool of water, mingling with hers. She looked up, brushing back tears, as the handsome Beltrán de la Cueva bowed to her.

"Your Majesty," he said, and had the effrontery to kiss her hand. "The Marquis de Villena mentioned that you spend a great deal of time in your garden. It is a fitting place for one as beautiful as you."

He helped her rise to her feet, gathered her into his arms and kissed her lips, the tips of her ears, and searched for what was not his to take. She slapped him hard across his face. He smiled back at her as red welts from her fingers spread across his cheek.

"I'll not let you waste your beauty on Enríque. The other day, in the field, it was just a show of my prowess, nothing compared to how I would fight for you in battle. I would die for you," he said as he knelt before her and bowed his head.

Juana wanted to run her fingers through his hair as she stared down at him. She thought of all the men, some of whom were well seasoned knights and guards, who had fallen to his blows.

"You may rise, Don Beltrán de la Cueva." She wanted to be held, to be ravished. She felt as if she were a prisoner in her own kingdom, in her own castle, in her own body. Beltrán lifted her and carried her away, seeming to know where he was going, though at the last moment she had to direct him toward her chambers.

As he skillfully undressed her, she asked no questions; she didn't want to know about him. She didn't care. She wanted to feel muscular arms hold her, to be passionately, hungrily kissed and ravished. Beltrán greedily fulfilled his queen's desire. She arched and beckoned for more until she fell exhausted to the deep sleep of satiated love. When she awoke, he was next to her, and she huddled close, enjoying the smell of his sweated skin. She woke him from his sleep and before she could speak, he was exciting her again, taking her again. Afterward, she could not sleep.

"Why aren't you sleeping, my beauty? Do you want more?" He laughed as she pulled away.

"No, I've had enough. What kind of man are you who would simply come and take his queen as though she were his prize?"

"Oh, my queen, I love you, would die for you."

"And what if I hadn't been willing, what then?" she said, stroking her hair.

"I took only what you offered." A grin spread across his face. She reached up to slap him again, but this time he caught her arm in his hand. She tried to scratch him with her other hand, but he caught that as well and pinned her against the silken sheets, her arms spread wide, his body still between her legs.

"You are caught, my love, and I will never let you go, never!"

He kissed her again and though she didn't think she wanted more, her body melted with his once again. She had never felt so alive. It was true; she was his and she would never want another. In the morning, she quickly changed the sheets on her bed before the servants came to wake her. Though she should have felt proud, she was embarrassed to let them see the blood stains on the pure white sheets.

CHAPTER 9

By 1460, the caravel had been perfected. A new lateen rigging made the ship more flexible, and with the newly invented astrolabe, navigation was more accurate. The ships sailed faster, exchanging goods in enormous volume. Isaac had replaced his father as treasurer for the Braganzas, and Judah was busy with the king's commerce. They were occupied tallying and taxing pepper, ivory and wood. Slaves were arriving from Africa while from India, Ceylon and Tibet came cotton cloth and spices: cinnamon, ginger, nutmeg and cloves. From the Far East, from China, came fine silks. Caravans traveling overland to the Guinea coast carried gold, and Portugal's caravels, Prince Henry's ships, brought the precious metal home. There was only so much Don Judah could do in a day; and though Isaac was nearly overwhelmed by his own share in the Braganza affairs, he often managed to find time to help his father. King Afonso had given his uncle, Prince Henry, free reign over the waters; the ships continued to set sail in search of Prester John. What Henry never realized was that he had found his treasures, the trade routes were established, and the kingdom of Prester John would remain an enigma forever.

Isaac had been in Evora working with his father for the king. Now prodding his horse, he galloped toward his castle and thought of Rebecca. He was anxious about her, for heavy with child, she was sleeping poorly. She told him she loved to feel the baby moving about in her swollen belly, but the kicking kept her awake. She had decided to give birth in Lisbon, in the Judería of all places! She said she wanted his brother, Samuel, to be by her side when she went into labor. Isaac knew she wanted to give birth in the Judería with her own midwives, and the security of Samuel nearby. Isaac's firstborn would begin life in the same home, the same room, the same bed in which he had been born. He had to dismount as he came to the Judería gates. It seemed strange that he had never felt locked in when he had lived there, so unlike Jonathan. He hadn't thought of Jonathan in a long time, but now that Rebecca was so near to giving birth, he missed him. The gatekeeper opened the heavy iron door as Isaac rode toward his old home. It had seemed so large when he was a child that he was surprised to find it a modest house though the heavy wooden door carved with grape leaves and the inner courtyard with its beautiful blue, cream, and orange tiles spoke of past grandeur. He took the steps two at a time, wanting to run into her arms, to smell her sweet scent, to lose himself in her. The house was unusually quiet when he entered. No one came to greet him.

"I'm home! Hello!" he called, then turned to see his mother and brother, their faces haggard and pale, come out of his father's library. Isaac felt the blood drain from his face—something was very wrong.

"Samuel, where's Rebecca?" He grabbed his brother and shook him. "Where is she?"

"She's upstairs." He pushed Isaac back more roughly than he had meant. "The labor started thirty hours ago, Isaac . . . ." He couldn't go on. Sarah began to weep and turned back into the library.

"Thirty hours!" Isaac sank onto the stairway steps and buried his head in his arms, seeming to fold into himself when he collapsed.

Samuel shook him gently.

"Isaac, listen to me, you must go up to her; I think she's dying. We're afraid the baby is already dead."

"Then why are you standing here? Why aren't you up there helping her? You're a doctor!"

"Isaac, I've been up with her all night. We've used herbs—brews—we've done everything there is to do."

"No! There must be something! You must be able to do something . . . . You've got to save her, Samuel. You can't let her die!"

"There's nothing more to do. She's exhausted. She can't go on. I'm sorry." He was hoarse from the strain of the last few hours.

Isaac ran up the long winding stairway and threw open the doors to the bedchamber. The room was dark and for a moment he couldn't see anything; then two women, midwives, scurried out of the room. They assumed he had come to say good-bye, that there was nothing more they could do for her. Isaac threw open the curtains covering the windows; the room was too dark and dank. Her eyes were closed, her face white, deathlike. Isaac sank at the side of the bed when he realized he might really lose her.

"No! Dear God, no, this can't be happening." He held her hand and cried. "It can't be true." He kissed her hand, held her limp, unresponsive body, and then he felt the monstrous swelling in her belly.

Rebecca woke with the pain. She saw Isaac, but it didn't matter that he was there; nothing mattered but the pain. She couldn't bear the terrible pounding. It had to stop! It had to!

"Push, my love, push!" he pleaded with her. "Fight for your life. You have to fight for it. Don't leave me, Rebecca! Please don't leave me," he whispered. He dropped to the floor by her side, choking on tears.

Seeming to hear him from the darkness into which she had descended, Rebecca tried once more to push with her last bit of strength.

"You can do this," he whispered to her sweated, pale face. "Don't leave me."

Rebecca's eyes fluttered open.

"Midwives!" he cried. "Samuel!"

Samuel and the midwives ran in. The baby had started moving again, and some progress had been made. Samuel escorted Isaac out of the room, and within the hour the baby came with a strong, loud cry. But Rebecca was bleeding heavily, and though the midwives usually tended the mother, Samuel cared for her. Isaac crept back into the room and stood against the wall. It had happened so quickly. His son was being washed by the women, but Rebecca was lying there still, white. He was afraid she was dead. Samuel pulled him from the room.

"Is she dead?" His voice shook.

"No, the bleeding has stopped for the moment, but it could start again, and then there won't be anything I can do."

"If anything happens to her, I won't go on."

"You're talking like a madman! You have to expect this with childbirth, Isaac; it happens. It's God's way."

"No, I will not accept that!" Isaac shouted. "God will not take her from me, not like this!" His face was scarlet. "How could God take her like this?" He doubled over against the wall.

"It's not yours to question, Isaac. She has a small pelvis, and it doesn't allow . . ."

"Stop your explanations . . . . I don't want to hear them . . . . She is alive. I will not let her die!"

"That's not your decision to make." Samuel was too tired to stand there and argue with him. "Look, please get some rest; the women will call us if there are any changes. We all need to get some sleep." Isaac clenched his fists as he watched Samuel stumble off to his room.

Sleep! His wife was hanging at the edge of life, and his brother told him to sleep? He gently opened the door and was angry to see that the midwives had closed the curtains and made the room dark again. One of the women came up to him and asked him to leave, explaining that Rebecca needed her rest.

He wanted to roar, but kept his voice under control and ordered them out of the room. He wanted to watch over her himself, and they were grateful that someone wanted to take charge, for they were exhausted. They were so old, their skin falling loosely over their bones. It was strange to see them holding the infant; for an instant, the babe seemed as old as they with his skin wrinkled around his tiny frame. They bundled the baby, placed him in his elaborately carved wooden cradle, and left. Once again, Isaac pulled back the curtains to let the sunlight fill the room. He knew she needed her sleep, but he couldn't bear to see her lie in the darkness as if she were already dead. The sunlight cheered him a little, for it seemed as if the warm rays could keep death away. He walked back to Rebecca whose breath was ragged, but she slept. How could God take her from him? It just couldn't happen. Her breath was so shallow, her eyelids and golden lashes hardly fluttered. Isaac fell to his knees to pray.

"Please, dear God, please don't take her from me. Samuel can't do any more for her. Our lives are in Your hands." He sat in the chair next to her and anxiously watched her sleep. He wept, not wanting to live without her. How could God bring death with the new life? None of his studying, none of his work, nothing prepared him for the void that opened before him as he watched Rebecca's shallow breathing, so fragile, not enough to ruffle a feather. Rocking back and forth he watched over her until, hours later, he mercifully fell asleep.

He awakened with the baby's cry. Sarah rushed in, afraid the baby would wake Rebecca. She lifted the bundle from the cradle, desperate to find a wet nurse. Before she left with the babe, she kissed her own dazed son. Isaac shook himself awake. How could he have slept! Rebecca was so still. He felt her head and panicked; she had a fever!

"Samuel! Samuel, she's burning! Please come, Samuel!"

His brother stumbled into the room, felt Rebecca's forehead, then put his arm around Isaac's shoulder and comforted him.

"I have something for this."

Isaac watched helplessly as Samuel prepared a mixture, and then roused Rebecca to help her swallow the medicine. Isaac was so grateful for Samuel's gentle ministrations.

"This should bring the fever down. If it doesn't, wake me in an hour," Samuel said as he left the room.

Isaac woke just as the sun was rising to see Rebecca still alive. He sat down gingerly on the edge of the bed and felt her forehead. She was slightly warm, but the raging fever had died down. She opened her eyes.

"The baby?" she whispered, for her throat was dry.

Isaac held her head as she drank some cool water.

"We have a wonderful boy, but you must grow strong so that you can take care of him. I need you, my love." Having been so close to losing her, he choked on his words. He buried his head in her breast. With what little strength she had, she held him for a moment until her arms fell to her sides.

"Where is he? I want to see him."

"Mother took him to a wet-nurse last night. I'll see if they are in the house." He rose and, for the first time, felt the fatigue of the terror which had seized him. He roamed the house until he found his mother, and the baby sleeping together in a chair by the large central hearth. Trying not to wake her, he took the baby from Sarah's arms, but the infant cried and startled her from her sleep.

"Rebecca?" she asked.

"The fever is down, and she wants to see the baby."

"Thank goodness I found a wet-nurse last night, but he'll grow hungry soon," Sarah mumbled, closing her eyes and drifting back to sleep.

Isaac carried his precious son back to Rebecca. She also had fallen asleep, so he settled into the chair next to her bed and tried to hush the baby by rocking him. The infant seemed to stare at him as if he were trying to recognize him.

"Do you know me? Perhaps we've met before." Isaac laughed, releasing some of the tension in his body. The baby nuzzled into Isaac's chest, seeking his mother's warm milk.

"I'm afraid this won't do," Isaac said as he kissed the small damp forehead. Frustrated, the baby began to cry, setting a knot in the pit of Isaac's stomach. He didn't know what to do, and sat there helplessly. Rebecca opened her eyes and tried to sit up. Isaac brought the distressed infant to his mother.

"Are you up for this?" he asked, feeling guilty about waking her.

Rebecca held her infant for the first time and she smiled as the babe rooted for her breast. Weary though she was, she pulled the sash on her gown and took the baby to her. She thought the infant would know what to do, but he had trouble grasping the soft nipple until she guided him. The baby sucked with a serious, thoughtful expression. When he was full, his little body relaxed. The nursing had lulled mother and child to sleep.

Isaac gently lifted the baby, terrified that he might wake again, and gingerly placed him in the cradle beside Rebecca's bed. He stared at the baby for a moment, trying to grasp all that had happened. She was going to be all right. His Rebecca, who seemed a part of his own body, his own soul, was going to live, and he had a son, a fine healthy son. The elation turned suddenly to fatigue. He felt so tired as if his head were an enormous weight and his legs would collapse under him. He tiptoed out of the room and finding an unoccupied bed, threw himself down and fell into an exhausted slumber.

The eleven year old Isabella, daughter of the late King Juan II of Castile, half-sister to King Enríque and god-mother of the Infanta Juana born in the year 1462, held Queen Juana's baby in her arms, and sang prayers for the child in a strong, clear voice before the noblemen of Castile. Her long red hair glistened in the sunlight filtering through the brilliant red and blue stained glass windows of the cathedral. The Archbishop of Toledo took the child from her as the ceremony continued. Throughout, Beltrán de la Cueva stood beside the king, not daring to look at the queen; the infant was already nicknamed *"La Beltráneja,"* daughter of Beltrán.

"Let them gossip," he thought as he arrogantly stared at the congregation gathered to see the Infanta baptized. "What does it matter? By tomorrow, seventeen cities will declare the baby heir to the throne."

Queen Juana had seen to it that the rumors about Enríque's impotence were squelched, and Enríque was so delighted to have a child that he convinced himself that Juana had conceived her on their wedding night.

The Princess Isabella and her brother, Prince Alfonso, kissed the baby's hand in homage before they were ushered out and quickly helped up on to the waiting mules, ready to leave for their castle in Arevalo. The archbishop watched the departure of the children, seemingly unimportant figures amongst the wealthy nobility, while the Marquis de Villena strolled up to him.

"Well, their station in life has just had a shift for the worse, wouldn't you say Carrillo?" His slicked mustache bounced above his lip as he spoke.

The Archbishop swung around to face the unctuous man. "The wheel of fortune is forever turning, Pacheco. They are still second and third in line to the throne."

"Yes, and wouldn't you like to see them moved up in that line of succession!" The Marquis laughed. "Cardinal Carrillo!" he continued. "I can see the ambition in your eyes. You'll never be satisfied with archbishop!"

Carrillo wanted to slap the man across the face, but, rather, in a voice affecting control, he answered.

"I will follow the path God has designed for me. If it is His will that I should rise within the Church, then so be it. I am here to serve the Lord and Castile whenever the need should arise."

"And I assume the need has arrived with the Infanta Juana!" Pacheco continued to bait the archbishop.

"Are you insinuating that Juana should not be declared heir to the throne, Pacheco?" He took the taunt in stride.

"Not at all! I am merely suggesting that it would be foolish for you to let your own ambitions cloud 'God's will.' The Infanta Juana will be declared heir. The Princess Isabella will wed my brother, strengthening my position with King Enríque, and I suggest you use your influence for young Prince Alfonso and place him in an order for the service of God!"

Now it was Carrillo's turn to laugh, and Villena's face reddened as he abruptly walked away. Rumor had spread through the court, throughout all of Castile that the Infanta Juana was Beltrán's child; and even if she was declared heir to the throne, there were many who would seriously doubt the justice of her claim. Fools like Pacheco, Marquis of Villena, thought the Infanta Juana would succeed King Enríque, but the archbishop kept his eyes on the little blond boy and lovely redheaded girl as they slowly disappeared over the horizon. The courts would never allow Princess Isabella to marry Pacheco's brother, a commoner in everyone's eyes. As for Alfonso, the archbishop had plans for Alfonso; perhaps it would be the young Princess Juana who would serve God, but Carrillo planned to see Prince Alfonso become King of Castile!

As the congregation left the cathedral, Don Beltrán pulled Queen Juana into a side chamber and kissed her passionately. She savagely slapped him across the face.

"Don't you ever kiss me in public! There is enough talk about the baby! Are you mad?"

He grabbed her cloak, practically choking her.

"You are mine, the baby is mine, and if you ever deny me, I'll tell Carrillo just whose bed you slept in the night you conceived the child! Where will your precious princess be then, my sweet?" He laughed. "Oh, Carrillo would treasure such a confession!" he said as he roughly threw her against the wall. Beltrán turned his back to her, kicked her guard in the shins for not bowing fast enough and strutted out of the cathedral. Juana stared angrily at Beltrán, the new Duke of Albuquerque, as he flung himself up across his horse and galloped away. She gracefully left the cathedral, and entered her litter, but as she leaned out to receive the baby, she noticed Archbishop Carrillo watching her. She nodded calmly and then closed the curtains. She could feel the litter being lifted off the ground and hugged the baby close to her breast as they made their way back to the lavish celebration already underway in the Alcázar in Madrid.

CHAPTER 10

Isabella felt as if a blade had pierced, pulled, and twisted her heart when she heard that her little brother, Alfonso, was dead. He was all she had, the only one she had loved. Her body convulsed with her sobs. Carrillo, the Archbishop of Toledo, had challenged the legitimacy of the Infanta Juana and crowned Alfonso king of Castile. A civil war had broken out and since then Isabella had been living in a nightmare. She felt as though she was lost in time, in her mind, and prayed to God to keep her upright as she stumbled along, but now in September of 1468, she lost the only person she loved without giving her the chance to make a separate peace with him. He had begged her to stand by his side, to follow his cause, but she had refused. She could not question the divine right of kings. As long as Enríque was her sovereign, Isabella would pay him homage, but through her tears she could almost see them, Juana and Beltrán, laughing at her. She had sided with them, and she knew they thought she was a fool. She had sided with them against her brother because Enríque had been granted the divine power to rule. As this thought crossed her mind, she ceased to cry. Though sobs caught her breath, she would not let them see her pain. Though her body ached as if from a fever, she managed to dry her eyes, dress herself in mourning robes, and walk barefoot to the antechamber of the castle's chapel. The room was cool compared to the stunning heat outside, and there on a stone slab he lay, his face white and peaceful. For her brother the struggle was over, and now with the cold reality of his death came the full awareness of its import. The rebels would try to pull her into the vortex of the storm, this raging civil war.

She knelt by Alfonso's side and held his slender, stiff hand. Alfonso had been her shield, had fought and died for her, protecting her from the rebels who would make her queen. Her fingers brushed aside the fine blond hair that fell across his forehead, and she touched his lips, so perfect in repose. How she had loved the sound of his voice when he called, "Isabella!" A scream was forcing its way up from the center of her body, but she held it back. Only silent tears escaped from the corner of her eyes. They told her that many had died from the pestilence this summer, but Isabella knew better. Her brother had been poisoned. Thinking of Joan of Arc, she stood. She had to be strong now, like her heroine, and for a wistful moment, she thought of El Cid, how Alfonso loved the story of the knight dressed in white who fought to purify Spain, and how Alfonso strove to be like him.

Fray Tomas de Torquemada was waiting for her in the chapel. The heavy woolen cloak of the Dominican Order fell loosely over his thin frame. His black eyes seared her, as if to question her soul.

"Father," she took his cold, bony hand and knelt before him. Torquemada basked in her homage to him—to God; he was sure it was a good sign for the purity of her soul.

"You must not grieve, my sweet child." He calmed her with his soothing words. "Your brother has ascended from earth's hell to the glorious kingdom of God. It is sinful to grieve for one who is with Him."

"Yes, Father," she whispered. "Please forgive my tears. I will not cry again." She dried her eyes and composed herself.

"Good! Isabella, you realize now, you must embark on a great journey to power; fearful power is within your grasp. Believe in Him, and He will not lead you astray."

"Father, they are coming for me; they want me to lead them against Enríque. What shall I say? Doesn't my half brother rule with the will of God?"

"Yes, he does. You must wait until the Lord commands you to take power, and then, when you do, Isabella, you must always have His cause foremost in your mind, body, and soul!" He bent over her and whispered, "Now is the time, my child, for you to prove yourself to Him, not to the men who would manipulate you."

She kissed his hand, and he bid her rise. She felt cleansed and certain now as to her course of action. The friar had guided her to her decision. If it was what God wanted, she was prepared to fight those adulterers who would flaunt their sins. Why hadn't she seen it before? She would do as God bid and not question His will again. Friar Tomas Torquemada had led her out of the darkness and onto a path that she could follow. The friar walked with her out to her mule, and she retreated to the convent in Avila where she prayed and waited for Archbishop Carrillo.

The archbishop was a fierce warrior as well as a servant of God, and the young woman was awed by his muscular figure clad in a scarlet cape with a pure white cross, as he entered her small, sparse chamber. "Isabella," he bowed to her, "all of Castile grieves with you. Alfonso proved himself to be a true king, a leader of men. But you must realize how desperate your people are for you to pick up his banner and fight his cause now that he is gone. It was his most fervent wish that you join us in ridding the land of the incompetent reprobate who calls himself king! You, so like your brother, follow the ways of God and must wear the crown to sanctify the throne that has been desecrated by Enríque."

Her heart pounding, she addressed the man whom she distrusted, who had led her brother to his death.

"I do not condemn Alfonso or the cause he fought. However, it is not my cause. As long as Enríque lives, I will not fight him; he inherited the throne from my father, and the divine right is his to honor or to tarnish. Though my sentiments may lie with you and those who fight against him, I will not join in your sanctimonious rebellion!"

"Whom are you accusing of being sanctimonious! Enríque is the most hypocritical, evil king a people has ever had to suffer, You sit there so righteous. Who are you to judge those who fight against him?"

She saw him grow tense as he moved closer to her. She knew he had to convince her to join him now or his cause would fail. What she still had to decide was if his cause was hers.

"Don't you realize men, women and children will die because of their treason, traitors now because they fought with your brother? You must pick up his banner and fight for justice. If you don't, Isabella, their deaths will be on your head. You must join us now!"

With a tremor running through her body, she stood and answered him, "I will not defy the King! If you think it is easy for me to watch Enríque, you are mistaken. I abhor Juana and Beltrán. But he rules by divine right, and therefore, it is sacrilegious to conspire against him!"

Carrillo grew noticeably pale.

"This is your final decision? You realize, of course, that they want you to marry King Afonso of Portugal!"

She could feel the blood drain out of her face. She had heard rumors, of course, but had not taken them seriously.

"Yes," she replied, "there has been some talk of my marrying the recently widowed King Afonso."

Seeing how she abhorred the thought, Carrillo spoke with more confidence.

"And this is what you want, Isabella, to leave Castile and allow La Beltráneja to rule someday? At this moment, there are still alternatives for you, one which will allow you to restore honor to the throne of Castile."

Remembering the aging King Afonso with his grey hair and protruding stomach, she realized the archbishop was the only one who could save her from Enríque's plotting.

"Are you referring to other suitors?"

"I have been informed that King Juan of Aragon is most anxious for a union between his kingdom and Castile. He has declared his second son, Ferdinand, heir to the throne now that the prince is old enough to marry. I will try to call a truce with Enríque, if you agree to this match, or perhaps you find the Portuguese king and life there more desirable." Isabella had already decided that she would never leave Castile. She had heard from her own informers that Ferdinand of Aragon was a valiant, handsome prince and had prayed that Ferdinand's uncle, a Castilian admiral, might make such a match for her. Now Carrillo had proposed to help her marry the one man she wanted. She answered in measured tones, for she trusted the archbishop only slightly more than Enríque, having learned a bitter lesson from her brother's death.

"If you can arrange it, then I will agree, though I know Enríque would do anything he could to prevent such a union."

Isabella saw the tension in Carrillo's body ease. She had given him what he had come for, but it served her purposes as well.

"You have my word that Enríque will not know about the marriage contract until it is sealed, and once that is done, you will have most of Castile, Leon, and all of Aragon behind you in any claim you make to the throne. I would, however, like to be assured that for my service you will promise to support me once you come to power."

She had been waiting for this and was well prepared when

"I will promise nothing, but I will always remember that you were my friend in time of need."

She knew it was not what he had expected to hear, but it would have to do. He gave her a perfunctory bow and left Isabella alone in her cold, bare room.

King Enríque saw them kissing in a dark corner of the courtyard. Juana's long black hair fell gracefully over her shoulders as Beltrán's hands caressed her back. His mouth brushed her ear then she rested her head on his shoulder as they made their way towards the queen's bedchamber. Enríque stood paralyzed in the doorway. He knew, of course, he knew, but seeing them together, flaunting their lust, was like being slapped in the face. Didn't they have the decency to keep it private! The depressed, gaunt man turned away toward his own chambers and was cursing the fate that made him king, when the Marquis de Villena approached him.

"Your Majesty," he bowed. "I've word that the Archbishop of Toledo, Carrillo, wishes to end the fighting and meet with you to work out a truce."

Enríque wasn't pleased with the idea, but he knew that many noblemen would not accept La Beltráneja as long as Isabella was unwed. He also thought the Marquis's brother would be a good match for Isabella.

"I, too, want to see the bloodshed stopped. Tell the archbishop I am willing to meet with him," Enríque sighed.

"He's here, Your Majesty. Will you see him now?"

Enríque stared at him in surprise, never sure which side the Marquis was on; he could trust the man with his slick hair and greasy mustache as easily as a cobra!

"Very well, Pacheco, I will see the archbishop now," he answered, though he didn't relish the meeting, alone at night like this.

He found the archbishop pacing the floor in the throne room. The archbishop bowed to him, and Enríque lifted his head haughtily.

"It is some small relief to assume your homage is in earnest after these years of battle. I must add that the mock coronation of my poor half-brother only heightened my anger at your treasonous acts. I even heard rumors, and I pray they were indeed just rumors, that you had the audacity to push my effigy into the dirt. That was highly insulting, don't you think, Pacheco? Do assure me, Carrillo, that those were just ugly lies. You didn't actually push my effigy into the dirt, did you?"

"Your Majesty," Carrillo answered with as much dignity as he could muster, "I come in peace. Let us not allow rash acts which may or may not have occurred in the past to jeopardize an agreement to put an end to the bloodshed. The question of your heir must be settled once and for all. That is where the disagreement lies. Will you claim the Infanta Juana or Princess Isabella as you legal heir?"

The sad king looked to the Marquis (as if he knew who was in Juana's bed the night she conceived) and then back to the archbishop and sighed once again. He thought of the lovers he had just seen. Whether or not he believed the child to be his own, he wanted peace at any cost. The kingdom was torn by rebellion, and the insurgents would never acknowledge Juana as long as Isabella was on Spanish soil.

"I will declare Isabella my heir," he answered, "if you swear allegiance to me now and forever more. I want an end to the fighting! I am the king, and if it will take my declaration of Isabella as my heir to stop the blood from flowing, then declare her I will. She, at least, believes in the divine right which so many have forgotten!"

The archbishop was not done with Enríque.

"We also want amnesty for the rebels and annulment of your marriage to Juana."

"You think it will be that simple for me to give her up?" Enríque said, gazing at him bitterly. He thought of Juana and La Beltrán. "But I agree," the king said, defeated not only by the archbishop and his rebels, but also by his queen.

Carrillo was elated. Years of battle had not settled as much as he was now extracting from the king. He was ready to execute the final blow: "And you must promise never to force Isabella to marry against her will."

"I will promise as much if she will promise never to marry without my consent," Enríque replied. "You know, of course, that I have spoken to King Afonso V of Portugal about her, and he is most anxious for her hand. A union like that could only strengthen our position against the Moors. Whatever your political ambition is, Carrillo, you must still want to see the Christian world united!"

The archbishop refrained from smiling as he thought of Enríque's mock crusade against Granada.

"I'm sure Isabella will honor you if you in turn honor her, my liege."

"Pacheco, see to it that the terms are drawn up, and I will sign them." Enríque wanted to end the audience. He was already regretting his denial of Juana, but he knew that as long as Isabella did not marry against his wishes, he was safe. If he could hand her over to the Portuguese, she would be out of the way, and he could declare Juana as his own once again.

The archbishop was staggered at how easily he had accomplished his mission. Enríque would acknowledge Isabella as heir to the throne of Castile and Leon and, with her marriage to Ferdinand, Spain would be united to fight the final crusade against Granada! Carrillo and the king parted cordially enough, both men satisfied that their own aims for the kingdom were well within reach.

The Portuguese delegation, arriving at a lonely stone fortress in Madrigal, was ushered into a room devoid of the rich tapestries and plush furniture they were accustomed to seeing. Here Isabella waited for them. She watched the men, wrapped in silken robes and decked with heavy gold chains, bowing to her and felt a certain satisfaction as she faced them in her simple, coarse gown. She was assessing this ostentatious group of men headed by the Archbishop of Lisbon, when her gaze met the fiery, black eyes of a man standing to the rear. Her heart stopped short, for she felt as if she knew the tall, lean man whose brown hair fell carelessly across his face, and whose slightly parted thin red lips formed a sly smile as if to say, "I know you will never accept this proposal." She was about to turn away from the handsome man when she saw the necklace hanging on his breast. The intricacy of the wrought gold differed greatly from the chains the other men wore. It was not the chain which fascinated her, but rather the gold scorpion with ruby eyes that hung from it, reminding her of El Cid's magical scorpion. She looked at the man's face once again, and he bowed slightly.

"It is with great pleasure that I have come to seek your hand in marriage in the name of my liege, King Afonso V of Portugal," the Portuguese archbishop abruptly addressed the princess. As you have already met our noble king, I do not need to enumerate the sterling qualities of the man. I beg you to give us a speedy reply to his proposal."

Isabella's thoughts of King Afonso kept returning to his strange language, and his son, João, who would someday inherit the throne. Her children, if she had any with the King, would never rule Portugal, and they would have to fight for their claim to the Castilian throne as her brother had done. Enríque had just declared her heir in the Treaty of Toros de Guisando, and now she must protect her rights. She had kept the counsel of Fray Tomas de Torquemada and was sure that God had brought her to this point. Castile, with its cold, harsh winters, its sun-beaten summer earth, its men willing to die for honor, was her land, and she would never willingly allow La Beltráneja to rule it. They had laughed at her long enough, the adulterers, the king and the rebels. Isabella had formed her reply.

"I am deeply honored by the suit of the King of Portugal, but you must be aware that Afonso is my first cousin, and I could not marry him in clear conscience without a dispensation from the Pope." There was an audible gasp from the delegation. She continued unruffled. "If it is God's will that I marry the king, then I will be happy to accompany you to Portugal."

"This is preposterous!" The archbishop fumed, "A dispensation from the Pope will take months to obtain. This marriage has been decided upon by kings! You have been ordered by King Enríque and King Afonso to accompany us to Portugal immediately. I can assure you our king will not wait for a dispensation." He stomped out of the little room, followed by his delegation, and all wondered how Enríque would react to her demur. As the noblemen shuffled out of the room after him, Isabella halted the man wearing the scorpion necklace.

"Your name, sir?" she inquired.

"Don Isaac Abravanel." He bowed stiffly.

"Your chain, it is most unusual. Where did you get it?" It was an absurd question at such a moment, but she could not let the man go without speaking to him.

His eyes opened wide in surprise and then seemed to sparkle with laughter.

"It was made for me long ago." Then it dawned on him why she was so fascinated by it. "I think it was fashioned after the fabled scorpion worn by El Cid. Of course, you know the legend."

"Yes, of course." She felt foolish now. How could she have taken it for the original one? But she was entranced by the man who wore the chain. There was something about the way he carried himself, the way he spoke, that intrigued her. "Your Castilian is excellent. Where did you learn to speak the language?"

Isaac felt trapped by this young beauty who had just defied the Kings of Portugal and Castile. He hesitated before he answered her, knowing she would be able to detect a lie.

"My grandfather was Castilian and once served your grandfather."

"In what capacity, Don Isaac?" She was clearly interested.

"He was . . ." he hesitated, afraid to reveal the identity of his grandfather who had fled Castile as a heretic. "He was a court treasurer, but that was long ago."

"And in what capacity do you serve this delegation?" She immediately sensed his anxiety and changed the subject.

"I am a treasurer for King Afonso and have come to see to your dowry. However, there doesn't seem to be much need for my service." He smiled at her, and she realized once again that he had not expected her to accept the proposal. It almost seemed as if this stranger knew her plans, as if he could read her thoughts, and an unsettled feeling crept over her. Was it all so very obvious? She quickly decided the interview must come to an end.

"There may not be a need for dowry arrangements, but then again there might. I have little to say in these matters. My future is in their hands." She nodded toward the archbishop. "However, if someday you decide to return to your ancestral home, I hope to be here and to have need of a fine treasurer." His steady gaze left her feeling weak, and she was sorry he was so formal.

"You are most generous, and I will not forget your offer." His eyes penetrated deeply into hers; he wanted to touch her soft white skin, to reassure her. She seemed so alone, so unprotected. The Portuguese archbishop called sharply, "Abravanel!" He bowed once again and then joined the noblemen preparing to leave.

She watched the men ride away and knew she could not hold them off forever. If Prince Ferdinand wanted her hand in marriage, he would have to come now. When Enríque learned her answer, he would order her arrest. He would realize that she would never marry King Afonso. She watched Abravanel ride away on his fine stallion. How she wished he was El Cid come to rescue her.

Gutierre de Cardenas and Alonso de Palencia, Isabella's informers, returned from Aragon without her prince. Beatrice de Boadilla, Isabella's closest friend, held her hand, for she was unsteady when she rose to meet them. She reached out to her friends. "Gutierre, what has happened? Didn't you explain my plight to him? I have no more time!"

"Forgive us, Princess, we have failed you miserably, but it was impossible to bring Prince Ferdinand. He is on a battlefield at this very moment. The French have invaded Rousillon, and he cannot leave his kingdom until the enemy is routed. He has given us his word that the instant he is free, he will come for you; he has sent you the most prized possession of Aragon," Gutierre said, bringing forth a necklace brilliant with gold, sparkling with rubies and pearls. "It is said that the center ruby belonged to the biblical King Solomon, my lady. This must prove the sincerity of the prince's proposal."

While she stared at the necklace, the creamy white pearls embedded in gold, the rubies causing the sun's rays to dance about the room, hot tears streamed down her face, and she whispered, "Pray, tell me how this necklace will save me from Enríque?" She felt desperate as she spoke. "Don't you realize he has ordered my arrest, and the Archbishop of Seville is already on his way with an army to carry me back to Madrid?" She felt as if a wind had pushed her over the edge of a cliff and that she was falling into a great abyss. "Leave me, Gutierre, Alonso, please. Beatrice and I will pray to the only one who can decide my fate. If my cause is just, then He will come to my aid."

Isabella and Beatrice retreated to the quiet chapel. They knelt on the stone floor before a wooden cross. They fasted, they refused to speak to anyone, and they beseeched God for deliverance.

Beatrice pulled a knife when they heard the hoof-beats in the distance. Beatrice, the faithful friend, stood before Isabella as the scent of the horses drifted in through the narrow turret window. But Beatrice could do nothing to comfort her when the soldiers clamored up the stairs, clanging and shouting as they forced their way past trusted servants, and broke down the door.

CHAPTER 11

The merchants' faces reflected the dismal gray of the inn where they had planned to spend the night. It was a small wooden building with only two cubicles for guests. A crude central room offered one large hearth and a long table and bench for those fortunate enough to have carried food with them. No meal was provided even at the outrageous sum the wiry innkeeper asked, but the merchants paid and were grateful for the roof over their heads. Their muleteer unpacked the dried salt pork and beans that had been their sustenance since they had left Aragon. The poorly clad muleteer struggled to keep his eyes open as he spilled the pork and beans into the black cast iron pot on the hearth. Soon the pork was simmering above the smoky fire. The muleteer closed his eyes for a moment; the aroma reminded him of happier, easier times. After the meal was served, he took his own portion and then turned his attention to the mules outside. Each arm felt like a heavy weight as he brushed the mules, watered, and fed them. He was vaguely aware of the holes in the barn siding where mice had whittled their way in, and the broken stalls which barely kept the mules and horses in place as he stumbled about looking for a place to sleep. The barn had not been cleaned, but he finally found a spot of fresh straw. As he closed his eyes, he felt as if his head were whirling with fatigue, while his torso, arms and legs seemed to float, they so sorely needed rest. The straw felt like feather down.

He had been asleep for an hour when the young blacksmith's apprentice, Jose, trudged in to share the lodgings. He too was exhausted after a day of burning himself on the molten iron and suffering kicks from the old mare he had tried to shoe. He threw himself down on a spot the muleteer had passed over and, just missing a large turd, he jumped up with a yelp, waking the muleteer, and danced about in a frantic effort to brush himself off, throwing about straw, chicken feathers and horsehair and dung. The muleteer chuckled at the poor lad.

"How dare you laugh at me? This is my barn, and you've taken my favorite place!" He whined.

"Sorry, lad," the muleteer answered. "I meant no offense. Here, I'll move to another section if you wish."

"No, don't bother, I'm all right," Jose said as he settled himself into a cleaner nook. A horse sniffled, a chicken ruffled its feathers, and then the barn settled into silence once again. Jose noticed that the muleteer had quickly fallen back into a deep sleep. Not a muscle on his thick frame twitched and only the soft rise and fall of his chest showed that he was alive. The boy studied the muleteer, for this man was not a thin, sickly peasant like those who usually tended to the beasts. He had fine black hair and beard. His clothes were faded and so badly torn that just enough strands clung together to cover the muscular body. The boy proudly pulled his own wool cloak about him as if it were rich velvet. His lot wasn't so bad, after all. He had a good future if he could only learn to control the hot fire, the bellows, and the iron. He continued to study the man before him. There was something he didn't trust about the group of strangers who were staying for the night. They were from Aragon, and that in itself was suspicious for soldiers had been searching for Prince Ferdinand of Aragon since early dawn. The boy inched over to view the man closely. To smell him one would never mistake him for anything but a muleteer! He was admiring the man's broad shoulders and thick arms when his eyes fell to his hands—fine, long, smooth hands, the hands of a nobleman. He stared at the unconscious face before him, as if he had found hidden gold. The narrow, almost delicately shaped eyelids looked as though they had been chiseled from the high cheek bones. He leaned forward staring once again at the man's hands and saw the distinct mark of a soldier where his palms were callused from heavy use of the sword. Without warning, the muleteer arose and pounced on the boy, pinning him to the floor and pointing a knife to his throat.

"What are you staring at, boy?" He whispered in his ear.

"Nothing, my lord, just walking staring, that's all. Please let me go. I meant no harm."

"What did you call me!" he growled. The boy could feel his own weak muscles bend to the might of the fierce young man. Terrified, he could not remember what he had said.

"I forget, my lord, I don't know."

"I'm a muleteer, boy, not a lord!" He cut each word through his teeth. "Where did you get the notion I was anything but?"

"Your hands, sir, they're so fine. I meant no harm. I was only looking at your hands."

The man threw the boy aside and stared at his hands. He had taken off his rings, but it had never occurred to him someone could see he was not a peasant by looking at his hands. He quickly covered them with dirt and then contemplated the lad before him. The boy was astute, and he liked that.

"Well, you see I am a nobleman." He straightened himself, dagger still in hand. "What news can you tell me, boy. What's going on in these parts?"

Jose quickly realized the man was measuring him.

"Two troops of king's men rode by today looking for Ferdinand of Aragon. An order is out for his arrest," he answered warily.

The man eyed the boy.

"And what news is there of Ferdinand's party?"

"There are rumors that they were seen on the high road heading for Valladolid," he answered.

"And the Princess Isabella, is she still there?" He seemed perturbed.

"Yes, she is still there and safe under the protection of the Archbishop of Toledo."

And with gusto he related the now famous tale.

"They say the archbishop found her praying before the cross. Then he lifted her in his arms, placed her on a fiery steed, and galloped away with three hundred of his men shortly before the Archbishop of Seville arrived to arrest her."

The stranger shuddered when he heard about the audacious rescue. The boy prostrated himself at the young man's feet. "You are Prince Ferdinand, aren't you? Please, Your Highness, please let me serve you. Your secret will be safe with me."

Prince Ferdinand had little choice. The boy obviously knew who he was, and this meant that Enríque's spies were everywhere, even a stable boy could recognize him.

"Tell me, lad, what is your name?" he asked with more kindness in his voice.

"Jose, your Highness."

"First of all, you must stop addressing me as 'Your Highness.' Do you understand?" Ferdinand asked as he slid his knife into its sheath. The boy nodded yes. "Do you know the old goat and sheep trails to Osma?"

"Osma? I thought you were going to Valladolid?"

"First we go to Osma. Do you know the way?" Ferdinand asked.

"Yes, and the trails are faster than the main road," he piped.

"Good, then you may travel with us, but I must warn you it will be dangerous, and there will be no rest until we get there."

"It will be a great honor to serve you; I would die for Isabella."

"Is King Enríque so hated that many feel this way?"

"There are some who would gladly turn you over to the king's men, for the ransom is high, but many will stand behind you and the princess." The boy answered honestly, and Ferdinand was grateful, for most young men would have tried to appease him with false security.

"Rest now, Jose, we have a hard trip ahead," he said. The boy settled back into the straw and quickly fell asleep. Now it was Ferdinand's turn to stare into the night; his disguise had been too easily detected and sleep might be costly.

Jose found the muleteer packing the beasts under the dim light of the moon and the stars. The disguised knights were quickly pulling their gear together, and they were off before the sun's rays could warm the earth. Grateful for the boy's knowledge of the land, they traveled quickly over the lightly trodden trails. The brown grass bending as if in reverence to the royal party was the only mark the small group made. Several hours later, they came, by necessity, dangerously close to the main road. The sun had risen when Jose spotted the royal banner of Aragon flying above a group of soldiers on the road. Jose was so thrilled to see them that he began to run ahead to flag them down when Ferdinand tackled him, covering him with his own body. At that same instant, they could hear the clash of Toledo steel striking steel, and the hideous screams that followed. Ferdinand could feel the boy squirm underneath him, but he moved not a muscle. Though torn with desire to rise and fight with his men, he remained motionless as if suspended in a tortuous hell; he would be spotted if he moved and that would mean his own instant death, but worse, far worse, his men, who had served as decoys, would have died in vain. Ferdinand and the boy could hear the hoof-beats of the king's men riding away, but they remained motionless for what seemed like hours, until the vultures descended upon the bodies of their dead warriors. Then Ferdinand could wait no longer, and he and his knights pulled their dead men off the road and buried them in a mass grave. Ferdinand made a wooden cross to mark them and promised himself that someday he would see them in a proper grave. In a somber mood, the party continued on to the borough of Osma.

Jose watched with admiration as Ferdinand pushed forward and realized that nothing would stop the prince from his quest, nothing but death itself. When they finally arrived at the gates of the fortress, Ferdinand pushed his knights aside and with great excitement called to the guard.

"Open up! It is Ferdinand of Aragon!"

"Ferdinand of Aragon is dead!" came the reply and a huge boulder was pushed from the watch tower. Ferdinand looked up to see the massive rock falling and thought, "Dear God save me," as it sent him crashing to the ground. Jose and the knights ran to Ferdinand and shook him. When they saw only the side of his head had been grazed, they angrily called to the guard to let them in. The guard ran to his master, the Count of Trevino.

"Who goes there?" the count called from the tower several minutes later.

In desperation Ferdinand found his voice, "It is Ferdinand, you bloody bastard! You nearly killed me!"

The count recognized the prince's voice, and the gates immediately opened for the weary travelers. Ferdinand slung his arm around Jose, and with the support of his men, staggered into the fortress which was friendly to Isabella and the rebel cause.

A few hours later, Jose, who had now been given the privilege of attending to the prince, carried water into a chamber decked with red and purple oriental rugs, gold wall sconces, and large tapestries hanging from the walls. Ferdinand was soaking in a tub, staring at the fire blazing on the hearth. Jose was sorry to break the spell and gently poured warm water. For the first time in many weeks, Ferdinand allowed his body to relax. He watched the grime slide off his body with the stench of the mules. It was so easy to wash away the muleteer, but not so easy to erase the death cries that haunted him. The screams of his men echoed in his head, of his valiant men today, of his men in Rousillon, and the agonizing cry he had heard from the first soldier he had ever seen die when he was a young lad on the battlefield with his father, King Juan of Aragon.

With a few quick splashes, Ferdinand shook himself and finished his bath. As he rose from the tub, Jose was struck again by the finely-tuned body, each muscle taut from the strenuous exercise of war. The prince dressed in a short purple robe and velvet breeches and donned a heavy gold chain with the crest of Aragon. For the first time in his life, Jose fingered velvet as he draped a cloak trimmed with ermine over Ferdinand's shoulders. The prince was ready to face Isabella's men.

Gutierre de Cardenas, Alonso de Palencia and Don Abraham Senior rose when the prince entered the great banquet hall. Count of Trevino bowed to the prince.

"My lord, please, once again accept my deepest apology for the mishap upon your arrival. We had most distressing news earlier in the day that your royal party had been ambushed, and that you had been dealt a swift death. Praise be to God that you are here alive and well."

Ferdinand's head still ached from the blow, but he would not allow anyone to see his pain.

"I realize the boulder was meant for Enríque's men. Fortunately, Princess Isabella still has her bridegroom." The guests felt the tension ease with his good humor and enjoyed a hearty laugh.

"You have met Don Gutierre de Cardenas and Don Alonso de Palencia, but I would like to introduce you to Don Abraham Senior, who is here to officiate over the dowry matters for the Princess," the count continued.

Don Abraham bowed to Prince Ferdinand, and somewhere in the back of his mind, Ferdinand remembered his grandfather mentioning Senior's name and saying something about old family ties. He wondered, for a moment, if he were related to the man, for his own grandmother had been a Jewess, but he if he were to ever ask, it wouldn't be before Isabella's men.

"My father has bestowed upon me the lands of Sicily in honor of my marriage to Isabella; I come to her as King of Sicily," Ferdinand announced to the small group.

The men bowed to King Ferdinand in tribute to his new title and eyed each other, wondering if this young king wanted new concessions in the marriage contract. Until now, Isabella had dictated the conditions. Though she offered a meager dowry, she was the legitimate heir to the throne of Castile, the most powerful kingdom in Spain. As the men sat down to the feast before them, Gutierre tactfully discussed Isabella's conditions.

"Your Majesty, there are a few points Princess Isabella has insisted upon, solely for the protection of the Castilian crown, you must understand, not for her own interest. Surely each kingdom will want its own sovereignty protected even though they will be united by the marriage. You must realize that with the weighty crown of Castile comes great obligations, and though Princess Isabella is not the sovereign, in her marital contract she must think as one." He held a paper high as he read, "You must promise never to leave Castile nor enter into war, nor form alliances without her consent. Only Castilians may serve in high offices. You must promise to honor the dowager queen, respect King Enríque and have as your highest priority the crusade against the Moors." There was no sound in the great hall as all waited to hear King Ferdinand's response.

Ferdinand sat with his elbow resting on his arm, his index finger rubbing his cheek as he listened, but no sign of any reaction could be read on his face. The silence continued until Cardenas could no longer stand the strain. "Your Majesty, will you accept these conditions or must I go back to my lady empty handed once again?"

Ferdinand was quietly seething at the insolence of the young woman making these demands. At first he wanted to stomp out of the room and return to his beloved Aragon. If he agreed, he would have to have her permission to go home. He thought of his mistress and infant bastard son, but he had suffered too much, his men had suffered too much to retreat now.

"I will accept the conditions as long as Isabella will respect these same rights for Aragon. Only Aragonese will serve in our courts, and she will make no decisions without my approval," he answered with only the slightest trace of anger in his voice.

"You will be equal monarchs in all respects. Princess Isabella will never sway from her duty to the crown of Castile, but she is also a beauty pining for love, Your Majesty, she prays for you." Cardenas tried to soothe the young king.

"Was she pleased with the necklace I sent her? You told her of its great value?"

Cardenas paused as he thought of Isabella's tears when she saw the necklace.

"She thought it very beautiful, Your Majesty, but was in desperate circumstances at the time. She was distressed that you yourself had not come for her."

"Well, I've come for her now, and I can promise you gentlemen, though we will rule with equal power in the throne room, my queen will bow to my wishes in bed!"

The men laughed and toasted King Ferdinand. Musicians played on recorders and lutes as wine was poured into golden goblets. Ferdinand's head continued to ache, cries from his dying men plagued him, and the merriment of those around him seemed bizarre when he thought of the cold facts. He was marrying a woman whose claim to the throne was insecure, their funds were pitifully low, and support for them throughout Castile and Leon was questionable. It would all be worth it though, for if she did inherit the crown, then he would be King of Castile, Leon, and Aragon, and they could turn their attention to the Moors in Granada. To rout the Moors had been the dream of the Christian kings for over seven hundred years. As the musicians bobbed up and down before him, smiling, dancing to their gay music, he stared at the red wine and wondered how much blood would be spilt before he and Isabella would rule Spain.

CHAPTER 12

King Afonso's face was drawn and tense; his fingers were tapping the side of his chair in Evora, Portugal, when Prince Fernando Braganza and Isaac entered the throne room.

"Your Majesty." Fernando bowed. "You sent for us?" He was annoyed to have been called back from his hunting party. For Isaac, who met with the King often, it was not unusual to have been summoned.

"You know that on October 18, 1469, a reception will be held for the newly-married couple, Isabella and Ferdinand, at Juan de Vivero's palace in Castile. I want you both to attend and to give King Ferdinand a message from me. If they insist on Isabella's claim to the throne after King Enríque's death, they will bring disaster down upon their heads!"

"But Your Majesty, Princess Isabella is the rightful heir to the throne! How can you threaten them in such a manner?" Fernando answered.

King Afonso continued as if he hadn't heard him.

"I have just received word from my sister, Queen Juana, that King Enríque has disinherited Princess Isabella since she broke the Treaty of Toros de Guisando by marrying Ferdinand of Aragon. I plan to marry little Juana and will unite Portugal and Spain!"

Fernando was taken aback, for even though the king was thirty-nine and, while it was not unusual for a monarch to marry a child, it was most unusual for an uncle to marry his niece! A dispensation from the Pope could make it legitimate, of course, but it was unsavory, to say the least, and to have to attend a wedding party with such a message would be most unpleasant! Gently, he tried to persuade the king to drop the idea.

"Your Majesty, King Enríque is not an old man and may live a long life. Is it so wise to marry this child, your niece, and threaten Isabella and Ferdinand in such a manner?" He miscalculated Afonso's passion.

The king pointed his finger at Fernando and shouted, "When I give you a command, I expect you to carry it out! Do you understand or shall I send someone else as my courier? Princess Isabella had her chance! She could have married me, but instead she has chosen this disastrous course of action which can lead only to more civil war, something Carrillo enjoys, I might add. It would be nice to see the archbishop praying a little more for his soul, instead of dashing about the countryside rescuing princesses! I will marry the Infanta Juana, the rightful heir to the Castilian throne, and Isabella and Ferdinand can go back to Aragon or Sicily!"

Fernando had never seen King Afonso so enraged and quickly realized it would be futile to argue further. Though he did not relish the idea of attending the celebration with such poisonous news for the young couple, he realized a mission of such importance had to be handled carefully and could become dangerous in the wrong hands. Carlos Málaga, Prince João's favorite, would be just the one to volunteer for such a mission were he to refuse. He turned to Isaac, who had allowed the scene to pass without making a comment, then turned back to the King, bowed again and said, "I will carry out your wish, sire. Isaac and I will leave at dawn tomorrow, and we will inform the couple of your plans to marry the Infanta Juana."

"One moment, Isaac!" the King bellowed.

Though he was raging inside at the King's plans, Isaac remained calm as he bowed once again.

"Your Majesty?"

"While Prince Fernando delivers my message to King Ferdinand, I want you to speak to Princess Isabella, privately. Tell her that I was truly disappointed with her rejection of my marriage proposal and will give up plans to wed the Infanta if she will reconsider."

"But Your Majesty, she and King Ferdinand have already made their wedding vows!"

"Yes, and with false papers of dispensation from the Pope!" Isaac blanched. "Shocked, are you?" King Afonso continued, "King Juan of Aragon had papers drawn up for Ferdinand, allowing him to marry a cousin, but it was not drawn up specifically for her. I'm sure she will look upon her marriage in a different light when she learns the truth, and perhaps when my plans for the future are made clear to her, she may be swayed to a different, more suitable course of action."

It was incredible to Isaac that Ferdinand could have been so deceptive with Isabella, but he wasn't pleased with Afonso's plotting either. He answered as honestly and as tactfully as he could.

"I don't think it is my place to inform Queen Isabella of a matter as intimate as this, Your Majesty."

"Not your place? I'm ordering you to inform Princess Isabella of Ferdinand's treachery, and perhaps you'll be able to save this headstrong young woman from a fatal mistake. I fully intend to take the Castilian crown when King Enríque dies, Isaac. If not with the Princess Isabella, then with the Princess Juana by my side. Make that clear to her!"

"Yes, Your Majesty, I will do my best." Isaac bowed once again to his king. There was nothing more he could say.

"I'm sure you will, Isaac, I'm sure you will." He nodded and Isaac was dismissed.

Fernando waited for Isaac while his nine-year-old son, Judah, handed him his sword.

"Take care of your mother, son," Isaac said as he bent down to kiss him good-bye. Judah nodded proudly. Isaac turned to his father, Judah, who had grown so old since his mother had died that his fine beard had turned from gray to white, his brown eyes so clouded that he could barely see. Isaac gently reached out to embrace the old man.

"I'm so proud of you, son! Such important king's business! You've grown so important, so important," he mumbled more to himself than to Isaac. "Good luck, boy, good luck!" He patted Isaac's breast, missing the broad shoulders.

"Thank you, Father. I'm sure all will go well," Isaac answered, more to reassure himself than the others. He bent down to hug his little girls, their smooth, rose petal cheeks brushing against his rough beard. "Bathsheba, Elisheba, behave yourselves and listen to your mother while I'm gone." Little Elisheba reminded him so much of his mother. How he missed her now that she was gone. Their serious eyes stared at him adoringly. He stood while Rebecca carefully placed his cloak over his shoulders as if each fold would stay in place until he reached Spain.

"Keep this on while you ride," she ordered. "We can't afford to have you sick." How she hated the idea of his going, even for the king. Only the Lord knew when she would see him again.

Isaac hugged her tightly, sharply aware of the children, Fernando, and his father, but wanting to feel her warmth, her soft breasts pressed against him. He loved the fragrance of her hair and even the little lines around her eyes that looked as if a hummingbird had landed there for a moment and left its footprints. He had to pull himself away—she wouldn't let go. He would have laughed but saw how anxious she was.

"It's only for two weeks, my love," he whispered, then kissed her on the cheek and mounted his horse.

Fernando, who loved her as he loved no other, blew her a kiss despite Isaac's jealous glance. The two men turned their horses to the east and galloped towards Castile.

"What did the king want after I left yesterday?" Fernando questioned.

"He claims King Ferdinand didn't have a proper dispensation from the Pope. He wants me to inform Queen Isabella, hoping she may change her mind, have the marriage annulled, and marry him."

"Ha!" Fernando laughed. "And does he think the crown is all she cares about? Afonso has grown old and fat! Why would Isabella choose him over a sturdy young man?"

"I can assure you, Fernando," Isaac answered, "the crown is all she thinks about. Not only is Ferdinand a more suitable husband, but through him, she can keep the Portuguese out of Castile."

"That makes two of us!" Fernando laughed, kicked his horse and raced ahead.

"It makes three, my friend," Isaac yelled as he caught up to him.

"Isaac, I can't imagine why you wouldn't want to see João on the throne in Portugal and Spain. Why, Málaga remembers you so well!" he laughed again.

"You can laugh all you want, Fernando. I just hope King Afonso lives a long, healthy life, with or without Isabella."

"I'm sure you do," Fernando said as he and Isaac galloped towards the Castilian border.

Two thousand people poured into Juan de Vivero's Castilian palace to celebrate Isabella and Ferdinand's wedding. The women, grouping and regrouping as the guests arrived, formed fantastic patterns of color as pink, red, yellow, blue and green silk gowns pressed against each other and then shifted again. Precious emeralds, rubies, and sapphires flashed around their slender necks. The *caballeros* were dressed in silks, brocades and velvets. Each carried a jewel-encrusted sword at his side and wore his family crest upon his breast. One by one, they were announced to the royal young couple. They bowed and then moved on into the gay ballroom where refreshments were being served and guests were already dancing to a roundelay.

"Prince Fernando Duke of Braganza, ambassador for King Afonso V of Portugal and Don Isaac Abravanel," the page called.

With Fernando a few paces in front of him, Isaac could feel all the heads in the crowded room turn to stare. A hush fell as the nobility of Castile and Aragon watched the two Portuguese men walk the thick red carpet and bow to the young couple. Isaac was hardly aware of the stares he received, for Isabella had captured his eyes, and he was fighting to control his racing heart. As emissaries of Queen Juana's brother, King Afonso, Isaac and Fernando were looked upon with suspicion and were quickly ushered past Ferdinand and Isabella to tables which were laden with fish and game, hot breads and dainty cakes. Noblemen and ladies swirled before them, their gold and gems sparkling, glistening in the candlelight.

"You look as if you could use a glass of wine." Fernando sensed his friend's distress at having to face Isabella.

"Yes, that's a good idea."

They headed for a large table laden with fruits, creamy cheese and wines, but before they had reached it Isaac stopped short. His heart jumped for the second time that night. He heard the laugh first and then saw him standing on the other side of the room, head bent forward as he listened to a well-dressed man with gold chains hanging around his neck and rings on his fingers. Fernando saw him at the same instant and was so very sorry that he hadn't seen Jonathan first. Isaac stared at his brother-in-law's golden hair. The color hadn't changed, not at all. His blue eyes were as full of life, of fun, as he remembered, and at the edges of those eyes were the same little bird-like marks that Rebecca now had. Isaac had never realized how much Jonathan looked like his sister.

When Jonathan looked up, their eyes met for a moment, surprise in Jonathan's, and a sad, sad look of deep loss in Isaac's. Jonathan watched as Isaac fled from the room followed by Fernando, then turned back to the nobleman as if nothing extraordinary had happened, though a blush crossed his face.

"Isaac, I'm sorry, I had no idea he would be here. It didn't even cross my mind. That must have been very painful." Fernando tried to soothe his friend when he caught up with him in the courtyard.

"You've seen him since he left, haven't you?" Isaac cried, spilling his emotions.

"Yes, I have, and why shouldn't I?" Fernando answered angrily. "Just because he is dead for you, doesn't mean he had to die for me. I love Jonathan; I love him as much as I love you, Isaac. You can't blame me for rejoicing in his conversion. I am Catholic, after all."

Isaac closed his eyes and bent his head back. Of course he couldn't blame Fernando for seeing Jonathan. It just seemed so deceptive.

"So this is how you get all your information. This is why you always know so much about Spain?" was all he could say.

Fernando bowed his head; he had not meant to deceive Isaac. That had never been his intent.

"Yes, Jonathan always has wonderful stories to tell. He is Juan Sanchez de Sevilla now and is one of the most respected jewelers in Castile."

"Juan Sanchez!" Isaac's eyes flew open. "He's taken my grandfather's name! My grandfather was Juan Sanchez de Sevilla. Doesn't he realize that! Doesn't he know my grandfather fled as a heretic?"

"Why are you worried? That was long ago. No one here is interested in who your grandfather was. What difference can it make?"

Fernando could not understand the fear that enveloped Isaac as he stood in the Spanish court. He was the grandson of a heretic, and for Jonathan to have taken this heretic's name seemed an act of madness, as if Jonathan were challenging fate.

"Is he married? Does he ever ask about the family?" he questioned, holding back tears.

"He says he will never marry. No one pretty enough . . . . You know Jonathan . . . ." Fernando laughed; then, seeing Isaac so distressed, he stopped. He wished he could bring the brothers-in-law together again. "As for the family, his first questions are always about you, Rebecca, the children. I've told him about you, Judah, Bathsheba."

"Stop . . ." Isaac interrupted him. "I don't want to hear any more . . ."

"I'm sorry," Fernando said in a soft voice. "No more." He quickly changed the subject. "I'm going to see if everyone has been presented. If so, we can deliver our messages and then leave." He was as anxious to depart as Isaac. Fernando left Isaac alone in the cool courtyard, where he drew a deep breath and tried to calm himself. He had buried Jonathan long ago, and it was difficult to see him so alive, so seemingly unchanged, and so happy.

"Well, my brother," he whispered to the night wind, "I hope you have found what you were after."

"Don Isaac, I'm delighted to see you again." Isabella startled him.

He turned to face her. She was radiant tonight, dressed as a queen should be, the fabulous ruby necklace shimmering against her white skin, her red hair piled high, almost hiding the gold crown.

"Your Highness." He bowed. She gave him her hand. Her skin was warm and moist. They walked down the steps into the garden maze of green sculptured boxwood until they found a corner where only a marble Greek goddess, standing by a bubbling fountain, could hear their conversation. They sat together on a stone bench meant for lovers seeking privacy.

"I'm afraid I have some distressing news for you," Isaac began. "King Afonso has learned that Ferdinand's dispensation was not properly obtained. He wants you to know that if you wish to annul the marriage, he would still be much honored to have you for a wife, his queen."

He spoke softly, trying to soften the blow, for he knew how important this information was to her.

She stiffened, as if he had sunk a knife into her, and she sat so still that he was afraid he had really hurt her. "Are you all right?" he asked.

"Yes. I will discuss this most distressing news with my husband."

"I take it then that you will not seriously consider King Afonso's proposal?"

"No."

"I didn't think you would."

"You didn't think so the last time either. Why did you have to try again?"

Isaac hesitated, knowing he must hurt her a second time.

"Because King Afonso has declared he will marry the Infanta Juana if you refuse him again."

"He would marry his niece! Will he stop at nothing to wrench the crown from me?" She stood, wringing her hands.

"I'm afraid there will be war if you don't marry him," Isaac said in a hushed voice.

"Marry him! Marry him! I am married—to Ferdinand! We will obtain another dispensation, that I can promise you, but he is my husband and nothing but death will ever separate us." Her eyes were ablaze as she spoke.

"It pains me to hurt you with this news, especially at your wedding celebration. I am truly sorry; forgive me, Your Highness." Isaac knelt before her.

"Oh, Isaac, I don't blame you for this." She put her delicate hand to his cheek, and he took it in his own. "But you must go back to Afonso and put an end to this madness of his. He must leave the Castilian crown alone. I will never allow La Beltráneja to rule; you must make him see that!"

He could not refrain from kissing her hand which had grown cold as the marble statue. He wanted to warm her.

"I will do my best to persuade him to change his mind." He could hardly hear his words above his pounding heart.

They jumped at the clanging of armed guards as King Ferdinand and Fernando entered the courtyard. Isaac quickly dropped her hand.

"How dare you come to us like this at our wedding celebration and threaten us with war!" Ferdinand raged. "You will leave immediately and not return! Tell King Afonso the crown will be Isabella's! If we have to fight all of Castile and Portugal, we will!"

He escorted his queen back into the ballroom while Fernando and Isaac were hurried through the servants' quarters by armed guards. They mounted their stallions and, surrounded by soldiers, rode through land where only tufts of wheat-colored grass sprouted. It was a long, hard ride. Little was said. They rode hard, stopping only to change horses, until they had crossed back into Portugal, when the soldiers turned and rode away. Fernando seemed relieved to see them out of sight, and then finally spoke.

"You seemed to be having an interesting discussion with Queen Isabella!"

"Well, you and King Ferdinand didn't get along very well!" Isaac retorted.

"Yes, he made quite a scene, but actually we got along rather well. You'd be amazed at how much we have in common."

"What is that supposed to mean? You were to inform him of King Afonso's plan to marry the Infanta Juana. I fail to see the common ground!"

"Ah, there we differ, that's true. However, it's not King Afonso whom Ferdinand sees as his threat, rather Prince João. Now, there we have a lot in common, don't you think Isaac?"

"Prince João's done you no harm, Fernando. You aren't plotting against him?"

"Don't be so naive, my friend. Neither King Enríque nor King Afonso will live forever. When they go, a new order will be ready to rise in Spain and Portugal."

He kicked his horse and took off, expecting Isaac to follow. Instead, Isaac pulled in the reins so suddenly that his horse reared. Isaac didn't like Fernando's insinuations. He watched his friend disappear over the blue crest of the hill before him. Each of them had to travel their own road, he realized, and shivered when he thought of the reckless path Jonathan had chosen. Fernando now seemed headed on a new and dangerous course, and, as it had to be, Isaac turned his horse down a different path and traveled the pitted, winding road towards home, alone.

Isaac found Rebecca sleeping. He buried his head in her breast, and she woke with a start.

"I'm home," he whispered and held her for a long time. When he thought she was asleep, he climbed out of bed and walked over to the window. He felt guilty about his neglected studies, his writings.

Rebecca saw him leaning against the window. She walked over to him and reached her arms out. He pulled her to him.

"Oh, Rebecca, I love you."

"What were you thinking about just now?"

"Nothing, really,"

"Isaac, something was calling you away from me."

He gazed down at her worried face.

"I was thinking about my writings, actually."

"Do you really expect me to believe that?" She slipped away from his embrace and looked out the window at the stars.

"Yes, of course! It's true!"

She felt a wave of panic rise. She couldn't bear to lose him to another.

"What is she like, Queen Isabella?" Her voice trembled when she asked.

She immediately sensed Isaac's stiff response. Rebecca was aware of Isaac's excitement at traveling to Spain and knew that it was Isabella who drew him there. She felt a pang of envy toward the young queen, unreasonably afraid of Isaac's falling in love with her.

"She's very intelligent, very sensitive." He looked into Rebecca's worried eyes and smiled. "And very beautiful," he added. "Do I see a little jealousy in those big brown eyes of yours?"

She stared at the floor.

"I love you. I can't live without you, Isaac."

"Isabella and Ferdinand are devoted to one another just as you and I are. Nothing can ever change that." He gathered her into his arms. "You silly little goose. No one could come between you and me." Holding her tightly, he gazed out at the stars. He kissed the top of her head. "How could you doubt me?" It was true that he had come under Isabella's spell, feeling bewitched by her like so many other knights—men who would die for her and her cause. But as he pressed Rebecca against him, he knew that he held the most important person in his life. Rebecca had become the central core of his inner being.

"Forgive me." She whispered, feeling relieved.

He led her back to bed, and they sealed their love once again.

CHAPTER 13

As warm sunlight washed the castle, Isaac wrapped his newborn, Joseph, in a light blanket and carried him outside. His little girls, Bathsheba and Elisheba, lifting their long gowns, ran to him and stared at the tiny face. The baby's bright black eyes stared back at them in grave wonderment, but the sisters quickly lost interest and ran off to play again in the cool shade of the yard. Grateful for this peaceful moment, Isaac settled into a comfortable chair to rock the baby. Since his father had died only a month before, Isaac felt this precious gift of life was God's way of easing his loss. He missed seeing his father's wrinkled face, his head of wispy white hair as fine as the baby's, and missed hearing his quiet dignified voice which always commanded close attention. His father demanded that he be a king's treasurer, and he had done so, had followed in his footsteps though he had really wanted to pursue his studies, to be a scholar. He kissed the baby's downy hair. The infant searched for his father's finger and began to suck. Closing his eyes, Isaac whispered, "Papa, this was all I ever wanted. Why couldn't you understand?" Isaac looked down at the baby and fondly remembered holding his older son, Judah. The moment of peace was shattered by young Judah's shrill voice and pattering of feet as he ran into the garden. The startled infant threw open his arms and began to cry. Isaac knew before Judah spoke that duty called, that quiet moments like this could not last.

"You must walk in quietly when I'm holding the baby."

Irritated by the thought, Isaac scolded Judah. Gently, he hushed the baby, the experience of raising three others helping him now.

"I'm sorry, Father," Judah whispered. "I didn't know you had him out here." He peeked between the layers of blanket to gaze at his brother. "He looks like an old man, a little like Grandfather, doesn't he? Papa, two men are waiting to see you. I brought them into your library. Is that all right?" His large brown eyes gazed at his father.

"King's men?" Too weary to acknowledge Judah's adoring eyes, Isaac asked. He wasn't in the mood to return to court again today.

"No, Father, they are from some foreign land. I think they said Morocco."

"Take Joseph for me," Isaac answered, handing the infant to Judah, "and carry him back to your mother." Judah held the baby in his arms as if he were a porcelain doll and inched his way out of the courtyard with his precious bundle.

Isaac rose and quickly made his way to the library. It was a large room scented with the clean, strong smell of leather from the manuscripts lining the walls, each one the masterpiece of a scribe. Isaac had inherited the collection from his father, and he already made some significant additions. The works of Aristotle, Plato, Maimonides, Thomas Aquinas and Jerome sat side by side on the thick wooden shelves. These volumes were his most treasured possessions. He entered the library and found two dark-skinned men facing him. For an instant, the men reminded him of exotic birds, for one was dressed in long yellow pantaloons, the other in blue, and they wore white puffy headdresses with huge plumes at the back in matching yellow and blue.

"Don Isaac." They prostrated themselves at his feet.

"Gentlemen, please, this is not necessary," he said as his face flushed red, and he bent down to help them stand.

"Don Isaac, you are too kind." The man dressed in blue spoke in broken Portuguese. "We are here to beseech your help for the Moroccan Jews. Two hundred and fifty of our people in Arzilla have been taken as slaves by the Portuguese crusading in North Africa. The crusaders have our men, women and children shackled, living in poor huts and subsisting on scraps of food. It is the children, Don Isaac, about whom we are most concerned. Their skin is soft and cuts easily from the iron bonds on their arms and legs. They develop sores and then die from the putrid wounds. Our children are dying! Our women are dying and only the strong men will survive."

The man dressed in yellow sank to his knees as his body shook with sobs.

"Excuse my nephew, Don Isaac, please excuse him. His wife and little daughter were torn away from him. He doesn't know where they are or if they are even still alive. Please forgive him, Don Isaac."

The man in yellow was slightly younger than Isaac, and when Isaac imagined his own family being savagely torn from him-his Rebecca, his children—he found it difficult to remain calm. He pushed back his own tears and knelt beside the man, staring at him with hope in his eyes.

"Your names?" Isaac asked.

"Forgive me, Don Isaac. I am Ephraim ibn Aknin and this is my nephew Moses ibn Aknin."

"Tell your nephew I will help." Gazing steadily at Moses he said, "Tell him I will do what I can to find his family and free the other people taken as slaves."

"Don Isaac, God bless you! You are our only hope! God bless you!" Ephraim sank to his knees, kissing Isaac's hands. He translated the good news to his nephew, who bowed.

Isaac stood and Ephraim continued, "I am afraid the ransom to give to the crusaders will be most difficult to raise."

"How much is it?"

The man hesitated. "Ten thousand gold ducats."

Isaac could feel the blood drain from his face and he sank into his leather chair. He held his head in his hands. Ten thousand gold ducats! Ten thousand gold ducats! He could launch three ships with that amount! Where would he raise an enormous sum like that? He looked up to see the two men staring at him as if he were about to pass a life or death sentence upon them. What could he say to these men? They had no one else to turn to. Isaac knew that even better than they. He didn't know where he would raise the money, but somehow he must.

"I will go and speak to the Lisbon congregation for you. This is an impossible sum, but somehow we will raise the money. You have my word."

It was as if he had blown life itself back into their desperate faces.

"Tamar, my wife, Dinah, my child," Moses said as he reached out to Isaac, grabbing his hands and weeping. Isaac gently released himself from the man's grip.

"I will do what I can."

He called for his servant, Simon, and the men were ushered to guest rooms where they could stay until he had some news for them. He threw on his cape and rode off to discuss the serious situation with the wise men of the Judería.

As the gates of the Judería opened, he was reminded again how caged and how very poor his own people were. The crusaders could so easily decide to enter these same gates and take his people as slaves. It seemed at times as if he alone stood between disaster and the Jews of Lisbon. It was a great burden to carry. One slip of the tongue before his king, one ledger balanced incorrectly, could throw him into disfavor and what would happen? He thought of Jonathan, who was not here to help him. He needed him now, had needed him with each new crisis, and missed him when his father had died, when each of his children was born-the uncle they would never know. He wondered where he was at this moment and then pushed the thought, and the picture of his jovial face in Castile, from his mind. At least Fernando had been there, could help, and he held great power. Fernando would never allow the Jews of Lisbon, of Portugal, to suffer, to be enslaved like the Jews of Morocco.

Isaac entered the synagogue at dusk just as the wise men were gathering. They made way for him to pass. He was an honored member, their most esteemed member.

Rabbi Joseph Chajun had filled Rabbi Heyyien's place after the old man's death. He stood to welcome Isaac and ushered him into his private chambers.

"It is an honor to have you here tonight, Isaac. What has brought you?"

"There is trouble from the crusaders in North Africa. Two hundred and fifty men, women and children have been taken as slaves."

"That's not so unusual. What is the ransom? Can't their own people pay it?"

"No, they can't, nor could we for that matter. It's ten thousand gold ducats."

"For this we need a miracle. That is too much to ask. Isaac, we can't raise that much; you know we are poor, we haven't the means!" The rabbi cast his eyes toward heaven.

"I have given them my word that we will help. I will give one tenth of it from my own coffers if I have to!"

"Isaac, that is most generous of you, but why bleed yourself dry for these people? You have no relatives there and no hope of ever being repaid. Our congregation can raise one thousand, maybe two, and then double that for the rest of the Jews in Portugal. You are still left with five thousand to raise. Where would you get it? It would take a miracle!"

"I don't know rabbi, but what if it were your wife, your child held in shackles, bleeding, dying! Wouldn't you do anything you could to save them!"

"I am sorry. Of course, you are right."

"If we don't try to help them, rabbi, who will?" he added in a softer tone.

"No one, Isaac, no one," the rabbi whispered. "I will do all I can to help you raise the money."

"Thank you, rabbi. All I ask is that you do what you can."

The men were collecting in the synagogue when Isaac and the rabbi joined them. As the old men shuffled in Isaac was reminded of the wise men with whom he had studied so long ago. He prayed that tonight they would respond to the plight of the Moroccan Jews.

"Rabbi, if I may present the grave problem before our congregation now?"

"Yes, Isaac, of course."

He waited until they were seated; then in a forceful tone he began.

"Two hundred and fifty men, women, and children have been taken as slaves by Portuguese crusaders. We must raise ten thousand gold ducats if we are to free them, and we will have to do it quickly for women and children are already dying."

"Ten thousand gold ducats!" was whispered around the room.

The rabbi stood beside Isaac adding his support.

"Isaac is not expecting all the money to come from us. But we must give what we can, a little from the candle money, a little from the money for rice. From here, from there, we must do what we can." His voice grew severe. "For if we do not, they will surely perish, and we cannot allow that to happen. Remember, if our brothers perish, then we ourselves are in danger."

Again there was a murmur in the room, and the awesome number, ten thousand gold ducats, was whispered over and over. Finally one man stood.

"Don Isaac, you can count on me to give what I can. It may not be much, a silver ducat, but I have been saving it for difficult times, and you may have it!"

Another stood to pledge money for the cause and then another and another until all the men in the room had offered something. Much of the money would be taken from allowances for food, but they wanted to offer something. Isaac left the synagogue, feeling they had a chance. He would raise the rest; he just had to.

When he returned home, it was late and very dark. He entered his library and took out his leather portfolio. He ran his hands over the precious white paper and then dipped his quill into the raisin-black ink and wrote a letter to Jehiel of Pisa, the great Italian financier. Though the men had never met, they had formed an understanding in their trade dealings between Pisa and Portugal. Their common ancestry had linked them in trade, and now Isaac hoped that perhaps the great man would feel for his brethren in a Godforsaken part of the world. If his own people in Portugal could raise five thousand gold ducats, perhaps Jehiel could somehow raise another substantial amount. He had to try, anyway, for there was nowhere else to turn. He prayed for Moses ibn Aknin as he wrote, for the children suffering in their bondage, and for his own sweet children sleeping safely in their beds.

After he was done writing, he stood and walked over to the window to gaze at the sea. The ocean was stormy, huge waves crashing against the rocks, white foam rising like the breath of a sea monster the sailors often spoke of who rose from the depths of the ocean floor to devour ships. He blew out the candles and retired to bed.

Rebecca was sleeping. Isaac pulled back her covers and marveled at her body, still so firm, like a young bride. As he undressed, lightning cracked and sizzled over the water. The storm was making its way inland. He slid into bed beside his wife and pulled the downy comforters over them. It felt good to press his body against her sleeping form, so soft and warm.

He ran his fingers down her back, and she opened one eye.

"I'm sorry, my love, didn't mean to wake you," he whispered.

"I was sleeping," she mumbled and turned over.

He grinned, "I know." His hands rubbed her back and legs.

"Isaac! It's too soon after the baby." Her complaint seemed unconvincing.

"It's been two months," he said as he rolled her over and began to stroke her arms, shoulders, breasts. Isaac flicked his tongue over her moist nipples.

"I don't think we should," she whispered, but he covered her mouth with kisses to stop the protest.

The storm hit the shore. Thunder rolled above them, an impatient calling, longing for release. The ocean rose only to come crashing down, pounding the earth. As lightening cracked the sky, Isaac entered her. He felt as if white lightening was coursing through him, each crack causing him to shudder. He could feel Rebecca's response, all encompassing warmth, a good place to die. It seemed as if the ocean's waves rose high, poised for just a moment before the onslaught of salty spray, flooding him, drowning him, drowning her. As the storm moved on and its rumbling clamored in the distance, he quivered with each charged sound. He held onto her, wishing he would never have to let go.

"I love you," she whispered and kissed him, holding him tightly.

"Rebecca . . ." her name, his breath of life. As he withdrew, he kissed her as if she were mother earth, discovered for the first time. Then an image of the still missing Tamar ibn Aknin, lying in shackles, bloodied, soiled, in pain, flashed before him. Please, dear God, please, not my Rebecca, never Rebecca, he silently prayed. He buried his head in her breasts and held her, pressing her to him as she rocked him in her arms.

For five months Isaac and Moses ibn Aknin searched the castles of the returning crusading knights for Tamar and little Dinah. They had freed many of the people taken as slaves, after which Isaac had brought the sick, destitute people back to his home until new homes and work could be found. It was an arduous task, for the knights who had brought them back from Africa weren't willing to let them go and often raised the price on their heads. Fortunately, after Isaac had sent his desperate plea for help to Jehiel of Pisa, monies came in from the great man, and little by little they were able to free first the children, then the women, and men. Isaac was glowing from the success of their campaign, but Moses had become more withdrawn as family after family was reunited, husband clasping wife and child, tears shed in the joy of their release.

Isaac and Moses had been riding hard when they approached a castle that sat at the top of a hill, surrounded by a wood. They had heard that within this gleaming, golden structure, white slaves were still being held. Arriving at the gates, they hailed the guard; Isaac identified them as king's men and the gates opened.

"State your business, king's men!" a guard spit at them. "Where is the Count Agrio? I demand to see him!"

"First state your business!"

"I will not discuss state affairs with a guard. Tell the count that Don Isaac Abravanel is here on urgent business. It has to do with the crusades."

"The crusades!" The guard bowed to Isaac. "I will call my lord immediately." He left them in the courtyard. Several minutes later, they were ushered into an elegant receiving room. The crest of Count Agrio was carved into the center of each chair that surrounded an enormous mahogany table. Isaac and Moses stared at four silken tapestries of a hunt hanging on the walls until finally the count entered and they bowed.

"Don Isaac? The king's treasurer? What brings you here? Taxes? I hope not! I've already paid handsomely!"

"Yes, my lord, I know. I am here for another matter. I'm interested in the slaves you brought back with you from North Africa. I would like to buy them."

The count whispered to Isaac, "They were Jews. All but one are dead."

"All dead?"

"They were skin and bones, walking skeletons when they were marched off the ship. Just one woman left! At least she has her uses. You're interested in flesh then, Abravanel? And your friend, too?" He looked carefully at Moses and noticed for the first time that his skin was dark. "This is your slave? Making a collection, Abravanel? You don't want to spend too much time around them or they'll send you to the devil as well!" His breath was foul, his stringy black hair hanging to his shoulders, his goatee bobbing at the end of his pointed chin.

"May we see the woman?"

"I'm tired of the bitch! Always a fight with that one! I'll sell her to you at a good price. She has some use left in her."

Isaac's hand squeezed the metal handle of his sword until his knuckles turned white and was grateful that Moses understood little Portuguese. He quietly, coldly answered, "I'm sure she has. Now if we might see her."

Isaac and Moses followed the count down a long circular stairway to the dungeon. While torches lit their way, the stench of urine and excrement grew stronger. Isaac was overwhelmed with nausea and prayed that Tamar wasn't here. Blood stains smeared the cold stone floor, and dead men's bodies were still shackled to the walls. Someone moved in the corner of the back cell, and Isaac prayed that it was not Moses's Tamar. The count ordered a guard to pull the woman out, screaming, fighting, kicking as she came.

Isaac watched as Moses and Tamar recognized one another. The horror, the pain, the violation was too much to bear. She grabbed the sword from the count's side and stabbed the count in the chest. As the guard lunged toward them, Moses pulled the sword from the dead count and slashed the guard across the neck, nearly beheading him.

"Where is Dinah?" Moses demanded of Tamar, shaking her. "Where is she?"

Tamar's wild eyes stared at him.

"Where is my child? Dinah? Where is Dinah?" he cried.

"Dinah," she screamed and collapsed weeping to the filthy dungeon floor.

Moses rushed toward the cell from which they had pulled her. Isaac tried to stop him, but he could not. Moses found a little heap in the far corner. When he lifted a putrid cloak, he found his Dinah, the body shriveled and decaying.

Aroused by the death cries of the count and his guard, guards came clattering down the dungeon stairs. Isaac pulled his sword. When Tamar saw the count, she pulled a dagger from one of the guard's side and stabbed the count again. Dragging Tamar and the dead child, they ascended the stairway, striking the guards as they climbed.

"Open the gates for king's men!" Isaac cried when they reached the courtyard.

In the chaotic frenzy, one old man opened the gates, and Isaac and Moses lifted Tamar and the child onto the horses, mounted and fled. Isaac never looked back. They raced through the wooded land, over rivers and into the hills. But as fast as the horses carried them, as clean and fresh as the afternoon air was, the horror of the castle could not be shaken.

King Afonso was pacing back and forth in his throne room when Isaac entered one week later. He abruptly walked to his throne and sat down. Isaac bowed.

"You sent for me, your majesty?"

"What happened at the Agrio castle? I've had a number of conflicting reports. You and your servant have been accused of murder!"

"We had come in good faith, with funds to pay for Agrio's Jewish slaves. But they were all dead, still hanging from the walls-" his voice broke.

"Take a moment," the king nodded to a servant to pour Isaac a glass of water.

"Thank you, your majesty," Isaac said, taking a sip of water as he tried to compose himself.

"Moses and I have roamed the countryside, finding the crusaders who had come back with Jewish slaves. Everywhere we went, the Jews were feeble, weak, broken in spirit, but the horror of that castle—Moses Ibn Aknin's wife, Tamar, was there. Ill used, sire, and out of her mind with grief for their little girl, Dinah, was dead. When she saw us, when her eyes met her good husband's, it was too much to bear. She killed the Count with his own sword. Moses and I had to defend ourselves as we fled."

"The count was a violent man, but you must understand that when my Jewish treasurer attacks a nobleman and his guards and cries king's business, I am put in an awkward position, to say the least! I must have all the facts; you know you have enemies at court. How am I to dismiss this? I'm afraid the story I heard was somewhat different. However, I am willing to forget certain facts, the deaths of several guards and the Count, for instance, if I can be assured that you will not be 'freeing' any more of your people."

"Your majesty, all of the Jewish slaves who were still alive are now free."

"That was ten thousand ducats! How did you raise such an enormous sum? Surely the Jews of Portugal didn't have that much to give." The king raised his eyebrows.

"No, they didn't. I sought aid from the Jews of Pisa, and they responded. There are no more Jewish slaves in the land."

"Ten thousand ducats! You were able to raise ten thousand gold ducats! Well, that is an amazing sum and in such a short time . I hope that if I ever have such a need, Isaac, you will serve me as well as you have served your people."

"Your majesty, I am always ready to serve you."

"I will depend on it. I am determined to bring Castile under my domain. There will be war between Castile and Portugal, and I'll need you by my side."

"You have my word. I will always be ready to serve you." Isaac bowed to the king.

"Just one more point, Isaac. The woman, Tamar, she will have to be brought to court to face charges concerning Count Argio's death."

"As we rode away, she threw herself from Moses's horse." Isaac looked away from the king when he answered,

"And?"

"She is dead."

The king stood and walked over to the window to look out upon his lands.

"Well, I suppose that's the end of this whole sad affair. Perhaps someday Moslem, Christian, and Jew will be able to live side by side in peace."

"My people and I pray for that day."

The king nodded, and Isaac was dismissed.

As Isaac mounted his horse, he looked up at a high castle window and noticed someone had been watching him. The figure quickly moved away from the window, but not before Isaac caught sight of the red hair and a black patch covering the man's eye.

CHAPTER 14

As the December ice ate its way into the cracks and crevices of the cold castle in Madrid, King Enríque opened his eyes and saw the fire snapping away at a log on the hearth. His lovely daughter Juana, now thirteen, sat beside him, holding his hand. She opened her mouth to say something, but he didn't hear her. His eyes froze, staring at her but no longer seeing; King Enríque was dead. Archbishop Mendoza was called and his daughter was rushed away; her security was of utmost importance.

Isabella donned her mourning gown and, though the sun had just risen, she walked to the cathedral in Segovia to pray for King Enríque's soul. She would have to face the day without Ferdinand, for he was on the battlefield in Aragon, fighting the French who were constantly making forays into their lands. She knelt before the great altar. She closed her eyes tightly, her body shaking from the cold air, and she beseeched God to help her, to give her the strength to rule. She had never felt as alone as she did now, kneeling before the altar. She could picture her brother's face as it had been in death, so white, so innocent. For one brief moment, when Carrillo crowned him, a moment that she had missed, her sweet brother had known glory. Glory—was it something that she was now pursuing, or was she truly serving the Lord? She prayed for His guidance, love and understanding. She was prepared to sacrifice herself to serve Him. Taking a deep breath, she crossed herself and secretly made her way back to her chambers, where her dear friend, Beatrice, and her ladies-in-waiting were bustling about, hurrying to ready her for the great occasion. She was dressed in a pure white gown and wore her necklace, the center ruby so large that it seemed to radiate a glow all its own, throbbed against her white skin.

"Isabella." Beatrice spoke quickly, for the nobility of Castile were already gathering in Segovia's *plaza mayor*. "You and Ferdinand have fought and prayed for this day. I know what a great burden it will be when you wear the crown, but be brave, have courage, and God will not fail you."

Though Isabella could feel a tremor running through her, she smiled and answered, "Let our enemies tremble, for Ferdinand and I will rule Castile!" She turned as Beatrice placed a white cloak trimmed with ermine around her shoulders. The ladies lifted the trains of cloak and gown, and Isabella walked out to receive her knights.

An enormous crowd had assembled, and the Archbishop of Toledo, Carrillo, held the jeweled reins of a white horse caparisoned in gold. He helped her mount as the people cheered, "Long live the queen!" A page carried the sword of justice which gleamed in the sunlight as Isabella rode through the city of Segovia. The procession made its way to the *plaza mayor*, where a platform had been erected for her to receive the nobility of Castile. One by one, the knights kneeled and paid homage to her: Gutierre de Cardenas, Alonso de Palencia, Ferdinand's uncle, the Admiral of Castile. Ponce de León, the Marquis of Cadiz, knelt at her feet and as he lifted his head and gazed at her for the first time, he was enamored. King Enríque had been successful in keeping her hidden, out of the reach of these knights, for he knew, and, rightly so, that her beauty would overwhelm them and bring them to her cause. Thirteen year old Juana had neither the beauty nor the charisma of Isabella. The knights beheld her lovely red hair, delicate nose and lips, slender figure, and they were all under her spell.

"I humble myself at your feet, Your Highness." Ponce de León's voice was husky. "I am your servant. All I ask is to have the honor to die for you in battle!"

Isabella answered him quietly, "It is with the aid of noble hearts like yours that Ferdinand and I hope to bring order out of chaos and a lasting peace for all of Spain."

He bowed and began to move on when a hush fell over the crowd. Isabella looked up to see her knights part like wheat blown in the field. Her heart raced with fear. The archbishop's hand went to his sword. The guards had drawn theirs. She braced herself, her face frozen white, as Beltrán de la Cueva proceeded toward her. He climbed the steps of the platform. The archbishop stood between him and the queen.

"I come in peace," he said. The archbishop stepped back. Beltrán knelt to Isabella and kissed her cool, smooth hand. His black eyes burned into her blue ones, which reflected the cold winter sunlight. Her body trembled at his touch, and then with a slight shiver, she felt warm, as if a great black cloud had been lifted and she basked in sunlight. How could the King of Portugal, Afonso, lay any claim to the throne now, now that Beltrán de la Cueva had come to pay her homage? Isabella took this as a sign from God, that Juana was Beltrán's child and not the rightful heir, that she, Isabella, was indeed, the one who must rule Castile. Beltrán said not a word more and left as quickly as he had come.

After all the knights had kneeled before her, the archbishop led Isabella to the cathedral, where the golden crown of San Fernando waited. As he placed the shining gold crown upon her head, she finally felt she was, at last, queen.

"Your Highness," Beatrice whispered.

Isabella opened her eyes in the darkest hour of the night.

"King Ferdinand has arrived. He wishes to see you."

Sitting up in bed, Isabella pulled her covers close. "Ferdinand," she whispered, more to herself than to the young woman, trying to pull her thoughts in order.

"Tell him he may enter."

With a dagger always hidden in her cloak, Beatrice hurried out as Ferdinand strode in, throwing his cape on the edge of the bed. He was tired, worn, covered with dust and mud from his frenzied travel, and enraged.

"How dare you take the crown without waiting for me!" he spit the words out between his teeth in a low growl.

Feeling his eyes upon her lightly clad body, her head still foggy with sleep, Isabella was not prepared to answer him and sat dumbfounded before his tirade.

"You could have had the decency to wait until I returned, and then we could have accepted the crown together—but no! No, you had to have all the glory for yourself!"

"Glory!" she said, letting the covers fall back, ignoring his eyes upon her. She stood, grabbing a robe, now ready to defend her. In a quiet but strong voice, she continued, "Do you think that's why I allowed myself to be crowned? Beltrán de la Cueva bowed before me, before everyone, practically acknowledging the Infanta Juana as his own in that one single moment. What would you have me do? Wait! Wait until you returned from your beloved Aragon—which, I might add, you would put before Castile! I will not wait, sir! Not when my own people cry for an heir!"

"And Carrillo! If you think for one moment I'd trust him as cardinal—I will not have it!" Ferdinand raged.

"All right then, we will have Mendoza," she said, stopping him short.

"You would agree—to Mendoza?"

"Yes," she said, knowing that she now had the upper hand, but still feeling stung by his first coarse, sharp words, she couldn't help but wonder if he had been with his mistress in Aragon, if her coronation had brought him back.

"But Carrillo crowned you. You would choose Mendoza over Carrillo?"

"I am prepared to do what I have to in order to present a united front." She needed Ferdinand, needed to be able to confide in him, and needed him to lead her armies, needed to be loved, needed to draw him away from his mistress and bastard son. "Besides, I trust Mendoza. I've never really trusted Carrillo," she added softly.

Incredulous, Ferdinand now also spoke in a gentler manner. "But he has always championed your cause. He fought to make Prince Alfonso king."

"It was not a just cause. Enríque had the divine right to rule, and Archbishop Mendoza has always been beside the rightful, divine ruler."

Though Ferdinand had been infuriated with her coronation, he felt disarmed by her quick capitulation to his demand for Mendoza as cardinal. She had him in checkmate; she gave him what he wanted, almost as good as an heir to the thrones of both Castile and Aragon. He sank down onto the edge of the bed. The fire was burning low on the hearth, filling the room with a soft glow. Isabella was standing so close that he was tempted to reach out and take her hand, but he did not move. He felt fatigued from the war in Aragon, and his maddening ride back to Castile, but he begrudgingly admired her courage and desired her.

"If you make yourself a little more presentable, I shall wait for you," she whispered, coming to him, stroking his black hair, kissing the top of his forehead.

He gathered her to him and said, "King of Castile—that's what they are calling you."

"You are my king," she answered and pulled away, but still holding his hand, she smiled. She had won this skirmish. "I cannot rule without you. Whatever strength I have, I gather it from you, my love."

He stared up at her, wanting to believe her words. There would be war, war with King Afonso of Portugal, Carrillo probably joining the Portuguese cause. Then there were still the infidels to face in the south, in

Granada. He sighed. He knew she needed him to lead those campaigns, but as a ruler, he knew Isabella needed no one. He let her go, and went off to prepare for the night with his queen.

Near the Portuguese border, in Castile, Isaac and Fernando watched King Afonso take the Infanta Juana, his niece, for his wife. The Marquis de Villena gave the bride way before a large gathering of noblemen: the Duke of Arevalo, the Count of Urena, the Master of the Order of Calatrava and many others. After the short ceremony, a hush fell over the crowd, and Isaac watched them part as the Archbishop of Toledo, Carrillo, approached the platform. The king's guards drew their swords, but the archbishop pushed them aside.

"I come in peace," he said. Isaac had heard that Isabella and Ferdinand had chosen Don Pedro Gonzalez de Mendoza for their cardinal, and he realized now that Carrillo was joining the noblemen whose allegiance was to King Afonso and the Infanta Juana. Carrillo knelt before them. The lines of sorrow had worn deep into his skin and his eyes, the red blood vessels like little cracks in glass, spoke of the sleepless nights he had passed before coming to his decision, but here he was, only a few weeks after crowning Isabella queen, kneeling to the King of Portugal.

Isaac rode with Fernando, King Afonso and an army of 20,000 men swiftly toward Arevalo, then marched into the city to the wild cries from a large crowd, "Long live the King! Long live King Afonso!" It was a declaration of war.

Isaac and Fernando stayed with the King Afonso for a short time in Castile before he sent them back to Portugal. Fernando was needed in the courts, and Isaac was ordered to raise money for this Spanish Portuguese war. Isaac's legs felt heavy as he walked down the long hall toward the throne room. Guards were at every door. Prince João was ruling the kingdom while his father was fighting in Castile. Isaac didn't know why he had been summoned and felt uneasy. When he entered the room, the sun was streaming in through the large windows onto the jester who was amusing the prince, but who stopped abruptly. Carlos Málaga was standing behind Prince João, his hand on his shoulder, and Isaac was instantly reminded of Don Pedro who had stood just like that behind King Afonso. Isaac had never noticed it before, but now he could see that Málaga was the very image of Don Pedro. Isaac bowed to Prince João. The jester was excused.

"You sent for me, my lord?" Isaac asked.

João waited for the jester to leave, then began in a quiet, tense voice. "There is trouble on the border. The Spaniards have invaded the country and most of our troops are in Castile with my father. I need to raise troops instantly to protect our own land now. We need more money, Abravanel; we need more funds!"

Isaac watched Málaga, his one good eye riveted on him, his hand clutching the gold encrusted sword at his side as if he were ready at any moment to strike him. Isaac trembled under the stare. He had never meant to hurt Málaga. Let him stare into my soul, he thought, and let him see what is there. He cleared his throat and addressed the prince.

"My lord, you have taxed the people as far as they can go. They have already cut meat and fish from their diets. If you ask more of them, it will be their bread!"

João stood. Enraged, he grabbed Isaac's cloak.

"I know what you did for the Moroccan Jews! You did it for your own people. Now raise that amount for your king!" He threw Isaac back.

"Ten thousand gold ducats!" Isaac croaked as João nodded with a smile, knowing full well it was an impossible task. "After all we have already collected, it will be most difficult!"

"Find it, Abravanel!" João said, "Or you and your people will suffer!"

Isaac had no choice but to bow, and he was dismissed with a nod. Where would he go now? The people would starve if he taxed them further. No, there was only one untapped source in the land. Isaac saddled his horse and rode toward the cathedral in Evora. When he arrived, he looked up at the cross, the sad figure of Christ, and entered. A priest greeted him at the door.

"Father, I have come to ask you a great favor in the name of the king," Isaac said, feeling the eyes of the Saints upon him, measuring him. The priest was a converted Jew. He gave Isaac his warm hand, and they retired to an antechamber to discuss the grave situation.

The Portuguese had been driven back to the Douro River after two years of fighting. In the dark of the night, King Afonso, aided by Prince João, moved his forces back toward Toro. Isaac rode with them as they came to a large field. The king held up his hand to draw his battle line. Isaac watched the troops forming, their armor gleaming in the misty dawn. Prince João was on the right, the Duke of Braganza on the left, King

Afonso and Carrillo at the center—Isaac waited for the pursuing Spanish. He saw the banners bobbing up and down with the movement of the swift horses. A glint of steel appeared and then the host. The enemy formed their lines and at the center, the very center, of the army rode Ferdinand, unmistakable, his helmet off, his black hair blowing in the wind. Isaac watched him raise his arm, his sword cutting through the mist, slashing down with a force that all could feel; the Spanish army charged.

Isaac had never been suited for battle. The mail cut into his sides and his vision was poor through the metal visor, but he could see the charging army. He rode next to Fernando, their horses carrying them swiftly into battle. He felt as if the ability to control his life were gone. He thought of nothing but the stampeding army approaching, growing larger until suddenly a soldier was before him, arm raised, sword high in the gray sky. Isaac slashed at the man, bring him down off his horse. Another soldier was right behind him. Again and again Isaac wielded his sword, as possessed by a demon. His sword was growing red with blood; his horse was slipping on the wet earth beneath him, tramping on the fallen bodies.

An enormous Spaniard stabbed him from behind, wounding his right side, like a hot iron the searing pain forced him to crumble to his right side, but he managed to stay in his horse. The sword hadn't fully penetrated the chainmail, but blood was oozing down his right side. He couldn't lift his sword. It was hard to breath; he had to retreat before he'd fall off the horse. Just below him was a massive moving ground of bodies, Portuguese, Spanish, all the same as they now fought back death as hard as they had fought each other. Isaac's head felt light, too light. The putrid smell of the battlefield surrounded him, men begging for water, for death, their bowels empting into the earth. Isaac pulled off his helmet and gagged. He could hear King Ferdinand's voice screaming, "Santiago!" but above that voice the cries of hundreds of wounded men, screaming, stuffing eyes back into sockets, torsos searching for limbs, blood everywhere, blackening the earth. And still soldiers rose up before Isaac. He raised his sword, which seemed to have grown much heavier. With every ounce in his body, his arms shaking badly, he slashed aimlessly at a Spaniard.

"No!" Fernando cried, seeing the Spaniard, arm raised, and the gleaming blade slicing down. "No!" he cried, racing to Isaac's side, slashing at the knight before the blade it Isaac's head. Within the next moment, he grabbed Isaac's reins and led him away from the bloody field. The Castilian army had broken through the Portuguese lines; their soldiers were retreating. He left Isaac by a grove of cypress trees and then returned to the battle, crying, "Back! Back to your lines!" But the Portuguese continued to flee. Up, up they went into the mountains. They ran from the carnage; they ran for their lives. Fernando chased them, crying all the time, "Back! Fight for Portugal, for King Afonso! Back to your lines!" He chased them into the mountains, but it was hopeless. From his protective spot, Isaac looked back to see King Ferdinand pick up the Portuguese banner of Aviz, his men cheering wildly.

"King Afonso? I don't see him on the field," Isaac asked when Fernando rode back to him.

"I don't know where he is. How badly are you wounded?"

"My side, it's burning? And you?"

"If we can find the king, I am fine; if not, I'm dead. Do you understand?"

Fernando took the reins of Isaac's horse again and they wound their way up the mountainside, all the while looking for the King Afonso's party. After hours of searching, they found a group of soldiers who had dismounted and were warming themselves around a small fire. They finally slid off their horses. Fernando unfastened his own armor and then pulled off Isaac's. Blood was oozing from Isaac's side.

"Let's get you closer to the fire," Fernando said.

"You've just fought side by side with João. Why do you fear him?" Isaac whispered as if his bloodied shirt was of no consequence, though his vision was now blurry and the pain in his side was burning so that he had trouble forming words.

Fernando threw Isaac's arm around his shoulder, and they limped along, continuing to search for the king.

"Because I am a prince, grandson of João I! Prince João sees me as a threat to his throne. Do you really think he will let me live in peace? He will not rest until I am dead! Only one of us will rule, my friend, only one," Fernando whispered, as they passed men helping others to staunch wounds, lifting heads for a cool drink, closing the eyelids of the dead.

When Isaac cast his eyes down, he saw a man crawling in the grass, bleeding into the earth, becoming a part of it.

"I am afraid for you, Fernando," he said quietly as they picked their way among the wounded men.

"We must find King Afonso. He has to be here!" was Fernando's reply.

Darkness had settled on the mountain, covering the bodies of men who had struggled upward to die. When Isaac and Fernando finally found the king, he was huddled over a campfire. Prince João stood over him, his armor covered in blood. Carrillo was nearby, his cape with the white cross soaked with blood as well. Málaga was there as well blood-soaked but not wounded.

Fernando knelt beside the king. "Your Majesty, we cannot give up now. We have all fought too hard and too long."

"You'd have my father and me die in battle so that you can rule. Is that it, Fernando?" João shouted at him.

"That's enough, João. Fernando fought by our side. You will not question his loyalty!"

João walked away in disgust. Málaga stared cold and hard at Isaac, unimpressed with Isaac's wound which Fernando set about wrapping, before he followed his prince.

Once the wound was bound tight, Fernando stood and walked in the opposite away. Isaac sat by the fire, near the king. After he had sipped some wine, Isaac winced as he got up. His side hurt like hellfire. He took a longer drink of wine and then limped off to find Fernando. He thought he'd find him resting nearby. He was not. Isaac limped down the path they had taken, calling for him in a hushed voice, but there was no answer; Fernando was gone.

King Ferdinand stood at the Douro River and watched the Portuguese retreat with grim satisfaction. He mounted his horse and rode back to his own encampment. King Afonso could not wrest his queen from him. The Castilian crown was now his to share with Isabella.

CHAPTER 15

When the sun rose red the next morning, Isaac awoke in the encampment to see Fernando standing above him with two fresh mounts.

"You've survived the night, I see," Fernando said, trying to sound as if all were well.

Isaac could hardly get up, but he didn't have a fever and the bleeding just under his ribcage had been staunched. The chainmail had protected him from a more serious wound. In spite of the pain, he was able to stand and wash. Though he didn't think he could get any food down, he ate the biscuit and cheese that Fernando offered. With Fernando's help, he mounted his horse. Isaac felt as if every bone in his body had been broken, but fortunately, the damage to his spirits was worse than to his body. Every jolt of the horse arched through him like flashes of lightening, but he grit his teeth and grimly followed Fernando. Fernando had a gash across his right thigh, but otherwise didn't seem to be too beaten up. Both suffered black and blues across the face, arms, torso, but the armor had done its job. They slowly descended the other side of the mountain in order to make their way back to Lisbon to nurse their wounds.

But from the moment, Fernando woke him; Isaac could sense a change in Fernando, an almost imperceptible distancing, a casting down of the eyes, a preoccupied stare. King Afonso had not yet surrendered, but Fernando and Isaac had done all they could for his cause. It was time to retreat.

A few days after their return to Lisbon, Isaac and Fernando, still stiff from their wounds and needing something to lift their spirits, decided to pursue a more peaceful occupation. They slowly rode their horses through the Lisbon streets down to the wharves to find a chart shop that had just received two of the newly printed Gutenberg Bibles. Vendors called to them from their stalls, showing them their plump tomatoes, clusters of garlic, green and black olives, stuffed with red pimento or garlic or hot peppers, purple grapes each one as large as an olive, bright yellow lemons, three different varieties of oranges, and figs, hanging in long honeyed ropes. Men in their spice stalls haggled over the price of cardamom, cinnamon, cumin, saffron, salt, and pepper. Noblemen bowed to the king's men, Fernando, now the Duke of Braganza, and Isaac, newly knighted grandee of Portugal, Don Isaac Abravanel. They acknowledged the greetings and rode on. As they approached the wharf, the scent of fish, seaweed, tar and salty sea grew strong. They finally came to the small shops which lined the great wall on either side of the gates which opened to the ocean. They hesitated, still on horseback, searching shop to shop, peering in at tile shops, glistening with cobalt blue, cherry red and golden colors, rope and barrel shops with coopers hard at work, bisque ware pottery, waxes and tars, as they searched for the Colón cartographer's shop. When they found it, they dismounted, Isaac letting a soft groan escape his lips, not wanting Fernando to see that he was still hurting. They tied the horses and entered. A tall, redheaded young man was seated behind the counter, gazing out toward the sea. The young man stood quickly.

"Can I be of service to you, sirs?" He said as if just awakened.

"Yes, we are looking for Bartoloméo Colón," Fernando answered. "I understand this shop has just received two Gutenberg Bibles, the printed Bibles. We are very anxious to see them."

"One moment, please." The young man turned to get his brother.

"You are not Bartoloméo, I take it, perhaps a relative?" Isaac asked.

The young man was now carefully eying Isaac and Fernando. "You are Don Isaac Abravanel and you sir, the Duke of Braganza?"

"Yes, the books," Fernando said, distractedly tapping his fingers impatiently on the counter.

"Allow me to introduce myself to you, Cristóbal Colón." He smiled, bowing to the two grandees.

"Zarco?" Isaac whispered; Fernando tensed.

"Yes."

"We are cousins?" Fernando asked, looking at the gawky young man.

"Yes, I believe, my father, the prince for whom you were named."

Fernando cast a cold stare at Colón. The youngest son of King João I, Prince Fernando, supposedly this young man's father, had died in a Moroccan prison, held as a hostage. Fernando may very well have been named for him, but this young man was just a bastard of the royal house, like so many others, and Fernando was now the Duke of Braganza.

Suddenly understanding his mistake, that the Duke of Braganza would not recognize him, in public anyway, Cristóbal quickly changed course and returned to the reason for their visit to his brother's shop.

"My lords, let me find my brother for you."

They watched the awkward young man, who was big boned, with long arms and legs, his red hair cut like a rag doll's falling unevenly down to his shoulders, walk to the back of the shop. A moment later, Bartoloméo appeared with Cristóbal tagging behind him. Bartoloméo immediately recognized Fernando and Isaac and bowed.

"What a great honor it is to have you here, my lords. My brother tells me you are interested in the Gutenberg Bibles. I thought they would sell quickly, but I'm afraid there are few nobleman interested in the printing press."

He brought forth a velvet covered box and opening it, displayed a beautifully bound Bible. Fernando took the volume and thumbed through it quickly and handed it to Isaac who turned each page as if it were a precious jewel, as indeed it was.

"Do you know about his new press?" Bartoloméo was anxious to make a sale, for it was not often that a Duke and a king's treasurer walked into his shop.

"Not terribly much, I'm afraid," Fernando said, clearly much less interested than Isaac. This whole excursion seemed to have been his idea.

"I understand each letter is on a separate wooden block, carved backwards," Isaac noted as he carefully thumbed the pages.

"Yes," Bartoloméo answered, turning his attention to Abravanel. "But the amazing thing is the way he makes his imprint. In the past he created the print by leaning on the blocks with his body weight. Then one day while he was out in the countryside, he saw some peasants squeezing wine on a press. He realized he could apply more pressure and get a better copy by pressing the letters with something like a wine press."

"Really? How ingenious!" Fernando declared, but wanted nothing more than to leave. He knew exactly who these two brothers were, and he wanted nothing to do with them.

However, Isaac was enthralled.

"This is very fine, indeed, compared to the other printed books I've seen. You know, of course, they are printing books in Castile."

"Yes, of course." Then the cartographer flushed red, for it was the Jews of Castile who were doing the printing. He quickly added, "But I've not seen any of those copies."

"Well, I have. I am a Jew," Isaac added, not surprised to see the relief written across Bartoloméo's face, though Cristóbal knew exactly who Isaac was, "and I can tell you these are superior. I would advise you, my dear friend, to buy one."

"Well, if my counselor feels this is of value, then I will," Fernando was patronizing all of them, anxious now to leave.

Bartoloméo bowed to the duke and Don Isaac.

"May I wrap it for you?"

"Yes, please." Fernando answered.

Bartoloméo returned to the back of the shop, and Fernando and Isaac were left alone with the strange young Cristóbal who had gone back to studying his maps as if studying for a great examination. Isaac was fascinated by the young man.

"Are you looking for a quick route to India," he joked.

"I'm sorry, I didn't hear you." Cristóbal looked up, his face turned pale, and he quickly rolled his charts, obviously not wanting to share them, and nervously drew his fingers through his bedraggled hair.

"I asked you if you were looking for a quick route to the Indies. You seemed so entranced with your maps."

Colón held the scrolls close to his chest and gazed at Isaac with deep, penetrating eyes.

"There might be other routes besides the one Prince Henry pursued," he answered warily.

"But surely that is the safest and most direct, if we can round the tip of Africa," Fernando said, now a bit more interested in the young man.

"Well, I've heard some say that India can be reached by sailing west," Isaac spoke softly.

"Where did you hear that?" Cristóbal asked, his eyes burning into Isaac's.

"There is a great scholar, named Zacuto, who has said that it's possible to sail the great western ocean," Isaac said, in a way testing Colón. Zacuto was Jewish. He was curious to see if he had heard of him.

"You've heard of Zacuto?" he blanched. "I'm sorry. You must excuse me." He pushed passed the two men, disappearing into the back of the shop.

He collided with his brother as Bartoloméo was coming back out with the wrapped Bible.

"Have you heard others write about a western route?" Isaac grabbed Cristóbal's hand, stopping him, his curiosity roused, discerning that Colón recognized the name Zacuto.

Trapped between his brother and Isaac, Cristóbal stopped short. "Yes, there are many." He seemed to think better of running to the back. "Of course, Aristotle wrote of lands west of the great ocean, and Marco Polo wrote that the lands of the great Khan are much bigger than we had supposed. But it is Toscanelli and Pierre d'Ailly who have calculated the land of Cipango to be much closer than previously thought."

"You seem to have made a great study of this," Isaac said, now truly interested.

"But Ptolemy doesn't speak of such lands and most of our great navigators have little use for Pierre d'Ailly's work," Fernando added. Fernando knew quite a lot about this, having studied with his uncle Prince Henry when he was young.

"Yes, yes, I know," Cristóbal answered. He had heard that argument far too often. He looked at Isaac and could see that at least one intelligent man was taking him seriously. So many had laughed at him, had asked him when he was planning a voyage to the moon, but here was a man who listen to him and didn't laugh.

"Well, perhaps someday I will be given the chance to prove I'm right."

Not wanting to lose another sale because of his eccentric brother, Bartoloméo said, "Is my brother driving you mad with his wild talk?" He laughed.

"Your brother needs to study his navigational charts a little closer," Fernando said, gathering the precious Bible into his arms.

"However," Isaac added, "Cristóbal, if you can support your calculations, come and see me."

"I will! Thank you, my lord!" Cristóbal bowed his whole body quivering, clearly unable to contain his excitement as he watched Isaac and Fernando leave the shop. Finally, someone from the king's court had listened to him.

They had just left the shop, when Isaac and Fernando were splashed with mud from a small party of horsemen who were galloping through the narrow street. While they brushed the mud from their robes, the party halted and the riders trotted back to them. Isaac looked up to see the banner of Aviz flying in the wind, Prince João peering down at them.

"Cousin! It seems I've bespattered you with mud. I'll send you another robe."

"You needn't bother!" Fernando's hand went to his sword; Isaac placed his hand over Fernando's lest he lose his temper. "It would be nice, however, to see you walk your horses when you are in the city streets. You could have trampled someone at that speed!" Fernando quietly raged. Isaac prayed his friend would not lose control.

João laughed as Málaga and his royal guard protectively surrounded him.

"My dear cousin, I'm on a mission that concerns the whole kingdom. Do you suggest I allow urgent state business to wait so that I will not bespatter the delicate garments of peasants and noblemen who frequent such places?" He leaned over and added, "Are you suggesting that the king's work be delayed?"

Fernando's face flushed red. "I'm not afraid of you, my lord. Beware your enemies!"

"Are you threatening me, Fernando?" João said, just above a whisper. Málaga began to pull his sword, but João stayed his hand.

Isaac interrupted, "Excuse me, my lord, but the duke is upset only because of his robes. Please excuse this angry outburst."

"Don't ever threaten me again. You think yourself a lord, a prince! Royal blood, is it, Fernando? Bastard's blood, I'd say, and so would the rest of the knights in the kingdom!" João turned his horse, and then galloped away. His party followed close behind. Carlos Málaga turned back to laugh at the bespattered Isaac, then rode after the prince.

"Why did you interfere?" Fernando fumed.

"My dear friend, we were surrounded by ten excellent swordsmen on horseback. What choice did we have but to pacify him?"

"Afraid of Málaga, are you?"

"No, I'm not afraid of Málaga," Isaac said quietly, trying to get the better of Fernando's rage.

"Let me tell you something, Isaac," Fernando whispered, though it came out more like a hiss. "There will come a time when I will humble this incorrigible young man. I promise you. There are those, more powerful than I, who do not want to see João inherit the throne!"

"King Ferdinand!" Isaac whispered. He was afraid, dreadfully afraid of confirming his fears about Fernando. "Where were you, Fernando, the night of the battle? I looked for you . . ."

"You know where I was . . ."

"I've guessed."

Fernando cast his eyes down. He had thought that maybe he could confide in Isaac. He was trying to hold King Ferdinand back from destroying King Afonso, but he could not stop what Afonso had set in motion, not if he wanted to live; João already suspected too much. After the two men mounted their horses, Fernando continued in a low voice, "I've been in contact with Ferdinand and Isabella. We've talked. There is much we could accomplish if I were . . ." He had grabbed the reins of Isaac's horse. "Work with me, Isaac. Do not fight this. You have as much to lose if João inherits the throne as I do!"

"No!" Isaac pulled his hand away from his friend. "I cannot be a party to your treachery. Do what you will, but I want neither to hear about it nor to have a hand in it!"

"I understand, but Isaac, you are a part of it whether or not you want to be. João is your enemy as much as he is mine, and he will see you in that light no matter what happens."

Isaac felt trapped, helpless. Perhaps Fernando was right; he knew his position would drastically change once João was king.

"Come, let us cool our tempers with a glass of wine," Isaac suggested. Grimly he wondered what his own fall from grace in the royal court would mean for the Portuguese Jews. He could see his father's face so enraged after he had wounded Carlos, his father's uplifted hand ready to strike. Ahh, papa, it's not so easy to navigate this treacherous world, he thought. He landed rather ungracefully as he dismounted, the pain in his right side sending a jolt through him. The old scars on his back felt unbearably tight.

As they entered an inn, Isaac's eyes adjusted to the dark, and he shook off the image of his father, of Málaga, of that beating he took that night in the Judería. A dog was barking at a goat which had wandered in and was chewing on a wooden bench. Angrily the innkeeper took his broom and swatted the goat outside. The dog, satisfied that he accomplished his task, whined for a reward.

"Your Highness," the innkeeper said, kicking the goat aside, addressing Prince Fernando, "you honor me by entering my humble inn. What may I bring you?"

"A pitcher of Sangria," Fernando ordered.

The innkeeper brushed the chewed wooden bench while an old man in the corner began to play a lively tune on a guitar. Isaac dropped a coin in his hat before sitting down next to Fernando.

The pitcher was brought to the table by a fetching young woman who stood wide-eyed, staring at the handsome duke and pale treasurer.

"What do you think of this Cristóbal Colón?" Isaac said, trying to take Fernando's mind off of João and the pretty girl whose breasts nearly spilled out the top of her blouse.

"I don't know," Fernando answered, still smarting from João's insult. He waved the girl away and spoke in a low voice. "You're impressed with Colón, aren't you?"

"Yes, I am. I've read Zacuto's work, and I believe that if someone were courageous enough to try it, there might well be a route to India by traveling west."

"My dear Isaac, if you want to go to the East, then you have to travel east to get there. Doesn't that seem logical? Besides, the man seems foolish. Don't you think so? I mean, the way he stares out the window and did you see him stumble across the room? He can't even navigate his way around the shop, never mind around an ocean." He laughed as he sipped his wine.

At that moment, a man came running into the inn.

"The war is over! King Afonso has surrendered to King Ferdinand. Some say King Afonso is leaving for the Holy land; some say he's gone mad!"

CHAPTER 16

After the defeat of the Portuguese army, Isaac was no longer called to court. King Afonso abdicated the throne to Prince João and prepared for a pilgrimage to the Holy Land. Then he unexpectedly changed his mind and returned to Portugal. Prince João begrudgingly relinquished power, but King Afonso no longer wanted to live. His hair turned dusty gray, his eyes clouded with despair, and he fell ill. Fernando, grandson of King João I, who had been loved throughout the land far more than Prince João, was in a dangerous position. So when Isaac's daughter, Bathsheba, dressed in her mother's wedding gown, walked in the procession to her groom's home, Isaac's heart was filled with the only joy he had known in a long time. His family had come to life once again like vibrant desert flowers after a rain. Isaac held his daughter's hand as they passed friends in the Judería. Bathsheba was marrying Joseph Abravanel, his brother Samuel's younger son. Isaac gazed at her as they walked; he had never been fully aware of her beauty. Her features were delicate, her eyes wide and blue, like Jonathan's, and her blond hair glistening in the sun resembled the woman for whom she had been named, Bathsheba Ben Ezra. Isaac had only heard rumors and muffled words behind closed doors when he was a child, but the tragic story of Rebecca's mother who died just after her birth was still a mystery. "Poor Bathsheba," Isaac remembered hearing his mother whisper as tears slid down her cheeks.

However, the sun was shining, reflective rays lightening Isaac's heart. They had reached his old home. His sister, Miriam, was handing out rice to Samuel and Joseph who threw the rice as well as coins, just as he had done when Rebecca entered this house. The canopy held up on wooden poles by his sons Judah, Joseph, Samuel and his nephew Jacob, was in the exact spot where he and Rebecca stood so many years ago. His little Elisheba dressed in yellow satin with yellow roses and pearls in her hair stood beside his Rebecca who was resplendent in rose red gown, roses and pearls. He passed them and then he had to let go of his Bathsheba's hand, their fingers reluctantly parting, and his daughter, his little girl, walked on without him. She seemed so happy as she stood beside Joseph.

Isaac couldn't hear the rabbi's words, his heart pounding, his head felt light. Visions kept leaping before him: little girls playing in the cool shade of the yard, adoring eyes gazing at him, small hands reaching up to him, tiny pink lips kissing him on the cheek. Where had those days gone? What kind of world had he shaped for them? Death and destruction was laying waste to all the peace and security he had tried to build. Life for the Jews was growing intolerable in Portugal. The old taxes levied by Don Pedro were being enforced once again. Under the heavy hand of Prince João and Carlos Málaga taxes on food, clothes and shelter—taxes on the right to exist on Portuguese soil—were reinstated.

The bride and groom sipped the red wine. Isaac looked at all the loving faces surrounding him, all but one were there, sharing in this joyous day. Isaac closed his eyes for a moment. Where, where was Jonathan? Why had he abandoned them? Why had he left all the responsibilities of the Portuguese Jews to him and just a few others? He missed his father's tired, wrinkled face. Isaac was trying still to please his father, to do as he had commanded, representing the Jews as his father had done before him. He had become the royal treasurer, as his father had commanded. But as he stood beside his grown daughter, instead of feeling satisfied with all he had accomplished, he felt tired, empty. He wanted to weep. He didn't want to lose his little girl, his Bathsheba. He wanted time to stand still; it was all going too fast. His throat constricted, tears rippled down his cheeks; he couldn't hold them back. How was he to defend the Jews when the old guard, the old powerful knights were constantly battling them with these incessant new taxes and religious laws that would barely let them survive. What would they do without the protection of the Braganzas? He didn't know. The sweet Hebrew words of the ceremony reminded him of his studies, his writings for which he had so little time. He yearned for a quieter life of study, of Talmud, of Torah.

Joseph smashed the glass; Isaac opened his eyes. His daughter was married. The young couple would have to build their own life now, just as he and Rebecca had done. He saw Rebecca standing amongst the women, receiving their congratulations. He was amazed to see some silver strands in her hair though her face hardly showed the passage of time. He walked over to her and tightly held her. He still loved to feel the warmth of her body pressed close to his. He was still as hungry for her as if he were still a young man. He loved the way her breasts had softened and kissed the tiny birdlike creases fanning her eyes. He released her before his manhood rose in front of the whole wedding party.

"I feel as if they are with us—the ones we've lost," he said, thinking of his mother, father, and Jonathan.

"I feel it too," she answered, "except one . . ."

He knew she meant Jonathan, for he was not with the dead. He kissed her and then they faced the celebration.

The musicians were playing on pipes and tambourines; the women danced, whirling about, flirting, and teasing the young men. Flaky white fish, puffy brown breads, oranges, melons, figs, dates, grapes, nuts filled bowls at every table and thick rice puddings were served with great dollops of whipped cream, raisons and cinnamon. After the meal Joseph approached Isaac, his new father-in-law.

"May I speak with you a moment?" he asked in a shy, quiet voice.

"Of course, Joseph." Isaac stood, and they walked into the old study. Isaac was afraid he was going to ask him some personal questions, questions he should have asked his own father, but he was taken by complete surprise when Joseph said, "I wish to leave my father's medical practice. I want to be a financier, like you."

"Joseph, it takes years to understand the world of finance, as many as it took you to learn medicine."

"I know. I'm willing to work very hard." He hesitated. "Judah, Judah wants to be a doctor, and I want to be a financier."

Isaac froze. Samuel had been teaching Joseph for years, and his own son, Judah, Isaac expected him to work by his side. Judah entered the room, not daring to look at his father.

"Why? Why today of all days did you have to make a decision like this?" Isaac fumed.

"Father, it's not a sudden decision. I've been studying medicine with Uncle Samuel for a long time now," Judah tried to appease him.

"A conspiracy then! Why was I not in on this great secret?"

"We didn't want to upset you. You've had so much on your mind with the war, and the duke," Judah answered in a small voice.

"So much that I wouldn't have time to discuss your future! You will follow me as I followed my father. Do you think this was what I wanted for a life?" Isaac was so furious he raised his hand, just as his father had done on the day he had wounded Carolos Málaga. And the thought turned into a violent cough, his whole body rigid in anger.

Samuel, Isaac's brother had followed the young men into the room and closed the door.

"I'll talk to him. You both go back to the guests," Samuel said in a calm voice. "Isaac . . ."

"Don't Isaac me!" he shouted. "Shouldn't a father be consulted before decisions like this are made? Don't I have a right to counsel my own son?"

"Listen to me. They only wanted to spare you. Don't you think we all know the burden you've been carrying these past years, the hours of riding through the countryside raising funds for the war, the tensions within the royal house . . ."

"The royal house does not concern me at the moment!" Isaac shouted again, and then looked up as he saw the worried expression on his brother's face. "Why am I yelling at you?" he asked in a quiet voice, shaking his head, sinking into their father's leather chair.

Samuel came forward.

"Judah couldn't face you. But my Joseph is very bright, and he has a tremendous desire to learn. If you will forgive me, he reminds me a little of you sometimes. And Judah, you should see your Judah with the sick, such love, such concern one cannot learn. A man either feels this or he doesn't. Judah was meant to be a doctor."

"He is my son and was meant to be a financier!"

"Judah is too sensitive, Isaac. Look, don't yell at me, not at me, Isaac. I know that father pushed you into being a royal advisor, that it was the last thing you wanted. Don't do this to Judah. He doesn't want it either. Joseph is your son now too. Let him help you. Goodness knows you need someone to help you."

Isaac sighed and slumping down further into the chair, said, "Yes, yes, I need help." He ran his fingers through his thinning hair. "All right, all right . . . . Joseph can work with me. The Duke of Viseu needs someone; it's become too much for me to handle myself. But let me tell you something Samuel, it's dangerous now, to work for the court. It's no secret that Prince João hates the Braganza Family. Fernando's older brother, the Count of Montemor, has fled to Spain, and the younger brother, the Count of Faro, speaks of leaving as well."

"I know Isaac, I know," he said, patting Isaac on this back. "Here, drink a little Madera." He poured Isaac a tumble of port. Isaac sat back and sipped on the sweet drink, letting this change in the family order sink in. Satisfied that his brother was calming down, Samuel quietly left the room. Isaac looked at the closed door. "Well," he thought to himself, "Papa, I'm so tired. Joseph? This must be your idea? Well," he thought, taking a final sip of the port, "I certainly need all the help I can get." He got up from his father's seat and joined the wedding guests.

Shortly after the wedding, Joseph, now working at Isaac's side, showed a tall, red-haired young man into Isaac's study. The man bowed, and Isaac was surprised to see Cristóbal with a trim haircut, a fine velvet suit of clothes, fine lace collar. The man was almost unrecognizable from the distracted young man in his brother's cartographer shop.

"Don Isaac." Cristóbal Colón spoke now as if he were addressing a man of his own class. "I have not forgotten your interest in my studies of a westward voyage to reach the Indies. Now I have mathematically proven my theory."

"Cristóbal, you look wonderful," Isaac answered. "Please first tell me about yourself. Your dress is so fine. You seem to be prospering since we last met."

"Yes, I've been most fortunate in marrying the late Captain Perestrello's lovely daughter, Dona Felipa, and she has given me a fine healthy son, Diego!"

"Well! You have my hearty congratulations! Shall we celebrate with a glass of port?" Isaac said, and called Joseph to bring them some glasses. Then as he poured the ruby liquor, Moses ibn Aknin knocked on the door and entered carrying papers for Isaac. "May I introduce my dear friend Moses ibn Aknin?" Moses bowed to Cristóbal. "Joseph, please, another glass."

"Not for me, thank you," Moses said. "I'll return later. I didn't realize you were with someone."

"Ah, well, we'll go over these later then. Thank you for bringing them in. And you, Joseph?"

"Thank you, but Moses and I are working on the current sums from the olive vineyards, if you don't mind, that is."

"No, no that's fine."

Moses bowed once again and then he and Joseph quietly left the room. Isaac turned back to Cristóbal.

"Now shall we have a look at these charts of yours?"

As Cristóbal unrolled his charts, Isaac could see scribbled calculations, none of which made sense to him. Pointing to the chart, Cristóbal began: "Toscanelli has estimated the miles separating Lisbon and the Great Khan at 2,500, which means that if we sailed west we could reach the first Indian port in just a few weeks." His long fingers moved across the mapped waters to an island labeled Cipango. "From my own calculations, taken from the work of Marco Polo and others, I estimate the land mass of Europe and Asia at 270 degrees, which would make the western ocean only 90 degrees." His eyes shining brightly, he added, "It is incomprehensible to me why the King and Prince João are so obsessed with an African route. The waters are known to be wild, and the trade winds unfavorable. I have spent much time of late on the islands of Madeira and Porto Santo and have studied the tides and trade winds of the western ocean. My late father-in-law was the governor of the island, as you may recall."

Isaac smiled, for he knew that the late Captain Perestrello had ruined the island by overrunning it with rabbits. Cristóbal chose to ignore the smile.

"I need an introduction to the court. As you can see I have married into a noble family and hope to present my case to Prince João, who, I understand, has great interest in expanding Portuguese exploration."

"Well, I'm afraid my own connections in the court are directly with the King, and he has not been well since he returned from the war. How large an investment would an expedition like this mean?"

"If I could have just three ships, money for sailors and supplies, I estimate about 6,000 gold ducats."

Isaac sat and stared out the window. A sea gull was soaring in a lapis lazuli sky, almost like the white sails of a ship against the water. What gold ducats could buy—the rescue of people from slavery, war, and peace? Isaac turned to face Cristóbal whose eyes never left Isaac.

"Prince João and I are not on the best of terms, but there are men I know, and I will try to arrange an audience for you. I am afraid my own education in the field of navigation is lacking, but your ideas make sense, for I am aware of Aristotle's reference to western lands, also of Zacuto's theories; I believe in you."

"I would be most grateful, Don Isaac, for any efforts you can make on my behalf."

Cristóbal bowed, but before he left the room Isaac said, "The name Colón, it is an old Jewish name. Are you sure you want me to use it in court?" He raised his eyebrows, wondering if Cristóbal would reveal anything about his family.

"The Jews of Portugal and Spain are very dear to me." He turned from Isaac, saying nothing more.

Isaac didn't press him. That day in the shop, the name Zarco was a whisper in the wind. Had anyone actually said it? He did refer to the young Prince Fernando, João I's youngest son, who died in a Moroccan prison, a hostage to political intrigue or was he an embarrassment to the powerful King João, because the young prince had a Jewish lovechild? Then again in Aragon, King Ferdinand himself was a grandson born out of a Jewish love. One thing Isaac clearly understood was that these liaisons had no influence on the fate of the Jews in Portugal, Castile, or Aragon. Isaac walked Cristóbal to the main courtyard, where he found Fernando dismounting from his horse and in deep conversation with Joseph, who had run out to greet him. Cristóbal bowed to the Prince. He had been hoping he might find Prince Fernando, the Duke of Braganza, at the Abravanel castle.

"My lord, it's an honor to see you again." Colón bowed to Fernando, but Fernando did not recognize the well-dressed young man.

"Have we been introduced?" He looked to Isaac.

"Yes, you remember the young cartographer who sold us the Gutenberg Bible. This is his brother."

"Oh, yes, yes of course. You seem to have improved your circumstances since we last met."

"Yes, my lord," Cristóbal answered. "I've had the great fortune to marry the late Captain Perestrello's daughter, Dona Felipa, and we have a fine son."

"Perestrello, wasn't he the one who brought all those rabbits to . . ."

"Indeed, the very same," Isaac interrupted, for Cristóbal had turned red, and he wanted to save him from embarrassment. "I want to introduce him to someone at court who might be able to obtain an audience with Prince João."

At the mention of João's name, Fernando's face turned white.

"On second thought, perhaps someone else would be better," Isaac quickly added.

Cristóbal realized to his great disappointment that Prince Fernando would be of no help in obtaining an audience with Prince João.

"Perhaps now that King Afonso is back from the Holy Land, he might have some interest?" he asked.

"I'm afraid the king is not well." Fernando glanced at Isaac but said no more; he wanted to speak with him.

Cristóbal sensed that the noblemen wanted their privacy, and he quickly took his leave. Isaac ushered Fernando and Joseph back to his library, and they closed the door. "Do you really think this man has any validity?" Fernando asked.

"He may have an interesting new route to India. The world is round—we all know that. But you didn't come here to discuss Cristóbal Colón or whether the earth is round." Fernando paced the room, then stared out the window.

"Does this have to do with King Ferdinand?"

Fernando stood like a statue. Little threads of sliver in his hair caught the sunlight as he stared out the window.

"I know you don't want to hear, to know, but as I've told you before, Isaac, the Portuguese will implicate you whether or not you are involved. I must have someone go to Castile for me; I have important papers that must get through to King Ferdinand. As long as King Afonso lives, we are safe from João, but once João is king, he will not rest until every nobleman in Portugal is crushed." He came close to Isaac and whispered, "Ferdinand wants to arrange a match between my daughter and his bastard son in Aragon. A marriage like that would only strengthen my position, as you can well imagine. Joseph will deliver the papers for me and negotiate the details." Joseph did not dare lift his eyes to see his father-in-law's reaction.

Isaac stared at Fernando. He loved him and thought of the young prince who had bravely come to his defense when he was a child, his friend who had freed him from the Judería and had graciously given him a life of luxury, a warm castle in the winter, a cool villa for summer.

"Joseph will not go. I will take them myself. There is nothing treasonous about a marriage contract."

At that moment, there was a knock on the door. Moses ibn Aknin entered.

"Some refreshments?" he asked.

"Moses, how would you like to repay Isaac? I have an urgent message which must get through to Ferdinand," Fernando asked without missing a beat.

"No, I forbid it. I must do this alone," Isaac said as Moses knelt before him.

"Let me go with you. When will you allow me to repay you? I want to do something of importance for you?" Moses spoke forcefully.

"It will be dangerous, crossing into Castile now. I can't send you with soldiers for protection, and the Castilian guards will draw their swords the moment they find you. Let them take you to the king as a prisoner. After he reads these papers, you have my word that he will let you go," Fernando said to Moses, but was glad that Isaac was hearing this.

"I consider it an honor to serve you, my lord. How many times have I heard my people cry out against Prince João? We pray for you, my lord, to someday be king," Moses answered.

Now Isaac turned to gaze out the window. He feared for them all. There would be no future for Fernando in Portugal, and he knew that Fernando would never live in exile. He wanted to reach out and embrace his friend. He didn't want him entangled with Spain. But when he saw the look of resolve on Fernando's face, he knew he couldn't change his mind.

"How sick is King Afonso?" he whispered.

"Gravely ill, I'm afraid."

"And the Infanta Juana? What have they done with her?"

"She's gone to a nunnery. They will not harm her. Isaac, if I thought João would let me live in peace, I would not be forced to take such action, but we both know he won't. João's son is in Moura right now with King Ferdinand's daughter. They are supposed to be married, but João is looking for an excuse to break the marriage contract. Ferdinand wants my assurances that I will support him should such a breach take place. I have no choice! I either support King Ferdinand, or I wait for João to stab me in the back." He came up to Isaac, his face an inch from his friend's and whispered, "And what future is there for you, with Málaga at his side?"

"I told you before I'm not afraid of Málaga, and I believe João would allow you to live in peace. If you enter into a secret pact with King Ferdinand, you will give João the excuse he's looking for to destroy you!"

"That's exactly why I must!" Fernando answered. "He will try to murder me whether I've got the support of Ferdinand or not. And you, my friend, will also be in grave danger. I'm afraid, Isaac, that sometimes you are too naïve," Fernando answered. "Come, Moses, we will speak of this as we ride."

Isaac and Fernando embraced as brothers. "God be with you, Fernando," he said, and they opened the door. Fernando was about to leave when Rebecca appeared in an upper balcony. His heart stopped for a moment. She wore a pale yellow gown and sunlight lit her golden hair.

Fernando loved her, but he would never hurt his friend, never let Isaac know just how much. "Rebecca," he said, bowing low and then fled.

King Afonso had withered to papery skin, his white bones clearly seen beneath. He lay in his bed attended by doctors, surgeons, servants, coming and going so that Prince João could barely squeeze into the room. When he saw his father, his first thought was that he was dead, but on closer inspection, he could see the covers slowly fall and rise with his father's labored breathing. João gazed impassively at the man he called father as if he were just a curious onlooker, not a man whose life would dramatically change with this man's death. King Afonso opened his eyes, saw his son, and struggled to sit up. With the aid of three men, he was propped up.

"I wish to be alone with my son," King Alfonso said.

Everyone left the room save his oldest and dearest physician, but he too was dismissed.

"You rarely come to see me these days," the king said.

"I am sorry father, but I've been so busy attending to court matters."

"So you are more interested in matters of the court than how your father is fairing."

"Father, I am advised about your condition every few hours."

"And how is my condition?" King Afonso asked, growing angrier each moment.

"The good doctors tell me that you will be up and about any day now."

"Liars, all of them liars!" King Afonso wanted to roar but his words were only a hiss, half of which were understandable. "You wait for my death like a vulture waits for its prey. You would not murder me in my sleep but circle until the last breath leaves my body so that you can take my crown."

"How can you say this to me, your son! I pray each day for your full recovery."

"Your prayers on that count will not be answered. However, there are two things that I have left undone, and I want my wishes to be carried out. I am still the king!"

"Yes, father." João bowed.

"I wish my bride, the Infanta Juana, to be sent to a nunnery."

"It has already been done."

"Come closer." João bent closer to his father. "There is also something that you must finally learn about Carlos Málaga."

"What about Carlos?" Suddenly, João was interested.

"This hatred of his for the Jews, it must stop."

"And I suppose you wish me to continue protecting your Jewish friends."

"Our friends. Listen to me, João. You will not be able to govern this kingdom without their help. This is something Don Pedro never understood."

"What does Don Pedro have to do with any of this?"

"Don Pedro was Málaga's father."

"I've guessed."

"But you did not know that Bathsheba Ben Ezra, Jonathan and Rebecca Ben Ezra's mother, was Carlos's mother."

"How can that be?"

"Don Pedro always took what he wanted, and he wanted that golden haired beauty."

"But this is madness. Carlos has hated the Abravanels all his life."

"Yes, your Málaga, who is so full of hate for Jews, is half-Jewish himself. Jacob Ben Ezra took the broken young woman for his wife, but Pedro kept the child that she bore, though never recognized him, nor told him the truth."

"Carlos does not know?"

"I doubt any of them know, save Ben Ezra, and he died in the riots Málaga inflamed. You have the information. Do what you will with it, but you must understand how intertwined our world is with theirs. To destroy the Jews within the kingdom would be destroying a part of us. This is something you must come to see, João. Now leave me for I am tired."

The prince bowed before his father, kissed his hand, and quietly closed the door.

Prince João sat on his father's gilded throne, wrapped in a purple robe trimmed with ermine but with no crown upon his head, and listened to Bartoloméo Dias discuss the possibility of cutting through the Senegal River, to the Gambia, the Niger, the Congo and hopefully connecting to the Nile. Carlos Málaga entered. João stared long and hard at Málaga and then nodded for him to enter. Dias bowed to Málaga, the prince's favorite. Málaga gave him a curt nod and waited impatiently for the audience to end.

"Captain Dias feels certain that the African rivers will connect to the Nile. What do you think of that, Carlos?" João asked.

"An interesting idea, my lord," he answered as he worked on a split fingernail.

The prince, however, seemed excited by the new proposal. He jumped down off his throne and threw his arm over Málaga's shoulder. "Just think! If we can cut through Africa, think of the advantage we will have over Castile, and there is always the hope, the dream that we may yet stumble upon Prester John's kingdom. Prince Henry was sure the kingdom was in Africa! Can you imagine, Carlos, stones that can heal the blind?" Carlos turned to him and stared with his one eye. The prince coughed and continued, "The fountain of youth, the precious gems, the gold, all waiting to be discovered. Imagine the power, the might of the kingdom that discovers it first! I would shake in my boots if Ferdinand were to find it before we do-the blood thirsty bastard!"

Málaga had heard it all before.

"Captain Dias, what do you know of Ferdinand's recent explorations?" he questioned.

"None, my lord. As far as I know he has been preoccupied with wars in Aragon and Granada. The French are keeping him busy in the north and the Moors are harassing him to the south. I'd imagine exploration is far from his thoughts at the moment. That's not to say he won't be interested in it in the future, of course."

"But at the moment, you know of no planned voyages coming out of Spain?" Málaga asked.

João quickly rolled up the charts they had been studying.

"That will be all for now, Captain. I will consider this plan further and think on it. I can tell you I think this seems most promising."

"Thank you, my lord." Dias bowed and left the throne room, beaming.

"What's this, Málaga? You're interested in exploration now are you?"

"Not really. You know how I feel about the subject. It's just that I was curious as to King Ferdinand's plans. It seems he has all he can handle at the moment, doesn't it?"

"Yes, it seems that way. Why? Are you worried about an invasion of some kind?" João sat down again.

Carlos bent over him and whispered, "I have a suspicion that Prince Fernando, your dear cousin, is corresponding with King Ferdinand."

"Can you prove it? I need proof!" He grabbed Málaga's black cloak. "And if you find it we will have to wait until my father is dead. We dare not move against him too quickly; he has too much support amongst the noblemen." He looked up into Carlos's face and added, "I need proof, not rumors! Do you understand? I'll not move against him without something concrete. The only blood that will flow this time will be by decree from the high court of Portugal. I would have civil war if I went after him myself and wouldn't the King of Aragon and Castile relish that!"

"Yes, he would," Málaga said, brushing the Prince's hand aside. "But I think I can find what you want, my lord." Málaga bowed.

As he rushed from the throne room, João contemplated all that he had been told at the earlier audience he had had with his father. João had sworn to his father that he would never reveal the identity of Málaga's mother. He was thinking about this when a guard rushed into the throne room, prostrating himself on the floor before João and cried, "King Afonso is dead! Long live the king!"

CHAPTER 17

During the next two years, King João II tightened the central structure of the Portuguese kingdom, drastically reducing the power of the nobility. In the spring of 1483, João summoned his royal cabinet to discuss the final plans for Captain Bartholomew Dias's exploratory trip through the African rivers. Fernando was summoned; it was not unusual for him to be present at a cabinet meeting. He was amazed at the meticulous attention João had given to the preparations—how many men on each ship, the pay, the cost of rope, canvas, food for the men. The sun penetrated the deep lines in Fernando's face and reflected off of his silver hair as he gazed out the window. It was warm for this time in May. He could see a swallow perched on a tree, its breast puffed up as it sang to the sun, and then he heard the sudden thunderous knock on the door. Carlos Málaga entered with the king's guard. A tense hush fell across the room, and all eyes turned to João, who sat back in his seat, letting the drama continue as if he had no part in it.

"Your Majesty." Málaga bowed to the king. "Excuse us for this intrusion, but we have been ordered to arrest . . ." he paused as some of those present gasped audibly—"Prince Fernando, Duke of Braganza."

Before any protest could be made, Fernando was pulled to his feet, as guards pointed swords at him.

"I demand to know why I'm being arrested!" Fernando shouted.

"Dear Cousin, I'm sure the truth will bring a just end to this most grievous accusation," João said, smiling, kissing his cousin on both cheeks as the guards marched him out of the room. The king then turned back to the other noblemen, who sat like stone figures, shocked by the outrage, but not daring to protest. Better to sit quietly and placate the king than face a court trial. João continued his discussion of Dias's trip as though nothing had happened.

Fernando was taken to the dungeons and thrown unceremoniously into a windowless cell. Only a torch burning near the prison guard shed light. He stumbled to the wooden bench and stared into the darkness. The strong smell of urine and feces made him feel nauseated, but he realized he had to pull himself together; he had to think clearly. João wanted to be rid of him; he knew that. But João also knew that King Ferdinand of Spain was not threatening the Portuguese throne, and he was surprised that João had actually moved against him. Then the cold reality became clear to him as a shiver rippled down his spine. "There will be no real trial! João was never afraid of an invasion from Ferdinand. I am the only threat to the throne."

As Fernando hunched forward on the edge of the seat, his muscles drawn like taut rope, he felt like a trapped animal. He could hear the clanging of chains, the soft moaning of a prisoner in another cell. He could not sleep, and hours passed before a guard brought him a cup of putrid water and a crust of moldy bread.

"I insist on knowing why I've been imprisoned!" he demanded, but the guard simply turned away. Fernando threw the food on the floor; a brazen rat scurried out to retrieve the bread, and he watched it race back into its hole. There was no place to relieve himself; he was forced to use the side wall, as many before him had done. Prison walls were foreign to Fernando; he was a prince raised to hunt, to run wild and free in his beloved Portuguese lands.

The next day, the guards came for him, unshaven, no change of clothes. He was pulled out of his cell and marched back to the living world. His eyes burned from the glaring sunlight as they shoved him into the courtroom. João was on his throne; the court was in session when he was brought in. He bowed to the king and took his place in the defendant's box.

"Do you wish the services of a court counselor?" the high judge asked. Fernando was surrounded by twenty-nine other judges.

"I decline," Fernando answered, feeling more secure with the presence of so many well-known faces, friends! There had been no treason; he was sure he could defend himself against any false accusations.

"Are we to understand that you will represent yourself before this court?"

"That is correct," he answered.

"Then bring forward the case against the defendant," the judge said. Carlos Málaga stood before the council.

"Prince Fernando, Duke of Braganza, is accused of collusion with King Ferdinand of Castile, León, and Aragon."

"The offense?"

"Treason of the highest order," Málaga said as he looked at Fernando with his one good eye. "High treason against the Crown."

"That is a lie!" Fernando shouted. "You have no proof! There is no case here, only jealousy and hatred!"

Guards grabbed Fernando's arms and the high judge said in a harsh voice, "The defendant will refrain from debasing this trial with such outbursts or he will be removed from the court and a king's man will try the case." The guards relaxed their grasp. "The accuser?" the high judge asked.

King João stood and a hush fell across the room. "I accuse Don Fernando, Duke of Braganza, of treason of the highest order and will submit documents to prove collusion between the duke and King Ferdinand of Castile, León and Aragon!"

Fernando's face turned white as he frantically wondered, "What papers could they have? I have not corresponded with Ferdinand in two years, and since he and João agreed on marriage terms for their heirs, there has been no threat of war. João knows that!" Fernando's heart was beating wildly. "Why was I so sure the danger was past?"

"Does the defendant wish to make a statement on his own behalf?" the judge asked.

"Yes, your honor, I do. These papers you have before you were stolen from my property. They are of no value and are dated more than two years ago. You will see they bear no royal stamp, neither mine nor the royal stamp of Castile."

"You do, however, acknowledge them as your papers?"

Fernando walked over to the council and looked carefully at the documents. There was no question that they were letters written to him from King Ferdinand. He had to defend himself; he had to make them see that these were not treasonous.

"Yes, they are mine, but these papers date back to King Afonso's reign. I had written to King Ferdinand at the request of King Afonso."

Fernando could see from the stern faces about the room that no one believed him or that if they did, they were not ready to defy the king. João would not rest until he was dead, and if he accomplished this through the courts, there would be no uprising, even though he, Fernando, was loved throughout the land. No one would challenge a court ruling of high treason. He looked at João now, his cousin, who was no longer hiding his hatred.

"Does the Duke of Braganza have anything more to add to his defense?" The high judge asked.

Fernando dropped his head; it was futile to defend himself.

"The court will recess until these papers have been carefully examined by the council. The court is dismissed." All rose as the king, followed by the judges, left the room. Fernando was jostled to the underworld once again. Though he was hungry now, he would not touch the poison they threw at him. When the molding bread hit the floor in his cell, he did not even notice the rat that sallied forth to retrieve it. Again he tried to clear his mind. What had he written in those papers? It was two years ago. How did Málaga get them? He was sure that they contained nothing incriminating, but the night dragged on into what seemed an eternity. He felt as if he were buried alive. Even the moaning in the next cell had ceased.

The sun cut him like a sharp blade when he emerged to the lighted world on the second day of his trial. The guards untied his wrists which had been bound so tightly that the circulation had been cut off. As he rubbed his arms and wrists, the high judge and King João entered the courtroom.

"How does the defendant plead to the charges?" the judge inquired.

"Not guilty, my lord. I must educate this court to the hideous conditions I've been subjected to in the last twenty-four hours."

"Silence! This court is not interested in the comfort of its prisoners."

"I have been served poisonous food! My wrists have been bound so tight as to cut off my circulation . . ."

"Silence or you shall be thrown back into your cell! May I remind you that you are here on the most serious offense in the kingdom? Treason! Treason which carries the sentence of decapitation! Let us not hear any more about your unsatisfactory accommodations. Do you have anything further to add to your defense? Is there anything further we need to know about the papers in question?"

Fernando, realizing he would have no chance to vindicate himself with a court full of João's henchmen, stood tall and held his head high as he answered, "No, my lord, as I have stated before there is nothing incriminating in those papers. Let justice be done—I have nothing to fear."

The judge raised his eyebrows and turned to the king. "The council requests more time to study these documents, your Majesty."

"Let the court take all the time it needs. Now that the culprit is in prison, the kingdom has nothing to fear from King Ferdinand. I do not wish a hasty judgment."

João was annoyed that the judges had not reached their verdict, rose to leave, when Málaga said in a low voice, "I'm going to arrest Abravanel."

"Not yet!" João whispered. "Everyone knows of your hatred. If Abravanel is to be arrested, my own guards will do it! Is that clear?"

Málaga pursed his lips and nodded then followed him out of the courtroom.

When Fernando was thrown into his cell again, it reeked from his own waste. He buried his head in his hands. They would find him innocent—they had to. It was a very good sign that they had not yet reached a decision. Obviously there was nothing incriminating in those papers. It was only a matter of placating the king. Finally, in complete exhaustion, he fell into a restless sleep. He dreamt he was riding his horse, the wind to his back pushing him onward. He raced on and on until he realized his horse had gone wild; he could no longer control the beast and panic filled his heart as he desperately held onto the animal.

On the third day of his arrest, he stood quietly and gazed at the sun, but its warmth no longer reached him. The king and Málaga were already in the room when the judges entered. The men shuffled to their places. The high judge addressed Fernando.

"Do you have anything further to add to your defense?"

Fernando shook his head no; his heart was too heavy to allow him to speak.

The high judge turned to the king.

"Your Majesty, after much deliberation and careful consideration this court finds the defendant, Prince Fernando, Duke of Braganza, guilty of high treason and condemns him to death."

Smiling, João turned to say something to Málaga and was surprised to find him gone.

Having been to the royal court on business for Isaac, Moses heard about the death sentence only moments after it was pronounced. Though the trial had been kept secret for fear of revolt throughout the land, the noblemen knew of the Duke of Braganza's imprisonment but were frightened for their own lives. Moses jumped on his horse and sped toward the summer villa where Isaac and his family were staying. As he raced, he could hear the hoof-beats of a rider not too far behind. He didn't look back but raced forward. He had to reach Isaac before the king's men! He had to warn him! When he reached the villa, he ran into the house crying, "Isaac! Isaac!" He saw Rebecca and cried, "Where is Isaac?"

"He was summoned an hour ago to court. Why, Moses? What's wrong?" His hysteria numbed her. "What has happened?"

"Fernando, Fernando has been convicted of high treason and sentenced to death!" He stuttered over the hateful words.

Rebecca felt a slow coldness creep over her, her body recoiling with the news. "No!" she whispered. Fernando, Fernando—a brother to them— their closest friend, their benefactor, their protector.

The door flew open and Carlos Málaga, surrounded by guards, entered.

"Where is Abravanel?" he raged, knocking over a vase, shattering it.

Moses bowed to Don Carlos.

"He has been summoned to court, my lord."

Málaga threw Moses against the wall, knocking the wind out of him. Rebecca backed up toward the end of the room.

"And where do you think you are going?" Málaga hissed.

"Nowhere, my lord," she whispered, her face deathly pale.

"Your beloved friend, Fernando, hasn't long to live. His head will roll, Rebecca!" Málaga raged.

She collapsed, leaning against the stone wall.

Málaga loomed over her, his great bulk covering her slight form in shadows.

"And Isaac is next. His head will roll across the floor like his friend's, or shall we get a bucket to catch it?"

She sprang at him like a wild cat, her fingernails racking him across the face.

Málaga hadn't come to rape her. He had come for the pleasure of escorting Abravanel to his death, but her wild, physical reaction excited him.

"Hold her!" he commanded his guards as he wrestled with her. They held her to the ground, assuming he just wanted to subdue her, but when he unbuckled his sword, they turned their faces from him.

"Don't you touch her!" Moses cried, breaking from the guards and pouncing on Málaga. Two guards pulled him back then delivered vicious blows.

"Stop, stop this madness!" Rebecca screamed as they dragged the unconscious, bloodied Moses from the room. "Don't you dare touch me!" she said to Málaga, stiffening in horror as he reached down to untie her gown. She started to scream, to kick and bite in order to break from the guards.

"Don't let him do this!" she pleaded to them, but they would not look at her, would not loosen their grasp. Cringing at his touch, she began to sob as Málaga forced her legs apart. Startled, he paused at the unexpected sound of horses and the clamoring of guards.

"Have you gone mad?" King João raged, exploding into the room. "Leave her alone!"

"I will have her, Abravanel's bitch!" Málaga cried.

"You take her, and you condemn yourself to hell and damnation!"

"For taking a damned Jewess!"

"For taking your half-sister!" he said as he pulled Málaga to his feet. "Release her at once!" João shouted and the guards let go.

Rubbing her bruised wrists, Rebecca rolled onto her side, but her sobbing had ceased with the king's words, "Your half-sister."

João had broken his vow to his father. The room was silent.

Málaga went to strike the king, but guards intercepted.

"You lie!" he cried. "You lie! My father was your uncle, Don Pedro!"

"And your mother was Bathsheba Ben Ezra," João answered. Now that he had revealed part of the tragic story, he could no longer withhold the rest.

"Pedro had to have her, the beauty with golden hair. He raped her . . . you were conceived. After you were born, Pedro took you away from her, brought you to court, and she never saw you again. Some say that she had lost her wits, but Ben Ezra married her, took care of her, and they went on to have two children. But she never recovered, and one day jumped from a tower in the Ben Ezra home. I promised my father that I'd keep this secret, but you've made that impossible."

"No!" cried Carlos. "No! You cannot be speaking the truth!"

"You dare question me, your king? You have only to look at Rebecca to see the truth!" João grabbed his arm. "I told you to stay away from Abravanel. But no, no you had to come here, directly from the court! Fortunately, I guessed where you were going. Now you will do as I say!" João pulled him out of the room, back outside.

Rebecca could hear the horses thunder from the yard. Alone, weeping, she stood, ran into the next room and found Moses lying on the floor. She lifted him in her arms, cradling him. He moaned as she wiped blood from his face.

"Did he hurt you?" he asked though his lips were black and swollen.

"No," she whispered.

"You must find Isaac!"

"But I can't leave you like this?"

"Help me onto a bed. One of the children will soon come home, but you must leave at once."

"The king has commanded Málaga to leave Isaac alone."

"The king himself will be looking for Isaac. You must find him and tell him to flee."

She helped Moses onto a bed in the next room and then took his advice. Grabbing a hooded cloak, she ran out to the horses, mounted and rode off, desperate to find Isaac. As she rode, João's words reverberated around her. "Jumped from a tower to her death . . . ." Her mother had jumped from a balcony in Jonathan's room—she could see the room, the window, imagine the fall. She kicked her horse. She had to find Isaac, reach him before Málaga! Her half-brother, Carlos Málaga! Isaac would be on his way home from Evora.

Isaac had stopped for the night at an inn on his way back to Lisbon. He was finishing a meal of bread and cheese when a man came running in crying: "Prince Fernando! Prince Fernando has been sentenced to death!" Outraged to hear this about their beloved prince, the men in the inn became violent, throwing plates and chairs.

Feeling as though he had been stabbed, Isaac stood, blindly made his way out of the inn and staggered down the road.

"Why?" he cried to the heavens. "Why?" He stumbled and, leaning against a tree, slipped to the ground. Fernando, his friend, his prince and benefactor, the protector of the Jews—sentenced to death! It seemed almost too much to bear. Fernando was going to die, and there was nothing, nothing Isaac could do to save him.

He did not know how long he sat there, but in the cold chill of the night, he could feel hoof-beats rapidly approaching. He rose and saw a rider racing toward him, a hood concealing the rider's face, so similar to his childhood night vision. "Let it be Málaga," he thought as he faced the rider. "Let me die now with my friend." The rider sharply pulled on the reins and called out, "Isaac!" It was Rebecca.

"Rebecca?" he whispered in utter disbelief.

She descended from her horse and threw her arms around him.

"You must flee for your life. Fernando has been condemned to death . . . ." She choked on the words.

He held her tightly; her warmth stopped the shaking that had been racking his body.

"I know. Rebecca," he said softly, his tears mingling with her golden hair. "How can I run? My disappearance would be an admission of guilt. I have to go to court, face the charges against me, and prove my innocence."

"You must flee. If they murder Fernando, what chance do you have in their court of justice?" She made no effort to conceal her anger. "They will murder you as well."

"I will not leave you and the children. It is impossible. Let them do what they will, but I cannot run."

"I am Málaga's half-sister . . . the king will not let any harm come to us." She heard Isaac suck in his breath then seem to stop breathing. His arms held her like iron bonds.

Without looking at her, he whispered.

"You've known this all these years?"

She broke from him so that she could see his face.

"No. King João told Carlos when," she stumbled with her words, "when he came to arrest you. Don Pedro and my mother . . ." Suddenly, she envisioned Málaga forcing her legs apart and weeping, she fell into Isaac's arms.

Isaac held her as she cried. They sat on the side of the road, and he rocked her back and forth in his arms until her tears had subsided.

She looked up defiantly and said, "For Fernando, for me, for the children, you must go! You must live; ransom us out. What good can you do any of us in a dungeon? Perhaps in Spain, you might even be able to help Fernando. Go, go quickly . . . . I'm sure Málaga and the king will soon be after you!"

The cold truth of her words stung him. He would be of no use to any of them locked in a dungeon. As Fernando had warned him so often, if he were condemned to death, Isaac would be too.

They stood, and he kissed her good-bye. He held her, not believing he had to let go, but finally took the reins of the horse she had been riding, mounted it, and made for the Guadiana River, the border between Portugal and Castile.

157

As Rebecca began to walk back to the inn, she heard the thundering hooves of a horse. She cowered to the side of the road when she saw a rider draped in black moving like the devil. It was early dawn, but the rider saw her in the morning mist. The cloak concealing her face did not hide her identity. He halted.

"Where is he, Rebecca? Don't think I'll let him go just because . . . ! Too much has come between us. There is no going back!"

"Why Carlos?" She ran to his horse and pleaded with him, with no fear for herself. "He never meant to harm you. Why do you hate him so? Because we are Jewish, Carlos? Is that a reason to hate? To feel nothing for another human being, but hatred is a sickness. I'm not afraid of you, Carlos, nor is Isaac."

"If you think for one moment that you are safe from me, you are wrong, and if your husband is such a coward that he has fled, then he has made a grave mistake. The courts will try him and his absence will only serve to strengthen the king's case against him. But I will find him and bring him back to see his head roll off the block like Fernando's!" Despite the king's admonition, he turned and headed for the Guadiana River.

Rebecca prayed that Isaac had already crossed. She walked back to the inn and found Isaac's horse. As she made her way back to Lisbon, she saw the king's men searching from house to house. She did not have to ask for whom they were searching. With a heavy heart she wondered if she'd ever see her husband, her beloved, again.

Isaac had traveled south all day, avoiding the roads and villages, for he knew king's men would be looking for him. As he stopped to rest by the river, he noticed the water was running high from the swollen streams that fed it. He bent over to take a drink, but when he turned, he saw Málaga standing just behind him, sword drawn.

"It would have been so easy to sink this into your back," Málaga said, "but we don't want to disappoint the king, do we?" The blade was now touching Isaac's chest, right above his heart. "To your horse, Abravanel!" he ordered.

Isaac slowly made his way to his horse, the blade now pressing at his back. If he went back with Málaga, he could defend himself. But then he thought of Fernando and how in the last two years he had tried to make his peace with João. No, there was no way out but to escape, and it had to be now, by the river, before they reached the main road and king's men.

As he mounted his horse, he threw one leg over the animal and kicked Málaga with his other foot. He held on to the horse, half on, half off, and began to ford the river. Málaga jumped in after him and pulled him off the horse, which was caught in the swift current and swept down the river. Málaga's arm closed tightly around Isaac's neck, but the two were caught in the current. Isaac was choking. He couldn't breathe as Málaga tightened his grip, water rushing over them. Isaac tried to pry himself free, but he could not budge the iron clasp, and then suddenly Málaga let go.

Isaac took a deep breath, dove under the water and let the current on the far side of the river carry him toward the Spanish shore. He turned once to see Málaga caught in the current, his form being tossed in the rushing water. Isaac tried to guide himself to the, east but as the river tumbled him about, he no longer knew which direction he was heading. On he continued, the water engulfing him. He came up for air and swallowed water, and felt as if he would drown but continued to push himself toward the shore; it was as if all the other elements in the world had vanished, nothing but water existed. Finally, wearily, he saw the shore and grabbed onto a rock, his legs dragging in the water. He inched his way forward onto dry land, praying he had reached the eastern shore. He crawled up the riverbank and looked around. There, on the far side, he saw Málaga stagger out of the water, walk over to his horse, and ride away. Isaac rolled over and stared at the blue sky; he had reached the other side; he was in Castile!

He collapsed, his strength gone, his body racked with fatigue and cold. After a long while, he fell into a deep, black sleep. He dreamt he was fighting the river again, his arms too tired to move; he sank under and then he seemed to float above the water, his body lifting free of living bonds. Rising into a night sky, he became lost in the heavens. From far away, a black cloud emerged and moved towards him, taking on different shapes as it came. Some of the forms it took were grotesque—Fernando's head, rolling. Then the image looked like a man on horseback. Slumped forward in his saddle, a black hood concealing his face, the rider seemed weary but the horse continued to move forward, lifting one heavy hoof after the other, and then vanished just as Isaac reached out to touch him.

When Isaac woke by the rushing river, he felt as if he were tumbling back into his body. He could not control his shaking, and he realized the dream that haunted him was the same he had experienced as a child, but now he guessed the rider was Málaga.

CHAPTER 18

Isaac felt stiff when he woke and then stood up, the river still churning just below him. Silt had dried on his clothes and looked like blood stains. He scooped his hands into the water in an effort to wash before he journeyed to the closest Jewish community in Segura. His hands trembled as he dipped them in and out of the water. Leaving Portugal, his wife and family alone, unprotected from Málaga and the crown, left him badly shaken. Málaga was nowhere to be seen, and the only noise he could hear was the rush of water. As he surveyed the riverside, he saw his horse, blood oozing from the left leg, all his belongings gone, but at least the mare was alive. He edged his way over to her, the old wound on his right side throbbing, the scars on his back tight once again, he gently laid his forehead against the mare's and just stood for a few minutes. He gathered up the reins and slowly walked the horse up to the main road.

As he set off, he thought about the little town he knew where he hoped to stay until his circumstances in Portugal were clearer. Only a few weeks before, he had heard that the town was swelling with Jewish refugees from Seville and Córdoba. King Ferdinand and Queen Isabella had ordered all the Jews out of these cities because of attacks against them, though the Jewish families had lived there for hundreds of years; Isaac's own family had been in Seville for generations. How ironic, he thought, that he would seek refuge in the same town as the Jews from Seville.

Walking past olive orchards, past old men prodding donkeys with long sticks, past rolling hills dotted with sheep, his despondent state left him feeling weak and slightly dizzy as his thoughts turned to Fernando and his perilous position. He would do everything he could to free him, and perhaps, here in Spain, he would be in a better position to help. He would find Fernando's brothers, the Count of Faro and the Marquis of Montemor, who had fled Portugal a few months earlier, and perhaps, working together, they could arrange his release. Yes, that was what he would have to do, he thought, walking the horse at a faster pace, as if getting to Segura quicker would release Fernando faster. He decided to write a letter to King João and defend his and Fernando's innocence. Feeling a little better, walking the horse briskly, he felt the earth begin to tremble beneath his feet and heard the sound of branches snapping as horsemen surrounded him. They drew their swords and demanded, "Your name, sir? Your destination?"

Perspiration breaking on his brow, he wondered if João had sent men into Castile after him. Drawing himself up, unafraid of going back to Portugal, he said, "I am Don Isaac Abravanel."

A man with a black goatee pointed a sword at Isaac's neck and said, "A Don? A grandee—and why should we believe you? Do you have papers?"

"No, I have come to help my brethren who have fled from Seville to Segura."

The man's mouth opened wide, his white teeth shining, and he began to laugh. The others laughed as well, for to see Isaac standing there with stained clothes, a bloody horse, the stubble of a beard on his chin, and claiming he was a nobleman, come to aid the Jews, struck them as funny. The men were, however, on business and had no time to waste on a mad beggar man.

"Well, my lord," he gave him a mocked bow; perhaps, you are just what your brethren need, another mouth to feed!" The men around him laughed again, turned their horses, and left Isaac alone on the dusty road.

Though he had nothing to eat, at the end of a long day, he settled down for the night by the side of the road, made a soft bed from pine branches, tethered the horse, and built a small fire. The dancing flames snapped at the wood and warmed his body, but not his soul. He had just closed his eyes when he heard someone approaching on foot from the woods that enveloped the small highway. Isaac stood and drew his dagger.

"Just some warmth, that's all I seek, some warmth by your fire." A man with a long shaggy beard approached Isaac. His clothes were ragged and dirty and his body reeked, but Isaac invited him to rest by the fireside. To Isaac's surprise, the man produced a pouch containing a loaf of bread and some fine cheese. He pulled apart the bread, offering a piece to Isaac, who took the bread and a bit of cheese and watched the man as he ravenously devoured the rest. He offered one last bit to Isaac, saying, "We must finish this quickly. Don't want to be caught with it!"

"Must you steal for your food?" Isaac asked the poor man.

"Yes, that I must do. In Madrigal, I stole a side of beef for my family. They were starving, my wife and three children. Afterwards, I had to run.

A thief's life is worth very little! The Hermandad has chased me all this distance. They know I'm heading for the Portuguese border. Is it far?"

"No, it's not far, less than a day's journey, but the river is swollen. Do you know how to swim?"

"Swim? No, I thought I'd be able to wade across or perhaps build a raft."

"I'm afraid the water is too swift for that."

The thief crossed himself then cast his eyes to the ground not wanting Isaac to see his tears.

"What hope is there for me then? I might as well give up."

"One must never give up," Isaac whispered as he thought about his own family and wondered if he would ever see them again.

"The Hermandad never loses a man. They will have their way with me."

"I thought the Hermandad was outlawed by King Enríque."

The thief looked at Isaac with his sad black eyes. "Queen Isabella has reinstated them. She says they will bring law and order to the land, but when a man cannot feed his family, what good is law and order?"

Isaac gently patted him on the back. The man rested for a moment longer.

"The firelight is dangerous for me, my friend. I must go back to the woods and head for the river. Maybe I will find a way to cross it. Thank you for your warm light. I am grateful."

He bowed to Isaac and then slunk back into the woods, dodging under bushes, making his way from tree to tree until he merged with the other dark shadows in the forest.

The Jews in the town of Segura opened their arms to Isaac though he entered as a tattered, penniless man. He was given the finest room in the rabbi's home and fresh clothes, for there was not a Jew in the town who had not heard of the great financier, Don Isaac Abravanel.

A few days after he had recovered from his ordeal, he woke at night, feeling restless and alone. He stood and walked over to a little window to gaze out. The moon threw twisted shadows off an old gnarled olive tree beside the house. Though his immediate needs had been met, he now felt desperate to ransom his family out of Portugal and was angry with himself for fleeing as he had. How could he have left them behind? He pressed his head against the cold white wall of his room. Still gazing out, he felt numb, hollow, empty inside. What if he couldn't get them out? What would his life be without them? Why didn't he demand that Rebecca come with him? He thought about her last words to him and wondered if what she had said about Málaga was true. And if it were, would Málaga really leave them alone? As he stared out at the tree, he saw something move, and then discerned the form of a man, then a woman. The man had been holding the woman in his arms. Isaac watched him gently kiss the top of her head. They laughed and moved away from the protection of the tree into the bright moonlight and walked away. Isaac stood back from the window and sat down on his bed. With his head buried in his hands, he knew he'd never survive without Rebecca, without the center of his soul.

His anxiety was not assuaged with the rising sun because now he was concerned for his son-in-law, Joseph, who was the financier and confidant of the Duke of Viseu, Fernando's cousin. If Fernando had been arrested for high treason, the duke and his courtiers would be next. Isaac had met with Count Faro, Fernando's brother, in Segura, and had been assured that every effort was being made to obtain Fernando's release, but the count told him that the Duke of Viseu was planning to overthrow King João. If these rumors had reached Isaac in Segura, he was quite sure that João must also have heard them.

With little hope, Isaac sat down at a thin wooden table in the rabbi's home and composed a long letter to King João in which he outlined his innocence, pleaded for the immediate release of Fernando and begged for his family to be allowed to join him in Castile. He had just put down his pen when he heard shouting, "Hang the thief! Hang the thief!" coming from the town's main square. He looked out a window to see the man he had met in the woods being dragged behind the horse of the man with the black goatee. As a riotous crowd of men, women and children gathered, the Hermandad were busy throwing a rope over the thick limb of a tree. The man with the black goatee placed the noose around the thief's head. The rabbi entered the room and stood next to Isaac. The crowd, enjoying the spectacle, watched the Hermandad quickly hang the man then riddle him with arrows, the man convulsing in death throes.

"This is a fine example of our new law and order," the rabbi remarked.

"I've met Queen Isabella. She seems to be sensitive woman, but she will stop at nothing to achieve her goal, a unified Spain," Isaac answered.

"Isaac, come, there is someone who has just arrived from Toledo to meet you." He ushered Isaac to the main room of the house, and Isaac saw a small, but distinguished looking man sitting by the fireside. He stood. The rabbi continued, "I have the honor of introducing Don Isaac Abravanel to Rabbi Aboab from Toledo."

The two men bowed.

"I believe God has sent you to us for a purpose, Don Isaac. We need you now more than the Portuguese do," Rabbi Aboab said, pausing for a moment, assessing Isaac. "Do you know that King Ferdinand and Queen Isabella have established a tribunal in Seville to investigate heresy within the church? Many new Christians are secret Jews, their loved ones are Jews; I know for they have confided in me. I shudder to think what will happen if these people are put to torture. The hand of God works in strange ways, Isaac. You have been sent here for a reason."

The Inquisition was something foreign to Isaac, and though he abhorred it from its inception, he had never had to deal with it. A terror he had never known stirred within him as he watched children throw rotten eggs and tomatoes at the lifeless form swinging from the limb of the tree.

"The Inquisition," he said, turning back to the two rabbis, "is the single greatest threat to our collective Jewish existence since the destruction of the temple. I will help you fight it any way I can." Isaac grimly turned back again to stare at the dead man. He knew that if people relished torturing this Christian man, their treatment of heretic Christians and Jews would be even more brutal.

Enveloped in what seemed a cold, black cloud, his soul suffocating, Isaac waited to hear whether or not his family would be released and allowed to join him in exile. Kind people offered him food and spoke soft gentle words of hope, but their voices didn't penetrate. He wrapped himself in his white Prayer shawls, sat in the synagogue and prayed to God for their release, morning, noon and night. He had lost all color in his face, had grown thin, and yet continued to pray. He could not go on without them. "Rebecca . . . oh dear God, please, please release her!" he beseeched over and over again.

After several weeks, King João relaxed his stance on Isaac's case, though it was not dropped from the court. His letter seemed to have had some effect, for Isaac finally had word that his immediate family would be allowed to join him in Castile. There was, however, no softening on Fernando's case as Count Faro and the marquis waged a hopeless battle to free him. King João was intent upon destroying the nobility of Portugal, and Fernando was his first victim. No nobleman in Portugal dared to come to his defense.

Two months after Isaac had fled into Castile, he now returned to the Guadiana River and anxiously watched his family cross on a flimsy wooden raft. His son, Judah, was poling it with a rough piece of wood. Most of Isaac's possessions were on the raft. He could see that Rebecca had even packed his books! He shook his head when he thought of how he had left her. His main concern, however, was for his daughter, Bathsheba. She had married his nephew, Joseph, and she was heavy with child. Carefully, the family slipped across the border without incident. Isaac helped Bathsheba and his sons, Judah, Joseph, and Samuel, and at last, his Rebecca, off the raft.

When their fingers touched, he felt his blood flow as if it had stopped until this moment. Tears surfaced, but he would not release them before the others.

"I would not have survived without you," he whispered to her.

She looked up at him, and he could see by the tears welling in her eyes, that she, too, was bravely holding back. Without another word, Isaac helped Rebecca and Bathsheba into litters he had waiting for them. He and the boys mounted horses, and as they rode back to Segura, Isaac felt wrapped in warmth he had not known since he was separated from his family.

Suddenly, he realized one member of the family was missing.

"Where is Elisheba?" Isaac suddenly asked. The boys retreated, and Rebecca firmly said, "She has stayed behind with your brother Samuel and Bathsheba's Joseph. You know that they have to look after family affairs."

"Yes, Joseph is still treasurer for Fernando's cousin, the Duke of Viseu. Elisheba, my Eli, no! She should have come with the family. How could you have allowed her to stay?" Isaac fumed

"Father," Judah stepped forward. "It's too hard for mother to tell you the truth."

"Too hard, what are you talking about!" Isaac shouted, beginning to understand that something unthinkable had happened in his absence."

"She's in love, father."

"In love with whom? Who would keep a young girl, not even eighteen, separated from her family?"

"Fernando's son, father, Diego," Judah answered.

"Diego?" Isaac said, feeling very faint. "Fernando's Diego?"

"Listen to me Isaac," Rebecca said, "I couldn't stop it, and you were not there. What was I to do?"

"In love! In love! No . . . no . . . . this I will not allow!"

"They are married. He's taken her as his wife. It is done," Judah answered, trying to ease his father's pain. "She is precious to him."

"Then she is dead to us!" Isaac roared, bending over in pain. "Dead to us!"

"Isaac, she's married to your best friend's son. Try to see it as they do," Rebecca was growing angry. She was not about to say Kaddish for her daughter.

"She is dead to us . . . . I will hear no more about it," Isaac said so softly, that none of them could hear the words, but they clearly understood them.

With his monies partially recovered, Isaac had purchased a villa in Toledo. From Segura, he now led his family across the Tagus River, into the ancient city that stood so high against the sky that the clouds seem to blanket it from the world below. The family followed him into a freshly white washed villa with a gay terra-cotta roof. At the center of the villa was a courtyard which boasted lemon and almond trees. Two stately nightingales sat in a wicker cage and greeted them as they entered.

The scent of lemon blossom reminded Rebecca of home, of Portugal. She turned to Isaac, and he embraced her.

"I will like it here, Isaac."

"Once we are all together again, we'll make a fine life for ourselves. I intend to get back to my scholarly work, Rebecca. It's what I've always wanted to do. It was my father who insisted I serve the king, serve my people. Well, now it's time to serve my family and God."

Rebecca looked up at him and smiled. She didn't answer him but wondered how long it would take for Queen Isabella to find out he was in Castile and call him into her service.

The family quickly settled into their new life in Spain. Rebecca spent hours learning the new language, for even though Isaac stated over and over again that he was devoting himself to the study of the Bible, she was sure that he would soon be in the service of the king. Isaac, however, was convinced that his family's misfortune was due to his neglect of his prayers, his Bible studies. He locked himself into his new library, surrounded by his beloved books and pushed the mortal world away. The wars in

Granada, the war in Aragon, were not his concern, for he was no longer a courier, a politician, a financier; he was a scholar, and now he wanted only to devote the rest of his life to his writings. He was writing commentaries on Joshua, the Judges and the books of Samuel. He was more convinced than ever that Maimonides was a heretic. How could one question the divinity of the prophets' visions! And once again he lost himself in the Book of Daniel, for the prophecies were so brilliant that Isaac was sure they referred to a great clash between the Christian and Moslem worlds. Were not King Ferdinand and Queen Isabella gathering their forces to fight the final crusade against the Moors in Granada? And what of the new advances the Moors were making against Rome—the fourth kingdom of Nebuchadnezzar's dream in the Book of Daniel? Would the Christian world ever rest until Constantinople or the conflicts in the Holy Land were settled? The answer was no! How could Daniel have foreseen all this without the help of God? It was simple: he could not have prophesied without divine inspiration.

One early afternoon, writing in his library, Isaac looked up, for before him stood Rebecca, Rabbi Aboab, and another older gentleman dressed in a blue velvet robe and wearing a gold and jewel-encrusted sword. This was most unusual for Jews were not allowed to carry swords.

"Isaac," Rabbi Aboab interrupted him, Rebecca looking guilty that she had led the rabbi to his study. "I am sorry to disturb you. It's important work, I know, but we've just received some very grave news."

"What is it, rabbi? You know I am indebted to you. What can I do for you?" He stood and held out chairs for the rabbi and another important looking stranger.

"First, I would like to introduce you to Don Abraham Senior, a treasurer for Queen Isabella." Isaac bowed to Don Abraham.

The powerful financier, who had helped arrange the marriage between Ferdinand and Isabella, spoke, "Your reputation has preceded you, Don Isaac. I am honored to meet you. I understand King Afonso rarely made a financial decision without your advice. I wish I had such power over Queen Isabella." He laughed.

Rabbi Aboab interrupted him, "I am afraid we are here to discuss a very serious situation." Don Abraham coughed and his eyes grew sad. The men took their seats. Don Abraham continued, "Fray Tomas de Torquemada, prior of the Dominican monastery of Santa Cruz, has just been appointed Inquisitor General for all of the territories under Ferdinand and Isabella and will rule the supreme council of the Inquisition. You know who Tomas Torquemada is, don't you?"

"No, I'm afraid I am not familiar with his name," Isaac answered, though he felt as if he should.

"He is a fanatic whose main objective is the destruction of Spanish Jewry!" Rabbi Aboab said.

"But I thought the tribunal was set up to investigate heresy within the Church. They have no jurisdiction over the Jews of Spain," Isaac answered.

Rabbi Aboab continued, "My friend, you were not here in 1481 to see the auto-de-fé, the act of faith. The 'heretics' were burned at the stake, but the Jews who were named by the tortured victims were arrested, condemned and slowly roasted on a spit over an open fire. Over three hundred people died! Over three hundred people! Make no mistake; Torquemada's main objective is to eliminate the Jews."

"And you, Don Abraham, do you think Fray Tomas is such a madman?" Isaac asked.

"Let me tell you about Fray Tomas de Torquemada, Don Isaac. The man is certainly a fanatic. He wears wool with no cloth in between to protect his skin as the other monks do. He sleeps on a wooden board, not on a bed; he wears a unicorn's horn around his neck to ward off evil spirits. He travels with fifty horsemen and two hundred soldiers because he is in constant fear that someone will try to assassinate him, and his stepmother, whom he abhorred, was a Jewess. Yes, I think the man is mad, and with him as Grand Inquisitor, the Jews are in a very dangerous position. Therefore, we must do all we can to surround King Ferdinand and Queen Isabella with Jews whom they can trust, and upon whom they can depend."

"One further question, if you please. If this Torquemada is such a madman, how did he rise to power? Surely Queen Isabella and King Ferdinand would want a just, righteous man in such a sensitive position."

"Fray Tomas was the queen's childhood confessor. She worships him as she would have worshipped the father she never knew. He is like a demi-god to her, but the real danger lies in the fact that she doesn't recognize the awesome power he holds over her. She does not see his demonic side or his worst of intentions for her Jewish subjects. She is like a little kitten, or rather, lamb, in his lap. Don Isaac, let me be brief. I am in a position to appoint someone as a royal tax collector. The Catholic Monarchs are now engaged in a crusade against the Moors in Granada, and monies are desperately needed. I'm afraid the Spanish-Portuguese war depleted our coffers. I know that you were effective in raising funds for the Portuguese, and I'm sure your services would be highly valued by the king and queen at this critical time when we need more Jews at court."

Though Isaac had already seen how easily a court appointment and all the power that went with it could crumble, he knew he had to accept this position. Perhaps it would mean a little more security for his family and his people, for Fernando. He could not refuse. He answered the powerful Don Abraham.

"I would be most honored to be in the service of the king and queen."

"Good! I will inform the king and queen that I have chosen my new treasurer. You will be called to court within the next few weeks." Don Abraham Senior bowed and left the room.

"God bless you, Isaac," Rabbi Aboab said, taking his hands in his own. The rabbi's hands were gnarled and wrinkled but felt warm, strong, like his old teacher's hands. "I told you when you first came to us, God works in strange ways. Though Torquemada has gained power through the Inquisition, we have our own champions to protect us!" He bowed to Isaac and followed Don Abraham.

Isaac walked over to the window and gazed up at the sky. A white cloud had just passed over the sun and then slowly its rays began to break out on the other side and light his face as he prayed, "Dear Lord, forgive me for wandering from Your work, but Your hand seems to be pushing me in a different direction. Please make me worthy to face such a task, and please, dear Lord, give me the strength to protect our people from the fury of Tomas Torquemada."

CHAPTER 19

Juan Sanchez de Sevilla was riding a pure white stallion through the verdant hills of Andalusia. The rolling land was dotted with olive trees, and the peasants, their heads wrapped in colorful scarves, brushing the smooth green fruit with long wooden paddles, bowed to him as he passed; for though they did not know who he was, they recognized the dress of a rich cavalier and all admired the magnificent animal that carried him. He had been traveling for several weeks and was looking forward to his return to his villa in Ciudad Real, where he often entertained the wealthiest Castilian families. His mind had been spinning visions of the beautiful Inés Lucena. With her raven hair, soft gray eyes and lips so red against her white skin, she was the most exquisite woman Juan had ever seen. Her father was a wealthy printer, and Juan felt he had finally found his perfect match, except for the one serious flaw—her father was a new Christian. Since the Jews had been exiled from Seville and Córdoba, the Inquisition was intent on rooting out the secret Jews, heretics hiding under the protection of the Church. Would it be wise to marry a girl whose family could come under investigation within the next few months? Not that he had anything to fear, for it was well known that Juan Sanchez de Sevilla had been high treasurer to King Enríque III, Isabella's grandfather. What had been lost, long ago, was the fact that Isaac's grandfather had fled Castile in order to revert to Judaism, a heretical act. Although Juan felt safe from the madness which was sweeping across the land, to marry a new Christian was something to seriously consider. It was clear that Señor Lucena was anxious for the match, and Inés encouraged his courtship, for what beauty in Andalusia did not dream about the rich and handsome Juan Sanchez de Sevilla?

As he rounded the bend in the road, his heart stopped short at the sight of the red glow that spread before him. His first thought was that a fire was rolling across the hills, but then the vision of thousands of fire red poppies, poppies as far as the eye could see, caught his breath. He turned his horse off the road and wandered through the natural garden. It was as if God, like a painter gone wild, had suddenly splashed this valley with the color of passion. The color was so vibrant that it beckoned Juan off his horse to touch the petals, soft as velvet, almost too delicate for such vivid color. Juan sat down and opened his leather pouch to lunch on some ham, olives, and rich red wine. The sun beating down on the field made him feel drowsy. He threw himself back against the flowers and drifted into a trance-like sleep. Inés appeared before him, her full red lips, the color of the poppies slightly parted, calling to him. The flowers rustled in the soft afternoon breeze, and though Juan tried to rouse himself, he seemed locked in a drugged-like trance. Inés was bending over him, sensuously pressing her white breasts against him. "Inés," he moaned in his dream and reached out to touch her, but as he did, she turned to fire—red, hot, fire—her hands and arms, her breasts, her hair all on fire!

Shaking violently, Juan roused and found himself drenched with sweat. How foolish to sleep in an open field of poppies, in the heat of the day; no wonder he dreamt about fire! He mounted his horse and made his way back to the road, trying to free himself from the vision of his Inés in flames. He could save her from such danger by marrying her, by securing her with his Christian name, and that was what he intended to do.

Juan stood beside three musicians he had hired to sing the traditional song of courtship. Wearing silk turbans and robes, the Spaniards played their guitars beneath the balcony of Dona Inés. He watched their fingers pluck the strings, vibrating the polished wood to create sounds that seemed to make the wind dance. The music lured Inés out onto the balcony. Accompanied by her mother, she drew a fan across her face, but Juan could see her smile. The music seemed to lift him to her, so that he was startled when Señor Lucena called and invited him into the villa. Juan tried not to let Señor Lucena see how impressed he was by the lavish surroundings. Gold cups and plates were set on the table, and blue velvet drapes with golden tassels hung at the windows. Señor Lucena offered him a large, intricately carved wooden chair and then sat across from him while servants offered honey cakes, dates, figs, oranges, red grapes and wine.

"Señor Sanchez, what an honor it is to have you here in our simple home. The music was most appreciated. It is amazing what music can do for the downtrodden soul."

"I'm sorry you are in pain, Señor Lucena. What has caused you such sadness?" Juan said as he munched some grapes.

"You surely must be aware of the horrors that are plaguing Seville and Córdoba, Señor Sanchez. Though you are of a Christian family, you must have some feeling for what we new Christians are made to suffer. Our relatives and closest friends have been thrown into prison, not knowing their crime! That the king and queen allow such outrages to continue is incredible to me! I have friends who have gone to Rome to make their objections known to the Pope!"

"I am well aware of the plight of the new Christians, not to mention the Jews of Seville and Córdoba. My heart goes out to them, Señor Lucena. However, I am here as the most respectful, most ardent admirer of your daughter, and wish to put such unpleasant thoughts aside for the moment." It hurt him, frightened him as much as any other new Christian, but he was committed to his charade. He stood, walked over to Señor Lucena, and bowed.

"I wish to ask for your daughter's hand in marriage."

He had to make Señor Lucena see that if she married him, she would lead a wealthy, secure life. They both knew how grave the situation was growing for the new Christians in Spain. Juan seriously doubted that the situation would change, even if Christian families tried to stop the dreaded Inquisition.

"I am sure that my daughter would be most honored to marry you, Señor Sanchez," Señor Lucena answered tactfully. "However, you cannot so easily dismiss our plight. I don't wish to frighten you away, but even as we talk, I have a brother who is being tortured in prison. The devil walks with these inquisitors—the devil! No one will marry my daughter who does not have some feeling for what the Inquisition is putting us though. The time may come," he said in a low voice, afraid his own servants might overhear, "when my own family may come under investigation. Only a man who truly loves Inés, who would go through torture to keep her from harm, will have her hand."

Juan sank to his knees and looked up into the father's eyes. Memories swam before him, a father's eyes shining on him so full of adoration, a sister's eyes so full of love, a brother-in-law—no! He had to push it all away. The truth was too painful to face. He had to continue down the path he had chosen. There was no going back.

"Let me assure you, Señor Lucena, your sorrow and your suffering are close to my heart. I do feel for the new Christians, for the Jews who are under investigation, and it is with this thought in mind that I entreat, I beg you to give your daughter to me. With me she shall be safe, and our children will carry a name that has been respected for generations in all Spain."

Señor Lucena pulled Juan to his feet and embraced him. "Juan, you and Inés have my blessing. May you enjoy a long and healthy life!"

Feeling lightheaded and happy for the first time in a very long time, Juan left the magnificent villa. He stopped at the balcony where Inés had stood, as if he could still smell her sweet fragrance in the air. "Inés," he whispered to the warm breezes, "I love you." He paused for a moment longer and then rode to his own villa which sat at the top of the highest hill in Ciudad Real. His horse climbed the steep path to the crest of his hill and as he viewed the countryside and the little town nestled far below, he felt like a king. He had won the admiration of King Ferdinand and Queen Isabella and now he had won the hand of the woman he loved. He had escaped the walls of the Judería, his unhappy past. Now that he would have Inés, he would have everything he wanted.

The whitewashed villa of Señor Lucena was pulsating with laughter and music as the guests celebrated the imminent wedding of Dona Inés to Señor Juan Sanchez de Sevilla. Ladies with long swan-like necks sat on the silken pillows and nibbled on almond candies. The men, dressed in satin and velvet, carried gold swords encrusted with emeralds, rubies, sapphires and diamonds, and discussed the latest campaign against Granada. Inés wore an emerald green gown, which revealed only the slightest crease of her breast. In her long black hair, piled high on top of her head, a small diamond tiara sparkled. Though Juan was forty-eight, his figure was still trim and his hair still full, with wisps of silver running through the gold. Inés had just turned nineteen, and as he stood besides her greeting the guests, he felt his life was finally beginning. He was comfortable with these people and felt that he had finally become an accepted member of the Lucena Family.

The musicians added a tambourine to the oud and recorders as a gypsy woman began to clack her castanets. Juan folded his arms in front of him and watched the woman weave snake-like between the guests as she made her way to the center of the room. Mesmerized by the music, he watched her body sway from side to side. Her arms and fingertips beckoned while a seductive smile crept across her lips. Juan smiled and clapped with the guests as her body swirled and became one with the music. Her hips and legs spun her about so fast that the orange, red, and pink of her gown seemed to melt into one hot color. Her long black hair rippled down her back as her body undulated over and over again until at last she threw her head back and all shouted, "*Ole!*" The thunderous clapping was joined by shouts for more and a quieter dance followed the fiery performance. Juan smiled as an ardent group of young men escorted the gypsy out into the night. Inés slipped away from her guardian, and Juan discreetly followed her outside.

"It was so hot in there!" she said, a little anxious about being alone with him.

Juan wanted to pull her to him, press her body to his, kiss her and take her! After gazing deeply into her grey eyes, he reminded himself that he could not so much as touch her cheek. In a hoarse voice he answered, "It was a very passionate dance." Then he gazed up at the sky, trying desperately to control his desire.

When she said, "Juan, we must have a moment to speak privately," a shiver ran down his back.

He moaned but gave her his arm, swallowed hard and led her down the smooth lawn and into the maze of jasmine gardens. They found a marble bench by a fountain and sat down. Against his better judgment, he pulled her to him and kissed her lips, her lovely white neck, the crease between her breasts. She gently pushed him away and said, "There will be plenty of time for that. First, we must talk. There is something that must be said before we are married." Her eyes seemed like dark, mysterious pools of water as she spoke.

He held her tightly sensing her deep distress and said softly, "What is it, my love? What has you so sad on this joyful occasion? Don't you love me? Don't say you don't want me!"

"Oh, Juan, I want you more than anything else in the world, but you will have to make that decision after you've heard what I have to say."

"There is nothing you could say that would change my mind. Nothing!" he whispered softly in her ear. She broke his grasp, stood, and walked away from him. She could not bear to see his face when she told him what her father had forbidden her to say.

"We are Jews, Juan. We are Catholic to the world, but in our hearts we are Jews."

Juan laughed. He stood by her side and pulled her to him once again. "Do you think this deep dark secret could keep you from me?" he said lightly, but he thought, "Coward! Now is the time to tell her, tell her about my own dark past!" but the words would not come to his lips.

"You don't understand, Juan," she said as she gently pushed him away again. "We are Jews!"

"I understand, my sweet, but what harm can come from hiding this in your heart. As long as you are a good Catholic, you didn't even have to tell me what lies at the center of your soul. There are some things that never have to be said, even between a man and his wife."

"That is what my father said, but I could never marry you that way. Our marriage would be based on a lie, and I couldn't live like that."

As Juan brushed his own truth aside, pulling her to him once again, he said, "Don't worry, my love, your secret will be safe with me. You have nothing to fear."

"No, Juan, you don't understand. We are *Marranos*! We are not just Jews in our hearts. Though we openly profess the Catholic faith, we are practicing Jews."

He let her go. He wanted to roar into the night like a madman. "Oh what a fine game you've played on me!" His soul cried to God. "What a fine game!" He turned to see her standing there like a statue. This confession could bring her instant death in the Inquisition. "Your uncle?" he asked more anxiously than he had intended, "will he speak?"

"Who knows what a man will say under torture," she said quietly.

When he saw the terror in her eyes, he drew her close once again. He gently rubbed her back as he held her.

"It will be all right, Inés. I couldn't walk away from you even if I wanted to, even if I felt it was too dangerous for both of us. Will you forgive me my weakness?" he whispered.

"Oh, Juan! Forgive you? Take me away from here, far, far away! I'm so frightened that sometimes I feel I can't breathe. I want to leave Spain."

"It will be all right, my love," he reassured her. "Once . . . I ran. I ran away from myself, and I cannot run anymore. We will be wed, and you will be protected by my name. You will be safe with me, Inés. I promise you."

He held her for a long time, caressing her.

"I love you Inés," he whispered, "I love you."

A black pain enveloped Juan as he tossed in bed that night. Memories flooded his mind—he and Isaac having bitter words. "Your God, Isaac, not mine!" echoed over and over again. He had only wanted to be free, and now he was trapped by his heart. Fernando's dark, curious eyes—how they questioned his intent, his sincerity at his conversion, he kept thinking. "Fernando," he mumbled over and over again in his sleep that night, but Fernando in his cell in Evora was not thinking about Juan Sanchez de Sevilla.

Fernando could no longer distinguish between the real world and the world he had retreated to in his mind. He was with Rebecca, yes, Isaac's Rebecca. Her golden hair sparkled in the sunlight, and her sheer white gown gently fluttered in a soft breeze. "Rebecca," he muttered as she held her hand out to him. He took it and pulled her close. He kissed her face and neck and breasts and merged with her and then her image faded. He was shaking uncontrollably when he was awakened by guards opening his cell door. The clanging of the iron echoed loudly against the dungeon walls. They roughly pulled him to his feet, and he stumbled up the long winding steps to the world of the living. His skeletal frame shook in the sunlight. He heard people gasp at the sight of him as he was hurried to the wooden platform in the center of the plaza. He stumbled as he made his way up the steps and fell, but he refused the guard's arm and carefully made his way up to the top. Instantly, everything came sharply into focus—João, the high judge, the priest, the executioner. "I want to live," he cried inside, but he clung to his last moment of dignity. He would not crumple before them! The high judge asked him if he had any last words, and he shook his head no. The priest gave him his last rites. He stared at João as the executioner pulled his cape off his shoulder.

His heart started to beat now, like the wild flapping of a great bird trying to escape from its trap. Suddenly, he thought of Isaac, of Rebecca, of his family, his brothers. He had to get word to them!

He was pushed down to his knees, and he could hear the shouts in the crowd: "Respect! A prince should be treated with respect! Fernando, Fernando, Fernando!" the crowd chanted, menacingly, anger growing against the king, against his entourage, the judges, the executioner. It almost seemed as if the crowd would have their way, would free their prince, but the king's bodyguard, then soldiers, came between the people and their prince. Fernando wanted to shout out to them, what, what could he say? "Freedom!" the word never left his lips. Fernando felt his head forced down to the rough wooden block. He saw the executioner's body reach up and felt the wind from the falling blade.

CHAPTER 20

Spain, 1483

His face gray, his heart pounding in his chest, Joseph Abravanel watched Prince Fernando die. Samuel, who had been standing beside his son in the crowded plaza, pulled him away. They stumbled down a narrow street to their horses, and, with the chilling wind at their backs, raced toward the Judería in Lisbon. After paying the tax to pass through the iron gates, they saw candles lit in the windows of every home; the Jews were mourning the death of their benefactor, Prince Fernando, Duke of Braganza. Loneliness enveloped Joseph and Samuel when they arrived at the dark Abravanel house, from which the inner life of a fire in the hearth, and the soft glow of candles were gone. The gentle rustling of dresses, the scent of perfume and of fresh baked bread were gone. Samuel poured Joseph a glass of sherry, but the alcohol burned in his stomach.

"I'm glad now that I sold Isaac's castle. Málaga paid a good price for it," Joseph said bitterly. Samuel had grown prematurely gray, and his back curved like bent wood as he sat hunched in his chair, cradling his sherry.

"Isaac must never know who bought the castle. Just tell him he got a fair price."

Joseph buried his head in his arms and cried, "All that Isaac worked for, all his hopes and dreams for the Jews in Portugal have come to this, a lonely house, prison-like walls for our people, the death of our prince." He lifted his head and gazed at his father.

Samuel paused for a moment before he answered. He thought of Joseph's wife and baby waiting for him in Toledo.

"Joseph, you have so much of your life ahead of you. We will join the family in Castile and begin again. I have had word that Isaac has been called to court. Surely, life will be better where Jews are still respected."

"As long as we fill a need!" Joseph answered him angrily. "And when that need is filled, when their coffers are overflowing, then we will be driven out, cast off once again. When will it end, Father? When will we find peace in this world?"

"When the Messiah comes, son! We must wait for his coming and the Everlasting Kingdom."

"I don't believe in the Messiah! I don't believe God cares for His people anymore!"

Samuel slapped Joseph and sent him sprawling across the floor. "Once! Only once before did I ever hear a man talk like that!" Samuel's face had turned red, his eyes full of anger. "He fled! Oh yes he fled from us!" Samuel stood and pointed his finger at Joseph. "But God will not forget! He will not forget his people!"

"Is that who my son is named after, this man who fled from us?"

Samuel collapsed back in his chair, "Yes, Jonathan," he whispered, "I wish Bathsheba had not named the infant after him, but I imagine she did it for Rebecca. He is her brother."

"So he is still alive?"

"For us, he is dead, and if you ever talk this way to me again . . ."

"Father, forgive me!" Joseph lowered his head. "I will never speak of him again."

Joseph left his father and climbed the stairs to his room and threw himself down on the bed where he and Bathsheba had slept, where they had conceived their son, his infant, Jonathan, whom he had not yet seen.

He was still awake when he heard the beating on the door. He lit a candle, made his way downstairs and admitted Moses ibn Aknin, his clothes spattered with mud. He had trouble catching his breath.

"The duke!" he cried.

"I know. I was there; Fernando is dead." Joseph had started to turn away when Moses grabbed his arm and sharply pulled him around.

"I know about Fernando." Moses paused still trying to catch his breath. "But the news is about the Duke of Viseu! King João sent for him shortly after the execution. He greeted him with a kiss and ushered him into his private chambers. As the door closed behind him, the king stabbed the duke in the back. We must flee!"

Joseph felt his skin crawl over his bones.

"I can't leave yet," he whispered. "I haven't brought Isaac's case to court! Our side must be heard. Málaga has spread vicious lies . . . ."

"Listen to me!" Moses shook him. "There will be no fair trial! Isaac is safe in Spain. You are the one in danger, my friend. Don't you see with the Duke of Viseu dead—you are his treasurer—they will be after you next. We must all flee now!"

"What of the years of service? Isaac served King Afonso for twenty years. Doesn't that mean anything?" Joseph shouted.

"King João has just murdered the Duke of Viseu; Prince Fernando is dead! What possible chance do you have of bringing a case to court? Even if you did, look at the men who are judging you. The same men who judged Fernando. We have to leave now before we are all thrown in the dungeons!"

Joseph stared at Moses. There was no time to make plans, to say good-bye to dear old friends, even to Elisheba. He woke his father and in the darkest hours of the night, Joseph, Samuel, and Moses fled.

Bathsheba saw them first. She had just put her infant in his cradle, when she saw the three men dismount. She ran out to them, in the courtyard, where she and Joseph embraced.

"We must never be separated again," he said as he kissed her forehead, eyes and cheek and held her close. Then he thought of the child.

"Where is he? I want to see him."

She smiled and led him back into the house, to the hugs and kisses of Rebecca and the family. Joseph then bent over the cradle and kissed his son, caressing the downy head and picking up the tiny hand.

"His fingers are so small."

He laughed and gazed at Bathsheba. As he stood and moved to embrace her, a shadow fell across the room. He looked up and saw Isaac standing in the doorway. Suddenly, all Joseph could see was Fernando's head severed from his body. He quickly handed the baby back to Bathsheba and hung his head not daring to look at Isaac.

"What has happened, Joseph? Why did you leave so soon? The court case?" Isaac asked.

"There will be no court case, Isaac," Samuel interrupted, dropping his bags in the doorway.

"What do you mean no court case? If I am convicted, we can never return to Portugal . . . . Our case must be heard . . . ."

"Fernando is dead, Isaac. Beheaded . . ." He could not continue.

Rebecca ran from the room. Isaac froze.

"No!" he shook his brother. "You're lying! It can't be true!" His sons pried him away from Samuel. "No!" he roared again and ran out after Rebecca. He ran into the courtyard and found her sobbing on the ground. He took her in his arms and held her.

"I loved him!" she cried. "Oh, Isaac, I loved him."

He closed his eyes and held her tightly. "I know," he said. "I loved him too. He was our protector, our friend, and our brother . . . ." He couldn't go on.

Isaac held Rebecca in his arms for a long time, rocking back and forth, trying to absorb the news.

"Isaac?"

"What, my love?"

"I want to find my brother, I . . . ."

"No!"

"He's here, in Castile. I want to see him."

"No," Isaac shouted, "he is dead!"

"He is not dead! He is alive! I thought we would be going back to Portugal, and I could live with it. I can't anymore. Now that I know we are here to stay, now that Fernando is dead, I have to find Jonathan." When Isaac refused to look at her she continued, "You don't know how it is for me. Every street I walk down, every corner I turn, I wonder if I will see him, standing before me. And Elisheba, you must accept that marriage now, after all the Braganzas have suffer . . . ."

"Stop it!" Isaac shouted. He stood up. "Elisheba is dead to us, and it was Jonathan's decision to leave. I begged him to stay. Jonathan turned his back on us, on you!"

"I can't help it. I want to see him again, even if it's just once before I die. And I want to see my precious daughter . . . ." She sobbed.

Isaac pulled her up to him. "Don't talk about dying. Please, let's not talk about dying."

"I want to see each of them, just once," she whispered.

"I don't know where he is, Rebecca."

"Promise me that if you hear his name or anything about him you will tell me."

"Yes, all right, but don't expect me to find him for you. I won't. I can't, Rebecca, and our Elisheba . . . . If they came here to Castile . . . . I don't know . . . . I don't know . . . . My little girl . . . ." he cried softly as he held her.

"I don't expect you to find Jonathan or to reach out to Elisheba, but now that Fernando is gone, don't deny me my dream of seeing either one of them, even it is it just one more time in my lifetime."

Several weeks later, Isaac was ushered down the long corridor to the throne room in the stone Alcázar in Tarazona. The smooth steel helmets and breastplates on the guards reflected the sun's rays so that they seemed to glow like human torches. The great carved wooden doors were opened. The throne room was stark compared to the Portuguese court. There were no tapestries on the walls, no drapes at the windows; the thrones were simple high backed, wooden chairs. The court was assembled to receive Isaac. The ladies-in-waiting were whispering to each other, eyeing the tall, slender man. Cardinal Mendoza in his red robes stood to the right of King Ferdinand. Though he still had the strong muscular frame of a warrior, Ferdinand's black hair had thinned, and he had gained some weight since Isaac had last seen him. Queen Isabella had also grown heavier, but her eyes were as blue as ever, and her red curls still played about her face.

Don Abraham Senior came forward, met Isaac and ushered him toward the king and queen. The two Jews bowed before the two monarchs.

"You may rise," King Ferdinand commanded.

"Your Majesty, may I have the honor of presenting Don Isaac Abravanel," Don Abraham said.

Isaac bowed once again to the king. Ferdinand smiled and bid him rise.

"Well, Don Isaac, I am glad that we finally have you in our court. I understand your aid was invaluable in raising funds for the Spanish-Portuguese war. It will be reassuring to have you working for us instead of against us this time." He laughed and then quickly grew serious again. "Our coffers are extremely low. We are engaged in a crusade against the infidels who occupy our most beautiful lands of Granada, but the power of the scimitar has grown weak. King Muley Hassan has been exiled from Alhambra by his wife, Zoraya. It seems she didn't approve his mistress!"

"I was unaware of King Hussan's exile, Your Majesty. Where has he gone?" Isaac asked.

"He is with his brother El Zagal in the hills of Málaga," the king answered. "We will be facing Boabdíl, King Hassan's son, in battle. He has joined forces with Ali Atar and has an estimated force of nine thousand infantry and seven hundred cavalry. I want to meet him with a force twice that size. We have to crush him now while the royal house is divided. I need funds! You are to work immediately with Don Abraham to raise the money and report directly to Don Luís de Santangel my high treasurer."

A distinguished-looking man with a gray goatee, dressed in long blue velvet robes, nodded to Isaac, who bowed back to the high treasurer.

"The queen and I would like to have a private word with you, Don Isaac."

The rest of the court was dismissed, and Isaac was ushered to the king's chambers.

"We were saddened by the news of the execution in Evora. I'm sorry. I know you and the Duke of Braganza were very close friends," Ferdinand said in a surprisingly gentle voice.

Isabella came up to him and put her hand on his shoulder. "We grieve with you, Isaac. You have our deepest sympathy."

He looked into her eyes and answered, "Thank you, Your Highness."

But now in a commanding voice, Isabella continued, "Isaac, you must put your past behind you. You know you can never return to Portugal. Think now about your future here in Spain. Help us fight for a secure land, and you will be rewarded."

Gazing into her eyes, he said, "I seek no reward, Your Highness."

"What do you seek, Isaac? Just tell us what will make you happy."

"I want peace and security for my people, Your Majesties," he said as he turned back to the king. "What kind of future can I have, can my people have here, with the Inquisition unleashed against us."

"Isaac, you are mistaken," Ferdinand said. "The Inquisition is purely an instrument of the Church to keep the heretics from destroying it. Surely you must respect our right to protect our faith, to root out the evil within which threatens its very existence. Your people are not threatened by the Inquisition."

"Your Majesty, for every heretic who is burned at the stake, three or four Jews die as well."

"Every man who is convicted has had a fair trial by secular law, Isaac. Are you insinuating that our system of law is corrupt?" Ferdinand grew angry.

"Isaac," Isabella interrupted, "in any system of law and order there will always be victims who are unjustly accused and convicted. However, you must make an effort to put your own interests aside, if you are to help us build a land where all can live in security and peace. You weren't here. You don't know what Castile and León were like under my brother's rule.

There was no law and order! Men died at the mere whim of noblemen. The monetary system was in disarray so that our people could not afford to buy the grain that was raised in their own fields. I rode the width and breadth of this land to raise money for our soldiers. They needed food, coats on their backs, boots, and money for their families at home." She paused for a moment. "I even lost a child, Isaac."

Ferdinand interrupted, "I will not have you discussing our personal tragedies with a court treasurer!"

Isaac cast his eyes down.

Ferdinand continued, "Isaac, you must understand that we have paid a high price for all we have achieved, and our battle is not over. Fray Tomas was not my choice for the Grand Inquisitor." He glanced at the queen. "If the friar is overzealous, then I personally will see to it that he is stopped."

Turning white as marble, Isabella said to Ferdinand, "I have the utmost confidence in Fray Tomas, Sire." Turning back to Isaac, she stated, "If you find proof that he ever unjustly sentences a man or woman to death, then I'd expect you to report it directly to me. Until such a grievous accusation is made against the Grand Inquisitor, I want to hear no more."

"Yes, Your Highness," Isaac said, and for the first time understood how powerful an influence the Grand Inquisitor had over Isabella, but not, he guessed, over the king. He secreted a look at Cardinal Mendoza who seemingly remained unperturbed but returned Isaac's gaze, clearly showing Isaac his support.

"By serving us, Isaac, you will serve your own people," Ferdinand said.

Isaac bowed and answered, "It will be my honor to serve you, Your Majesties."

"I knew we could count on you, Isaac." Ferdinand dismissed him with a nod.

Isaac bowed to Isabella, Ferdinand, and Mendoza, and he left the hall.

As Isaac quickly made his way down the long corridor of the Alcázar, he just missed colliding with a gaunt man cloaked in the brown robes of the Dominican Order. A guard whispered to the friar, and he instantly recoiled. Isaac left the Alcázar as Tomas Torquemada entered the king's chambers.

"You've gone against my wishes! Abravanel is in your service?" he lashed out at the king and queen.

"Fray Tomas, you are indeed the Grand Inquisitor of the Inquisition, but I will not be dictated to in state affairs! Don Isaac Abravanel is an outstanding financier, and we need him to raise funds for us!" Ferdinand fumed.

"The Jew will try to twist your minds into believing his people have a right to stay here in Spain. Once the Moors are routed, the Jews must follow or you will never achieve true peace in the land. They will continue to influence the pious souls and send them to the devil. Extricate yourselves from this grasp. Do not become dependent upon the Jews! Do not give them access to your coffers, or your souls will be tarnished by your denial of His wishes!"

Cardinal Mendoza walked up to Torquemada and staring at him straight in the eyes, he said, "Let me make myself very clear to you. It is not this court's policy to persecute the Jews in this land. If I should hear of any wrong doing by your office, I will personally write to the Pope and demand you resign from the office of Grand Inquisitor!"

"As if you haven't done so already!" Torquemada raged.

His face glowing red with anger, Mendoza bowed to the king and queen and left, Ferdinand close at his heels.

Torquemada walked up to Isabella, who had sat rigid through his tirade. He took her hand and said in a more controlled tone, "Don't be influenced by the king or cardinal, Isabella. You know Ferdinand has Jewish blood running in his veins. He can be easily swayed by money, by the Jews, by the devil."

She wanted him to let her go, but was afraid to offend him. He had been her friend, her confessor since childhood. He had advised her before her coronation, and all that he had predicted had come to pass. Though she feared his dark, brooding, angry eyes, she trusted him as she trusted in the Lord, and it was painful for her to protest his accusations. Slowly pulling her hand away from his, she said, "Father, I am sure that the king and cardinal will always be true to our cause. As for Don Isaac, he has been a good friend."

"Beware Abravanel . . . Beware Senior . . . their cause is not our cause."

"Don Isaac realizes his people must abide by our laws and respect our faith if they are to continue to live in Castile. We need the Jews. They are our doctors, our lawyers, goldsmiths, tanners, weavers, merchants. They are a most industrious people, and we cannot afford to lose them. If we expel them, as you would have us do, we would never have the means to continue the crusade against Granada. Father, please concentrate on your great work within the Church and leave the ruling to Ferdinand and me."

"Someday you will see that I am right. You will see that you can never have a true peace while either Moslems or Jews remain in Spain." He turned and left the queen without waiting to be dismissed.

When Fray Tomas de Torquemada finished his evening prayers, he sent for Fray Domingo Gomez. The friar had been at his side when three hundred men and women were sentenced to die in Seville. The Church would not allow blood to be shed, and so, the heretics were relaxed into the secular arm in an Auto-de-fe, Act of Faith. Torquemada was pleased with the records Gomez had kept and found himself relying on the man more and more. After all, one could never be too careful. Heretics had even infiltrated the priesthood.

Having just finished his meal, the rotund friar entered Torquemada's private chambers.

"You sent for me?"

"I want you to begin an investigation that must be done with the utmost secrecy. I want no one, no one at all, to know what you are doing."

"Fray Tomas, you know you can count on me in these delicate situations."

"Very well. I want you to investigate the family history of Don Isaac Abravanel. The king has just granted him a position in the court, and we must know everything we can about the man. Trace the family as far back as possible. I want every detail of the information recorded, no matter how trivial."

"Of course. I will begin immediately." He bowed and waddled out of the room. The sound of young seminarians chanting the evening prayers enveloped Torquemada as Gomez retreated to ancient church archives.

CHAPTER 21

Flames licked the burning effigies of Isaac and Joseph Abravanel. Cristóbal Colón watched mournfully as the human shaped straw burned in the central plaza in Evora. Dona Felipa Perestrello Colón rested her head on her husband's shoulder as she watched. She pulled her five-year-old Diego close to her skirts so that the black smoke wouldn't hurt his eyes. Cristóbal looked up at the royal balcony and saw that King João had come to witness the effigies burn. His golden crown caught the sunlight and flashed as he bent his head to speak to the noblemen gathered around him. The flames quickly died, leaving only the black stubs of the stakes. The smoke slowly rose, painting a gray wash across the clear blue sky.

Cristóbal and his family shuffled along with the crowd leaving the plaza. His heart was heavy as he thought of Isaac, of Joseph, of Prince Fernando. They had befriended him, listened to his plans, his dreams. With Isaac gone, what would become of the Jews of Portugal, he wondered as he glanced over his shoulder, pulling his cape around his wife and child. His feet felt like lead, his head ached, his eyes smarted from the black smoke.

King João remained in his box for a while longer watching, with satisfaction, as the last of the smoke curled upwards. It was done. He had consolidated his power and wealth within the land. His enemies were eliminated, and now he could dictate his policies. The voyage he had been planning for so long would commence. Bartholomew Dias would soon set sail, and the flag of Portugal would ride the high seas as it had under Henry the Navigator.

Carlos Málaga bent over the king and said, "I received an interesting letter last week from a Fray Domingo Gomez in Castile, requesting information concerning the Abravanels."

João smiled at Carlos, "Fray Domingo Gomez? What could he want? I understand Isaac is already well entrenched within the Spanish court."

"Yes, that's true, but it seems Fray Domingo Gomez is not associated with the court. He is an inquisitor for the Church. His mission is sacred, not secular." Málaga's smile was broad.

João laughed. "Well, what information will you send to the good friar?"

"That Isaac's grandfather was Samuel Abravanel, a court treasurer to the royal house of Castile. I have supplied the inquisitor with family names: Judah, Rebecca Ben Ezra and her brother, Jonathan. I believe her brother is in Castile as well."

João looked up at Málaga.

"My dear friend, I am grateful that you are not my enemy. Perhaps this fire today is only a precursor for the Abravanels in Castile. I want you to inform Fray Domingo that Isaac Abravanel has been found guilty of high treason in the Portuguese courts. We are willing to make available any records the friar might need to further his investigation."

"Very good, your Majesty. I will send as much information to Fray Domingo as I can gather."

When in his haste to leave, Málaga bumped into a guard, he threw him to the ground and kicked him. João laughed until tears streamed down his cheeks.

The monastery in Segovia was unusually cold. Even the fires on the hearth could not warm the stone walls. Wrapped in a woolen cape so enormous that he looked like a shaggy bear puffing clouds of smoke in the bitter cold, Fray Domingo Gomez waddled down the corridor to the Grand Inquisitor. He knocked on the door and found Fray Tomas de Torquemada kneeling on the stone floor before a simple altar. Torquemada turned to see the friar waiting, and then slowly turned back to his prayers for several minutes before he stood and addressed the friar.

"What brings you to Segovia on this bitter winter's day, Fray Domingo? I understand the roads are so glazed with ice that horses are slipping and breaking their legs."

"I have finished my initial investigation on Don Isaac Abravanel, and as you requested, I have made a detailed report." He placed the papers on the wooden table before him.

Torquemada fingered the papers. "Good. Have you found anything that should be made known to the king and queen?"

"Most of the information I received from the Portuguese court was of little value. I am sure the king and queen already know that Abravanel was found guilty of high treason. However, my meticulous research within our archives did bring to light something which most definitely calls for further investigation."

Torquemada was leaning over the wooden table between them. "Yes? What is that? I told you no detail was too insignificant."

"A Carlos Málaga wrote that Abravanel's grandfather was Samuel Abravanel. It was well know in Portugal that he had been a high treasurer to King Enríque III. In my investigation, I've found documents dating back to King Enríque's court. There was indeed a Samuel Abravanel who was high treasurer. However, he was baptized Juan Sanchez de Sevilla, here in Castile. There is no record here of the man after the attack in the Jewish quarter in the year 1391."

"A heretic?" Torquemada whispered. "Abravanel's grandfather was a heretic?"

"Of course, that is not enough to call him before the Inquisition," Gomez added.

"No, of course, you are right," Torquemada conceded.

"However, there is a Don Juan Sanchez de Sevilla living in Ciudad Real. He has served the queen on several occasions as a jeweler. Don Carlos mentioned in his notes that Don Isaac has a brother-in-law, Jonathan Ben Ezra, who also lives in Castile. Perhaps this Juan Sanchez is related to Abravanel?"

"Most interesting. So you intend to call forth Juan Sanchez before the Inquisition?"

"No. I had something else in mind, a little more subtle." He glanced at his papers. "It seems Juan Sanchez is engaged to Inés Lucena. Her uncle was burned at the stake last year as a heretic. It seems the family may be Marranos. I thought it might be of interest to question this young woman. She might have the kind of information we are looking for in reference to Juan Sanchez . . ." he paused, "and Abravanel."

Torquemada gave him a cold nod. "I'm pleased with your work, Fray Domingo. It will not go unnoticed."

The friar slowly eased his massive body to the stone floor and kissed Torquemada's hand. "Father, my greatest desire is to serve you."

Inés floured the wooden bread board while her mother mixed the egg dough in a large bowl. Her mother rolled the dough out and together, with their fists and elbows, they beat the dough so that it would rise and bake light as a feather in the brick oven. They had to prepare the bread a day early, for to bake before the Sabbath would be far too dangerous. Flour was drifting in the afternoon sunbeams when their servant girl ran to them. Her face was white.

"What is it, dear? What's wrong?" Inés's mother asked, but before she could finish her sentence, Inés saw the men dressed in dark robes like demons of death standing at the door. Her heart seemed to stop beating.

"What is it? What do you want with us?" her mother asked.

"Inés Lucena has been called forth by the Inquisition."

Inés heard her mother scream and watched her crawl to the men, begging them to take her instead. Her mother threw herself at their feet and clung to their robes until one kicked her away. The man who had spoken held his hand out to Inés and added, "Simply to ask some questions. No need to worry."

Inés felt so small that the men seemed to envelope her as they escorted her from the house. From the moment he held out his hand to her, from the moment they surrounded her with their black capes, Inés felt as if she had passed from this life and into some hellish nightmare of the next.

Inés felt cold as she was ushered into the tribunal. The men sat behind a high wooden bench and stared at her with their black eyes. She shivered under their stare. "What do they want from me? Why haven't they taken Father? He, after all, would have been the one they wanted if poor uncle had confessed under torture. Torture!" The word reverberated in her mind, the word for something that happened to others, poor victims. Though she had lived with fear, she had never seriously thought that these men of the Church would want to harm her. Her heart thudded painfully against her chest, but when the Friars asked her name, she couldn't speak.

"This is good," she thought. "At least I won't say anything that will hurt those I love."

"Do you swear to tell the whole truth?"

She nodded yes and crossed herself.

"You must answer yes or no. Do you swear to tell the truth?" the prosecutor for the tribunal asked.

"I do," Inés answered.

"If you do, may the Creator have mercy on you. But if you fail to do so, may the Creator destroy you. Is your name Inés Lucena?"

"Yes," she answered, looking from Inquisitor to prosecutor.

"Are you a native of Ciudad Real, Castile, nineteen years of age, the daughter of Señor Lucena of Ciudad Real?"

"Yes."

The prosecutor continued, "We want to ask you some questions, my dear. Answer us honestly and no harm will come to you. We want to ask you some intimate questions about your family and your fiancé, Don Juan Sanchez de Sevilla."

"Juan!" she thought. "They are after Juan!" but she said nothing to the men.

"How does he come by the name Juan Sanchez de Sevilla?"

It was a question she had never asked herself. His was an old Andalusia name, or so she thought. There could be no harm in answering such a simple question.

"I don't know," she said in an inaudible voice.

"What? Speak up!"

"I said, I don't know. I just assumed it came from his father and his father before him," she answered in a stronger tone.

"You were not aware then that Juan Sanchez de Sevilla, high treasurer to King Enríque the III, was a converted Jew? His name at birth was Samuel Abravanel, and he fled to Portugal as a heretic in the year 1391!"

"No! It cannot be true. It must be another you speak of!" she cried. "Oh Juan," she thought to herself. "How could you have kept this from me after all I confessed to you?" The blood drained from her face.

"You are telling this tribunal that you did not know that Juan Sanchez is from Portugal, and that his name by birth is Jonathan Ben Ezra—the very same Ben Ezra family that is connected to the Abravanel's? How absurd, my dear!"

"I know nothing! Nothing!" She cried, more from the pain of not knowing the truth than from the fear of torture.

"Your family—do they observe the law of Moses?"

"I know nothing! Nothing!" Now they were attacking her own family.

A heavy set friar leaned forward and whispered to the man in the center who had been questioning her. The inquisitor nodded his head in agreement. Without another word the men rose and began to leave.

"What is it you want from me? What do you want to know? I know nothing of this Jonathan Ben Ezra! He has nothing to do with Juan, with my Juan!" Inés, in panic, threw herself at their feet. The hateful eyes of the inquisitors stared down upon her, and then the men turned and walked away.

A guard wrenched her to her feet and pulled her out of the tribunal, gripping her arms so tightly that the circulation was cut off.

"Please. You're hurting me," she pleaded.

The guard ignored her. She stumbled after him, tripped, and was dragged by her arms. He pulled her down a long winding staircase which led to the inquisitional dungeons.

"Where are you taking me?" she asked, her voice becoming hysterically high. "I haven't done anything wrong! I am here to be questioned—that's all. Where are you taking me?"

The guard turned on her, his face wrinkled in hate, and he spit in her face.

"You didn't answer the questions to their satisfaction! Down here we will get some answers!"

He opened a great iron door, and she was thrown into the torture chamber. A huge knotted rope hung from the ceiling, large rust iron hooks lined the wall, and a long wooden table with cuffs for hands and feet stretched out before her. An inquisitor sat on a chair in the far corner. His face was puffy and sallow from lack of sunshine. A scribe sitting at his right did not look up when she entered. Two guards stood before her.

"Her clothes," was all the inquisitor said. The guards held up a *sanbenito*, yellow sack cloth painted with devils. "Change," the inquisitor demanded.

"No!" she cried. "No, I've done nothing wrong!" She ran to the inquisitor and fell at his feet. "Mercy, father, please have mercy on me. I will tell you everything you want to know. Please, just please let me out of here."

"That's a good child," he said. "We don't want to hurt you. If you cooperate, there will be no pain. We will let you go home."

"Yes, please, father, I want to go home."

"Of course, you do, child. Just tell me what you know of Jonathan Ben Ezra."

"I know nothing of this man! You must believe me! There has been a terrible mistake. I am engaged to Juan Sanchez. He is not a Jew! He is of a fine Christian family."

"The court will not be mocked." The inquisitor grew icy cold. Change into the sack cloth.

Inés whimpered as she changed into the horrid gown. Once she neatly folded her own clothes, the guards led her to a wooden table with iron cuffs for legs and arms. She was so small that her arms and legs were pulled to their limit. Then they clasped her nose with iron prongs, and she had to gasp for breath through her mouth.

"What? What have I done? Why are you doing this to me?" she wept.

"You are not cooperating! We don't want to hurt you," the inquisitor said. "Answer our questions, and we will let you go home, Inés. You can go home. We won't hurt you."

"Yes!" She cried. "I want to go home. Please let me go home. I have done nothing wrong. Please," she begged.

"Is Juan Sanchez de Sevilla, Jonathan Ben Ezra?"

"I don't know!" she sobbed. "Oh, God, have mercy! Please, dear God, have mercy. I don't know—I don't know."

"Does your family follow the law of Moses?" His face was next to hers.

"No, I know nothing, nothing!"

"Gag her," he commanded.

The guards stuffed a bloody cloth down her throat, so that she couldn't breathe. Her body began to writhe as she struggled for breath, and her eyes grew large with terror. A guard was pouring water on the cloth. She was drowning . . . . Her lungs felt as if they would burst. Then, suddenly, the guard pulled the gag from her throat. She gagged on the blood that came up with the rag, gasping for air, sobbing.

The inquisitor looked down at her disdainfully.

"Well now, that was most unpleasant, wasn't it? I don't want to hurt you again, but you must cooperate. Now, Inés," he bent over her again, "who is Juan Sanchez de Sevilla? Is he a Jew?"

"I know nothing!" she cried, choking on the blood in her throat.

"Very well! Then there will be more of the same. The truth will come!" he said before he left the room.

Inés was uncontrollably shaking as the guards stuffed the cloth back down her throat.

Señor Lucena held his head high and marched to the tribunal to demand the return of his daughter, but he was coldly refused. It was as if she had been devoured by the ugly stucco building where the tribunal sat in Ciudad Real. When he returned home, he found Juan standing at the entrance to his villa. He stood like the Greek hero Orpheus alone and lost without his love. The father's heart broke.

"They've taken my precious, precious child! Why? Why didn't they take me?" He embraced Juan in his agony. "Forgive us, Juan! My brother must have spoken before he died. They must know that we are Marranos. Forgive us!" He slid to the ground and sobbed.

Juan bent down and held the man in his arms. Señor Lucena thought his brother had betrayed them. A throbbing pain reverberated through Juan's body for he sensed that they knew, that the Inquisition had found him out, that he too was a Jew, pretending to be a Christian.

"Inés is gone," he choked, "Inés is gone because of me!"

CHAPTER 22

Blood red and white Moorish arches seemed to pulsate above Isaac's head as he searched for Cardinal Mendoza in what had been the Córdoba Mosque, now consecrated as a Cathedral. He passed peaceful alcoves where children used to sit with their teachers and listen to the wisdom of the Koran. Isaac found Mendoza at the center of the church where the cardinal had sanctified an altar. The cardinal made the sign of the cross, then stood, and walked with Isaac to a private room.

"I'm glad we finally have an opportunity to speak privately with one another. I want you to know how impressed I am with your financial wizardry. I know the king and queen are very grateful for all you've done in the past few months," the cardinal said.

"Thank you, that means a great deal to me. The treasury had sunk at one point to 885,000 reals, but is now over 13,000,000. However, this is still insufficient for the expenses appropriated for the crusade. Will the next campaign begin soon?" Isaac asked.

"Yes, I think so. Though King Ferdinand is fighting the French in Aragon, once again, we will rally behind the Count of Cabra. The queen wants to push forward, now. I've advised her to wait for King Ferdinand's return," Mendoza continued.

"I never understood why you did not support Isabella from the beginning. I know that you admire her as I do. Why was it Archbishop Carrillo and not you who came to her rescue and crowned her?" Isaac asked.

"I always prayed that Isabella would see her way to the throne, but I was the Archbishop of Madrid. King Enríque ruled Castile by God's decree, and I was with the king when he died. Though I wanted to support Isabella, it was my duty to stay with my king until he was in His hands once again. I will not deny that I dreamed of wearing these red robes, but I never allowed my own ambitions to interfere with my duty to the king. I think in the end, Queen Isabella respected my decision." Mendoza paused for a moment. "I'm not sure I would have crowned Isabella that day, without King Ferdinand by her side."

"And yet you became the cardinal, and Archbishop Carrillo fought with the Portuguese and Princess Juana."

"Isaac, may I call you that?"

"Please."

"I cannot answer for Archbishop Carrillo, but I am not a man to be bribed or swayed by power. As I see it, my purpose here on Earth is to serve Him first, my king and queen second; but please, let us return to the present. I respect you. I feel you are a man of great integrity and want you to serve as my own personal treasurer. Do you feel this is asking too much? With all the work you are now doing for the king and queen, I don't mean to burden you."

"It will be a great honor to serve you," Isaac answered.

"Fine. I am afraid my records are in disarray as I have been traveling with the queen in preparation for the next campaign."

"I'm sure I'll have no trouble. I've heard the queen has a new weapon. Will it be ready for this battle?"

"Yes, it's called the lombard. It throws rocks, boulders, iron balls with devastating effect. I'm sure it will crush anything in its way."

"I imagine Boabdíl will be quite unprepared for that!"

"His force far outnumbers ours; we'll need it." The cardinal confided.

Reassured by Mendoza's personal tone, Isaac braced himself. He felt compelled to discuss the Inquisition with the powerful man.

"Your Holy Eminence, there is something I feel I must bring to your attention."

"Yes, Isaac, what is it? Please feel free to speak."

Perspiration was forming on Isaac's forehead.

"It concerns the Inquisition."

Mendoza's face flushed red.

"I cannot believe that God intended his work to be carried on in such a manner."

Isaac felt encouraged. "Right now in Ciudad Real another tribunal has been established. Thirty-four new Christians and Jews have been condemned to be burned alive at the stake. Surely, you cannot believe that all these people are heretics bent on destroying the Church. Can you intervene on behalf of these poor souls?"

"Oh, that I could, Isaac, but I'm afraid I have little to say in these matters. The tribunal works in complete secrecy. I do not have access to their records. Without records, how can I judge who is innocent and who is guilty? The only one who can halt the Acts of Faith is the Grand Inquisitor."

"Forgive me, cardinal, but can't you intervene when you feel injustice is being done?"

The cardinal bent his head for he could not look directly at Isaac as he spoke.

"I'm afraid I am powerless. Fray Tomas de Torquemada has complete authority over the Inquisition. He answers to no one, not to me, not even to the king or queen."

"But surely there must be something that can be done to save some of these people. I plead for the Christians as well as the Jews."

"This must be kept the strictest confidence, Isaac," the cardinal continued in a hushed voice. "I've taken it upon myself to go above the king and queen in this matter. I have written to Pope Sixtus IV. I feel that Fray Tomas was a poor choice for Grand Inquisitor. It's as if the friar has cast a spell over the queen. She will not discuss the matter with me. I suggested to the Pope that two other inquisitors be appointed to sit beside Fray Tomas in order that his judgment would not necessarily be the final one."

"That was very courageous. I'm sure the Grand Inquisitor will not look favorably on such a proposal."

"Isaac, if you fear for me, then you must also fear for the king and queen."

"Still, it could be years before any action is taken. What about these people who are condemned to die?"

"For them, I am afraid there is no help."

There was a soft knock on the door. A guard opened it and the Count of Cabra, one of Queen Isabella's knights entered. He bowed to Cardinal Mendoza and kissed his ring.

"If I may have a word in private with you, Your Holy Eminence."

"Isaac may hear what you have to say."

Isaac's heart ached for the condemned in Ciudad Real, but knew there was little he could do. He was honored that he was included in the highly secret meeting. The count less pleased.

The cardinal waited for the count to be seated, and then asked, "Where is Hassan now?"

"He is still with his brother El Zagal. From what my spies tell me, he has the backing of all the caliphs but has lost control in Granada. You'd think he would try to mend his differences with his wife and son. However, I've been informed that Zoraya wants Boabdíl to march, now that King Ferdinand is in Aragon."

The cardinal looked from Isaac to the count, before he said, "we are weak without the king. Hopefully, Boabdíl will tarry, and King Ferdinand will soon return. However, if the Moors begin to march, you must be ready to counter them. Hassan is the sly one; his son does not know how to fight. I'm sure the father is waiting for us to eliminate the suckling. Then, he can return to Alhambra with the full support of his kingdom."

"How can a father turn against his own son?" the count asked.

"The man's lust will bring about his own downfall. The entire Moorish empire will crumble, fall to ruin, not so much from our might, our determination to carry the cross and the sword, as from the decay within it. We will face Boabdíl with or without King Ferdinand, and we shall prevail!"

The vehemence with which Mendoza uttered these words gave Isaac a glimpse of Mendoza's iron will, as strong as Queen Isabella's.

In the southernmost portion of the Iberian peninsula, the snowcapped peaks of the Sierra Nevada glistened in the sunshine like sliver stepping stones ascending to heaven. They protected the Moors' fortress, Alhambra, and blessed it with perpetual beauty. Alhambra, red and gold in the shimmering sunbeams, was Isabella's dream, the prize for which Ferdinand fought, the chalice Mendoza pursued. The Moors within its walls had fought off Hassan when he tried to retake it, and his son, Boabdíl, sat on the throne, having taken the title of caliph.

Boabdíl was a slender young man who had inherited blond hair and blue eyes from his mother. Hassan had loved Zoraya's firm, supple body when she was young, but as her skin wrinkled from the cruel sun and her muscles softened, he found his comfort in his younger wife, Ayesha. It was now Zoraya, the first wife, who turned her son Boabdíl and the people of Alhambra against Hassan.

Zoraya intently watched her son as he sat on his father's throne. His fair hair fell to his shoulders when he leaned forward to play with his dark-haired little boy.

"Have I ever told you the story of the sorcerer and his cave?"

"No, father." The child's black eyes grew large.

Boabdíl laughed.

"A long time ago, before Alhambra was built, there was a king-"

"Was he a Moslem, father?"

"Yes." Boabdíl laughed again. "Now be quiet and let me finish the story." The little boy settled into his father's lap and nestled his head into the strong arms that held him. "The king's name was Aben Habuz. The king had many powerful enemies who tried again and again to take this land upon which Alhambra sits. One day a very old man with a long white beard and tiny black eyes came before the king. He was a sorcerer and claimed that he could protect the kingdom from all its enemies. The king listened to the old man and built a large tower. In the room at the top of the tower, he and the sorcerer arranged a chessboard with large hand-carved figures. Each knight carried a sharp lance. The sorcerer crowned the top of the tower with a talisman and softly chanted an ancient incantation. The talisman was a Moslem knight, and he watched out over the kingdom. When an enemy army approached, the talisman pointed to the direction of the danger. The king and the sorcerer would run up to the chess room in the tower and pierce the enemy chess pieces with the lances from their own knights. To the king's amazement, time after time the sorcerer's magic worked and all his enemies were defeated in battle. The kingdom prospered as never before, and the king granted the sorcerer his dearest wish, to build a cave at the very bottom of this hill upon which we now sit. The sorcerer had the walls of the cave draped with damask, expensive incense wafted about the room. Oil burned in crystal lamps, and beautiful girls danced before him. The king was well satisfied until one day a beautiful Gothic princess was taken as hostage."

"Like Queen Isabella?" The prince interrupted his father again.

"No, not like Isabella. Queen Isabella is fair, but this princess was a dark beauty with raven hair and black eyes. She wore a sliver lyre around her neck. When she played upon her lyre the notes rippled through the throne-room like the sweet song of the nightingale. The king was bewitched, but the sorcerer recognized her as a sorceress."

"Didn't he tell the king?" the child asked.

"Yes, he tried to tell the king, but the king had fallen in love with the beautiful woman and would not listen to him. The sorcerer decided that he must have this beauty for himself. He conjured the kingdom of Irem, a paradise filled with fig, pomegranate, orange and lemon trees, wild red roses blossoming so that the colors and scents of the enchanted land were irresistible. After he conjured the land, he fashioned an entrance with a large archway. At the top of the arch he engraved the holy hand reaching for a key."

"I know the archway, father!" the child cried with delight.

Boabdíl smiled and continued.

"The sorcerer brought the king and the princess, who rode upon a donkey, to this paradise. He said to the king 'If you could have one wish what would it be?' The king, enchanted by the sights and scents of what lay before him said, 'Surely to live peacefully in a land such as this. And you, my sorcerer? What is it that you most desire?' The sorcerer smiled and answered, 'I desire the first beast and its burden that enters this land.' The king laughed and said, 'That is all you wish for? It shall be done!' Well, no sooner had he said this than the princess riding upon her donkey entered the enchanted land. 'She's mine!' cried the sorcerer, 'She's mine!' The king was furious at being tricked and told the sorcerer he could have anything, anything he possessed but not the princess. The sorcerer became so enraged that he entered the enchanted land, and with a bolt of lightning, he and the princess sank into the hill.

The paradise disappeared, and all that remained was the arch with the hand reaching for the key. The king had men dig for the sorcerer and the princess. They tried to enter his cave and found it had been completely sealed. The talisman no longer pointed to approaching enemies and, within a few years, the king died in battle. Many years later Alhambra was built, but if you listen very carefully you might still be able to hear the princess playing her lyre for the sorcerer in his cave."

The father and child walked over to the balcony in the throne room. From here Boabdíl could see his land stretched out before him. The hills were lush and red roses ran wild, dancing in the balmy breezes.

"I think I hear her, father," the child whispered. Boabdíl laughed, but then was startled to hear Zoraya clapping three times. A servant came to take the child away.

With Zoraya's heavy gold chains undulating around her neck, thick bracelets jingling on her arms, red silk scarf flowing behind her, jasmine perfume filling the air, she strutted up to her son.

"It is time for you to prove yourself a man. When are you going to fight for your kingdom? When are you going to stand up to your father and show him that you are no longer a child, but a man to be reckoned with?"

"Ali Atar advises us to wait. We will wait until he decides it's time to move."

"Since when do we have to wait for Ali Atar! What does he know of war? Ferdinand is in the north. Now is the time to move . . . now, while the Christians are without their king!"

"I have had so little experience. I must bow to his judgment in these matters."

"What kind of a leader are you? What kind of a king will you make if you cannot decide when to lead your own armies into battle? I say now is the time to move . . . . if you wait, you will be defeated!"

Boabdíl was a gentle man and tears came to his eyes at his mother's wrath.

"Perhaps, then, I was not meant to rule."

She slapped him across the face.

"After all I've done for you! How dare you talk to me like this, like a child with tears in your eyes? You are a man, you are the son of Muley Abou'l Hassan! You were meant to rule!"

His hand went to his cheek which was growing red.

Zoraya changed tactics.

"My sweet, sweet prince, it is time for you to shape your own destiny and the destiny of all Granada."

"Then let me rule as I see fit. I shall decide when we will march!" he said with surprising force.

"Yes, it is for you to decide," she said, furious, and left the throne room, her heavy perfume, her red silk scarf, flowing behind her.

As Boabdíl rode with Ali Atar out of Granada, he knew his father, Muley Hassan, and his uncle, El Zagal, watched like vultures waiting for the kill. He knew that they prayed for his death and then they would descend from the mountains and lay claim once again to the throne. The hoofs of seven hundred horses pounded the ground, and nine thousand foot soldiers behind them followed Boabdíl into battle. The Count of Cabra waited for him with a pitiful army; however, Boabdíl was no warrior. He fought bravely beside his men, but they quickly fell into disarray. They had no battle lines and fled at the sight of blood. Boabdíl raised his scimitar and many a man fell to his blade. His hand was covered with blood as he wielded his weapon forcefully. Horses convulsed in death, their eyes wild, their guts spewed wet and slimy on the ground. Boabdíl called to his men to fight; he prayed for strength and wielded his scimitar, thrashing, slicing off arms, heads. After several brutal hours, the Count of Cabra encircled Boabdíl and a small group of men in a dry riverbed. The Christian army began to move in on the Moors, who were now completely outnumbered. Boabdíl realized he could command his men to fight to the death, and they would gladly die for him, for Granada. He hesitated for a moment and then made his decision.

Isaac had been called to court just as King Ferdinand returned to Isabella. He stood beside Don Abraham Senior and watched the king approach the throne. Queen Isabella was sitting on a golden dais, and no one was sure of the reception King Ferdinand would receive. He had, after all, left her in the middle of a campaign, to chase after the French in Rousillon once again. King Ferdinand knelt at her feet.

"Forgive me for leaving you," he said humbly. "You were right; you were the wiser one. I should never have left you while you are waging this holy war. But someday, Isabella, someday I swear I will rout the French, and that land will belong to Aragon once again."

"To Spain," she said softly and gave him her hand. She was grateful he had returned. Her knights had fought valiantly, but without their king, she knew they would never achieve complete victory. She realized Boabdíl was not a serious threat. He was a young, untrained warrior and obviously still ruled by his mother. It was Hassan and El Zagal who kept them from Alhambra and a complete *reconquista*. Only Ferdinand had the strength to lead such a perilous campaign. He kissed her hand tenderly, lovingly, and as Ferdinand looked up at Isabella, Isaac could see the love that flared between the Catholic Monarchs.

The heir to the throne, Don Juan, and his sisters, the Princesses Isabella and Juana, were ushered in to see their father. It seemed to Isaac that the four-year-old prince ran up the dais as if he knew it was meant for him. He hugged his father before the court. The knights and ladies-in-waiting smiled at the exchange between father and son, an intimacy rarely exhibited. The princesses bowed to their father, and then the children were quickly ushered out. A page announced Cardinal Mendoza. After the cardinal and the king greeted each other, all except the high counselors were dismissed; Isaac was leaving with the others, but held back by guards to stay.

"It is good to have you back, Your Majesty! We are waiting for your wise counsel. Boabdíl is here in Córdoba. What would you have us do with him?" the Count of Cabra asked.

"What is your suggestion, Cardinal?" Ferdinand asked.

"Some would execute him immediately, Your Majesty."

"I said, what would you do?" he repeated.

"I believe the man is worth much more alive than dead—alive and back in Granada." He was interrupted by gasps in the room. "If he becomes a vassal to Your Majesties, then Granada will still be divided. Eliminate Boabdíl and Hassan will return to Alhambra and a united kingdom."

"Your Majesty, I must object to this preposterous scheme!" cried the Count of Cabra. "Valiant Christian soldiers have just given their lives to capture this infidel! Would you have us just let Boabdíl go?"

"You have formidable foes in Hassan and El Zagal. Keep the enemy divided," Cardinal Mendoza insisted. Then turning to Isaac, Mendoza asked, "What do you think?" and Isaac realized he had been ordered to stay to strengthen Mendoza's position.

"I quite agree with Cardinal Mendoza, Your Majesties," he said and bowed.

"Your Majesty," Cabra continued, clearly angry with Mendoza, and his second, Isaac. "We fought a hard battle. Though we captured Boabdíl this time, I would not scoff at the man's courage! He slew many a Christian soldier. His father has offered a ransom for him, dead or alive. I think he would prefer him dead." The king laughed. "I say we should send the scoundrel back to his father."

"There is another proposal," Isabella added in a voice which immediately brought a hush to the room.

"What is this, my lady?" Ferdinand asked. Isaac smiled to himself for he knew Ferdinand respected her opinion above all the others in the court.

"His mother has also offered to pay the ransom and suggests, as Cardinal Mendoza indicated, that he declare his loyalty to us and become a vassal king. We would hold his child, the heir, as a hostage, should trouble erupt."

Wistfully, Isaac thought of the little boy, Don Juan, who had just pranced out of the room. Boabdíl's son was the same age. What a sacrifice, what a humiliation it would be for Boabdíl to accept such a proposal. The same thoughts seemed to run through Ferdinand's mind, but it was obvious that this was indeed the best solution. Boabdíl was worth more to them in Granada, and they would have the child.

"Very well. I accept Zoraya's proposal. We will receive Boabdíl as a king," Ferdinand answered without hesitation.

Boabdíl watched the Moorish noblemen ride toward him as he waited beside Ferdinand. The banners of Castile, León and Aragon flew above him as he saw his own banner flap with the wind of the approaching men. There were children in their midst. He squinted his eyes and saw his own son amongst them. It was part of the ransom—his son and the sons of twelve noblemen for his own release. It was a ransom he would never have agreed to pay. Only his mother could have thought of it. The Catholic Monarchs had been gracious. Greeting him as a brother, Ferdinand had received him as a king with embraces and kisses. He had lavished silver armor, fine horses and jewels upon him, and Boabdíl had accepted the gifts, the false honor, stoically. He knew they were not afraid of him. He knew they felt they could control him, and he let them believe this. He would be their vassal. He would pay them homage, and annual tributes, but in his heart he believed he would face them again in battle someday. He had fought with his men and bled with them, but he still had to prove that he was a leader of men, a king! His mother had bought his freedom with his son, and as he saw the boy pulled from his horse, he wished he had died in battle rather than to see him in their hands. Seeing his father, the child bravely broke away from his captors and ran to him. Boabdíl dismounted and embraced him. They held each other for only a moment as Boabdíl felt the piercing eyes of his noblemen. Twelve of their sons were to be held hostage as well, and they were incensed at this display of emotion. Boabdíl carefully pried the child's arms from around his neck and said, "Be brave, my son." He mounted his horse, savagely kicked the animal, and the Moors galloped off toward Granada. Though Boabdíl could hear his child cry out for him, he dared not turn back. The wind blew the tears from his face as he raced back toward the red fortress on the sorcerer's hill.

Ferdinand turned to Isabella and was surprised to see tears in her eyes. "Is it possible that you feel for this man, this barbarian?"

"He is not a barbarian. He is an intelligent man," she said as she wiped her eyes. "It is a pity that he does not know the light, the purity, the truth of our Lord."

"He doesn't have the strength to rule," Ferdinand said quietly. "I can tell you, my love, he values the life of his men more than the glory of victory. I will not fear meeting him in battle, if it ever comes to that."

"I don't think it will," she answered.

"No, neither do I."

CHAPTER 23

As Isaac wove through the green slopes of Andalusia, he enjoyed watching the mules carrying heavy sacks of olives, swatting the flies with their scrawny tails, their large brown eyes looking to their masters' for consolation. Isaac watched millers cracking and pounding wheat. As Isaac journeyed toward Castile, the lush greenery, the sweet scent of rose and jasmine, and the song of the nightingales faded. Plateaus undulated before him in soft rose, tans and dark leathery browns. Dots of olive and cork trees brushed the countryside, and still the land stretched out across the wide horizon in an unending palette of earth tones. Isaac drew his cloak about him, for he had never felt so desolate as he now did on the plains of Castile. The land spoke to his heart and reminded him that in the end, each must travel alone. He passed farms where men were cutting the earth with their hoes, looking up for a moment, waving, mopping their foreheads, and then turning back to their work.

When Isaac had reached the town of Ciudad Real, he sharply pulled on the reins of his horse, his mind not wanting to believe what his eyes saw. Before him stood thirty-four auto-de-fé stakes set on pyres just outside the town walls. He had thought that the church would stop this madness from within. But no . . . they were actually going to burn people, women as well as men, at the stake! Hoping in some way to stop the horror, Isaac kicked his horse, entered the city, and found his the way to an inn. Upon dismounting, he was swirled along with the swelling crowd that had gathered to see the heretics stand trial. The crowd moved towards the *plaza mayor* where Isaac saw benches, ten rows deep, lining the square, and in front of the church stood a platform which had been erected for the Dominican friars who would conduct the trial. At the very top of the platform was a second level with one wooden chair covered with a canopy, looking like a royal throne.

All the benches were filled, and Isaac stood in the back of the crowd watching as a long procession of Dominican friars solemnly marched in, followed by clergymen carrying crucifixes, incense, and candles. The noblemen of Ciudad Real entered and were seated up front; then a hush fell over the crowd as the Grand Inquisitor, Tomas Torquemada, took his place on the throne.

Some of the defendants walked into the plaza, some hobbled on canes and two were so deformed by torture that they had to be carried in cages to the center of the plaza. They all wore the *sanbenitos* and yellow caps with pictures of devils cavorting in the flames.

Isaac watched as a short stocky man, naked except for the yellow sack with an obscene laughing devil painted on it, was brought before the tribunal, and as he gazed at his naked feet, Isaac saw him shiver.

"Your Eminence," the man wept. "I have never broken the law, never stolen, never missed payment of taxes. My only crime is that there was no smoke coming from my chimney on the Jewish Sabbath. I am not a heretic. I have not relapsed. Have mercy on my soul!"

Fray Domingo Gomez stood and said, "The defendant has already been tried, Your Excellency. We have been informed that he was indeed practicing his old faith."

"Who is my accuser so that I may address the accusation," the man cried.

From on high, Torquemada said, "We will not divulge such information! Would you have us playing traitor to the good people who have brought forth the information we need in order to conduct our search for heretics? I assure you it is a most difficult task even when such information is divulged. I find you guilty! Guilty as charged! Next!" Torquemada sat back in his seat.

"Mercy!" cried the man, falling in the dirt. "May the Lord have mercy on my soul! I repent! I confess to Judaizing! I confess and I repent!"

Torquemada nodded and said, "Very well. You shall be released to the secular law. You shall be garroted before your body is consigned to the flames."

A friar bent over the defendant as he lay weeping in the dirt, and gave him his last rites, then had him dragged away.

"Next case!" Gomez called.

A dark haired beauty leaning on a cane was brought forth.

"Your crime?" Gomez asked without looking up.

"I cooked meat in oil and refused to eat pork."

Isaac frantically looked about him for others outraged by these proceedings. Couldn't these people see the injustice being done? Why was no one crying out? Why were no objections raised? Feeling, desperate, wanting to cry out against this mockery of a trial, he searched faces, hoping to find others in the crowd who were as enraged, but then he realized that the fates of the defendants had been sealed before they had entered the plaza. This trial was simply their last chance to repent and be granted garroting before they were burned at the stake.

"Have you opened your soul to Lord and begged His forgiveness? Have you confessed your sins?" Gomez was saying.

She would not answer but only stared at the dark robed friars.

"Repent!" Gomez roared from his bench. "Repent your sins, and you shall find mercy and salvation!"

The young woman just stared at the friar without responding.

A hush fell over the spectators, some stricken-faced Jews and new Christians, who now seemed to Isaac to be uneasy with the proceedings, but still the Christians sat back comfortably, but listening intently.

"We must stop this madness!" Isaac whispered to the man next to him, but the man suspiciously turned to look at him.

"The woman is going to die a Jewess!" he said to Isaac.

"A martyr," Isaac whispered in awe as murmurs of the pending martyrdom ran through the crowd. One by one, thirty other men and women stood before the tribunal and refused to repent. Despite the beseeching of the clergy, all, except the first man, had decided to die as martyrs.

Isaac followed the condemned in the *sanbenitos*, as they marched out of the *plaza mayor* and through the city streets. People jeered at them as they walked, throwing rotten eggs and tomatoes. Just as a lad was about to throw a tomato, Isaac grabbed him and shook him, all of his anger spilling out. "These people are suffering enough! Must you make their agony worse! Have all of you gone mad!"

A huge man suddenly pulled Isaac away from the lad and punched him. Isaac staggered back, bleeding from his nose. Pressing his nose to stop the bleeding, he allowed himself to be pushed along with the crowd as they made their way outside the city's walls. Isaac could see that some of the condemned could barely walk, so grotesquely disfigured had they been by torture. One young man was completely bent over, his head almost touching the ground as he hobbled by; his back had been broken as if he had suffered a great fall. Isaac saw others with fingernails and toenails black from the spikes that had been driven into them. He stared into their vacant eyes, and guessed that the pain from their torture had crippled their minds. He saw the beautiful woman limping amongst them. Though her head hung low, she was to die a martyr. She stumbled when a rotten egg was thrown against her breast, but she went on. Someone in the crowd screamed "Inés!" but she did not respond. She continued, caught in this nightmare. When Isaac heard the scream a second time, the sound of the voice echoed inside him. He knew the voice, Jonathan's voice, though he had never heard it in such pain. Desperate to find him, Isaac began pushing people aside. Feeling an unaccustomed wave of panic, almost the same feeling he had had on the wharf as a small boy, facing Málaga for the first time, his sense of desperation quickened. He had to find Jonathan, but there were hundreds of people. He finally stopped fighting the crowd and allowed himself to be hurried along.

Rotted tomatoes and eggs were hurled again and again at the condemned heretics. Other new Christians who had repented also wore the yellow sacks, and they flagellated themselves, causing blood to flow as they were forced to join the procession and watch the autos-de-fe. Isaac was now in the middle of the crowd as it drew to the town walls, and then stopped. At this point mostly family members and the condemned moved beyond the walls to the stakes.

Still searching for Jonathan, Isaac ventured past the city's walls to witness the auto-de-fé. The men and women were suddenly grabbed by guards. One woman screamed, reaching toward her little boys who were held back by their father. Others were docile and were led to the stakes. Isaac watched the young beauty as guards forced her up onto the straw surrounding a stake. They bound her wrists so tightly the cord cut her skin. Her legs were tied so close to the stake that she hung rather than stood. Again Isaac heard Jonathan scream, "Inés!" He turned, and now with fewer people separating them, he saw him, forcefully being held back by guards. His face was red, his body straining forward as he cried out to the dark-haired beauty. An older gentleman and woman, standing next to him, held each other up as they wept. Her parents, Isaac guessed, as he pushed his way toward them. Again Jonathan screamed, "Inés!" and the beauty looked up as if she were awakened from sleep. The fire was lit at her pyre. Her eyes locked with Jonathan's for a moment then she cast them up to the sky and cried above the flames, "Shema Yisraeil, Adonai Eloheinu, Adonai Echad!" The flames touched her toes, and she screamed at the searing pain. At the last moment some of the victims confessed and were granted the mercy of garroting. They did not feel the fire, but Inés, dying as a Jewess, was very much alive. The fire slowly crept up her legs. Her face contorted, and she screamed uncontrollably. Jonathan broke from the guards and lunged toward the inferno of burning stakes. It took five guards to subdue him and drag him away from the flames. When Isaac looked back up at the stake, Inés was enveloped in flames, smoke rising from her pyre, merging with the mass of smoky cloud. Jonathan lay on the ground as though lifeless, while the old man and his wife tried to lift him and carry him away. Isaac finally reached them, bent over Jonathan and heard the shallow sound of his breathing.

"Jonathan," he called softly. "Jonathan, you must rise and come away from here. You must."

Juan Sanchez de Sevilla lifted his head and looked at Isaac with madness in his eyes. Leaning upon Isaac, he stumbled away with Señor Lucena and his wife. Fray Domingo Gomez grimly watched as Isaac Abravanel helped Juan Sanchez de Sevilla away from the grisly scene.

"My brother must have said too much under torture," Señor Lucena said in a broken voice inside his home. He had given his grief-stricken wife a sleeping potion, had put her to bed, and now sat next to Isaac and Jonathan by the fire, his hands supporting his head as he wept. "They wanted my wife and me to see our precious child burn. Oh how I wish I were the one, not my Inés!" he cried, raking his head with his hands. "Poor Juan! Our poor Juan! How he loved her!"

Jonathan stared into the fire and would look at no one. A servant offered food, but none of them could eat.

"It was kind of you to help us. I don't even know your name," Señor Lucena continued. "I'm sure we would still be there if you hadn't come."

"I am Isaac Abravanel. I spoke with Cardinal Mendoza in an effort to stop this atrocity, but there was nothing the cardinal could do." Isaac, trying not to collapse into tears as well, shook his head.

"Don Isaac, forgive me, I did not recognize you. Do you know Juan?"

"Yes, I know Juan, but we haven't seen each other in many years."

"For you to find him today, like this, makes one believe in fate. My daughter died as a Jew, Don Isaac. We are Jews. All of us, even our Juan."

"Yes, I know." Isaac answered though he could hardly speak.

"I must go to my wife. You will excuse me." He wept as he ascended the stairs to comfort his wife.

Isaac then walked over to Jonathan and knelt by his side.

"Jonathan," he whispered. Jonathan stared vacantly into the fire on the hearth. Isaac had never felt Jonathan's need to flee the Judería. But he thought he understood why Jonathan had left, though not fully able to forgive. However, he could see that Jonathan had found the happiness he sought with this family, and the beautiful woman who had just died, destroyed because she was a Jew. Jonathan's hand touched Isaac's shoulder. Isaac looked up.

"I thought you were a vision, a spirit, but I see now this is really you!" Jonathan said.

"Yes, I was on my way from Córdoba to Madrid when I saw the stakes . . . ."

Jonathan turned his head and stared back at the flames. "Señor Lucena thinks she died because her uncle admitted to Judaizing, but I know differently. The inquisitors are after me! I should have been the one to take the flame! I should have been the one to die, not my beautiful, beautiful Inés-" His whole body wrenched as he wept.

Isaac held Jonathan. He held him for a long time until gradually the tears subsided, his body shuddering with his grief.

"Come home with me now. Come back to us. Rebecca misses you. She often speaks of you."

"Rebecca?" he asked.

"Yes, we are all here in Castile. I fled the Portuguese court when Fernando was imprisoned. You know about Fernando-"

Jonathan nodded yes.

"Come home with me."

"No!" he wrestled himself free of Isaac's grasp. "I can't! Don't you see? If I have anything to do with you, I will place all of you in danger. Jews who meet socially with Christians come under investigation. How I have imprisoned myself! I meant to be free from the walls of the Judería, but I am far more bound now than I ever was," he said bitterly. "Tell Rebecca that I love her, but it is much too dangerous for us to be seen together."

"I have power in the court. Perhaps I can persuade the king and queen to . . ."

"Are you mad? Do you want to burn at the stake as well! All communication between us must be severed. Do you want to see Rebecca burn?" Jonathan's eyes were wild with anger.

Isaac stood and tried to remain calm.

"Very well, Jonathan, my brother . . . ." He choked on the words. Then regaining his composure, he added, "You will always be in our prayers!"

"There is no God for me, Isaac! I've told you that before. If there were a God, he would never have let this happen!" Jonathan cried.

Enraged, Isaac raised his hand to strike him, but he held back and then dropped his hand.

"God save your soul," he whispered, turning his back on Jonathan as he had done in the Ben Ezra home so long ago and left him.

Rebecca was in the courtyard when Isaac returned. He found her carefully pruning the rose bushes which had been neglected by the previous owner of the tranquil garden. She pricked her finger on a thorn, and it began to bleed. Isaac held her hand in his. The blood slipped between their fingers for a moment and then stopped. She sensed Isaac's distress.

"Are you having trouble raising funds?" she asked.

Isaac answered, "No, for once monies are coming in. Cardinal Mendoza has been a great help. He has asked me to manage his own financial affairs as well."

"Won't that be too much, Isaac?"

"No, I'll manage. It's a very great honor. Can you imagine a Jew controlling the monies of Cardinal Mendoza?" he said, distraught, he turned away from her.

"Isaac, don't keep your burdens to yourself. I know when something is disturbing you. What is it?" She was concerned. She had never seen him like this, so agitated, so tense, ready to snap in two.

He brushed a silver strand of hair from her face, and it blended in with the honey gold. He could no longer keep it inside, and it came spilling out.

"I saw him." He could see her body tense, knowing full well that he meant Jonathan. "He lives in Ciudad Real . . . ." Isaac choked when the vision of Inés in flames jumped before him. "He was to marry a beautiful young woman, a Marrano. The Inquisition found her guilty of heresy, of relapsing to Judaism." Rebecca turned away from him.

"Oh God, I don't understand your ways!" she cried. Shivering, she imagined the grisly auto-de-fé. She closed her eyes and a vision of Jonathan in despair, as he had been after their father's death, rose before her. Feeling dizzy, she opened her eyes and stared at Isaac. She let him fold her in his arms and felt the warmth of his body, but it did nothing to stop her trembling. After a long while she said in a more controlled voice, "I suppose now it would be too dangerous for me to see Jonathan again." She looked up at Isaac.

"Yes, I'm afraid it is."

"Is he in danger of being investigated?" she asked, pulling away from him and wringing her hands.

"He feels sure that they will want him next."

She picked up her pruning shears and continued to cut furiously at the roses until she pricked herself again. She dropped the shears and wept. Isaac held her in his arms once again.

"What kind of life can we have here, Isaac?"

He rocked her back and forth in his arms then suddenly let go. He felt as if a tidal wave were swallowing him alive as the horror of the auto-de-fé still held him in its grip. "What choice do we have?" he answered in desperation. "Where would we go? Fires burn all across Europe. We have to stay here and try to build a life for ourselves. Jonathan cannot retrace his steps and neither can we." He took a deep breath, trying to blot out the vision of Inés, burning, and then gathered Rebecca into his arms. Shutting his eyes, still trying to block the vision, he said, "Ferdinand, Isabella and Cardinal Mendoza respect my work, and that affords us and the Jews of Spain some security." The vision gone, he opened his eyes and walked away from her. "Perhaps we can fight the Inquisition and see it abolished before it destroys all of us. We have to try, Rebecca."

He thought of how powerless even Cardinal Mendoza was to halt the auto-de-fé, and he knew that Torquemada could not be stopped unless the queen herself intervened. "The queen must be made to see his madness," he said, taking hold of Rebecca's hand and pressing it. "Someone has to wake her to the terror that has gripped the land."

"Will she listen to you, Isaac?" Rebecca asked.

"I've tried to talk to her about it, but it's as though she herself is afraid."

"Afraid of what? Of Torquemada?"

"No, I think it's more a fear of being wrong. So many have already died. Their deaths are upon her head as well as upon Torquemada's. Perhaps that is why she cannot see how terrorized her people are."

"Then you will have to make her see, Isaac," Rebecca said, "and then perhaps someday Jonathan can come home."

CHAPTER 24

King João, who appeared to have aged greatly since the deaths of Prince Fernando and the Duke of Viseu, stroked his grey streaked beard, while he and his counselors sat and listened to Cristóbal Colón's proposal to sail the western ocean to find Cipango.

Colón was saying, "Marco Polo declares that the land of Khan is much larger and the latitude of the Earth is at least 30 degrees more than we had supposed. Therefore, I suggest that the island of Cipango is significantly closer. I would like to present before the court a letter from Señor Toscanelli. He calculates that Cipango is just off the great shore of the land of Khan. It is a land rich in gold, silver, pearls and gemstones. The temples are built of precious metals and glisten in the sun like jewels. Think of the souls waiting to be saved."

"What would you require for such a voyage?" João leaned forward as he questioned Cristóbal.

Seeing the king so interested, Cristóbal stood erect, carrying himself like a cavalier and waved his arms as he spoke.

"Three or four ships to be equipped by your Majesty. For undertaking such a daring enterprise, I would expect to be made an admiral and receive one tenth of the profits."

Having listened intently, João sat back on his throne.

"You expect to be made an admiral! You haven't the means to outfit your own ships and yet you have the audacity to ask to become an admiral? The admiralty is reserved for the nobility, the royalty in this land? Your conditions are outrageous. I will not seriously consider such a proposal."

"If it pleases Your Majesty, I would put aside all my own ambitions if you would set up a committee to study my proposals, I beg you . . . think of the wealth, the souls to be saved . . ." Cristóbal replied, keeping his head down, but watching the king waver.

João settled into his throne. "Very well," he snapped. "I will appoint Diego Ortez de Vilhegas, Master Rodriego and Jose Vizinho to study the matter." Each nobleman bowed as his name was called. "However, Señor Colón, their word will be final, and you, for your part, will have to come up with more modest requests."

"I am forever indebted to you, Your Majesty." He made an extravagant bow, and then was dismissed.

The plague swept through Lisbon in the summer of 1485, taking with it Colón's wife, Dona Felipa. She had lain in a fever for days and, though Cristóbal wiped her brow, changed her sheets, and lifted her head as he fed her clear broth, the disease proved too virulent. After suffering for three weeks, she succumbed on a stifling hot summer's night. The next day, little Diego walked solemnly behind the funeral procession; plague victims were buried as quickly as possible. The musicians played the dirge all the way to the cemetery where they had to wait for the burial. So many were dying that a line had formed to enter the graveyard where Dona Felipa would rest. As Cristóbal waited with his son, it seemed that all Lisbon was mourning. Everyone he met had lost someone dear. Finally, they were allowed to enter the graveyard. There were mounds of freshly dug graves all around them. Diego's small hand held tightly onto a red rose, and Cristóbal was saddened to see that the flower had withered before the coffin slid into the ground. He tried to stop his trembling as the grave diggers shoveled the earth over the coffin, but the grating sound of the dirt and gravel hitting the wood increased his despair. Finally, he watched Diego throw the wilted rose into the fresh mound, and then as the musicians began to play the funeral dirge once again, he led his little boy away. Clinging to Diego's hand, he wondered if they would survive the summer. It seemed an interminable amount of time as he waited to hear whether or not King João's committee would approve his plans. He turned back for a moment to stare at the fresh mound of earth left behind, then pulled the weeping Diego along.

Standing in their Spanish courtyard, Isaac pressed Rebecca close to him. They smiled shyly in remembrance of the night just past, and then he kissed her one more time, for he had just been called back to court. His experience with Jonathan had left him badly shaken, but now after a few days with Rebecca and his family, the warm sunshine and soft green velvet growth of spring's new leaves did much to strengthen him. He released Rebecca and took a running jump onto his horse, but when he landed, he felt the old, familiar sharp pain stabbing in his back.

"Since when do you mount a horse like that!" Though Rebecca was worried, she tried to make light of it, chastising him.

"I've always mounted my horse like that!" Isaac said, more hurt in pride than in pain. He wanted to rub his back but was determined to hide the pain from her.

Instinctively, Rebecca rubbed it for him.

"Isaac, we are not young anymore. You just can't do everything you used to."

"Nonsense! I'm as fit as I ever was. I just twisted it, that's all!" He pulled her hand from his back and kissed it. "I hope to be home before the end of the month."

"Just make sure you wear your cape," Rebecca called as he turned his horse toward the road. "And don't jump on your horse like that anymore. I've only got one husband!"

Though his back throbbed, he trotted away and waved without turning; it hurt too much.

From the way he held himself, Rebecca could see that he was in pain.

"The stubborn fool . . ." she muttered to herself. "He could have waited another day before he left, but, no, he has to start now." She watched him disappear over the crest of the hill. Life would be lonely until he returned. She would keep herself busy with the garden and her embroidery. Her family would bustle around her, and she would pretend to be content. Her little grandson, Jonathan, was chubby now and pitter-pattered about the house, chatting constantly. Her son Judah was in love with a beautiful Jewess, Rachel; her father was Rabbi Aboab, and both families very much wanted to make a match. Isaac would have to see to that when he returned. She helped her own daughter, Bathsheba, with the baby and supervised the cooking, but without Isaac at home, she always felt empty deep inside. She sat by the window at night and looked up at the moon and the stars. She felt closer to him when she gazed at the night sky, and after a long while, she felt sleepy. Sometimes she even found herself asleep by the window and realized the stars had grown soft with a kiss from the rising sun. At times like these, she smiled in the early morning light for it was one day closer to his return. He was her strength, her very life and breath. She realized, in the pain of his absence, just how much she loved him, and that she was bound to him as if he were the other half of her own body.

Isaac had to walk his horse all the way to Madrid. His old wounds ached, for the muscles had never really healed properly. He shifted his weight back and forth as he rode. He leaned forward, then backward, but nothing helped. Rebecca was right. He just wasn't as young as he used to be. He would have to mount his horse now like a stately old gentleman. It was humiliating.

The high treasurer, Luís de Santangel, greeted Isaac warmly. Abraham Senior and his son-in-law, Melamed, had already arrived. They tapped their fingers on the table, and it was obvious they had been waiting for him. Isaac winced as he sat down. The two days of riding had done nothing to improve his back. "Are you all right?" the high treasurer asked anxiously.

Isaac looked up, surprised by the concern in the man's voice. "Yes, I'm fine, just not as young as I used to be." The other men laughed.

"Isaac, when you consider the alternatives to growing old, a little pain now and then isn't so bad," Don Abraham said.

On a more serious note, Luís de Santangel began, "I've had a message from the king that preparations are being made for an attack on Málaga within the next year. Our most Catholic Monarchs are sure they will never be victorious while Muley Hassan and his brother roam freely in Granada. I want you to raise three million reals within the next two years. Isaac, you will have complete responsibility for the Siguenza and Guadalajara regions. You may appoint whomever you please to assist you, but the revenues must be collected quickly. This war on Málaga may prove to be the most decisive one."

Isaac tried to keep his face from showing any trepidation, but the name Málaga reverberated inside him, making the task of raising such an enormous sum seem overwhelming.

The high treasurer continued, "I understand you are now high treasurer for the Mendoza family. I sincerely hope you have adequate assistance for such a demanding task. I know that the family has some seven hundred and fifty castles."

"Eight hundred," Isaac quietly corrected him.

"Eight hundred!" The high treasurer's eyebrows lifted, and he let out a gasp. His reaction made Isaac wonder if indeed Mendoza's estates surpassed the king and queen's. It was, however, not a question to be asked, and only the high treasurer knew the answer.

"My son-in-law, Joseph Abravanel, was the treasurer to the late Duke of Viseu. He is used to dealing with large estates, and his experience will be invaluable to me now."

"Good! You will report directly to me."

"Yes, of course," Isaac answered. Don Abraham and Melamed, nodded. "That will be all then. Report to me as soon as the funds begin to come in. Enough business. I hope you will join me in a simple repast." The men stood and went into a private but luxurious banquet hall. A table had been prepared with a feast fit for twenty men. Silver candelabrums graced both ends and the candles flickered. Steam was still rising from hot breads and delicate rolls. A fish baked in a cake of white salt was served with saffron rice, and the aroma of the enticing dish reminded Isaac how hungry he was. The serious problems of the kingdom seemed to mellow with the aged red wine which had been poured into golden goblets.

As they ate, Abraham Senior turned to Isaac and quietly said, "I have the most fascinating news for you, my friend."

"Indeed?" Isaac asked after he had taken a long drink of wine.

"Yes. Just before I left the court in Cordova, I was asked to dine with Don Luis de la Cerda, Count of Medina Celi. He is a wonderful man, though rather stout for a knight. He has a large estate at Puerto Santa Maria. Many *cavalieros* and extraneous couriers were invited. A most curious fellow, a Cristóbal Colón, was amongst the guests. He claims he knows you."

"Yes, I know the man," Isaac answered, surprised to hear that Cristóbal was with the Count of Medina Celi in Spain.

"I am amazed, Isaac, that you would know such a man. He dresses in a simple brown friar's robe. I imagine his circumstances must be drastically reduced since you made his acquaintance. His red hair was poorly cut, shaggy, down to his shoulders, his sandals worn thin. He had a hungry look about his blue eyes, but the man could talk! My how he talked-"

"Of sailing the western ocean to find the lands of Khan."

"Yes! The men listening to him, myself included, didn't take him very seriously. Someone wanted to know if he might not try reaching Eden first, India second!" Don Abraham laughed.

Isaac asked, "And the count, did he laugh?"

"No, not at all! Can you imagine! He's even considering underwriting the enterprise! He asked me my opinion," Abraham Senior answered as he pulled a small bone from the fish.

"And what did you say?" Isaac asked as he sipped his wine, so intent on the conversation that he was not eating.

"I told him I thought the whole idea was preposterous! Imagine backing a voyage venturing out into that wild ocean. Even if there is land on the other side, how would one get there?" He laughed again and continued eating.

Isaac sat quietly, slowly rolling the red wine around the golden goblet. Don Abraham put down his knife and fork and wiped his lips.

"Isaac, you don't think such a voyage is possible do you? You would have advised against such an unsound investment wouldn't you? Imagine, sending this Cristoforo or Cristóbal, or whatever his name is, off into the green ocean."

"His name is Cristóbal, Cristóbal Colón, and I believe someday he will succeed in finding the land of Khan."

CHAPTER 25

Boabdíl, awakened by one of his servants, dressed in his white satin pantaloons and jacket, and quickly strode to the Hall of the Ambassadors to receive a courier. The courier, who was still dusty from the road, had not taken the time to change his clothes before addressing the caliph. He prostrated himself before Boabdíl, shaking from the fear of bringing bad news.

"I come with grave news, my caliph."

"What is it? Speak up! I wasn't roused just to have you prostrate yourself before me!" Boabdíl answered angrily.

"The caliph, your father, Muley Abou'l Hassan is dead!"

Boabdíl sank back onto his throne. The blood drained from his face, and when he looked up he saw his mother staring at the courier in disbelief.

"No!" she screamed. "No! It can't be true!" She pulled the hair on her head as she cried. All that she had done had been in a desperate effort to get Hassan back, to tear him away from his younger, more beautiful wife. She had thought if she were strong, if her son were strong, Hassan would crawl back to them someday. He would throw himself at her feet and beg forgiveness. But now it was all over; Muley Abou'l Hassan was dead. She stared up at her son. Boabdíl was the caliph, and he alone would rule.

"How did it happen?" Boabdíl asked the man, who had not dared to raise his head off the marble floor.

"Poison!" the man croaked.

"Who poisoned my father? Who?"

"Your uncle, El Zagal."

Boabdíl's astrologer and his high counselor had run into the room when they heard he had been awakened.

"My father is dead. This man says my uncle poisoned him. I will have my revenge." His hand went to his scimitar.

"No, sire, that would not be wise," the high counselor answered. "The Catholic Monarchs are ready to march against Málaga." Boabdíl turned to the astrologer who was consulting his charts of the stars.

"What do you see?" Boabdíl asked him. The old man brushed aside his long white beard and poured over his charts for a long time. His cracked brown lips moved as he silently read the stars and held up his wrinkled hand for all to wait. Then he pointed to the charts.

"The lion and the wolf will meet in battle. They will tear each other apart while the sly fox waits in his den. When the fighting is over, the fox will rise and lick the bones of his enemies." The old man looked up into the blue eyes of Boabdíl and then continued. "The stars say you must wait. Let your enemies destroy each other."

Boabdíl breathed a sigh of relief. He was rid of his mother's plotting, his father's vengeance. He sat back in his throne and allowed the full satisfaction of the evening settle over him.

Isaac rode beside Rebecca, who was seated in a litter, as they traveled across Castile to Andalusia. It was late September, and the sun beat down upon them as they swayed to the gentle rhythm of the horses' hooves. The flat land was parched under the summer sun, the grass standing out of the earth like brown thistles, the leaves on the olive trees brown and thirsty and the lazy white windmills crowning the few hills. The dust from the horses' hooves coated Isaac and his party until they appeared to be a part of the land as they traveled. Every hour, Isaac turned to look at Rebecca. He knew that her throat must be dry from the dust and the heat, but she had not complained. Isaac was escorting Rebecca to court so that she would finally be presented to the king and queen. Isabella had just recently passed a law allowing women to ride on horses rather than donkeys, but Rebecca had told Isaac that she preferred to be discreet and travel in her litter. The queen had requested Rebecca's presence at a ball to be given in honor of the Marquis of Cadiz and the Count of Cabra for their victory over the Moors on the banks of the Lopera River. Rebecca had never been to court, and both she and Isaac were anxious to make a favorable impression, not only for themselves but as representatives of the Jews of Spain.

Isaac ordered the litter placed gently on the ground and helped Rebecca down. She thanked her servants for their help and insisted that they drink before she did. Other servants were busy erecting a large tent just outside the small town they had passed. Silken pillows were spread out on the ground cloth, and the servants brought forth smoked rainbow trout, cheese, olives and wine, which had been purchased for their luncheon. Isaac took a long drink of water before he entered the tent. His face, streaked with dust and sweat, had tanned from the long exposure to the sun. There were bright silver strands in his dark hair, and wrinkles near his eyes that gave the impression that he was smiling. He was indeed pleased that he had regained the power and prestige he had known in Portugal. Though the dark cloud of the Inquisition hovered over them, he was content with all that he and his family had achieved. Bathsheba and Joseph were settled in his castle in Alcalá de Henares. Joseph was a great help to him in the tax collecting he had to do. Judah was establishing a fine medical practice and had spoken to him about marrying Rabbi Aboab's daughter, Rachel. That Isaac still had to arrange, though he was quite sure the rabbi would be pleased with the idea of such a match. He and Rebecca ate the delicate fish which came from the local rivers and rested for a few minutes before resuming their journey. A breeze blew the tent flaps open and, as he rested his head on Rebecca's lap, he could see the hills near Ciudad Real in the distance. He cringed to think of how close they were to Jonathan at that moment, but he dared not tell her. He had purposely made a wide circle around the city so that she would not search for him. Also, he could not bear to see the walls of the city where the lovely young Jewess, Jonathan's Inés, had died. He closed his eyes to shut out her anguished face, an image he was sure would never fade from his memory.

"If we start now, we'll cover more ground before nightfall," he said.

"I'm so grateful for the rest, Isaac. Though I'm anxious to get there, I don't think I can travel any faster. I'm slowing you down, aren't I?" she said, stroking his cheek.

"I wouldn't want to make this journey any other way, my love." He reached up to kiss her hand, then rested back in her lap. "This land makes me aware of my own mortality. As much as I love you and share my life with you, we must in the end part."

Rebecca looked deeply into his eyes and then a smile crept across her face.

"It is a barren land, isn't it?" she said. "And yet when I see it day after day like this, I do begin to appreciate a beauty here."

"Only you, Rebecca! Only you could see beauty here!" Isaac laughed.

"At the end of the day just before the sun sets, the land becomes red and pink and purple. It's almost as if a magic transformation takes place, and this dry brown becomes a rosy world. I almost expect to see fairies dance before me at that hour."

"You've gone mad!" he said, and they laughed. "Do you know I'm never so happy as when I'm with you?" Isaac confided.

"Is that so? We're such an old married couple. How boring, really! I'd imagine by now you've known a few other women?"

"There's never been anyone in my life but you. You know that," he whispered as he kissed her.

"I know," she whispered as she held him close, relieved to hear that there had never been anyone else. They kissed again, rose, and continued on their journey.

Seated on a dais draped in gold brocade, Queen Isabella and King Ferdinand were holding court in Córdoba. They both wore golden crowns and purple capes trimmed with ermine. Ferdinand held the golden scepter and wore a jewel-encrusted sword. Isabella's dress was of gold brocade. They appeared truly omnipotent and invincible as they sat there together. The Marquis of Cadiz and the Count of Cabra were seated on satin cushions to their right. Rebecca felt out of place amongst the ladies-in-waiting, clustered together in their bright dresses. The marquis' wife was dressed magnificently in a peacock blue gown, a high collar laden with pearls and a high pointed cap to match. Rebecca was dressed in a simple grey gown, and, though it was elegant, she knew it was not the fashion of the day. The women laughed and gossiped about the latest female conquest of King Ferdinand, and Rebecca sat discreetly to the side, only to join them when they curtsied to the king and queen and then to the marquis and count.

Isaac was one of the many *cavalieros*, and courtiers who bowed to the king, queen and honored quests. He found Rebecca an hour later leaning against a tapestry all alone looking like a dove lost amongst fine, exotic birds. He took her arm and escorted her to the center of the room, where they joined in the stately court dance. Isaac was so enamored that he didn't notice the many eyes in the room turning to them. Because Rebecca was new to the court, the noblemen were entranced by her beauty. King Ferdinand's eyes continuously turned to her. Rebecca's golden hair glistened in the candlelight as Isaac guided her about the room. Graceful in dance, her form was bewitching as she enjoyed the music.

Isabella also was watching, fascinated. She felt as if she had met Rebecca before, but couldn't put a time or place to their meeting. The extraordinary color of Rebecca's hair, the little creases in the corners of her eyes, the way she laughed seemed familiar. Then, suddenly, Isabella made the connection. She searched until she found the man, in the back of the room, engrossed in conversation and paying no attention to the dance. Isabella was surprised at the way the man had aged. Only a few months before he had fashioned the scorpion necklace she wore, but now the beautiful sheen in his golden hair was gone, his eyes were dull. As Isabella continued to watch him, she saw him lift his head, casually glance at the dancers, when suddenly his face turned white. He excused himself from his conversation and inched his way toward the dance floor, then stood not four feet from the gay dancers, his face frozen in pain. Isabella watched Isaac and Rebecca dance, oblivious to this steady stare, but as Isaac turned with the music, and saw him standing there, staring in disbelief, their eyes met for an instant. Isaac stumbled and tripped over Rebecca's feet. Isabella watched Juan Sanchez de Sevilla flee from the room. Turning to see what had so unnerved Isaac, Rebecca caught a glimpse of the back of Juan's head. Isaac, seeming to have recovered from his shock, discreetly escorted Rebecca from the dance floor. Fascinated, Isabella continued to watch Isaac as he looked about him to see if anyone had noticed them; then he glanced up at the throne, and they stared at one another. She smiled; he bowed, and then led Rebecca back to the dance.

"That was he, wasn't it?" Rebecca whispered as they continued to dance.

"Yes." Isaac had difficulty finding his voice. "I should have known he would be here."

"Oh, Isaac, it's so wonderful! I must find him!"

"No, Rebecca! You must not seek him out. The queen has made some connection between us. There are inquisitors in the room. We must keep dancing." He glanced over his shoulder at Fray Domingo Gomez, who was helping himself to roast suckling pig.

"I must!" she answered. "I must find him, just this once."

Breaking away from the other dancers, they made their way out of the room and into the courtyard of the Alcázar. Isaac was afraid to look back at the queen. Guests were still arriving, *cavalieros* giving directions to their servants. It was almost as crowded outside the great hall as inside. Isaac held Rebecca's hand firmly and guided her through the maze of people, but Jonathan was nowhere to be seen. As they headed toward the stables, they passed beautiful stallions caparisoned in shining armor and golden brocaded cloth, the plumes on their heads bobbing up and down as they pranced. A magnificent white stallion suddenly reared before them as they were about to enter the stable.

"What are you doing, you fools?" the rider shouted.

Isaac pushed Rebecca back and almost took the horse's hoof in his face. The rider pulled sharply on his reins as the horse reared again, and was about to turn and race away when he saw Isaac and Rebecca. Juan's face paled, and he dismounted, trying to calm the horse.

"There, there," he said quietly as he held tightly onto the reins. It's all right, my beauty, it's all right." He patted the horse until he grew calm. "You gave us quite a fright," Jonathan said when he turned back to Isaac.

"I'm sorry. I wanted to let you go, but Rebecca-" They turned and saw her standing against the cold stone wall, her eyes riveted on her brother.

"Rebecca." Juan held out his arms to her.

She rushed forward and embraced him.

"Oh I've missed you, Jonathan! I've missed you!"

He pried himself away from her, lifted her chin in his hand and gently kissed her cheeks. He whispered in a hoarse voice, "Rebecca."

"Come home, Jonathan. Please come back to us. I have children, a grandchild named after you . . . ."

Jonathan looked up at Isaac in surprise.

"I'm amazed you allowed a child to me named after me." He laughed without humor. "Rebecca," he continued, "I never wanted to leave you behind. I wanted to take you with me. I wanted to set you free as I was going to set myself free."

"You never understood, did you, my dear, dear brother? I had what I wanted; I didn't have to go beyond our Judería to find my happiness."

"Oh, yes, I did know Rebecca. I knew you wanted Isaac, and I stayed until I saw you were united with him." He looked up at Isaac. "It seems your happiness is a sweetness I can never share. I was in love-" his throat had tightened when he turned back to Rebecca, and he choked as the vision returned to him of Inés burning.

"I know. Isaac told me about her. What was her name?"

"Inés," he whispered his face taut with pain.

Rebecca folded her brother into her arms and rocked him back and forth as Isaac had done so many times for her.

"I'm sure I would have loved her, your Inés."

"We must never, never be seen together again. Too much suspicion would fall upon us if you, a Jewess, were seen talking to me, a Christian. Do you understand?"

"No, I don't understand!" She turned her angry eyes on Isaac. "Why must we stay here? Why can't we flee to another land, another kingdom where we can live in peace?"

"Because there is nowhere else to go! There is no land where Jews can live in peace and security!"

"Isaac is right. We have to live our separate lives and hope that no one will ever make a connection between us. You must promise me that you will never, never try to see me again."

"Yes, I promise."

After he and Isaac embraced, Jonathan mounted his horse and trotted out to the courtyard.

As Isaac and Rebecca made their way back to the ball, he accidentally brushed shoulders with a heavyset man standing in the dark shadows, and he shivered when he recognized Fray Domingo Gomez.

Once inside, Isaac and Rebecca were about to be seated when Isaac was approached by a page with the message that Isabella wanted a word with him, in private. Rebecca was seated alone, and Isaac was ushered into a small room draped with red and blue silken tapestries where Isabella sat on a simple wooden throne.

"You're not wearing the scorpion's sting tonight," the queen said and smiled.

Isaac looked down at the chain he was wearing.

"No, I haven't worn that chain in a long time." He was trying to assess just how much she had guessed when he noticed the necklace she wore. "May I?" he asked as he fingered the gold scorpion with ruby eyes.

"I have a very fine jeweler, Juan Sanchez de Sevilla."

"Really?" Isaac hedged.

Isabella took Isaac's hands into her own.

"Isaac, why are you so afraid of me? Do you think I couldn't see that your wife and Juan are related, brother and sister perhaps?"

"We have nothing to hide. Juan is my brother-in-law, but Rebecca and he have not seen each other in many years—until tonight."

"Then why are you so afraid? Do you think the inquisitors are after every Converso and his family?"

"No, Your Highness."

"Well, that is not the reason I've called you here. I want to know how your meeting went with my high treasurer. He's given you the figures?"

"Yes."

"And can you raise the sum?" When he hesitated, she added, "Isaac, when we are alone like this I expect your honest appraisal, not a court answer."

"It's a tremendous sum."

"I know that. Can you raise it?"

"The sun has been merciless on the crops this summer. We must have more rain. I think this heat also is aggravating the sickness that is ravaging the peasants. If the plague sweeps through all of Andalusia, it will cut down the number of workers in the fields, and the yield will be smaller."

Isabella knitted her brow.

"The crusade must not fail for lack of funds! We must find a way to pay for the arms, the ammunition, the bread for my men." She stood and grabbed his shoulders. "God has chosen me to unite our land. You must help me, Isaac. You must!"

"I will do all I can, Your Highness, but my work would be so much easier if this black cloud which envelops the land were lifted."

She pulled away from him and sat down again on her chair.

He knelt before her.

"The autos-de-fe, the Inquisition, it has gone too far. They have paralyzed your people with fear. In the fields, the peasants are afraid to talk to one another for fear of being accused of heresy."

Isabella held her head high.

"Do you know of anyone unjustly accused or burned at the stake, Isaac?"

He thought of Inés, a Marrano. In Isabella's eyes, she was guilty of heresy and deserved to be burned. And then he thought of his father, his arm uplifted to strike him when he was a child. This was no political game he was playing now, his people, Jewish people's lives, were at stake, and he had the power to influence a queen, if not a king.

"No, Your Highness," he whispered.

"God will not allow us to achieve our victory unless we cleanse the land."

Again he thought of his father, his stern words echoing around the room, "You will represent our people."

He tried again, "But even Cardinal Mendoza has condemned the auto-de-fé."

"What would you have us do, Isaac? Find these heretics and then just release them back into society so that they can continue to eat away at the foundation of the Church! No! We will never succeed; God will not allow us to triumph, if we do not carry the cross as well as the sword."

Still he would not give up, "Then perhaps another Grand Inquisitor . . . ."

"There is no one more dedicated to God's work than Fray Tomas de Torquemada! You shiver at the word torture, but you do not know the enemy he has to face. He must exorcise the devil and redeem souls for salvation. We must oust the Moslems and heretics, and then the land will be sanctified for God. I want Alhambra, Granada!"

He lifted his eyes to face her and was dismayed to see her face had turned red, her eyes ablaze with her passion.

"Yes, Your Highness," Isaac bowed. He could not bring himself to look into her eyes again. He knew he couldn't reach her, couldn't make her see the terror that was choking her people. He also wondered what would happen to the Jews once the Moors were ousted. After the *reconquista*, would they be the next to go? Defeated, he began to leave when she abruptly called him back.

When finally, he looked into her face again, her coloring has resumed its pale, seemingly undisturbed complexion. He was amazed at how quickly she gained control of herself. He did not think Rebecca could do that so quickly, but then again, Rebecca often surprised him with her emotional strength and power.

"Isaac, I'm prepared to sell everything, all my earthly possessions, to raise the sum for this great task. My jewels . . . ." She was fingering her golden scorpion. "Would you be able to sell my jewels if the need arises?"

"I will raise the funds, Your Highness. There will be no need to sell your jewels."

Queen Isabella nodded and then gazed out the window and looked as if she had turned to marble.

CHAPTER 26

After the long journey back from Córdoba, Rebecca was resting in the castle in Alcalá de Henares. The sun dappled its light against the rich red and blue tapestries hanging on the walls. Rebecca looked up from her embroidery as a bumblebee buzzed against the wall and then clumsily made its way back outside again. She was working on a fine linen tablecloth with pink, red and yellow roses. A long thick green vine wove the colorful flowers around the border of the cloth. She enjoyed working on the flowers more than the vine, but she decided she had better get on with that part and leave the colorful work for another day. She smiled as she stitched. Happy thoughts of the impending wedding of her son Judah with Rabbi Aboab's daughter, Rachel, filled her with joy. The cloth was for the bride's wedding chest. Rebecca was picturing a beautiful family scene with Judah at the head of his table, when her servant burst into her room. The girl's face was beet red, and she stammered as she spoke so that Rebecca could not understand her. She didn't ask the girl to repeat herself because she saw the men standing behind her. Recognizing the brown robes of the Dominican Order, Rebecca stood, though she felt weak.

"Why are you here? What do you want from us?"

"We want to ask you some questions. Please come with us, and if you answer to our satisfaction you may return home soon."

Blood was pushing so hard against her ears that she was sure she hadn't heard the friar correctly. "You want me? You want me to come with you? But why? Why would the Inquisition want me? I am a Jewess, not a Marrano, not a Christian heretic!"

"Only to ask some questions, my lady. You have nothing to fear. Please come with us now."

"But my husband . . . . I can't just leave here. My husband will be home soon. You can talk to him. He will tell you I have done no wrong. He is treasurer to the king and queen. Surely you've made a terrible mistake."

"Are you Rebecca Abravanel?"

"Yes," she scarce whispered.

"Then there is no mistake. The Inquisition wishes to ask you some questions. There is no need for you to be afraid. As you say, you've done no wrong."

"Then why must I go with you now? Why can't you wait until my husband returns? I am sure I can answer your questions right here. Why must I go with you?" she begged. She knew few if any ever returned from the inquisitional dungeons.

"These are delicate matters that can be discussed only in the private chambers of the tribunal. The Grand Inquisitor himself has requested this investigation."

Rebecca's heart seemed to stop beating with the reference to the Grand Inquisitor. "Tomas Torquemada," she whispered in disbelief. "Why, why would he want me?" she asked herself as the men enveloped her.

Suddenly her younger sons, Joseph and Samuel, ran into the room.

"Mama! Where are they taking you?" Samuel cried as Joseph held him back.

"Mama?" Joseph whispered. "Mama . . . they're not taking you . . . ." But before he could finish his sentence, she was quickly escorted outside.

Just arriving home, Judah was dismounting from his horse when he saw them ushering his mother into the courtyard, his two younger brothers clinging to one another. "What are you doing?" he shouted angrily at the friars. Menacing with their spears, five guards left the horses they had been tending and surrounded Judah. "Where are you going with my mother?" he shouted again.

When she heard Judah's voice, Rebecca looked up.

"It's all right. Tell father what's happened. They want to ask me some questions, and then they will let me come home. Reassure the boys, Judah. I will be all right . . . . isn't that right, father?"

"No harm will come to your mother if she answers our questions."

"No harm! No harm!" Judah roared. "Then tell me, tell me why no one ever returns from these interrogations?" His face was red, every muscle in his body was straining as he lunged at the friars. The guards forcefully gripped him. He kicked the strong men holding him in a vise-like grip. Breaking free for a moment, he was brought crashing to the ground by another guard, who then stood over him pointing a spear at his heart.

"No! Judah, no!" Rebecca screamed. "Judah, it will be all right. I have nothing to fear. I will tell them what they want to know, and then they will let me come home."

"No one comes home!" he cried as guards held his arms and legs. "Mother!" he cried, "Mother, don't let them take you away, don't let them." Writhing, he struggled to free himself. But his efforts were futile. He watched as she mounted a horse and was escorted out of the castle.

Isaac returned home with his nephew Joseph and Moses late that night. From the far distance, he could see that something was wrong, for the castle was aglow. It was obvious that no one inside was asleep. He galloped into the courtyard and ran into the main hall, where his family waited. They fell silent upon his entry, and as he glanced from Judah to Bathsheba to Joseph, realizing Rebecca was not among them, he thought she was dead. He closed his eyes, praying it was not so.

"What has happened?"

Judah stepped forward, the two Josephs and the youngest son, Samuel, all standing behind him.

"They've taken mother. I was here when they took her away," Judah said.

"Who took my Rebecca?" Isaac shook his son. "Who!" he cried.

"Guards of the inquisition."

Isaac's hand went to his heart, and he stumbled backwards. His son, Joseph, ran to catch him while the other two young men held Judah, who had fallen to his knees.

"I tried to stop them," Judah continued in a broken voice, weeping. He looked up at Isaac's white face, "I tried, but she screamed when they forced me to the ground with a spear . . . so . . . so they took her . . . ."

Isaac saw specks of lights before his eyes, and a blinding pain shot through him. Joseph and Samuel ran to Isaac, helped him into his study, and gently laid him down. Isaac closed his eyes. He had to wait for the pain to stop. It was precious time wasted, but he could not fight down the pain which was so severe it blinded him. Judah ran to his medicines and mixed some herbs. Samuel and Joseph lifted Isaac so that he could drink the brew, and then gently eased him back down. Bathsheba sat by her father's side. His eyes still closed, Isaac gently stoked her hair.

"What will we do, Father? We can't let them keep her."

"I will see to it that she is immediately released."

Though he tried to fight the drugs, Isaac fell asleep. Judah kneeled beside Bathsheba and gently rubbed his father's damp forehead.

"Will he be all right?" she asked.

"If Mother is released, he will be fine. If not . . ." his voice broke . . . "then I don't know."

"She was working on a cloth for Rachel," Bathsheba began to say, but she choked on her words. "She was always doing something for someone else, always."

"She is not dead!" Judah answered forcefully. He stood and started to leave the room. His brother-in-law stopped him.

"Where are you going?" Joseph asked.

"To the tribunal. I'll enter hell itself if I have to in order to bring her back."

"You'll go to hell and won't come back if you leave tonight. Wait until tomorrow and then I'll ride with you."

"And let her sleep with the devil!" Judah shouted. "It's my fault that she's there, and I will release her!"

"It's not your fault." A cold, unfamiliar voice startled them. "It's mine."

The children turned to him as he stood in the doorway, and though they had never seen him before, he could see that each one silently recognized him and cast their eyes away. Judah and Joseph walked over to him, so startled that for a moment they were unable to speak.

"You come to us now? Tonight of all nights! Do you think we don't know who you are?" Judah finally found his voice.

"My child was named for you!" Joseph shouted. "I spit on you!"

Bathsheba ran to her husband and slapped him across the face.

"You will not talk to him this way!"

"Your mother was just taken by the inquisition because of him! You'll not tell me how to talk!" Joseph answered.

Bathsheba ignored Joseph and walked over to Jonathan.

He stared into her eyes and shivered. They were his eyes, his mother's eyes. He stepped back, for the resemblance of this young woman to his mother was striking.

"Bathsheba," he whispered.

"Yes," she said, smiling, "and you are Jonathan."

"Yes," he answered as if he were speaking to the dead. These young people—ach of their faces reminding him of someone he had loved—had grown to adulthood without him. He entered the room and touched Joseph's shoulder, but he cringed.

"So like Samuel," he said sadly. "Where is your father?"

"Father died a year ago," he answered curtly.

"Here or in Portugal?"

"Here." He cast his eyes down.

Jonathan moved on and gazed at Samuel, then stopped at Judah.

"You were here when they took her?"

"Yes." Judah also spoke curtly to his uncle.

"Did they say why they were taking her?"

"No, only that they wanted to question her."

"Why did they take her? What do they want to know?" Jonathan cried, on the verge of unraveling. Why did he think he could just come back into their lives. No, Isaac was wrong, he could never come home.

"To question her about you, I suppose!"

"Judah!" Bathsheba cried. "Stop . . . stop it! You know the man has suffered enough. You know that." She pleaded with her brother.

Judah didn't heed her.

"Why has he suffered? Why did the Jewess from Ciudad Real die . . . ."

There was an audible gasp around the room.

Bathsheba slapped him and then in her fury turned on all of them.

"What is the matter with you? With all of you? Jonathan has come home! He has come back! Isn't that enough? Isn't this what Mother and Father have dreamed about all these years. What greeting is this? What a way is this to treat our uncle!"

"I deserve no better," Jonathan said softly. He walked over to Isaac, who was well sedated. He kneeled before him and took his hand in his own. "Forgive me," he whispered to Isaac, kissing his hand, tears streaming down his cheeks. "I deserve my welcome and not the loving embraces I would have received from you and Rebecca. They are right, my friend, my brother. I deserve no better from my family whom I deserted so long ago. But forgive me, Isaac. Please recover from this terrible shock and then find room in your heart to forgive me. I didn't know Rebecca had been taken, but I was worried. So I came, too late to keep her safe, but not too late to save her." He kissed Isaac's hand again, rose, and left the room.

Bathsheba threw on her cape as she ran outside after him, grabbing his arm.

"Don't go, Jonathan. Father will be furious with us, when he finds out what has happened. Please, my brothers-my husband, they are angry. This was a terrible night for you to have returned. But in the morning, father will go to the tribunal and have her released. If you go now, they will have both of you. Please, please, just stay the night."

Jonathan held her face up to the moonlight.

"You're so like my mother. Do you know that?" She nodded yes. "You must promise me something, Bathsheba. You must promise me to be happy. Be happy for me, for my dead mother, for all of us."

He kissed her cheek, the tears streaming down, mounted his horse, and rode from the castle toward the tribunal.

"Stop, please, don't go! Please don't go . . . ." Bathsheba cried, falling to the ground weeping.

Jonathan rode across the countryside, the wind swirling around him. The faces of the young people, the only people in the world who would ever know that he had existed, kept flashing before him. They held no love for him, but thought of him as traitor—all except for Bathsheba. He smiled when he thought of Bathsheba. He had run so far that he had come full circle, but everything he had left behind was gone. There was only one thing in his life that mattered. There was only one thing left that could right all the mistakes of his past. He had to free Rebecca. If it took every ounce of his own blood to do it, he would prevent her dying for his sins. His mind was bent on this one thought as he galloped on his white stallion, Pegasus, toward Toledo, toward the tribunal of the Inquisition, toward Rebecca.

The dawn was just breaking when he arrived at the walls of Toledo. He had to wait for the gatekeeper to open the heavy doors of the city. He waited as old men pulled wagons and guided donkeys out into the fields for a workday to begin. Dogs barked merrily and nipped at their feet. Goats, chickens, and geese scurried in front of his horse. Well-dressed merchants were coming up the dusty road, having traveled through the night like Jonathan, to be there when the gates opened. As Jonathan passed into the city that morning, Pegasus was admired by all who saw him. Jonathan made his way up the twisting, narrow cobbled streets, up toward the tribunal. He arrived at the cathedral and slowed his pace. The sun was warm on his back as he rounded the bend to the building behind the great church. He dismounted and tethered his horse on a grassy knoll.

He gazed out beyond the stone walls of the city and watched the water of the Tajo River gently roll. It seemed so peaceful, so cool, and crystal clear from where he stood. A hawk circled gracefully above him in the blue sky.

"I wish I could be like you, my friend," he whispered. "I wish I could fly through blue sky and clouds and never have to face the misery we have made for ourselves here."

He turned away from the great bird, from the rolling river, and pounded upon the doors of the dreaded tribunal.

When Isaac woke the same morning, the blinding pain in his head had eased. He felt weak and had trouble sitting up. The left side of his body wouldn't move the way he wanted it to. He looked at his fingers and forced them to open and close. He had no trouble moving his right arm and hand, but he could hardly move his left. Bathsheba was holding him as he sat on the edge of the bed. Judah was standing before him. He looked up into his son's concerned eyes and noticed he was dressed to ride.

"Where are you going at this hour?" His words were slurred, but his mind was sharp as he gazed closely at his son.

"Was Jonathan here last night?" he asked.

Judah looked at Bathsheba, then back at his father. "Yes, we thought you were asleep."

"I dreamt he was here and that he spoke to me, but I can't remember what he said."

"He asked you to forgive him," Bathsheba answered softly.

"Forgive him? I told him once before, it's not mine to forgive." He answered, feeling angry at his inability to move as he wanted. "Where is he now? I want to see him."

Judah glanced at Bathsheba again. She answered for her brother.

"He's not here, Father. He left."

"Where? Where did he go?" Isaac felt as if hands were squeezing his heart.

"Toledo," Judah answered.

Outraged, Isaac stood, Bathsheba holding him so that he wouldn't fall over. With all the strength left in his body, he shook Judah.

"You let him go? You know that's why they took her, and you let him go!"

Judah lowered his head. Isaac limped toward the door, his heart pounding like a heavy hammer. How could they have let him go? His own

233

children let Jonathan go, he thought as Judah ran to him, grabbing his arm, stopping him.

"Where do you think you're going? You must lie down. Father, this attack will get worse if you don't rest! Joseph and I are ready to ride to Toledo. Younger Joseph and Samuel have already left for Córdoba to inform the queen and Cardinal Mendoza about mother's incarceration. We will have her released in no time. I promise you I will not leave Toledo without her. You must rest or this condition will worsen."

"I will bring my wife home!" Isaac pushed past Judah. Joseph had been waiting outside. The two men had to help Isaac onto his horse; then they mounted their own, and the three riders turned toward Toledo.

Rebecca had spent the night in a clean whitewashed room. Though there were no luxuries, it was not a cell. She felt somewhat relieved by her decent accommodations and hoped that they would indeed let her go after she answered their questions. The door was locked from the outside, however, and she could hear the guard who was stationed there. When the dawn broke she was given a clean bowl of water for washing and some porridge, which she didn't touch. She sat quietly on the edge of the bed she had hardly disturbed, trying to stay calm as she waited to be called. After what seemed to be several hours, she heard the footsteps of several guards. A key ground against the rusty lock, and she was ushered out of her room and into the courtroom of the tribunal.

As Rebecca stared at the friars dressed in the dark robes, seated at a long wooden table. One friar sat above the others on a wooden throne. He was extremely thin and his eyes seemed to burn right through her as if he were examining her soul. She felt naked before his glaring eyes. Fray Domingo began the questioning.

"Do you swear by the Creator who made heaven and earth and the sea and the sands and wrote his name in four letters Jot, He, Vav, He and gave the law to Moses on Mount Sinai to tell the truth in answer to the questions which may be propounded to you by this tribunal?"

"I do," she answered in a very small voice.

"If you so do, may the Creator have mercy on you. But if you fail so to do may the Creator destroy you!"

A friar of the tribunal stood.

"Her name is Rebecca Abravanel. She is a native of Lisbon, Portugal, recently settled outside Toledo. She is forty-five years old and wife of the queen's treasurer, Don Isaac Abravanel. She was arrested yesterday on the suspicion of influencing a new Christian to relapse and was committed to one of the secret rooms of this tribunal."

The friar asked, "Is this the truth?"

Intimidated, she answered in a stronger voice, "I am Rebecca Abravanel, but I have influenced no one to relapse."

"You are a Jewess."

"Yes, I am a Jewess," she answered.

"Your maiden name, please."

The question was so unexpected that she couldn't answer. "What?"

"Please state before this tribunal your maiden name."

"Rebecca Ben Ezra," she whispered her throat so tight she could barely speak.

"Speak up!" he demanded.

"Rebecca, Rebecca Ben Ezra Abravanel is my full name," she answered in a strong, clear voice. She had done no wrong and guessed that they had arrested her to harass Isaac, but now she realized this was much deeper, more insidious. She stared at the man who sat upon the wooden throne—the man she knew to be Tomas Torquemada. In her anger, she found strength she had not known she possessed, and she no longer felt afraid.

"Are you related to Jonathan Ben Ezra, known in Spain as Juan Sanchez de Sevilla?"

The question was so unexpected that she felt as if they had thrown cold water over her. What did they know of Jonathan, she wondered frantically.

"I don't understand the question," she answered.

She suddenly realized what they were after—that Jonathan was her brother, that they had spoken, that she had begged him to come home to them, to Judaism, the crime that demanded the death sentence, that with her confession of heresy, Isaac would be forced to leave Isabella's service, and she herself could be burned at the stake.

Suddenly, the door to the tribunal flew open. Having stabbed two guards at the door, Jonathan stood before the friars, pointing his blood stained sword.

"I will have my revenge," he cried as he ran toward the inquisitors, who tried to flee from their seats. Fray Domingo could not budge and began to scream for the guards. Five ran into the room, overpowering Jonathan, holding him to the ground with swords pointed.

"Kill him!" Gomez roared. "Kill him!"

A guard was about to stab him through the heart when the Grand Inquisitor stood and shouted, "No!"

Everyone in the room froze. Torquemada's veins stood out like ropes wrapped around his head and his voice was tight as if there were a vise around his neck. He turned to Rebecca.

"Is this man your brother?"

Staring at Jonathan with a sword at his heart, she could not speak.

"I said, is this man your brother?" Tomas Torquemada repeated. "If he is your brother we will spare his life, if not, we will be done with him."

"I've never seen this woman in my life!" Jonathan interrupted.

Torquemada's face turn beet red.

"Then why, why did you kill my guards and threaten our lives like this, Juan Sanchez de Sevilla?"

"Because you murdered my fiancée! You murdered my Inés!" he said vehemently.

"Take him away," the Grand Inquisitor said in disgust. As Jonathan was dragged out of the room, he stared at Torquemada, not daring to look in Rebecca's direction.

"I am unconvinced. He is your brother, and we have a witness who saw the two of you together in Córdoba," Torquemada said, trying to regain his composure.

"I have done nothing wrong." Rebecca said, her head held high though guards were holding both of her arms.

"If you don't cooperate with this tribunal, it will grow most unpleasant for you," Torquemada said before storming out.

"Take her away," Gomez said, following Torquemada as quickly as he could.

The two guards wrenched Rebecca to her feet. They held tightly onto her arms as they tripped over the dead bodies of the men lying in the doorway. They dragged her down a hallway and a long winding stairway to the dungeons below. She was thrown into a dark, foul cell. She slipped on something wet and slimy, but it was too dark to see what it was. Aware that Jonathan's violent act could only complicate her plight, Rebecca felt a despair she had never known. Cold, alone in the dark putrid cell, she wept for Jonathan, for Isaac, for herself. The walls seemed to close in around her so that she wanted to scream, but she knew they wanted to hear her cries for mercy, for help, so she stifled them. They wanted her to confess, to say that she had begged Jonathan to return to the family, to Judaism. Slowly, carefully, feeling around the edge of the cell, she made her way to the back where she found a rotted wooden bench. She sat down, wrapping her arms around herself to quiet her racing heart.

CHAPTER 27

Isaac's sons Joseph and Samuel, raced to Cordova to inform Queen Isabella of Rebecca's incarceration, while he, Judah, and his son-in-law, Joseph, rode to Toledo to demand her release. As the horses trotted along, Isaac felt some sensation returning to his left arm and hand. He looked down at his fingers, still clenched in a tight fist from his first effort to hold the reins, and flexed and relaxed them until he could move them. He knew he had been gravely stricken but would not give in to it. He stretched his neck and twisted his head back and forth to try to feel some sensation, but the numbness would not go away, and it left him feeling frightened, vulnerable.

"Are you all right, father?" Judah asked.

"Yes, I'm better." He tried to kick his horse in an effort to ride faster, but his leg didn't move the way he expected it to. A lump rose in his throat, but he would not give into the feeling of desperation creeping over him.

"Let's not go too fast . . . ." Judah tried to soothe him. "We'll get there." He paused a moment. "When we do, father, what are your plans?"

"I intend to speak to the Grand Inquisitor and insist on her immediate release. When did Joseph and Samuel leave for Cordova?"

"About twenty-four hours before we did."

"If they rode continuously with only short rests and a change of horses, they could arrive in another two days."

"Do you think Queen Isabella will intervene if we cannot secure Mother's release?"

"Quite sure," Isaac answered

"And Jonathan?" Joseph interrupted the conversation between father and son. "What will become of him?"

Isaac looked at Joseph, then back at Judah, but said nothing. With an enormous effort he kicked his horse, which took off in a gallop, and Judah and Joseph followed close behind.

They arrived at nightfall just before the great gates of Toledo closed, and then headed for the Judería and Judah's bride in Rabbi Aboab's home. The rabbi opened his arms to Isaac, embraced him as a brother and offered the three men a simple meal of mutton and bread. After the meal, Isaac, the rabbi and Joseph discussed Rebecca's perilous situation while Judah and Rachel talked quietly by the hearth.

"I'm going to take you far, far away from here, my love." He kissed the top of her forehead and held her hands in his.

"Where? Where would we go, Judah? With Luís de Santangel, Gabriel Sanchez and Abraham Senior the Jews are safe. They will protect us. They will not allow the Inquisition to destroy us. I'm sure your father will secure her release.

"They are determined to oust the Moors from Granada. Can't you see that we are next in line for expulsion? Father just doesn't see this? And do you also think they will release my uncle?" Judah grimly added, "I don't think so."

As Judah stared at their hands so tightly intertwined, he said, "I have something for you." He took out a slip of paper and handed it to her.

"Judah, my poet," she said softy as she unwrapped the paper and began to all the pain he kept hidden in his heart over losing little Isaac. She began to weep. He held her in his arms.

"It's not finished," Judah said before she could say anything.

Rachel folded the paper neatly and tucked it next to her heart.

"Wherever you must travel, wherever you go, I will follow you, Judah," she whispered.

"We will find a land where we can raise our children and live in peace. I promise you," Judah replied. He looked up when the rabbi broke into their conversation. "You won't leave us, Isaac! We need you desperately. I'm sure the queen will secure her release. She will not forsake you."

"And Jonathan? What will become of him?" Isaac said bitterly, though he couldn't look at the rabbi, who also had turned his face away. Both men knew the answer to that.

"Do you want me to go with you, Isaac?" The old man's lips quivered.

"No. If I don't return, see to it that the children are wed." He glanced over toward Judah and Rachel. "See to it that their children know who they are, and the glory of their past."

"Even if it has to be underground as secret Jews," his son Joseph interrupted.

"Never! Never!" Isaac answered him angrily. "We will die first. Let them burn us at the stake if they will, but we will not forsake our Lord."

"I'm afraid our future may lie with those who hide our sacred traditions in cellars and at the bottoms of false wells," Joseph said in disgust.

"No! If it ever comes to that, then we must leave this land. We will wander the face of the earth as foretold in Isaiah, and someday, someday our people will return to the Promised Land, and it will be our kingdom once again." But Isaac felt the strength in his arm and leg failing. He flexed his fingers, which were growing stiff again.

Rabbi Aboab took a deep breath. "Yes, Isaac, you are right. We will wander the earth if we have to, but we will never forsake Him." He was growing alarmed at Isaac's sallow complexion and the slump of his shoulders. "Come, now you must lie down. Judah!" he called sharply.

Judah ran to Isaac's side. Leaning heavily against Judah and Joseph, Isaac turned to leave.

"Where are you going at this hour?" the rabbi demanded.

"We will sleep in our own home on the other side of the plaza," Isaac answered.

"No, I forbid it. Judah, you will not move your father another step. You will all stay here. Isaac will sleep in my room tonight."

Isaac was too weak to resist. They guided him into the rabbi's chambers, and Judah held his hand until he fell asleep.

There was no day or night for Rebecca as she sat on a wooden bench in the filthy four-by-six foot cell in the dungeons of the Inquisition. Horror overwhelmed her as she gazed beyond the iron bars at dead men hanging from hooks in the stone walls. Gently swinging back and forth, their bodies were slowly decaying. A woman who had been moaning in a cell to her right when Rebecca was first incarcerated now lay silent. Rebecca brought her legs up close to her body, for she didn't trust the putrid smelling ground. Her body tensed when something scurried across the floor. The hairs on her back rose as another and another scurried back and forth in front of her. Suddenly, she felt a bite on her leg, and she screamed. She stood on the bench, and as she struck at the dark, her hand brushed against a hairy creature. The long skinny tail of a rat slithered through her hand as it raced away. Not a moment after that, another rat ran across the bench, and Rebecca began to scream and wave her arms out of sheer panic in an effort to keep them at bay. She stopped when she sensed they were gone. Her eyes were growing more accustomed to the dark, and she could see the hairy bodies with beady red eyes staring at her from all directions. She sensed now that she was the invader; she was in their lair. They began to swarm again, more brazen, and Rebecca began to scream again and again until above her own voice she heard, "The earth is the Lord's, and the fullness thereof; The world, and they that dwell therein. For He hath founded it upon the seas, And established it upon the floods. Who shall ascend into the mountain of the Lord? And who shall stand in His holy place?"

She knew the voice, her brother's voice. "Jonathan!" she cried. She ran to the cell's iron bars and screamed, "Jonathan," but he continued as if he hadn't heard her.

"Psalm 24, Rebecca, recite it with me, He that hath clean hands and a pure heart . . . ." His voice rose, "Who hath not taken My name in vain, And hath not sworn deceitfully." His voice now reverberated throughout the dungeon. "He shall receive a blessing from the Lord."

"Jonathan, Jonathan." Rebecca's sobs echoed in the silence that followed. "I love you! Isaac loves you. Don't confess that you were a Jew. Don't break down before them. Isaac will secure your release. I know he will."

In a voice so quiet that it frightened her, he answered, "God will not forsake you, Rebecca, but I must do my penance. I must humble myself before Him, and then He will take me back into His fold. I have sinned against Him, Rebecca. In the torture of the flame, my soul will be cleansed and I will be a Jew once again."

"No! Jonathan, no!" Heedless of the filthy floor, the rats, she fell to the ground and began to weep, then finding strength she did not know she possessed; she clung onto the bars and pulled herself back up. She had to make him see that all was not lost. She loved him, her beautiful, golden-haired brother. "You must not give in to them. Say what you will about Isaac, about me, but don't give into them. Then you can at least become a Marrano, secretly, secretly . . . ." She began to weep.

"There is hope for you, Rebecca, my sister . . . ." He was sobbing. He will not desert you in your hour of need. Isaac will secure your release. I know he will."

They could hear guards clanging down the stairs.

"They have come to release you!" Jonathan said, his sobbing ceased, and his voice was full of hope as it echoed from the back of his cell.

241

Grasping the iron bars, Rebecca watched the guards walk past her cell. She seemed to have turned to stone as she watched them drag Jonathan, like a dead man, toward the torture chamber. She fell to the floor and cared not that rats ran over her. "I love you," she wept. "My brother, I love you."

With Judah and Joseph standing at his side, Isaac knocked on the wooden doors of the tribunal. Rusted iron spikes jutted out every three inches in the wood so that no intruder would be able to push it open. Perspiration ran down his cheeks as he waited. He flexed his fingers back and forth trying to feel the muscles work. As the sun rose higher in the sky, he noticed a pure white stallion tethered on a grassy knoll nearby. He walked over to the animal, the young men close behind. He had begun to stroke it gently, when suddenly he recognized him. "Jonathan's horse." They walked back to the door and pounded on it again. "King's men! Open up!" The thick, heavy doors creaked open.

"Your names?" a friar asked.

"I am Don Isaac Abravanel, the queen's treasurer. I wish to speak with the Grand Inquisitor."

The friar's eyes opened wide. "No one can see the Grand Inquisitor without proper papers."

With his one good arm, Isaac grabbed him as three guards surrounded them.

"You tell the Grand Inquisitor that the queen's treasurer is here and wishes to speak to him, now!" He threw the man back against the wall. The friar brushed himself off, rearranged his dark robe.

"I will inform His Eminence that you are here." He nodded to the guards who continued to surround Isaac, Judah, and Joseph.

Fray Tomas de Torquemada was kneeling before his altar when the friar lightly knocked.

"Enter," he said.

"Your Eminence." The friar knelt. "Don Isaac Abravanel is here and wishes an audience with you."

"Have him searched and then bring him to me," Torquemada said without looking up.

"Yes, Your Eminence. There are two other young men with him as well. Shall we let them all in?"

"No, just Don Isaac."

The friar bowed and left the sanctuary. Torquemada stood, pulled the dark hood over his head and made his way toward the tribunal's bench. He sat down with great satisfaction on his high throne.

The friar returned outside to Isaac.

"Only Don Isaac may enter," he informed them.

"I will not let my father go in there alone!" Judah began when Isaac interrupted.

"I will be all right. Wait for me here."

When the thick, heavy doors creaked open, Isaac limped forward into the tribunal, flinching as the doors slammed shut behind him. He was escorted down a long corridor, and then roughly shoved by a guard into a room where suddenly he was face to face with Fray Tomas de Torquemada for the second time in his life. Torquemada's eyes seemed redden, his lips so thin Isaac could barely see them move as he spoke.

"Don Isaac, we meet again."

Isaac suddenly felt as if he had fallen into some sort of trap, wondering if Torquemada would release him or if he had taken Rebecca in order to incarcerate him. He didn't care. He couldn't stand being on the outside if Rebecca was in here, somewhere in here. Suppressing his rising fear for her, which was threatening to overwhelm him, he thought for a brief moment of David facing Goliath; David had been able to slay the giant. He thought of his father and how he had always been so proud that they were descendants of David, half expecting Isaac to be a King David. But he wasn't David, he was only Isaac, Isaac Abravanel. He could feel the hot breath of Torquemada when he shouted, "What? What do you hope to accomplish? Do you think I will allow you to corrupt my beautiful Isabella? Her soul is pure! It is white, but each day that you serve her, each day that you stand by her side, she is tarnished in the sight of the Lord!"

"It's a pity that Cardinal Mendoza doesn't see this tarnish," he heard himself say in a voice much stronger than he ever thought he could muster.

"Mendoza!" Torquemada hissed from his throne. "Mendoza has Jewish blood. He cannot see what I see."

"And what is it that you see? What evil do I and my people represent to you? We do not want to convert you. We only ask to live here in peace."

"No, never! Every day you and your people remain, souls are turned away from Him. You steal away to dark places to worship your God, and like the devil, you take souls with you. I will not allow this blasphemy to continue! I will not rest until every heretic has been routed and burned."

"But my wife is not a heretic! Let her go!"

"She has been seen conversing with a heretic. She was trying to wrestle his soul away from God. However, I will let her go on one condition and on one condition only." Isaac held his breath. "You resign from the queen's service; then you can have your bitch!"

Isaac's hand went for his sword, which had been removed. The friar's eyes continued to beat down upon him as he turned and left the tribunal. This Goliath had not been slain.

The congregation had been assembled and were praying for the release of Rebecca Abravanel. The service over, Rabbi Aboab placed the Torah back in the Ark. A young moon was rising, shedding a dull light on the blue and gold tiles in the synagogue, El Transito. The Hebrew letters of the psalms written across the walls glowed in the soft candlelight. The rabbi had closed the Ark and turned to face the congregation when he saw Isaac, like a lifeless stone figure, standing in the doorway. The old men turned to stare at Isaac and his sons, Judah and Joseph, a few paces behind him, as they walked up to the front pew and sat down.

The rabbi concluded the evening prayers; the congregation quietly got up and let the great men alone. Rabbi Aboab sat quietly in the back pew, and Isaac walked up to the Ark. As he kneeled before it, only the soft flicker of the candlelight lit the room. He prayed for Rebecca's release, shuddering to think of her locked up with that madman. He ran his fingers through his hair and prayed:

"Dear Lord, release her, please dear God, tell me what to do. Should I give up my position? Is this what you want? I cannot let my wife languish in prison! Please tell me what it is that I must do!" His eyes closed, an image of David bringing the sword down upon Goliath's head swam before him. The young hero raised the bloody head for all the warriors to see, but suddenly the head was Prince Fernando's then the hair in his hand turned blond and the head was Jonathan's.

"No!' Isaac cried. "No!" and he collapsed.

Isaac lay in his villa in Toledo. He had prayed and fasted, waiting for some word from his queen. If anything happened to Rebecca, he did not want to go on living. He no longer fought the numbness from the stroke but allowed his body to grow stiff. When he closed his eyes, he pictured himself sleeping next to her and thought of the warm soft curves of her back that touched him when she slept. Occasionally, he'd wake, tortured by dreams of the night of Judah's birth when he almost lost her. How frightened he had been then, but not so feeble and hopeless as he felt now. He had had the strength to fight, but now tears filled his eyes when he wondered how he could save her. The days had rolled into weeks when at last Joseph and Samuel rode through the stone gates of Toledo and to their father's house. Isaac was so weak that he could barely lift his head to greet them. Joseph kneeled by Isaac's side and gently stroked his father's head.

"The queen was enraged when she heard that mother was incarcerated. Fray Tomas de Torquemada has been summoned to Cordova, and mother is to be immediately released."

Isaac closed his eyes and cried, "Shema Yisraeil, Adonai elo heinu, Adonai echad."

Rachel came in with a bowl of steaming broth, and Judah held Isaac's head while he sipped the nourishment. "Everything will be all right now, father. She will be here soon. Joseph and I will bring her home now." Judah stroked his forehead again, and Isaac closed his eyes.

He opened them a few hours later at the sound of hoof beats. He rose and stumbled over to the window to look out. Far below, he could see a religious army dressed in brown, crossing the bridge over the Tajo River. A silver cross was held at the head of the party, and Isaac could make out the narrow, bony figure of Torquemada as he raced southward on the dusty road. Isaac was so engrossed in the sight of the entourage leaving that he did not hear the sounds of joy within his own home until he suddenly turned from the window and saw Rebecca, thin and pale, standing alone in the doorway.

CHAPTER 28

All of Cordova celebrated the great Christian victories in Benamaquex, Coin, and Cartama. The bulls ran through the cobblestone streets toward the bullring. Men drank wine from earthenware jugs and strummed guitars while their women danced, and the children cried out in delight. Though not as boisterous as the festivities outside the Alcázar, music and laughter filled the great banquet hall. Isabella and Ferdinand sat at the head of the table as the celebration swirled about them. Noblemen and their ladies danced. Jesters somersaulted and capered about the room. Roast suckling pig, chicken, quail, swan, flaky white fish, crusty bread, fruit and cheese were being served. Isabella turned to Ferdinand and noticed the frown on his brow.

"Are you all right?" she asked?

"I'm fine." Startled by her question, he forced a smile and patted her hand, but could not shake the visions of the battles flashing before him, the haunting eyes of the dead men glaring up at him from where they lay. "Will they never let me rest?" he asked himself as he sipped his wine. Cardinal Mendoza and Fray Hernando de Talavera sat beside the king and queen smiling and toasting the knights who were enjoying the celebration.

Heavy with child, Isabella was lost in thought as her eyes searched the room for the man for whom she was waiting. She saw Torquemada enter with his guards. She leaned over to whisper in Ferdinand's ear, and then excused herself from the table. Two guards followed her out a rear door. Few noticed that she had left.

She was seated on a high-backed wooden chair when Torquemada entered, but was so furious with him that she did not rise when he entered. She watched his cheeks flush red with the humiliation, but Torquemada knelt before Isabella.

"Your Highness has sent for me," he said in a low voice.

"Father, with all my heart and soul I have followed your sagacious words. I know that your ultimate desire is to bring the word of God to all men, but you have been overzealous. You will not threaten the security of the throne with the power I have given you."

"The power that you have given me? Given me! My power, Your Highness, comes from the Pope."

"It was at my request that you were appointed Grand Inquisitor, and I accuse you of abusing your power!"

His eyes burned into her as he asked, "What spell has Abravanel cast over you that you should speak to me this way?"

Isabella blushed and answered angrily, "I am not under a spell. My concern for Don Isaac is strictly political and practical. We simply cannot carry on the crusade without him. Our funds are so tight that Cardinal Mendoza has begun to sell church jewels for the cause. Ferdinand is ready to fight unto death to liberate our people from the heathens. We have dedicated our lives to consecrating the land for our Savior, but we need funds to continue. In this last campaign we had to pay an army of thirty thousand men and nine thousand cavalry. We brought soldiers in from England and Switzerland. We have to feed these men, put clothes on their backs and weapons in their hands. We need Abravanel to raise funds. I will consider it an act against the crown if he or any member of his family is called before the Inquisition again. Is that understood?"

"Even if that member has confessed to heresy and will not repent?"

"Abravanel's wife is not a heretic, and she is a Jewess!"

"I am referring to her brother, Juan Sanchez de Sevilla. His Hebrew name is Jonathan Ben Ezra."

"You have proven this?"

"I have his confession," he lied.

Shaken, Isabella cast her eyes to the ground and then whispered, "I will not have Don Isaac harassed. See to it that Don Juan Sanchez repents. Let the man do his penance, but do not burn him at the stake."

Torquemada took a deep breath before continuing. "My sweet child, you do not understand the insidious nature of this case. The Abravanels want him to return to his old faith. They use incantations and magic to wrestle his soul from God."

"I do not believe this. Don Isaac would not force his own beliefs upon another."

"I've seen the books! They use black magic to work their evil mischief. Take heed, Isabella, my child. Take heed or the man will be after your soul as well!"

"I have no fear of Don Isaac Abravanel. I would trust the man with my life. Do not trifle with him or his family. Juan Sanchez will repent, and then you will set him free. That is my command, Fray Tomas."

"I will not be dictated to by you or by any other secular ruler. Juan Sanchez will be freed only if he repents and does his penance. I warn you, Isabella, you are already under Abravanel's spell. Beware the purity of your own soul!" Without another word, he turned and left the room.

Shaken by the confrontation with the Grand Inquisitor, Isabella sat as though frozen to her throne, where Talavera found her with her head in her hands. He startled her when he spoke.

"Forgive me, Your Highness. I didn't mean to frighten you." He took her hand. "You are troubled?"

"I had summoned Fray Tomas. My treasurer, Don Isaac Abravanel, is being harassed by the Inquisition. They had imprisoned his wife and are still holding his brother-in-law."

"I see. Were there grounds for the incarceration?"

"Yes, it seems Juan Sanchez is a heretic. I'm hoping he will repent. He can do a penance and then, I hope, the whole affair will be over."

"Why was Abravanel's wife incarcerated?"

"She had been speaking with her brother, but there is no proof that she influenced him in any way."

"And do you think this man will repent?"

"I pray to God that he does. I pray for his soul, Father."

"And if he doesn't?"

Isabella cast her eyes away from the friar.

"We cannot afford to lose Abravanel. I shudder to think what might happen if Juan is burned at the stake."

"Do you feel Fray Tomas has become omnipotent, Your Highness?"

"No!"

"And if he does become so? What then? I don't need to tell you that I hear complaints every day about the Inquisition. It has created an atmosphere of fear and distrust throughout the land."

"What am I to do? There are so many new Christians who do not believe in God, who are heretics. Shall we let them continue to profess their belief in the Church and then, underground, secretly practice their old faith? How are we to distinguish the true converts from the false?"

"It is a difficult task, I agree. Perhaps it is too great for any one man to undertake. Perhaps there should be more than one Grand Inquisitor," he suggested.

"No," she whispered.

"Your Highness, are you afraid of Torquemada?"

"I am not afraid, but if he has been wrong, overzealous, then his sins are my sins, aren't they, father?"

"If Fray Tomas has sinned, then only he is accountable for what he has done. If you feel that he has become too powerful, then Cardinal Mendoza and I will petition the Pope and have him removed."

Terrified that she might hurt her confessor, she cried, "Only he can search out the heretics! Only he can fight the devil." Images of Torquemada, standing over her as a child when she was alone in the dark, of Torquemada her confessor, of Torquemada, the man who had guided her on the day of her coronation, swam before her. He was the only one who could cleanse the land of heretics and though she feared him, knew she couldn't control him. She needed him. She freed Rebecca Abravanel, but Juan Sanchez would have to pray to God for his salvation.

"*Yes,* my lady." Talavera bowed and left Isabella alone, cold and trembling.

Shortly after Rebecca's release, Isaac was summoned to court. Though he had recovered somewhat from the stroke, he was exhausted by the long ride and limped into the Cordova Alcázar. As he entered the Alcázar, he rubbed his hands against the smooth colorful wall tiles and gazed up at the white lacelike designs created by the Moors. "The magnificent Moorish culture is being destroyed," he thought as he slowly made his way to the throne room, and the private audience that Isabella had requested. "And are we next?" he wondered as he approached Isabella with only two guards standing beside her.

"Don Isaac, thank you for responding so quickly. News of your illness has reached us, and we were most distressed. I hope that you are feeling better now," Isabella said as he bowed to her.

"Thank you, Your Highness, much better."

"Your mathematical wizardry has astounded us." And she added, "we are grateful, Isaac."

"And I am grateful to you, Your Highness." His voice broke off.

"Has your wife recovered from her ordeal?"

"She's feeling much better, thank you."

Isabella noticed that his color was indeed sallow, and that he had a tremor in his left hand.

"Isaac, have we asked too much? Are you overwhelmed with all your responsibilities?"

"No, Your Highness. I am honored to be in your service, and my son-in-law, Joseph, is a great help to me."

"I'm afraid your position with the crown has endangered your family. I am sorry. In the light of what has just happened, I'm afraid to put this question to you, but I must."

"I am prepared to do anything for you, Your Highness. All you need to do is ask."

"I want you to handle my personal financial affairs." Isaac's face turned white. "I know how busy you are with the Cardinal Mendoza's estates and fund raising for the crusade, but I need you. I trust no one as much as you, not even Luís de Santangel. Please help me, Isaac. All my funds, estates and jewelry must go to the cause. Only you can direct it properly. I will not have my treasures lining the pockets of adventurers. You are the only one I trust."

Isaac hesitated before he answered. It wasn't so much the responsibility of the queen's estates that disturbed him as the animosity of Tomas Torquemada. He would endanger his family once again if he took this position. The queen had come to their rescue once, but would she be strong enough to counter Torquemada a second time? He thought of the Jews of Spain. How desperate they were now for men in power to stand up for them as the Moors desperately clung to what was left of their land, Granada. But now, for the Jews, each day brought more terror into the hearts of those whose loved ones were taken by the Inquisition. He could not refuse this most honored position—personal treasurer to the queen.

"It is my greatest honor to serve you." As he knelt before her, she gave him her hand. He looked up into those startling blue eyes and found them to be sad and serious.

"He will not harm you or any member of your family again. I promise you," she reassured him.

"My brother-in-law," he whispered.

"He must repent. He must do penance, but I have commanded that if he does, he is not to die."

"And will Fray Tomas listen to you?"

She couldn't look at him, and Isaac shuddered. He knew Jonathan would never repent, never do a penance.

"We must pray for him then," she said as if she could read his mind. "We must pray."

Hands tied behind his back, Jonathan hung from a rope on a hook on a cold stone wall. His arms and hands had grown numb; his head had fallen against his chest.

"Cut him down," a guard called from outside the torture chamber. An ax slashed through the rope that held Jonathan, and as he fell, he moaned, his head smacking the floor.

"Is he still alive?" one guard growled to another.

"Yes," came the answer as guards lifted the unconscious Jonathan and dragged him back to his cell.

Hours later, Jonathan sensed a stabbing pain as blood returned his arms and hands. Semiconscious, he curled up.

"Why am I still alive, dear God," he whispered to the bloodstained walls that surrounded him. "Why am I still alive? Please God have mercy, take me back into your arms. Release me from this hell. Have mercy on my soul."

As he lay on the stone, a vision of Isaac's serious, solemn face as a child rose before him. The rabbi was there too, smiling at Isaac, not at him. Pushing the vision away he wondered, was this why I turned my back on who I am? Jealousy? Jealous of Isaac? He wept. He thought of his sister, of his beautiful sister whom he had given to Isaac. Rebecca, he thought, I must try to protect Rebecca. He had no sensation of time passing, but other visions haunted him—a Sabbath dinner, his mother whispering a blessing over the bread, his father pouring red wine into a silver goblet, Rebecca, little Rebecca, sitting beside him, smiling up at him. Suddenly the sound of his mother's scream, Bathsheba, as she fell to her death, enveloped him. He could smell the smoke from the burning synagogue as it collapsed around his father. He saw Inés, burning. "Forgive me," he wept. "I have betrayed you. I wanted a better life . . . . I wanted to be free, but in seeking that freedom for myself, I betrayed all of you, myself."

The thudding of boot against stone reverberated through the dungeon, right down into his bones. He knew that they were coming for him. When he looked up, the skull-like face of Tomas Torquemada was staring at him.

"You will confess your sins! You will repent!" Torquemada demanded.

Jonathan rolled back, closed his eyes a beseeched God, "I abandoned You, but can You not forgive and save me in my hour of need?"

"Yours is not the true faith! Accept the Lord once again, and your prayers will be answered. What evil spell has your sister cast upon you that you can no longer see the light?"

"No one has cast a spell upon me. I am a Jew," he reaffirmed not only to Torquemada, but to himself.

Jonathan felt the crack of Torquemada's boot against his face, and he fell back into darkness.

Torquemada left the cell and ordered, "Take him back to the torture chamber."

The guards nodded. They waited for the Grand Inquisitor to leave, and then carried Jonathan back and tied him to the rack. The subterranean room was lit only by the torches on the walls, and though it was washed down each day, the stench of blood, vomit, excrement, and urine had seeped into the stone.

Jonathan opened his eyes as he was tied down and felt blood oozing down the left side of his face. He tried to move but realized he was back in the torture chamber, strapped against the large wheel, his hands lashed above his head, and his feet tied tightly, curving his body against the wheel. He closed his eyes and clenched his teeth against this new agony.

"We needn't go through with this" said Gomez. "It's very simple. Confess to your sin of relapsing to Judaism, acknowledge your sister's influence, and you will be forgiven. God is merciful if you will reach out to him."

"No one has influenced me. I am a Jew," Jonathan whispered.

"Turn the rack," Gomez ordered.

The guards slowly turned the wheel, and Jonathan's muscles were pulled in opposite directions, stretched so that he had trouble breathing. Sweat ran down his face as with all the strength left in him, he tried to counter the force of the wheel. Suddenly the pulling stopped, and he was suspended with his muscles stretched to their limit.

"Will you repent? Will you cast off your old faith and find mercy in God?"

"No!" Jonathan wept.

"Rebecca, Rebecca," Gomez whispered in his ear, "Rebecca Abravanel, the Jewess, has stolen your soul!"

"No!" he cried again. "I have only just found my soul."

Infuriated, Gomez cried, "Turn the rack!"

As the guards turned the rack, Jonathan cried in bitter wrenching sobs, "Shema Yisraeil . . . ." and then lost consciousness.

CHAPTER 29

In a shady grove of olive trees standing beside the Henares River, just beyond their Castilian castle in Alcalá de Henares, Judah and Rachel spread out a simple white muslin cloth for their siesta. While Rachel was setting out the wine, bread and cheese, a small flock of sheep meandered by, their black, shiny noses sniffing the ground for sweet shoots of grass. A ewe looked up for a moment as her lamb wandered off after a butterfly. She bleated and the lamb stopped short on its wobbly legs, then pranced back and nuzzled against her. Rachel smiled as she watched the sheep make their way further up the hill. Judah swam with long sweeping strokes in the river to cool off from the relentless sun.

"Come into the water with me!" he called.

"Judah! It's indecent! How could you suggest such a thing!"

"I am your husband now, and I insist!" He clapped his hands twice.

Just two weeks married, Rachel was not used to orders.

"No, I won't!"

"Indecent or not, if you don't come the next time I clap my hands, you'll regret it."

"You can say anything you want, but I'm not going in the water." She swatted a fly that was buzzing around the cheese. "The food will spoil if you don't have your meal now."

"Rachel, I want you to swim with me. Now come down here." He clapped once.

"Judah, I can't swim. I didn't grow up near the ocean. I've never even seen the ocean."

"That doesn't matter. I'll teach you."

"I won't go in. Come have your lunch."

Judah clapped a second time. Rachel didn't move. Dripping wet, Judah emerged from the river and began to walk toward her slowly.

"You don't want me to throw you in do you?" She stood and began to walk backwards.

"Judah! You wouldn't!"

"Oh, wouldn't I?" He laughed.

"Judah, don't." She put her hands up to push him back, but he caught her and then pulled her to him. She started to laugh. "I know you won't do that. You would never be so cruel."

He kissed her. He held her so tightly that she felt she couldn't breathe. She parted her lips from his for a moment, and then suddenly she was lifted into the air. "Where are you taking me? No! Judah, no, don't do that!" She slapped his back as he walked to the water. "Judah, don't." She was so nervous that she couldn't control her laughter. "Please don't." He gently put her down when they got to the water's edge. "Judah," she whimpered softly between laughs, "don't." He held her tightly and kissed her again. She could feel the tension in his body.

"When I get like this," he whispered, "there are only two things that can cool me off."

"Is that so?"

"*You* have a choice, my love. Come into the water or suffer the consequences."

"Judah, we can go home. We can pack up the lunch and go back."

"No," he said softly. "Now which will it be? Swim with me!"

She had slipped from his arms and begun to run away when he caught her, picked her up, and ran into the water.

"No," she cried, "oh Judah How could you!" She fumed as she stood waist high in the cool clear water. He embraced her again. At first she pounded on his back, but as he pressed his lips against hers and the cool water caressed her skin, she returned his kiss. They began to lean further and further into the water and just as she was about to protest again, they were submerged. "Oh Judah, I'll never, never forgive you. Oh look at me . . . . I'm all wet . . . . Look what you've done."

Judah was swimming in the shallow water, laughing.

"Stop it . . . . Stop laughing at me." She was in tears.

"Don't cry, love." He swam back to her and held her. "I love you so much."

"Oh no! That won't work a second time. I trusted you once; that's it." She refused his kisses.

"Come, come over here, and I'll teach you how to swim."

She had lost the battle and grudgingly moved closer.

"Now, lie back. I'll hold you."

"Ha!" she said but did as he ordered. She floated on her back while Judah held her up. The sky was a silky blue and white puffy clouds drifted by like the sheep on the hill. "Oh, it is beautiful, isn't it?"

Judah looked up at the sky for a second, lost his grip, and dropped her.

"Oh Judah!" she cried. "Oh how could you do that?" She stood up and trudged out of the water.

"Rachel, I'm sorry. I didn't mean to let go, I'm sorry. Please, let's try again."

"No! I've gone swimming, just as you commanded." She bowed, turned and missed his smile.

She tried to dry herself off, but her dress clung to her body. Judah came up to her from behind. "You'll have to take that off, you know."

"I will not. It's your fault that I'm in this horrid state, and you'll just have to look at me like this for the rest of the afternoon."

"Just take it off for a few minutes and let it dry."

"Are you suggesting I sit here in my shift? What if someone comes by?"

"No one is coming," he said as he undid the back of her gown.

"Judah, no! Don't! What has gotten into you today? No don't," she pleaded as he forcefully pulled the gown off. He gently rolled on top of her.

"No one can see us."

"Oh Judah, I can't believe you are doing this. You've gone mad . . . ." He stopped her protests with another kiss.

Rachel looked up as the clouds slipped by across the infinite blue. She held his head and caressed his shoulders as he gently kissed her delicate small white breasts.

"Oh, I love you, I love you." She felt wild and free as he took her under the blue sky. She felt as if she were rising into the sky like the white clouds. They fell asleep and woke when a bee buzzed above them and then flew away.

"There now, you see, your gown is dry," he said as he got up to take another swim. Rachel quickly dressed. She looked around the hillside, and to her very great relief, she saw no one. She cut a thick slice of creamy white cheese and spread it on the fresh bread. The white wine was still cool in the earthenware jug. Judah came back, dripping water over the cloth and helped himself to the wine and cheese. Lying on his back, he laid his head on her lap and gazed up at the sky.

"We are so close to God now." He reached up to touch the sky. "I believe that God's ultimate purpose is for us to love, that to be an integrated part of the universe, one must know love."

"Then we indeed are with God." She bent over and kissed his cheek.

"God is the constellations, the stars, the universe," he went on, ignoring her kiss. "Matter is the world that we know—the trees, the earth, man and animals. He created it out of love, and it's his love that sustains all this."

"But what about men who hate, men who do not know love or mercy? How do you explain the evil in this world with a philosophy like that?"

"Ah!" he rolled over onto his stomach. "They are a part of it all. It's part of the imperfection in matter, in man, the lowest form of the great unity between man and God."

Rachel smiled and with her fingertips followed the outline of his lips. She kissed them. "I taste the wine."

He sat up and held her hands in his own.

"But you, my love, you are at the very center of the circle of love. We are with Him now."

"Oh, my prince," she sighed. "You are one of the stars that God promised to Abraham, Isaac and Jacob and King David."

He laughed. "A prince, one of a thousand princes."

"No," she whispered, "You are the Prince, the one through which the line shall be carried until that time shall come when the Earth will be no more."

He pulled her down to him, and, in the sweet summer grass, they united again.

Judah and Rachel were leading their horses into the castle stables when Joseph ran out to them.

"Where have you been? Father has been looking everywhere for you."

Rachel blushed.

"We were by the river taking a siesta. Why? What's wrong?" Judah answered.

"The queen is sick and dissatisfied with her physicians. It seems she wants you."

"Me? The queen wants me? Why me?" Judah's mouth hung open.

"It's not too difficult to figure out where the recommendation originated."

"Father? Why would he do that? I can't attend the queen."

"She has heard that Don Isaac's son is an outstanding physician."

Judah stood speechless and stared at Rachel until finally she pushed him.

"Well go inside and find out what this is all about." Handing the horses' reins to a servant, they went directly into the main hall where Isaac was pacing back and forth.

"There you are. I've been out all over the countryside looking for you. The queen is residing in Cardinal Mendoza's castle. She is suffering from swelling in her legs, and I've recommended you."

"But I can't tend the queen."

"If I can serve Her Majesty, then you most certainly can!" He left the room, preparing to leave.

Judah turned to Rachel.

"I don't know when I'll be back." Rachel laughed. "It's not a death sentence, you know. It's a very great honor, and you'll only be a few miles away." When she thought of all that Isaac had done for the queen and then thought of Rebecca's arrest, Jonathan's incarceration, she wondered what this new "honor" would bring? The sensation of fear rose at the nape of her neck.

"I'll return as soon as possible," he said as he hurriedly kissed her good-bye. He flew to his chambers, gathering all his medicines and books. Rachel followed him and raced to pack some clothes, his very finest for his audiences with Queen Isabella. Within the hour, Judah was following his father out into the courtyard.

"This is a great opportunity for you, Judah," Isaac said as he mounted his horse.

"One I'm sure I could live without," Judah answered as he tied his bundles on the back of his horse.

Isaac leaned down and pointed his finger at his son. "Never, never shrink from your duty to your medicine, or to your people."

"Perhaps I can serve 'my people' better without being so close to the queen."

"You can refuse to come with me, Judah, but if you turn your back on this it will catch up with you someday."

"That's just exactly what I'm afraid of, father—that this will turn against me someday." He too was thinking about his mother's incarceration, his uncle. But there was no questioning his father. He mounted his horse and took off, following his father toward Mendoza's castle.

Isabella's fair skin was extremely white as she lay in her bed. She was staring at the tapestries in front of her, but her mind was on Boabdíl and Alhambra. Her servant knocked on the door and announced that Don Isaac and his son had arrived. She nodded, and the two men were ushered into the chamber. She held out her hand to Isaac. He knelt by her side and kissed her hand.

"I have brought my son, Your Highness. He is an excellent physician, trained by my own brother."

"I have the utmost confidence in your son, Isaac." She gave her hand to Judah, who had also knelt beside her bed.

"Your Highness," he whispered, "I am your servant." He was amazed by the silken complexion of her skin, her vivid blue penetrating eyes, and soft red hair. He had heard that she was fair, but she was more than that; she was mesmerizing.

"I will leave you then," Isaac nodded to Judah who turned his attention to his medical bag.

Three ladies-in-waiting fussed about Judah, taking his cape, offering cold lemonade. Isabella was near term with her fifth child. She had miscarried again the year before, as a result of her hard riding to raise supplies and morale for her troops. This year her physicians insisted that she not ride.

With the ladies-in-waiting surrounding him and Isabella, Judah examined her. Her legs were extremely swollen. As he lifted them, she winced but made no complaint.

"Forgive me for hurting you," Judah said softly. "Is the pain very bad?"

She looked up at the women around them and said, "No." She forced a smile. "Judah, you must be honest with me. My physicians will only tell me what they think I want to hear. Do you think this will hurt the baby?"

"No, Your Highness. I'm sure the baby will be fine, but you must rest. I have a salve for your legs, and I'll wrap them."

"When can I get up? I can't stay like this!"

"Yes, I know," he answered as gently as he could, his nerves stretched, one false move, one wrong word, "Oh my God!" he thought, "I'm tending to the queen!" He tried to remain calm, wished his hands weren't shaking. "You'll have to stay in bed for a while."

"How long?" She was clearly perturbed.

"At least a week."

"A week! I can't stay in bed for a week."

"Oh no!" he thought, "I've said the wrong thing." As calmly as he could he took a deep breath and continued, "Your Highness, you want me to be honest. I could tell you my potion will cure you by tomorrow and each day say the same until you are better, but I must be honest with you, honestly is the very least I can do for you. It will take about a week for this to subside."

"I'm sorry, Judah," she said and a wane smile lit her face. "I'm glad I can trust you as I trust your father. Forgive me for being such a horrid patient."

"You are the bravest woman I've ever had the honor of meeting. Your condition is severe and must be very painful."

"Judah, when you've seen men die in battle, as I have, it tempers your desire to cry over a slight discomfort."

"Well, you must take my advice and rest. Within the week, the swelling will go down, and the pain will subside." He bowed to her and to the ladies.

"Thank you," she said. As he stared at her eyes and lovely red hair, he began to realize why his father had risked so much for her. She was beautiful, even in her pain, she was a beauty.

"It is my honor to serve you," he replied. He rose and joined his father outside the chamber.

"Is it serious? Will the baby be all right?" Isaac questioned him.

There was a concern in Isaac's face that Judah had only seen when he worried about his mother. Judah wondered what exactly Isaac felt for Isabella, and he cast his eyes to the ground.

"She'll be fine. She just needs to rest." He looked back at his father again. "I don't think this will affect the child. She is handling the pain very well. She's a brave woman."

"I've seen her ride to the front of battle lines. I've seen her tend wounded men as they lay dying. Pain and suffering are not foreign to our queen."

Their eyes met.

"I will stay by her side as long as she needs me. I just hope and pray, father, that the Inquisition doesn't descend upon us again, now that another Abravanel is in the queen's service."

"And if it does, she will stand behind us as she has done in the past."

"I hope so, father. I truly hope you are right."

Judah gingerly unwrapped Isabella's legs and smiled when he saw that the swelling was dramatically reduced.

"I think Your Highness will be much more comfortable now."

Isabella smiled. She let him exercise her legs. "Now, I'll help you up," he said as he lifted the queen heavy with child.

Unsteady at first, Isabella held onto Judah and walked around the room. "Thank you, I don't know what I would have done without you this past week."

Judah laughed.

"Your Highness is an excellent patient. There, now," he said as he helped her lie down. "How do you feel?"

"Fit to ride!"

"And ride you will, after the baby is born," Judah answered firmly.

"If only childbirth were as simple as ruling a kingdom," she laughed.

Again Judah laughed, and then he gently rubbed her forehead.

"You'll soon have a strong, healthy child, and the kingdom will be blessed."

Isabella took his hand and held it for a moment.

"Let us pray for a male heir. You and your father have been such good friends. I hope that you have many children, Judah."

"Thank you, Your Highness. I certainly will try. Now you must rest. You must stay confined to these apartments until the baby comes."

"Yes, Judah," she said, closing her eyes, wondering how she would run state affairs from her bed. One lady-in-waiting ushered him out.

Two days later, on December 15, 1485, Catalina, Aragon, was born.

CHAPTER 30

"An adventurer!" King Ferdinand thought. He rubbed his hands across his face and shifted about in his seat as he listened to Cristóbal Colón estimating the measurements of the ocean and the earth, discussing the possibility of crossing the great ocean. He glanced at Isabella and was surprised to find her captivated by the man. Her eyes were opened wide, her lips slightly parted as if she were drinking in every word. Ferdinand turned his attention back to Colón, who, he guessed, was about his age of thirty-four, maybe a year or two older. He was unimpressed by the simple brown velvet doublet he wore.

"Not a man of great means," the king thought. "He probably can't afford to outfit such an enterprise, though the Duke de Medina Celi certainly can."

Colón seemed to be able to read the king's thoughts and said, "D'Ailly claims that the east is rich in precious stones and has mountains of gold." Ferdinand sat up in his throne and was attentive now.

"According to the prophet Esras there is not as much water on the earth as our men of science would have us believe. If this is the case, then the ocean is only one seventh of the total earth's circumference. From my calculations, the ocean is not 8,125 miles wide as has been supposed but rather 2,550 miles. I believe that the riches of the orient are within our grasp. Let the Portuguese waste their time rounding Africa. I say that the fastest way to the East is by sailing west." Colón paused for a moment. Ferdinand shifted about on his throne; Isabella was waiting for him to continue. Colón knelt before her.

"The fabulous wealth of the Orient awaits us. We can trade glass beads for emeralds, rubies, sapphires and diamonds, and mirrors for gold! Think of the crusades that could be financed with such treasure! Not merely Granada, Your Highness, but the Holy Land as well."

Isabella looked to Ferdinand then back to Colón.

"We have not the means to finance such an enterprise at the moment. You must understand that all of our funds are going directly to the crusade."

"If I were to leave within the next few months, I could be back with shiploads of gold."

"We haven't the means," Ferdinand said curtly.

"However, I would like to suggest that we set up a council to discuss this proposition further," Isabella added.

Ferdinand hesitated then said, "Very well."

"I would like Fray Hernando de Talavera to organize a commission, perhaps at the University of Salamanca. I will speak to our treasurer, Alonso de Quintanilla, and see to it that you are paid a stipend until a decision has been reached."

"I am your humble servant." Cristóbal bowed to the Catholic Monarchs.

Cristóbal was ushered into the treasury room. Isaac looked up and was startled to see him standing there.

"Cristóbal, I am delighted to see you. I had heard a few months ago that you were in Spain."

Alonso de Quintanilla coughed as he waited for an introduction. Isaac turned to the treasurer.

"Excuse me, Your Excellency, I would like to introduce you to Señor Cristóbal Colón." Isaac quickly looked at Cristóbal to make sure he said the correct name. He was relieved to see Cristóbal bow to the treasurer.

"I am honored, Don Quintanilla."

"Well, Isaac, since you seem to know what this is all about, why don't you explain it to me?"

"Señor Colón has done some interesting research on the distances of the Earth's waters, and he is quite sure we have overestimated the size of the ocean. Have I stated that correctly?" He turned to Cristóbal.

"Yes, exactly. Fray Hernando de Talavera is to set up a commission to study my proposal, and I devoutly hope I will soon set sail."

"I would like to know where the king and queen expect to find the funds to finance such an expedition," Quintanilla exclaimed, staring at Isaac for an answer.

"The Duke de Medina Celi can finance it from his own pockets, but he wishes the honors from such a discovery to go to the king and queen," Colón replied.

Quintanilla laughed and continued, "I'm afraid the duke always finds an excuse not to spend his money."

Cristóbal looked anxiously at Isaac.

"Is this true?"

"A good part of the expenses would have to be financed from royal funds, Cristóbal, and those funds are extremely low. I'm afraid any expedition like this will have to wait."

"To wait! But the treasure I find will more than pay for the expenses. There would be plenty for the crusade."

"Well, for the moment, Señor Colón, we can extend a stipend of three thousand maravedis a month for you to live on until a decision is made. That should be sufficient," Quintanilla said.

Isaac saw Cristóbal brace himself at the mention of the meager sum and cast his eyes to the floor as he humbly accepted the offer.

"Let me see you out." Isaac took Cristóbal's arm.

Once they were out of the treasury, Isaac turned to him.

"You were lucky to have received any funds at all. We are trying to raise money for the next campaign. What happened in Portugal? King João turned you down?"

Cristóbal gazed at Isaac and then said, "I fared only slightly better than you did, my friend. I was in the main plaza when your effigy was burned."

Isaac's eyes were sad as he looked out across the countryside which spread before them.

"I miss the ocean. I miss the smell of the salt air and the cool breezes that carry the gulls."

"Sometimes the air is so dry here that I feel I can't breathe. Don Isaac, you must help me. You must speak to the queen and make her see the necessity of this voyage. If Spain doesn't send me, I will go from court to court until I find a sponsor."

"How did she receive you?"

"The queen is interested, of that I am sure. It's the king who seems to be against the idea."

"The king is waging war, Cristóbal."

"Of course."

"He knows that at the moment there are no funds in the treasury for such an enterprise."

"You must find the means then, Don Isaac. If I find a route to India and the East, it might prove valuable to the Jewish people as well."

"In what way?"

"There, perhaps, the Jews can live in peace."

It was something Isaac had not thought of, and he stared at Cristóbal, wondering about his Jewish ancestry. "Yes, well, of course, I'll do what I can. You know that, Cristóbal."

"I am very grateful." He patted Isaac on the back and then left the Alcázar.

Queen Isabella wanted to see Isaac when he returned to the treasury. He hurried down the long hall to her private chambers and found her gazing out the window.

"You sent for me, Your Highness?" He bowed and kissed her hand.

"What do you think of this Cristóbal Colón? Have you spoken with him?"

"Yes. I knew him in Portugal, but at that time I was unable to obtain an audience for him with King João. As you can imagine, my position in the court had changed with the Duke of Braganza's imprisonment."

"And that tragedy brought you to us." She turned to face him. "King João turned him down. Do you know anything about that?"

"No, by that time I was here. I've seen his charts. He has a different way of calculating his distances, basing it more on the reports from Marco Polo and Aristotle than on Ptolemy."

Isabella was watching a man herding his goats across the rocky land toward a pasture which had dry little shoots for grazing.

"Our Castilian soil is so rocky, so barren compared to Granada. The Moslems have ruled there long enough. Their time is short. We will not tolerate them much longer."

She turned to face Isaac.

"Colón claims the land of Khan is rich in gold and precious gems, enough to pay for the crusade. I am determined to see him set sail as soon as possible."

"I agree. However, I'm afraid then you will have to let the Duke de Medina Cell finance the voyage for we don't have the means."

"And the campaign in Málaga? Do we have the funds for that?"

Isaac turned his eyes away from her. It was his turn to watch the goatherd. Isabella walked over to an intricately carved wooden armoire and carefully opened the doors. On a large shelf sat an exquisite ebony and gold jewelry box. She took a key from around her neck, unlocked the box, pulled out a gold necklace with a large diamond, sparking in the center.

"Will this help?" she said, handing it to him.

Isaac shivered as he held the royal jewels in his hand. The diamond seemed to vibrate, to dance about as if it were alive. Isabella gave him a cloth bag, and the treasure was slipped inside. Isaac put the bag inside his cloak.

"How much will that pay for?" she asked.

"I'm sure it will help."

"It's not to be destroyed. As soon as Colón returns with his treasures, I want it back."

Isaac took her hand and knelt before her.

"I will have to go out of the country with this, but you have my word that it will be returned whenever you desire."

"I would give you all the contents of this box if I thought it would buy me Granada."

"Let us pray that that won't be necessary, but there is little left in the treasury. Luís de Santangel has spoken with Cardinal Mendoza, and church treasures are now being melted down."

"Yes, I know. I ordered that. We will have Granada, no matter what the cost, Isaac. We will have Granada!"

In May of 1487, King Ferdinand launched his attack against the city of Málaga. Trumpets blared; swords clashed against scimitars; lombards blasted the stone walls of the city while cannon fire from ships battered it from the sea. Eventually, Ferdinand had it completely surrounded. Málaga was the last of the ports of Granada to be taken, and without a lifeline to Morocco, the Moslems would be isolated from their brethren in Africa. Ferdinand laid siege to the city, and it was only a matter of time before Boabdíl's uncle, El Zagal, would have to surrender. Isabella and her dear friend Beatrice rode out to the seaport when news reached them that the siege had been laid. The half-starved inhabitants looked out over the walls when they heard the thunderous cheers of the Christian army as Queen Isabella, dressed in red, with a wide rimmed black sombrero, rode into the camp. Filled with dread, they watched her review her troops, Ferdinand by her side. The handsome Don Alvaro, Prince Fernando's brother, the Count of Faro, who had been by their side ever since his brother's death, Fernando Duke of Braganza, rode with them.

"She is magnificent, isn't she?" the Count said to Beatrice as they rode. Beatrice smiled, for she had seen Isabella face her enemies before. No one knew better than she the strength that lay beneath the delicate frame of Isabella.

As the fiery orange sun set behind the olive trees, the royal party settled into their silken tents. Beatrice and Don Alvaro were playing cards in the tent next to the king and queen. Alvaro had pulled a joker from the deck when a Moor slipped into the tent, and taking Alvaro for Ferdinand, stabbed Alvaro in the neck. Beatrice screamed when the Moor then lunged at her, but the dagger glanced off the necklace she was wearing. Before he could lift the dagger again, the guards were upon him, and he was quickly hacked to death. Isabella and Ferdinand ran into the tent and helplessly watched as doctors tended to the bleeding Alvaro.

Ferdinand bent over him.

"My friend, are you all right?"

"It was meant for you, the blade was meant for you," Alvaro whispered.

"You must not talk. The doctors will stop the bleeding. You must rest." Ferdinand stroked his head as he spoke softly to him. Alvaro closed his eyes, while Ferdinand stood above the camp bed. He and Isabella helped Beatrice out of the tent.

"Will he be all right?" Isabella asked.

"It was a deep wound, but he is conscious. That's a good sign," Ferdinand answered.

"The dagger was meant for you," Isabella choked on her words as she held the sobbing Beatrice in her arms.

Ferdinand kissed the top of her head. "One man with a single blade!" He laughed and left them. Isabella rocked Beatrice in her arms and tried to comfort her, but deep in her own heart she was afraid. She knew that at any moment a madman could appear and suddenly destroy all they had worked for, could destroy her beloved Ferdinand.

In August, El Zagal fled, and the city of Málaga surrendered. The Moors, men, women, and children who had been left behind, were sold as slaves and separated from their loved ones forever.

King Ferdinand and Queen Isabella walked at the head of the procession to what had been the mosque but now was the newly dedicated Cathedral in Málaga's plaza mayor. Ferdinand wore a purple silk suit and a long velvet cape trimmed in ermine. The golden crown of Aragon sat snugly on his black hair, and he carried his father's golden scepter. His gilded sword hung at his side and showed no trace of the blood that had washed it. Isabella was dressed in a golden gown, and upon her breast she wore the pearl and ruby necklace Ferdinand had given her so long ago. Prince Juan and the Princesses Isabella, Juana, and Maria walked behind their mother and father. (The babe, Catalina, had been taken to the safety of Madrid.) Behind the king's party, cavalieros and their ladies followed the procession. They were met by Cardinal Mendoza and Talavera. The voices of a hundred young men echoed the Te Deum against the walls of the new cathedral. As the king and queen knelt before the altar, they prayed for the souls of their dead men, for the strength to fight on, for Granada.

CHAPTER 31

Ferdinand had closed his eyes and drifted off to sleep when in his dream a horse suddenly reared and a bloody scimitar was raised above his head. He sat up and shivered, though it was a warm spring night. Isabella slept soundly. Jealous of her slumber, he watched her for a moment, kissed her forehead and climbed out of bed. He walked over to the tent flap and stared out at the black landscape until his eyes grew heavy, but he dared not close them, dared not seek the rest he sorely needed, for the dream scimitar was sure to rise again. During the winter of 1488, El Zagal had taken much pleasure in harassing the Christians whose land bordered Granada, stealing flocks of sheep and goats and setting fire to the land. Ferdinand was determined to eliminate him.

Before the sun rose, he was dressed in his armor and ready to mount his horse. Their banners flying only slightly lower in deference to the king's. Ponce de León and Gutierre de Cardenas rode by his side. The wind seemed to wail and moan as Ferdinand raced across the plains of Jaen, leading his army of fifteen thousand on horse and eighty thousand on foot. He looked neither to the right nor the left but pointed his sword forward in the direction of Granada. The sun glanced off the armor of the knights and caused the approaching Moors to shield their eyes from the glare. El Zagal raised his scimitar and charged the Christian host. Ponce de León split to the right and Cardenas to the left while Ferdinand and his men met the force full center. He braced himself as his sword slipped into the belly of a Moor, quickly pulled it out as the Moor fell, and again wielded it with deadly aim. He felt like the vortex of a storm; the sun and blue sky above him faded with nothing before him but steel and sweat. Horses reared, flesh was torn, and men, their eyes reflecting the knowledge of their death, fell before him.

He could feel them fall, feel the weight of their bodies as they hit the earth, feel the blood flow into the ground. He looked up and saw the scimitar raised above him. Blindly he swung around and cut down another Moor. Again the scimitar was raised, this time dripping blood. Ferdinand had no time to strike. He ducked as the sword came down, splitting his horse's skull and throwing him to the ground. He stood and, surrounded by Moorish horsemen, plunged his sword into a horse's side. It reared and threw its rider. Again and again he went for the horses until he was surrounded by the men now on foot who, when he stopped for a moment to catch his breath, like vultures slowly circled in. He raised his sword, ready to take on each one in turn. Suddenly Ponce de León and twenty knights charged, coming to the king's rescue. Three dismounted as the others drove the Moors back. They helped him up onto a fresh mount; then they rode away from the battle.

"Are you all right?" León called over his shoulder, but Ferdinand was so breathless he couldn't answer. They pulled over to a grove of cork trees and dismounted.

His knights at his side, Ferdinand dismounted, pulled off his helmet. Sweat was dripping down his face, and he bent over to cough. Ponce de León dismounted, put his hand on Ferdinand's back and anxiously asked again, "Are you all right?"

Bent over and still unable to speak, Ferdinand shook his head yes, and at last he straightened up to face his concerned men. Still slightly winded, but not daring to show any signs of physical weakness, he took the reins of his new horse, mounted, and shouted, "Why are you all standing around here? The enemy is over there!" But just before he placed his helmet on his head, he stared at Ponce de León and added, under his breath, "I owe you my life, my friend. I shall never forget!" He put the helmet on, pushed the visor down and immediately led another charge, crying "Santiago!"

Now under Ferdinand's fierce charge, the Moors were pushed back, eventually five miles into the hills, where the fighting raged on as Ferdinand's knights pursued them through the thickly wooded mountain side. Slowly, relentlessly, Ferdinand's army advanced until at last the mountains surrounding Baza were his. Ferdinand watched El Zagal retreat across the valley before them and disappear into the fortified city.

A black bearded man slipped into the war council's tent, took off his Moorish garb, and knelt before the king.

"And what news have you, Señor?" Ferdinand asked his spy.

"Baza is well fortified. There are approximately ten thousand troops within its walls and provisions for fifteen months. Should you decide to lay siege as you did in Málaga, you must take into account that they have learned from their past mistakes. This city will not fall as easily."

Ferdinand looked up at Cardenas and León. "We could build fortifications down in the valley and just wait it out."

Ponce de León's voice was tense.

"I know this valley. You have two rivers down there, the Guadalentin and the Guadalguiton. When they swell, the land turns to mud and becomes impassable."

The spy continued, "The dense woods also help to make the city impregnable."

"Leave this vulture in his nest to sulk. Let us move on to Boabdíl in Alhambra," León forcefully interrupted.

"Retreat! Retreat!" the knights agreed.

Ferdinand looked at each of them and then asked, "And you Gutierre? Why are you silent?"

"Your Highness, it is not easy for me to question my brothers, who have fought so valiantly by my side, but I think it's a mistake to retreat."

"How can you say that?" León interrupted. "You must see how impossible our position is."

"Yes, as it stands now, it most surely is, but if we had more support, more men, more food, I think we could take him. With El Zagal still here in Granada, we can never fully concentrate our efforts on Alhambra."

All eyes turned back to the king.

"We will hold our position for the moment," Ferdinand decided. "I will find out what our resources are and then make a decision."

The candlelight flickered, throwing long shadows against Ferdinand as the men stood to leave. He sat and watched the flame dance about while the tent folds opened and closed. The lines in his face had grown deep, and he worked his hands, now grown rough, back and forth until he was alone with the candlelight. He took out pen and ink and wrote to Isabella: if she could come up with more men and supplies, they would lay siege. If not, the campaign would be lost.

Isaac found the queen praying in a small chapel in Jaen. She crossed herself and rose to meet him.

"We must talk," she said softly as she led him out into the spring air.

"We are desperate for more men, musket-balls, arrows, horses, mules and grain, and we need them now. How are we to get them?" she asked, as if she were about to go to a market to purchase the goods.

"We have no more funds. We've just financed an army of eighty thousand, not to mention the cavalry." He dropped his eyes, not daring to look at her.

"What personal backing can we get? How much can we expect from our nobility?"

"They have already given a great deal. Your Highness, I am prepared to give you a substantial amount from my own personal funds. I've already contributed seven hundred fifty thousand maravedis. I've been waiting for a desperate moment such as this to give you the rest. I can add another seven hundred thousand to that."

Isabella sat very still; not even the Duke Medina de Celi had given so much. Her eyes downcast, she said, "I'm very grateful. However, I know that in itself won't be enough. Come, please."

She led him into her private chambers. She took the key from around her neck and unlocked her ebony and gold jewelry box. She hesitated a moment, then lifted the false floor of the box and pulled out Ferdinand's pearl and ruby necklace.

"Certainly not the most beautiful of gems," she said as she held it up. "It's the center stone, Isaac, the ruby which makes it priceless."

Isaac looked at the ruby as it swung from her hand. It was as large as an ostrich egg with a small knot on the edge.

"Why? Why is this ruby so valuable?"

"It belonged to Solomon, King Solomon."

Isaac straightened up, grew stiff, as he watched it gently swing back and forth.

She was puzzled by his response.

"What's wrong?"

He turned his back on her, on the gem and doubled over.

"Isaac, why are you so disturbed? It's only a ruby, just a stone."

"Just a stone!" he whispered. Then gaining some control, he knelt before her and gazed at the ruby.

"I'm a direct descendant of David—King David and King Solomon."

Isabella brought her hand up to still the gem's swing. "It's almost as if I knew, almost as if I've always known," she said. She placed the necklace in his hands and closed his fingers over it as she gazed into his eyes. "Take good care of it, Abravanel."

He nodded as he slipped the necklace into a bag and hung it around his neck, then kissed her hand and stood to leave.

"Isaac, you have everything now . . . all the royal jewels . . . all I possess . . . all that Castile and Aragon have to give. We wait for you to return with the needed funds and supplies."

"How much time do I have?"

"Ferdinand is waiting for an answer from me now. Do we lay siege or give up the fight?"

"I'll be back within the month. Tell Ferdinand to hold out. You'll have your funds."

Isaac traveled with Moses ibn Aknin, whom he had asked to act as his personal aide. After they had been on the road for several hours, they ordered their servants to pull up for the night. When the two men lay on their backs, the smoke curling from their campfire into the dusky sky, Isaac took the sack from around his neck and pulled the ruby out of its hiding place. It seemed to pulsate in his hand as he stared into it.

Moses gave a low whistle, "That is a beauty! I've never seen a ruby like that." Moses touched the ruby, his fingers caressing it, as they stared at it.

"Strange, that it should be in my hands now. So many, many years ago this was ours, Moses."

"It's just a stone."

"No," he whispered, "it's not just a stone. It belonged to King Solomon."

Moses looked up from the ruby and watched grey clouds drift across the moon.

"Yes, but now it's Isabella's, and it's needed to pay for their war."

"And our peace," Isaac added as he slipped the necklace back into its sack.

"Oh, I hope you're right, my friend. I hope you're right," Moses said. He rolled over to go to sleep.

Isaac watched the moon emerge from the other side of the grey clouds. "I hope so too," he thought to himself.

Isaac felt as if someone were tapping him on the shoulder when he woke to rain. The clouds had burst open in a fury. Lightning streaked across the sky, and thunder cracked above him. They quickly packed their gear and began the long ride to Valencia. When the terrified horses reared in fear of the thunder and lightening shattering the sky, Isaac and Moses dismounted. The servants followed, patting the horses to calm them as they slowly walked down the road.

"We had better pull up at the next inn," Moses called. "*You* can stop with the servants," Isaac answered above the pounding rain, "but I must go on. Catch up with me near Barcelona."

"If you go on, then so will I."

As they walked, the road turned to mud, and the horses labored, struggling with each step. At long last they came to a dilapidated inn and went inside to rest, but it was almost as wet inside as out. The tile roof was in disrepair, and buckets had been placed around the room in a futile effort to catch the water. Isaac, Moses, and the servants rested by the fireside for an hour and then continued on their way.

By noon, the rain had turned into a light drizzle, and finding patches of grass that had not been washed away, they mounted their horses and rode hard across the long, lonely plains in an effort to make up their lost time. Their horses slipped and skidded in the mud, but Isaac bent forward, determined to waste no time in getting to his destination.

Several days later, they arrived in Valencia, exhausted, their clothes spattered with mud. At an inn, an old woman greeted them with a wide, toothless smile before she showed them to their rooms. It had been awhile since she had had guests, she said. The roads had been washed out days before, and few had ventured out. She was glad to have her rooms filled again.

Moses threw himself down on the straw mattress and closed his eyes.

"I really wasn't sure we'd make it!" He looked up when Isaac gave no answer and opened his mouth wide. Isaac was busy dressing in his finest clothes.

"What are you doing? Surely this business can wait until tomorrow. We haven't had a night's sleep since we left."

"I didn't come here to sleep," Isaac said as he fastened his white shirt and threw his cape around his shoulders. "*You* rest. I'll be back in a few hours and then we will be on our way again."

Moses smacked his hand against his head and fell back down on the bed.

"This time, my friend, you can go on without me. But wake me when you are ready to leave the city."

"I will," Isaac said as he shut the door.

When Isaac returned several hours later, Moses was snoring, his mouth hanging open, his eyes slightly parted as he slept. "Wake up . . . ." Isaac shook him. Moses sprang to his feet.

"Where? Where are we?" he asked, trying to gather his thoughts.

"We're on our way to Barcelona," Isaac said and threw him his gear. Moses fell backwards as he caught the flying bedroll and clothes.

"The ruby? Do you still have it?" he asked as they left the room. Isaac jingled coins that were now in the bag he was carrying, and the men, joined by their servants, paid the old woman and left the inn.

Three weeks after they had first left, Isaac and Moses dismounted from their horses in Jaen, and Isaac began to direct the wagonloads of grain and weapons he had purchased in the name of the king. A royal guard found him waving the wagons into the Alcázar.

"Her Majesty wishes to see you immediately, Don Isaac Abravanel."

Moses continued to direct the wagons while Isaac was ushered into the Alcázar and was immediately shown into the throne room. Cavalieros and their ladies-in-waiting lined the room, and Isaac quietly took a place in the back. Two friars were kneeling before Isabella. They also had just arrived, for one of them began to address the queen.

"Your Royal Highness, we have come from the Holy Land as bearers of grave news. The Sultan of Egypt has received distressing tidings from Boabdíl and El Zagal. He accuses you of harassing the Moslems and warns that if such activities do not immediately cease, the Christians in the Holy Land will in turn be persecuted. We beseech you to show mercy and halt your crusade against the Moslems of Granada."

Isabella looked up and saw Isaac standing at the back of the room. She stared at him for a moment, looking for a sign that he had secured the supplies they needed. Isaac pulled a sack of coins from his cloak, and, seeing the sack was full, she turned her attention back to the friars.

"Tell the Sultan that we will not be swayed from our mission. The Moors who live within our Kingdom are ruled by the same laws as Christians. We expect the Sultan to treat the Christians in the Holy Land with equal justice. No one, no power on Earth will stop us from conquering the land which was taken from our fathers. No one," she said again as she gazed at Isaac and a smile crossed her lips. The friars were sent back to the Holy Land, laden with gifts for the Sultan but with no promise of peace.

On December 7, 1489, two years after the defeat at Málaga, El Zagal rode out of the city of Baza and surrendered it to Ferdinand and Isabella. Whether because of influence Isaac had brought to bear or because of the sultan's threat, he would never know, but the Catholic Monarchs were much kinder to the Moors in Baza than they had been to the Moors in other cities they had conquered. They were allowed to remain in their homes and told they would not be sold into slavery. El Zagal left the Iberian Peninsula for Morocco.

Sitting in the Hall of the Ambassadors in Granada, surrounded by his advisors, Boabdíl grimly received the news of the fate of his uncle and the Moors of Baza. Granada was his alone to rule and to defend.

CHAPTER 32

The constant danger of Moorish ambush and forays led King Ferdinand to establish a camp several miles away from the red fortress, Alhambra just outside of Santa Fé, there to prepare for the final conquest. Anticipating the adventure and glory of the last crusade, noblemen were gathering there from all over Europe, and the banners of counts, dukes and marquises flapped in the winds that blew down from the Sierra Nevada.

Isaac was on his way to the queen's tent when he stopped abruptly at the sight of Dominican friars standing outside it. Torquemada was in private audience with the queen. Turning before the friars saw him, Isaac had begun to walk away when someone called. He looked up and saw Cristóbal Colón, his red hair streaked with grey, striding toward him. The men embraced.

"It's been a long time! How many years?" Isaac asked.

"Five, my friend. Five of the most frustrating years of my life. The king and queen have been playing with me as if I were an amusing toy. I was finished with the Spanish Court, through, when they called me back again, so here I am. I'll tell you . . . ." He looked over his shoulder and then lowered his voice, "if they won't support my enterprise now, I'm leaving for France. I think King Charles VIII may have the funds Ferdinand and Isabella lack."

"If you can wait a few more months," Isaac said, "I'm quite certain you will get backing from them. I know for a fact that the queen wants to see you set sail under the Flag of Castile and Aragon. If you go to France now, you don't know how many years it will be before some other committee decides your fate."

Cristóbal sighed. "Yes, of course, that's true. If they had let me set sail years ago, I could have been back by now with treasure. How much longer will it be, Isaac? When will they conquer Granada?"

"The time is near. Though officially Boabdíl is a vassal king, King Ferdinand and Queen Isabella will not stop until all the Moors are gone from Spanish soil. Boabdíl can't hold out forever. Each day brings reinforcements from all over Europe. They are, for the most part, opportunists, adventurers, men seeking a quick reward."

Cristóbal looked around at the colorful tents, the knights jousting, the jesters and troubadours, the merchants selling produce, spices, leather, pots and trinkets of all kinds. "It's as if a city has grown up here overnight. One has many friends when one is on the winning side, isn't that so?"

"Yes, I'm afraid that's true, and many enemies when one loses." Isaac looked anxiously at the friars surrounding the queen's tent.

"Is Torquemada in there with her?"

"Yes."

"I don't know if you took me seriously years ago when I said my voyage could be of great importance for your people, Isaac. I care about the Jews . . . . I care very much, more than you can know."

Isaac knew better than to penetrate those blue eyes. It would be far too dangerous for him to know any more about Cristóbal than he was willing to share.

"I have always believed in you, you know that. But what good can you do for the Jews? If Torquemada has his way, we will be expelled along with the Moors. So far, the queen has not taken his preaching too seriously."

"Legend has it that one of the lost tribes of Israel wandered to the land of Khan. If I can find a quick route, it might be a kingdom where the Jews will be accepted and allowed to live in peace."

A great sadness enveloped Isaac as he thought about what the Jews had endured since the time of the destruction of the temple in Jerusalem, Solomon's temple, and they had lost their kingdom. Were they cursed to wander from land to land, always strangers, fumbling with new languages, cultures, and customs in order to survive, until a new king decided they must go, move on again? Cristóbal had a strong argument, to find a land where Jews, Moslems, Christians, and people of all religions and cultures could live in peace, side-by-side with one another. A fool's dream? Maybe not.

"There will come a time when Jews will live in peace. We'll find a land where people of all races and religions can live together as one, function as one nation, and be an example for others to follow. Until that time, Cristóbal, the Jews will bow to the wishes of monarchs wherever we wander."

His black shadow covering her face, Torquemada stood above the queen, who shivered, staring up into his eyes as he continued to rave.

"You need funds! This is your answer! You have allowed God's work to go undone for lack of money! All of our precious silver and gold has been melted down to pay for your cowardice. You belittle yourself and beg for money from your pawnbrokers. They have the treasure, and you have nothing. Each Jewish family that is found guilty by the tribunal has forfeited thousands of maravedis to the crown. Let me have full authority, full power to exorcise the devil, and then you will see money flow as never before. And you will achieve complete unity of church and state."

Fray Hernando de Talavera walked into the tent, and Torquemada bowed.

Talavera angrily demanded, "What is this talk? What evil mischief are you up to now? How can the Jews have money when they pay more in taxes than everyone else? They have given more to the crusade than many of the noble houses! Why Abravanel himself has given over a million maravedis to the cause. How dare you make such accusations?"

"Don't speak to me about Abravanel!" Torquemada's white skin was stretched so tightly across his skull that it seemed paper thin. His pulsating veins stood out, and his eyes looked ready to pop from his head. "He has worked his evil magic long enough. We must rid the kingdom of the Moslems and Jews if we are to consecrate the land in His name!"

"You are the root of evil! The Moslems and Jews are an integral part of this land. Without them we would not be productive." Turning to Isabella, Talavera continued, "Expel the Jews, expel Abravanel, and Granada is lost. It is against His will to show no mercy to the heathen." The outraged Talavera stormed out of the tent.

"He is under Abravanel's spell, and if you are not careful you will be too. I can see it in your eyes," Torquemada said, regaining his composure, neatly pressing down is brown robe.

Isabella cast her eyes to the ground, not daring to look the Grand Inquisitor in the eyes.

"What has happened to Juan Sanchez? You have not passed sentence on him, have you?"

Torquemada's face was just inches from hers when he said, "He is a heretic and will suffer for his sins!"

Without another word, Torquemada left her.

Isabella remained huddled in the corner of her tent. Trying to stop shaking, she folded her arms about her. Then she stood and walked to the enormous tent where she and Ferdinand held court. Isaac was ushered in and knelt before her. He could see her trembling and guessed its cause.

"Does he think I would harm you?"

She could not look at him.

Still on his knees, Isaac looked up at her and continued in a soft voice, "Your Highness, I have served you for eight years. Have I ever once failed you? Have I ever once betrayed your trust?"

"No, not once. You have fulfilled my every wish. Oh, Isaac, open your heart! It would all be so much easier if you could only accept His love. God is merciful."

Isaac looked away.

"I would die for you," he whispered, "but you must never, never ask that of me again."

"But why?"

"Because it is the one thing I cannot do for you. I am a Jew. Would you have me baptized and then burned at the stake for heresy?"

"I would never allow that to happen."

"And my brother-in-law? He's been imprisoned for five years. I pray each day that the Lord will take him back into his bosom. No matter what sins he may have committed, he has surely paid for them in full measure."

Isabella looked away. "I'm afraid I can't save him."

She sat up straighter on her throne and continued in a more controlled, colder voice. "Fray Tomas claims the Jews have money that has been held back from the cause. Is this true Isaac?"

"Your Highness, if you could but see the poverty your Jewish subjects are forced to live in, you wouldn't question the madness of such an accusation."

Isabella rubbed her hands against each other and said, "I have called Cristóbal Colón back to Santa Fé. The Count Medina Celi claims Colón is prepared to leave for France if we don't agree to finance him immediately. Have you seen him?"

"Yes, I have."

"And do you think we will lose him to Charles?"

"Right now, he still hopes to sail under the Flag of Castile and Aragon, but he has grown impatient with these long delays."

"We haven't the funds, have we?" she asked.

"No. However, I think if you reassure him that in the near future you will patronize such an expedition, he will wait."

She nodded. "Call forth Cristóbal Colón."

A guard left the tent and a moment later Cristóbal entered. He bowed before her, his eyes quickly searching Isaac's for some clue as to how the audience would go.

"Señor Colón, it is good to see you again."

"I am your humble servant, Your Highness."

"I have had several letters of late from Fray Juan Perez and the Count Medina Celi, who, I understand, are ardent admirers of yours. They have implored me to reconsider your proposal for a westward voyage to the land of Khan and the Indies." She looked at Isaac. "I have decided to have the proposal studied by my royal council of Castile."

Colón's throat tightened so that he thought he wouldn't be able to breathe.

"Another committee, Your Highness! My proposal has been in the hands of different committees for five years. Living off the generosity of my friends, I have felt imprisoned as I wait for the privilege to serve you."

"Señor Colón, I understand the hardships you have been forced to suffer over the past few years. But we have all sacrificed. We have all suffered to accomplish the great task before us. When Granada is conquered, we will have the resources to finance your voyage. Until then, the merits of your enterprise must be carefully evaluated."

There was nothing more Colón could say. He had waited for this audience for years, and now knew he would have to wait even longer. Enraged, he thought to himself, "I will wait for you, my lady. I will wait a month, perhaps two, perhaps until Granada has fallen, and then I will wait no more!"

Ferdinand had spent the day reviewing the inventory of foodstuffs. The last sale of royal jewels had bought supplies for a long siege. After enjoying a light supper, he and Ponce de León settled down to a game of chess, and were resting, the king's head in his hands, concentrating on the board, when Isabella entered. León stood and bowed. Ferdinand took her hand. "It's been a long day."

"Yes, indeed it has. I saw Señor Colón today."

"Is he willing to wait or is he going to France?" Ferdinand asked as he knocked off León's bishop with his knight.

"He will wait for the moment." She sighed, "But I don't know how much longer we will be able to stall him."

"I understand Fray Tomas was also here. Did you see him? Damn!" He swore under his breath when León took his knight with the queen, then looked up when Isabella didn't answer. "I asked did you see him."

"Yes," she whispered.

He stood up and drew her into his arms.

"He's upset you again, hasn't he? I don't know anyone else who can affect you so. What power is it that he has over you, my love?"

"No power," she whispered, but her eyes seemed glazed; she wouldn't look at him.

"I think you should retire for the night." He kissed her forehead.

"Yes, I'm very tired," she said as she left.

Ferdinand sat down to the chessboard and smiled as he knocked León's queen off with his bishop.

Isabella had drifted off into a fitful sleep. A man in a black robe appeared before her. She fell to her knees, she cried, she pleaded, but he wasn't listening to her. Then, in her sleep she smelled smoke. It seemed to rise slowly from the feet of the man. The smoke was enveloping his black figure, when she began to cough in her sleep. Then suddenly she woke. She was coughing, trying to catch her breath, her eyes smarting from the smoke which she saw now was filling her tent. The flame from her candle had set fire to the silk curtains. The fire, its hot tongues reaching out to burn her, hungrily devoured the fabric all around her. She ran through the fire to the children . . . Why had she been so foolish to have take the baby? They were coughing, rubbing their eyes and crying.

"You must get up!" she screamed, "Quickly! There's a fire! Quickly, quickly! Juan, take Maria out . . . . I have the baby." She reached over the cradle and lifted little Catalina. Juan guided Maria out of the tent when, as if from the sudden breath of a dragon, a wall of fire leaped before him. He put up his hands to ward off the fire, which fanned out and burned him. He was blinded by the heat and smoke; Maria was crying. Still holding onto the baby, Isabella grabbed Juan and cried, "Hold onto me and Maria. Don't let go of her hand!" She blindly led them in the opposite direction, but the crying, heat and smoke were making her dizzy and confused. She screamed, "Fire . . . fire!"

Suddenly Ferdinand was with them. Ponce de León carried Maria and the baby, while Ferdinand pulled Isabella and Juan from the inferno. Blinded by the smoke, she fell against Ferdinand when they made it to the open air.

"The children?" she cried, her face black with soot.

"They're all right. It's all right. No one was hurt." Ferdinand held her as she fought to regain control. Rumors spread as quickly as the fire that the Moors had started it. Soldiers readied themselves to do battle with the hidden infidels. Isaac and Ponce de León quickly organized a fire brigade and stood side by side as they threw buckets of water on the fires, for the flames had leaped from tent to tent and stretched up into the sky. Isaac's face also blackened with soot, his hands blistering as he swung bucket after bucket of water onto the flames. It seemed hopeless, as the fire continued to spread across the camp. When Isabella recovered her breath, she laid to rest the rumors that Moorish spies had stared it. The fire had indeed started from her single flame.

Torquemada and his clergymen emerged from their tents to watch the spectacle. Isaac was running to a nearby stream for water when he recognized the thin black figure of Torquemada outlined by the raging flames. He was so taken aback by the sight that he stopped for a moment and stared at the Grand Inquisitor surrounded by fire.

"Water! Water!" came the cries all around him, breaking the spell, so that he continued to fetch more water.

Hours later, it seemed as if the sun had not risen for the smoke had hidden it, creating the image of a smudge in the sky. Men and horses suffered burns, but no one died from the Santa Fé fire. Bleary eyed, Isaac, along with Ponce de León, and the king and queen, surveyed the damage. It seemed all was lost. The colorful tents had been reduced to black shreds gently fluttering in the wind. Ferdinand knelt down and picked a sword from the charred debris.

Isabella put her hands on his shoulder and said, "We will not be defeated. We will build houses and barns, markets and liveries. We will build a city of mortar and stone in the shape of a cross. Let them look down at us from Alhambra and know that we are here to stay."

Ferdinand stood, raised the charred sword and cried, "We will not be defeated! Alhambra will be ours!"

Disheartened and exhausted from the disaster, the soldiers were slow to rally. They began to cluster around the king and queen chanting, slowly at first and then raising their voices until the sound swelled throughout the camp: "Alhambra! Alhambra! Alhambra!"

CHAPTER 33

Isaac and Rebecca had not seen each other for almost six months when he returned to the castle in Alcalá de Henares. Since the crusade had become the overwhelming force in his life, Isaac had been home for only brief periods of time. They embraced.

"How long can you stay?" she asked. She wanted to hold him close. She was feeling frail, weak, and his tall warm body felt reassuring pressed close to her. At these moments of reunion, she sensed how much she missed him when he was gone.

"For only a week." He kissed her gently on the lips.

"Oh, Isaac When will this war be over?" she asked, pulling away. "When will you come home for good?"

"I think the end is near. Boabdíl is now cut off from any aid he might have expected from El Zagal or his brethren in Africa, and I believe Ferdinand has him in check."

Judah ran out into the courtyard, and father and son embraced.

"Well, it's good to have you back! How long will you be here?"

"Just a week." Isaac picked up his gear and walked into the main hall.

"Just a week? Father, you haven't been home in over six months. Surely the king and queen can spare you for more than a week?"

"I'm afraid it's only for seven days; and then, Judah, I'm going to leave Moses here, and you will accompany me back to Granada."

"Me? Why me? I'm needed here. I can't leave Rachel and the baby."

The journey had taken its toll on Isaac. Leaning on Rebecca as he walked, his back aching from long hours in the saddle, he turned and in a voice much sharper than he intended, he said, "When the queen requests your medical care, you will gallantly honor her!"

"The queen wants me again? But why? She has other physicians . . . ."

"Judah!" Isaac shouted and then in a more controlled voice added, "Son, I'm sorry. I'm very tired. She wants you. She trusts you, and that's why I'm here, to escort you back to Granada." He turned, and Rebecca helped him up the stairs to their private chambers.

Judah turned to Moses. "This is true? She wants me in Granada?"

"Ever since the fire, she has suffered headaches and dizziness. Her physicians have been brewing and mixing every known medicinal herb, but without success. She wants only you. It's a great honor . . . . I'll be here to help the family."

Judah patted Moses on the back. "You've been a good friend. We were blessed when you came into our lives."

Moses said softly, "God works in strange ways." Shaking his head, he retired to his own chambers.

Early the next morning, the family celebrated Isaac's return with a picnic in the countryside. Judah and Rachel led the family to their favorite place beside the river Henares. Bathsheba and Joseph glowed as their son, Jonathan, led his horse to the water for a drink. He was eight years old and muscular for a youngster his age. Isaac walked over to the child and rubbed the horse's back with his hand as the animal drank the cool water. He gazed back at his family. They were all there—except the older Jonathan and Elisheba: Moses, Rebecca, Bathsheba and Joseph, their Jonathan, Judah and his Rachel with their two-year-old son, his namesake, Isaac. Then Isaac gazed at his other two grown sons, Joseph and Samuel. He would never admit it, but oh, he missed his Elisheba, wondered if she were well, but never daring to breathe a word of these thoughts to Rebecca; he'd breakdown to her pleas for reconciliation if he told her his true feelings. Then brightening to the gifts of the day he thought, "How Father would have loved this moment!" He let the sun warm his back, soothing its ache.

"Jonathan, you handle this horse very well," he said, turning to the boy.

"I love to ride, grandfather. We can go faster than the wind!"

"So like Jonathan," Isaac thought. Then he continued, "What is his name?"

"His name is Pegasus. When we ride out across the plains, I feel as though I'm flying."

"Pegasus!" Isaac said. He patted the pure white mare. Suddenly he stopped, his hand flying away from the horse's side.

"What's wrong, grandfather?"

"Your uncle . . . his horse also was a white mare."

"Yes, I know. This is his horse. Uncle Judah gave him to me. My uncle's name is also Jonathan, but he must be a wicked man."

"Why do you say that?" Isaac asked, feeling the innocent words as sharp stings.

"Because he's been imprisoned for so long."

Isaac decided it was time to explain, in as gentle a way as possible, what had happened to his uncle. He sat down by the river's edge.

"Come here, Jonathan, come." He waved to the boy, who settled next to him, allowing his small frame to rest against his grandfather's. "You must not think that about your uncle. He is a good man. He was once a very happy, strong man, the best of us, really."

"But why is he in prison?"

"Because he was not happy with who he was and what he thought he wanted out of life. He tried to become someone different and that led to serious trouble." The conversation was suddenly interrupted by little hands clutching Isaac's back in an effort to climb it. Isaac grabbed the chubby arms and swung little Isaac over his head to land in his lap. The two-year-old squealed with delight.

"More!" he cried. "More!"

Judah, who had pursued little Isaac to the water's edge, now sat down next to them.

"How old is he?" Isaac asked, hugging the child, kissing the top of his forehead.

"If you weren't away so much, you'd know . . . ." Judah chided.

"I'm two!"

Isaac held the child's small hands in his own and kissed the fingers. Little Isaac traced his grandfather's lips. They stared at each other for a moment, and then the boy hopped down from his lap and ran toward the water. Jonathan jumped up and caught him. Again the child squealed with delight as Jonathan swung him around in circles. Laughing, little Isaac tottered before he sat down next to his big cousin. Jonathan had picked up some sticks, and they made designs in the mud near the river. Judah looked up quickly and blushed when he caught Isaac's gaze.

"He means everything to me. I never realized what a miracle birth is. It still seems so incredible that Rachel and I created another human being who can look at the world and discover its beauty."

"He is God's gift, Judah. Never forget that."

"I won't, father. I shall never forget. Isaac!" Judah called. Startled from his play, the child looked up adoringly at his father and grandfather. "Come, Isaac! Mother has something good to eat." Little Isaac took his father's hand and pumped his legs as quickly as they would go in order to keep up with him.

Brushing the dirt from his hands, young Jonathan came and sat down next to his grandfather again. They sat there peacefully watching the roll of the water.

Isaac whispered, "Hold this moment, Jonathan. Hold onto this and never let it slip from your memory. Life isn't always so sweet."

"Do you know what I wish, grandfather?"

"No, what do you wish for?" Isaac turned his gaze back to his older grandson.

The boy seemed mesmerized by the flowing water, and he spoke softly. "I wish my horse was Pegasus. I wish I could free my uncle, and we could ride away up, up into the sky."

Isaac stood feeling agitated. How he wished he could free his closest friend, his brother.

"That's a very good wish, Jonathan." He patted the boy on the back, but turned from him, seeking the company of the others where he would be protected from thoughts of Jonathan. "Jonathan!" he wanted to scream. "Where has it all led? You held so much in your hands—what has happened to you?" He felt like weeping, but the others brought him round again to this present, precious moment.

Two days later, Isaac and Judah strapped their gear onto their horses, ready to ride for Granada.

"It seems as if you just arrived," Rebecca sighed, holding tightly onto Isaac's hands. Usually she was more at ease with their partings. "Isaac?"

"What, my love?" He sensed her anxiety.

"When Granada is conquered, when the Moslems are routed, do you think we will be safe? Torquemada preaches that the land will not be secure until both the Moslems and Jews are expelled. The king and queen would never contemplate such a thing, would they?"

Isaac was holding her tightly when he answered, "I don't know. The king and queen are certainly dependent upon Don Senior and me. Queen Isabella was adamant about Judah accompanying me back to Granada. It would seem they respect and need us, but Torquemada has been drumming his diabolical ideas into her head. However, I don't believe that either she or the king will issue such an edict."

Rebecca relaxed, a little.

"Well, then, if you must be off, you must. Take care. Judah," she turned, "Don't ride too fast. You know your father suffers a great deal of pain in his back."

Isaac laughed, but gingerly climbed onto his horse. Judah was holding little Isaac in his arms. He put the child in his father's saddle. Little Isaac kicked his legs which barely made the spread of the saddle; then he turned and reached his arms out to his grandfather. Before handing him back to his father, Isaac embraced the child and kissed him.

"Enough! We must be off!" Isaac said and thought, "How many times have I had to say good-bye to my little ones!"

Little Isaac began to cry when Judah handed him back to Rachel. She tried to cradle him in her arms, but he was crying out to Judah and Isaac. He screamed, his arms reaching out toward them, and continued to scream until Rachel had to take the inconsolable child inside.

Isaac and Judah headed for Toledo before turning south toward Granada. Isaac wanted to reassure the Jews of Toledo that the Catholic Monarchs still considered them loyal, faithful subjects. They passed through the stone walls of the city, and for a brief moment Isaac's heart cried out for Jonathan, who was still imprisoned by the Inquisition. They wound their way through the narrow cobblestone streets. Here, as in other cities throughout Spain, the Jews lived in their own Judería. The buildings were fragile white structures, the texture of bleached bones. The windows seemed like vacant eyes staring down upon Isaac, begging him for sustenance. From time to time, he'd see the face of a child or old woman peeking out, watching him and his son pass on their way to Rabbi Aboab's house.

A group of twenty men met Isaac and Judah in the small main room. A fire was crackling on the hearth, and the scent of beef filled the room. The men bowed to Isaac, and the rabbi insisted that they all eat before they spoke of serious matters. Rabbi Aboab raised his arms above the bread and the stew, blessing the meal. Quietly, the men helped themselves, though sparingly, leaving large portions for Judah and Isaac. Dressed in coarse woolen cloaks, the men whispered among themselves and stole glances at the great man who broke bread with them. After the dishes were cleared away, the rabbi began to question Isaac.

"So, you are off to Granada again. The king and queen must hold you in high regard if they insist on your constant presence. And now Judah?"

"Yes, the queen has also insisted on Judah's medical care once again. At the moment, I'm sure there is no need for alarm."

"Excuse me, Don Isaac," a young man with a long woolly black beard said, "but surely you must be aware of the Grand Inquisitor's recent sermons. Other clergymen throughout Spain have been preaching the same; 'Once the Moslems are out, then the Jews must go!'"

"Yes, yes, I know I've heard it often enough, but what would become of Spain if they really issued such an edict? Look at the men gathered here tonight. What would Spain do without her bankers, lawyers, doctors and merchants? We are critical to the welfare of the Kingdom. Without the Jews, Spain would grow weak and crumble," Isaac answered, trying to sound reassuring.

"Yes, but do the Catholic Monarchs see it that way? I understand the queen is under a spell, that Fray Tomas de Torquemada has complete control over her," Rabbi Aboab said, as murmurs ran through the room.

"I cannot guarantee our security. All I can tell you is that the king and queen have high regard for my service, for Don Abraham Senior and his son-in-law, Meir Melamed, and we have great support from Luís de Santangel, and Gabriel Sanchez. Even Cardinal Mendoza and Fray Hernando de Talavera have been preaching moderation on the Jewish question. They are powerful friends. Some even call Mendoza the third king."

The rabbi pressed him further.

"But, Isaac, do you think it could happen? Do you think the king and queen would really consider expulsion of the Jews?"

"Where would we go? What about our wives, our children, our old people? They would never survive as strangers in a foreign land?" the young man with the black beard cried angrily.

"What about our dead? What about the graves of our dear departed?" asked an old man with a long white beard? Wild, angry voices filled the room until at last the rabbi lifted his arms to silence them.

"Isaac, can you reassure us that our fears are unwarranted?"

"I can make you no promises. I have dedicated myself to serving the king and queen; I have offered up my son, jeopardized the safety of my family."

"Your brother-in-law, Juan Sanchez de Sevilla, is a traitor, a heretic, a blasphemer and should be burned at the stake!" a man yelled from the back of the room.

Isaac lunged toward the speaker. His hands went around the man's neck, and he watched the face turn beet red, the eyes bulge.

"Is there no mercy in your heart, no room to forgive one who has suffered more than you will ever know!" Judah and three other men pried Isaac away from the man who rolled away, choking. Isaac shook them off as if they were annoying flies, and stood over the man. "I pray that the king and queen have more mercy in their hearts than you, you fool."

"Isaac, the man doesn't know what he says! He speaks from ignorance . . . . Please, don't leave us like this. Promise us you will not allow such an edict to be issued!" The rabbi had grabbed Isaac's cloak as he and Judah headed out the door.

Isaac turned and looked at the rabbi. He looked at the frightened faces of the men in the room, like sheep lost on a hillside with no shepherd, even the man, still on the floor, rubbing his red neck.

"I don't think we are in that kind of danger, but you have my word that if such an edict is issued, I will do everything in my power, everything," he repeated as he gazed at the man still lying on the floor, "to protect the Jews of Spain."

CHAPTER 34

The Christian army rebuilt the entire town of Santa Fé within three months. On January 1, 1492 Isaac watched Boabdíl and his entourage of knights, his mother, and his wife, ride out to meet Ferdinand and Isabella. Isaac saw that Boabdíl prepared to dismount when the king lifted his arm to halt him.

"I salute you as a king," Ferdinand said.

Boabdíl handed the golden key of Alhambra to the Catholic Monarchs. His son and the other noblemen's children were released. Isaac saw a gentleness and pure love in Boabdíl's eyes, eyes that were brimming with tears, when his sturdy little boy rode up to meet him. The entourage turned and swiftly headed for the Alpujarra Mountains.

Ferdinand was about to proceed when Isabella held him back.

"We will not enter the citadel until it has been dedicated to our Savior, the Lord Jesus Christ." She nodded her head, and Cardinal Mendoza and a small party of clergymen galloped up to the fortress and disappeared under the sorcerer's archway.

Isaac could feel each beat of his heart as he, Cristóbal Colón, and the entire army silently waited for Mendoza to sanctify Alhambra. Cristóbal and Isaac glanced at each other as they waited in the crowd. The air seemed so heavy that Isaac felt as if he couldn't breathe. The sun's rays bounced off the silver cross, almost blinding him, when Cardinal Mendoza set it on top of the highest tower where the old talisman had sat guard for centuries. The army's cheer was deafening as the golden lions and castles fluttered from the towers. Passing under the sorcerer's arch, Ferdinand and Isabella rode triumphantly into Alhambra. Granada, all of Spain, was theirs. The *reconquista* was complete.

Ferdinand and Isabella were seated on the throne in the Hall of the Ambassadors when Fray Tomas de Torquemada entered. He bowed to the Catholic Monarchs.

"The time has come now for a complete victory for God! The land must be cleansed. All infidels must be cast out."

Isabella turned to Ferdinand and said softly, "I cannot lose Isaac, Judah or Abraham Senior. I simply cannot run the government without them."

Torquemada knelt before her.

"Order their baptism. If these infidels mean so much to you, then command that they be baptized or expelled."

"I think Don Abraham Senior might *accept* the Lord. What about Abravanel? Do you think he would consider conversion?" Ferdinand asked.

"I know he would not," Isabella replied. "We have already discussed the matter."

Concerned over losing his treasurer, Ferdinand frowned as a page announced Fray Hernando de Talavera. Torquemada stood and moved to one side of the hall as Talavera bowed before the king and queen.

"Your Majesties, I have just met with Señor Cristóbal Colón. He is most distressed that you have still not given him an audience. He will travel to France within the week if he isn't granted his mission. He has, after all, waited for six years for you to accomplish your most glorious task."

"Fray Hernando, we still have not the means to send this man into uncharted waters backed only by theory," Ferdinand answered.

"I beg you to consider the mission once more before he leaves for France. If indeed this proves to be a short, direct route to the Indies, think of the power, the wealth France would have. Sire, your own provinces, Rousillon and Cerdange, would be in danger once again," Talavera pleaded. Torquemada stepped forward and spoke. "Your Majesties, there are untapped sources of money still in the land, if you would only listen to me. You would have all the gold you need if you expel the Jews and confiscate their properties."

"Why was I not made aware that the Jews still have resources?" Ferdinand asked, and he glared at Isabella, wondering for the first time if the friar was right

"Because this vast source of funds does not exist," Isabella said firmly, gripping the arms of her throne until her knuckles turned white.

"Fray Hernando, do you think the Jews still have wealth we do not know about?" Ferdinand asked.

Talavera shook his head. "No, sire, only the simple houses that they live in, the necessities of life. That is all. Would you expel your doctors, lawyers, merchants simply to confiscate their property?"

"It is you who say that Colón is ready to deliver the Indies to France!" Ferdinand shouted. "I need funds! Immediately!"

Again Torquemada interrupted. "There is more, much more than the simple necessities of life in the Jewish homes! I know! I've seen what the church has already confiscated. Silver candlesticks, golden plates and goblets, ornaments for their sacred scrolls. I tell you there is still great wealth, if you would only tap it, Your Majesty." He turned from Ferdinand and addressed the queen. "If this Abravanel is so stubborn not to accept conversion there are other ways of convincing him to stay."

"What other ways?" Isabella asked angrily.

"Nothing is more important to Abravanel than his family. Perhaps you can convince him to stay by offering him his brother-in-law's life."

"I will not listen further to this blasphemy! If, Fray Tomas de Torquemada, his brother-in-law is indeed a heretic, then he will, as you have said so many times, have to pay for his sins. Burn him at the stake! Do what you will with Don Juan Sanchez, but Don Isaac Abravanel is not to be treated in such a manner."

"Then he must be expelled along with all the Jews."

Isabella stood. "I will not lose Don Isaac. He has been my most faithful servant, sacrificing all his monies and energies to help us achieve this victory."

"Very well then, Your Highness, you might as well dismiss Señor Cristóbal Colón now, for without an immediate new source of funds, he cannot set sail."

"But he must sail under the Flag of Castile and Aragon!" Isabella said and turned to the king.

Surprising everyone in the room, Ferdinand stood and said, "Señor Cristóbal Colón will set sail under the Flag of Castile and Aragon!" Then he abruptly dismissed the court.

Isabella quickly retired to her chambers, but Ferdinand caught Torquemada before he left the hall.

"A word in private," he said and led Torquemada to his own chambers. Closeted alone with the friar, Ferdinand continued, "What my wife says about Abravanel is true. I value the man and his wizardry with numbers. I do not want him expelled along with the others."

Torquemada frowned. This was not what he wanted to hear. He thought that at last he would be able to separate the Jew from Isabella's service.

"I see no other way, Your Majesty."

Ferdinand frowned, scratching the side of his face. "What if we were to kidnap one of his children, hold him hostage as I did with Boabdíl's son?"

"To what end?" Any plan to keep Isaac in Spain was distasteful to him.

"Boabdíl capitulated quickly enough when his own son and heir was threatened. Perhaps Isaac could be made to see the light that it is in everyone's best interest for him to convert and remain in Spain. Besides, once Isaac converts, many more Jews will follow. I, like my queen, do not relish the idea of losing so many valuable subjects all at once. Still, I think many Jews would cling to their old beliefs and leave the kingdom, and we'd be able to collect enough funds for Colón's voyage. If this works, we have won two victories. We will still have Don Isaac in our court, and Colón will set sail under the Flag of Castile and Aragon."

Torquemada carefully considered this new idea. It certainly would be a great victory to see Don Isaac Abravanel, direct descendant of King David, accept the Lord Jesus Christ.

"If you agree to the expulsion, I will arrange the abduction of one of Abravanel's grandchildren."

Ferdinand nodded his head in agreement.

Upon leaving the king, Torquemada retired to a small chapel where, to his consternation, he found Talavera, along with several other friars, praying. Talavera looked up for a moment, nodded to Torquemada, then returned to his prayers. Torquemada knelt beside Fray Domingo Gomez who had been kneeling directly behind Talavera and said in a low voice, "You are to leave at once and seize the youngest grandson of Don Isaac Abravanel."

Gomez did not answer, but looked at Torquemada in surprise.

"By order of the king," Torquemada said, and then closed his eyes in prayer, not noticing Talavera stiffen.

Dressed in his dark robes, Talavera watched Gomez mount his mule and ride out in the blackest hour of the night. Talavera silently walked down several corridors until he came to a closed door and softly knocked. There was no answer, and again he knocked. He heard a cough and then a voice said, "Come in."

Isaac had been asleep and was not sure he had heard the first knock on his door. He sat up and watched in amazement as the door creaked open. Hidden behind his robes, a man said, "Your child is in danger."

"Which child?" Isaac asked, startled, fully awake now, his heart racing for he recognized the voice and wondered at the secrecy.

"The youngest, the one named for you . . . ." was all that the cloaked figure whispered before closing the door, leaving Isaac in total blackness.

CHAPTER 35

The stars were dimming as Isaac quickly made his way to Judah's room. He knocked softly on Judah's door. When there was no answer, he opened it and entered.

"Judah," he whispered.

Judah rolled over.

Isaac shook him. "Wake up! Isaac is in danger!"

"What?" Judah quickly sat up. "What's happened?"

"I've been warned that my grandchild is in danger. The king and queen must be preparing to expel the Jews, and this is their attempt to keep us here."

"But why? Why would they want a little boy?"

"To force us to convert," Isaac answered, his head throbbing with anger.

"I told you our services to the queen would lead to trouble, but, no . . . no, you wouldn't listen . . . ."

"There is no time for recrimination. Now listen to me. Whoever is after him has probably already started out, so you must leave now!"

"Where shall I take him? To France?"

"No, they will be expecting that. I'm afraid you will have trouble at the border. Instead, I want you to send him to Portugal. Let Moses take him across the border and claim him as his own child."

"I will take my child to Portugal and bring him to Elisheba."

"And be arrested the moment you cross the border! What protection will he have then? Don't argue with me. There isn't time."

Isaac helped Judah quickly dress and prepare for the journey. When he was ready to leave, Isaac embraced him and said, "May God protect you, son."

"And little Isaac? Why isn't God protecting him?" Judah asked bitterly as he turned from his father.

"He is, Judah. In His own way, He is," Isaac answered, thinking of the warning.

Judah rode furiously each day in an effort to overtake the king's men or friars, he was not sure, but, as the evenings closed in around him, he was forced to stop, for fear that his horse would not last the journey. He made himself chew the dried cheese and crust of bread he had hurriedly packed, and rested for a while each night under the stars. After traveling almost nonstop for four days, he dropped to the ground at night and fell into a deep sleep. Visions of his little boy, crying as men in dark robes carried him away, haunted him. Waking in a sweat, trying to ignore the ominous nightmare, he quickly saddled his horse and rode as if the phantoms in the dream were just in front of him, just beyond his grasp. He covered the enormous distance from Granada to Acalá de Henares quickly, and reached the Abravanel castle before the friar.

Rapidly dismounting, he cried, "Rachel! Rachel!" and when she came running, her face beaming at first then quickly growing pale as she took in his disheveled, agitated state. He tightly held her to him. With Moses and the rest of the family gathering around him, Judah quickly explained what they must do to protect little Isaac. He was grateful that Rachel did not protest but set about getting Isaac prepared for his ride. Rebecca and the others hastily prepared food and horses for their flight. With their bodies bent forward, savagely kicking their horses, Judah, little Isaac strapped to Rachel, and Moses rode away from the castle. Afraid of delivering the child into the bosom of the Inquisition in Toledo, they headed south, their horses racing across the dry, flat plains. The land rolled by, but still they saw no one pursuing them. When they came to a fork in the road which would take them west, Judah pulled up short. He took little Isaac from his mother and folded the child in his arms, holding him tightly. Little Isaac radiated a sweet warmth, and Judah didn't know how he could let him go. He turned to Moses and, trying to catch his breath, said, "You will have to take him across the border to Portugal."

"Portugal! Are you mad? He will be seized the moment we are on Portuguese soil," Moses protested, thinking they were heading for France.

"Not if they think he is your son. The king's men don't know who you are."

"But why not go north to France?"

"Father is sure the border in that direction will be closely watched. They won't expect us to head for Portugal. You won't make good time with the child." He handed him a heavy sack of coins. "Find Elisheba. You will be safe under her protection. Once the danger has passed, you will be able to return." He felt as if he were tearing his heart when he handed little Isaac to Moses, strapping him onto the saddle. "May God go with you."

"We will be just fine, my friend," Moses said, though he had little faith in this plan, that the Portuguese crown wouldn't find them.

Suddenly realizing that she might not see her baby again, Rachel ran to her son and grabbed his outstretched arms. She kissed his fingers.

"I love you! Your mama loves you!" She wept as the little boy reached out for his mother, suddenly realizing that something was wrong.

"Now go!" Judah shouted, glancing anxiously over his shoulder.

Isaac began to cry when Moses turned the white mare, Pegasus, and headed west. Judah and Rachel clung to each other as the cries of their child slowly faded in the distance.

Entering the main hall of the Abravanel castle, Fray Domingo Gomez and his guards were confronted by Rebecca, flanked by her sons Samuel and Joseph.

"What do you want with us?" she asked. Upon seeing the friar, images of the tribunal, of Gomez and Torquemada's omnipotence behind those walls, of the rat infested cell, of Jonathan's tortured soul assailed her, but she clasped her arms tightly around her, and held her head high.

"Haven't you caused us enough pain?"

"I am here to demand that you hand over your grandchild, Isaac Abravanel," Gomez answered unperturbed.

"Why do you want the child? Take me," Samuel said. "If you must have an Abravanel, take me. Little Isaac is just an infant and has harmed no one."

"We don't want you or your mother. We want the child," Gomez continued. He turned and in no particular rush said to his guards, "Search the castle."

The guards swarmed through the castle and within an hour, one guard returned, holding young Jonathan by the scruff of his neck. Bathsheba and Joseph were escorted into the room by other guards.

The guard presented Jonathan to Gomez.

"Here he is."

"That's not the boy I want! I seek the little one named Isaac!"

"There is no one else in the castle," another guard answered. Gomez walked over to Joseph. "Where is the child? Where is the child, Isaac Abravanel?"

As Joseph turned his face away, Gomez lifted his arm as if it were an ax, and struck Joseph, sending him crashing to the ground. Joseph moaned; the side of his lip bled. Jonathan tried to run to his father, but the guard held him fast. Rebecca and Bathsheba, however, were quickly at Joseph's side, cradling him.

Jonathan cried, "What do you want from us? Take me, instead of my cousin!"

"Let him go," Gomez ordered in disgust. The family huddled protectively over Joseph.

Gomez clenched his fists and glared at Rebecca.

"You think the child has escaped us? You are mistaken."

Samuel protectively put his arm around his mother as Gomez began to rage, "We will track him and find him!" He walked over to the window to stare out at the countryside then slowly turned back to face them. "They won't head for France. No, of course not, that would be too logical." He pointed his finger at Rebecca and said, "Someone has betrayed the Church! Someone has warned you, but we will find the child. We will have him!" Surrounded by his guards, Gomez stormed out, leaving them shattered in his wake.

"Oh dear God, please protect our baby," Rebecca whispered as she clung to her children surrounding her.

Cristóbal Colón had finally been called to court. He entered Alhambra and was ushered past the fountains and pools into the Hall of the Ambassadors. Framed by the Mudejar arches and white marble pillars, Ferdinand and Isabella gazed down upon him. To the right of the king stood Luís de Santangel and Francisco Pinelo, and to the left of Queen Isabella stood Abraham Senior and Isaac. Cristóbal bowed.

"Your Majesties, though I have had to wait these six years, it is still my most fervent wish to serve you."

"You know, Señor Colón, that our resources are still extremely low," Ferdinand said. "How much will your voyage cost?"

"We need at least three ships, supplies to last several months and money to pay the sailors. I would have to estimate at least two million maravedis."

Ferdinand raised his eyebrows and then turned to Luis. "Do we have anywhere near that?"

Luís de Santangel bowed and said, "I'm afraid, Sire, we do not."

Ferdinand frowned and stroked his beard. Isaac stepped forward. Before he spoke, Isaac's gaze fell on Pinelo and suddenly a memory was reawakened. Pinelo was the man with the black goatee who had questioned him when he first crossed into Spain. Pinelo was the leader of the Hermandad, the one who had hanged the thief and Isaac felt a chill run down his backbone.

"Yes, Isaac, what is it?" Ferdinand asked impatiently.

Isaac turned back to the king. "Your Majesty, there are still some funds which have not yet been tapped." He shot a glance back at Pinelo.

"What is this? What funds? I thought you said the Jews had no more money!"

"Sire, there are funds are never touched by the crown," Luis said.

"What funds?" Ferdinand roared.

"There are approximately 1,400,000 maravedis appropriated for the law enforcers, the Hermandad, Your Majesty," Isaac answered, not daring to look at the king nor Pinelo. Pinelo's face reddened, and he stepped forward, glared angrily at Isaac, and then bowed to the king. "Excuse me, Your Majesty, but were you to touch those funds, you would be left with no law and order in the land."

"Law and order!" Ferdinand roared again. "There will be no law and order if the French have the means to invade! Let us keep our priorities in order!"

Pinelo paled and quietly answered, "Yes, Your Majesty."

Luis insisted, "But that would still leave six hundred thousand to raise."

Ferdinand turned to Isaac. "I understand the Jews still have some resources. If you expect to be secure within this land, then I imagine you can come up with the needed funds."

Isaac's throat had grown so tight he couldn't speak and could only nod yes. He and Cristóbal exchanged glances.

"I believe the Count Medina Celi also wishes to contribute to the enterprise," Cristóbal added when he saw Isaac's distress.

"Well then, Señor Colón, perhaps we are not so far apart as we had thought. What other stipulations do you have for such a voyage?"

Cristóbal took a deep breath. If he asked for too much, he knew he risked everything. Yet he had to think about his sons, Diego and his infant bastard, Fernando.

"I request one tenth of all the silver, gold and precious gems that I discover. I want one eighth of the treasures brought back from future voyages." Ferdinand was listening carefully, but Cristóbal could not read his thoughts. He continued, "I want to be made a Viceroy of the lands I conquer. The title is to be passed down to my heirs and," he took a deep breath, "to be made Admiral of the Ocean Sea."

"Admiral!" Ferdinand exploded. "The Admiralty is for royalty! My grandfather was an Admiral! Surely you are mad!" Ferdinand stood and pointed his finger at Cristóbal.

"I'll tell you what you can do with your enterprise, Señor Colón! You can take it to King Charles, and let him send you off on your madman's mission!" Ferdinand had begun to march out of the room when he turned and yelled, "And may the devil take you!"

Isabella stood and cried, "My liege!" But it was too late; the king was gone.

Cristóbal's eyes were glued to the floor, his face scarlet.

"I am sorry, Señor Colón," Isabella said, her voice failing her. "It seems we cannot meet your conditions."

Cristóbal bowed curtly and quickly left the hall.

Isaac, Abraham, and Luis retired to the treasury room while, Pinelo headed off in another direction. Luis closed the door and said in a hushed voice, "You had better start raising all you can in Seville, Cordova, and Toledo. Ferdinand will be expecting that money whether Colón sets sail or not."

Isaac and Abraham looked at each other with grim expressions and solemnly nodded in agreement.

Pinelo rapidly walked to the cold dark room where Torquemada prayed. He bowed to the Grand Inquisitor.

"Colón has been dismissed and is leaving for France."

"Why? What has happened?" Torquemada asked.

"He had the audacity to ask for an admiralty! Can you imagine? And Abravanel! Abravanel suggested we use the money from the Hermandad to help Colón set sail."

"It doesn't surprise me," Torquemada said calmly. "My battle with the devil is not yet over. Who is with the queen now?"

"She is alone."

"Good. I must speak with her." Torquemada pulled his cape across his shoulders and left his quarters.

He found Isabella sitting still as a stone, as if under a spell. As his shadow fell across her body, she shivered, looked up and reached her arms out to him.

"Come, my child. Come to me." She knelt at his feet and rested her head against his bony legs.

She said, "The victory I thought would be so sweet has turned bitter. Colón will not sail under the Flag of Castile and Aragon."

"You are being punished for your sins, my child. How often have I told you to repent and to cast the devil from the land, but you have not listened to me."

"I cannot govern without Abraham and Isaac."

"I have spoken at great length with Don Abraham Senior, and I believe he will convert. Perhaps Abravanel can still be persuaded, but if not, then he must be expelled with his people. Your victory will not be complete until this has been accomplished."

"I cannot do as you ask. I cannot expel the Jews."

Shrinking away from him, she stared up into his eyes. It seemed as if a mask had been pulled from his opaque face as it twisted in hate, the eyes aglow, sweat beading his bald head.

"I resign my position as Grand Inquisitor! I cannot continue to fight the devil alone! Your soul will writhe in constant pain for you will be forever damned! I am done with you!"

As he began to walk out of the room, Isabella cried, "No! Father, no! Please don't leave me! Please!" but he did not turn back. She sobbed as she watched his reflection glide across Boabdíl's pools. She sat there for a moment and forced herself to cease crying. Then she stood and hurried to Ferdinand's chambers. She found him pacing back and forth, ran to him, and he held her.

He felt her body trembling when she said, "Oh, my love, we have fought so long and so hard, and it seems now as if it was all in vain."

"Hush, my Isabella." He kissed her, forehead, her lips and brushed away the tears on her cheeks. He held her for a moment. "I cannot give into Colón's demands."

"We have achieved victory because we have always fought His cause. It is His will that Colón shall go forth. It is His will!" Her body still trembled; her eyes were wild as she spoke.

Ferdinand sat down. He rubbed his hands across his brow, across his chin. "Believe me; I don't savor the idea of his going to Charles in France. Haven't I given my whole life over to keeping them out of Aragon! With the riches from the east, Charles will be impossible to stop."

"All you can think about is your damn Aragon!" She raged. Then in a more controlled voice, she pleaded, "Then reconsider, my lord. Think of your provinces, think of the Holy Land still in the hands of the infidels."

He had grabbed her arm and tightened his grip.

"If Charles takes Aragon, everything we have accomplished here will be for naught!" He had to calm himself. "The audacity of the man is not to be tolerated—to be made an admiral! His demands are outrageous!"

"He is willing to risk his life. Does that not make him noble, my lord?" she said softly.

Ferdinand shook his head, and then kissed her forehead again. "Were I to ennoble all who have died for Spain, my love, we would have only noblemen."

Isabella smiled for the first time.

"And the Jewish question. What are we to do about them?" Ferdinand asked. The question caught Isabella's breath. She looked up into his eyes and said very quietly, "They will stay. We will all live in peace."

"I'm afraid it's impossible. You know very well that Abravanel cannot raise the money needed for Colón's voyage. We must do something to get the funds."

"They are one tenth of our population! We are speaking about 300,000 people! Where would they go?"

"Portugal, Turkey—I don't know . . . . All I know is that we have to raise 1,400,000 maravedis, if we decide to accept his proposal."

Isabella gazed into the fire burning on the hearth and, for a moment, saw faces burning in the fire—Jewish faces. She desperately wanted them to convert and felt helpless because she knew that most of them would not, that Isaac would not. "We would be condemning them to death."

"We would be saving the souls of all those who convert, and though your dear Isaac seems obstinate, he may still change his mind, as will others."

Isabella looked up at Ferdinand. "I wish it would be so. Then it is decided?"

"If Isaac raises the six hundred thousand maravedis, then we will let them stay. If not, then I'm afraid, my dear, we have no choice. It is imperative that Colón sail under our flag,"—and he paused—"even if I must give in to his demands."

"Shall we recall Colón then?"

Ferdinand hesitated for only a moment. "Yes, recall Colón. If he reaches the East, then I will grant him his admiralty. I cannot afford to lose him to France."

CHAPTER 36

Swaying back and forth on his mule, Cristóbal had just reached the bridge near Pinos. His head hung so low that his red beard touched his breast, his watery blue eyes reflecting the despair within it. He lifted his head and let the sun warm him. He smiled sadly at little Diego. "No!" He said, more to himself than to the child, "I will never give in! I will travel to every court in Europe until I find a sponsor for my mission. I will carry Christ upon my back, carry his words across the ocean to the lands of Cipango and Khan!"

As the two mules' hooves click-clacked across the bridge, Cristóbal heard the galloping hoof beats of a horse close behind. He pulled his son to the side to let the rider pass and recognized the courier from court.

"Señor Colón, the king and queen have requested your presence before the court," the courier said, trying to catch his breath.

"Why? Why should I return with you? I will not be humiliated again."

"Don't be an arrogant fool! They have reconsidered your proposal and wish to speak with you."

Cristóbal sighed. He gazed up at the sapphire blue January sky as if he were looking for an omen, a sign, but nothing disturbed the infinite blue. He looked at the courier again. "Very well," he said at last and turned his and his son's mules around.

Ferdinand and Isabella had moved back to Santa Fé, so for Cristóbal, the trip back to court was much shorter. It was here that he was received once again. He bowed to the king and queen.

"We have reconsidered your proposal and decided you shall set sail under the Flag of Castile and Aragon," Ferdinand said.

"And my conditions?" Cristóbal asked, not believing he had heard the king correctly.

"They will all be met, provided, of course, that you do indeed reach the Far East."

"Of course, Your Majesty."

Isabella gave Cristóbal her hand and said, "I have always believed it to be your destiny to deliver the word of God to the heathens. Let us pray that you do indeed find your western route and return with riches, with the means to liberate the Holy Land."

"I am your humble servant, Your Highness." He kissed her delicate white hand.

"You are God's servant, Cristóbal," she said as she smiled down upon him.

A Jewish network of communication had been established over the centuries between Seville, Cordova and Toledo so that when Isaac arrived in Seville to deliver the grim news that 600,000 maravedis had to be raised immediately, the news quickly spread to the two other great Jewish centers. Old women carefully wrapped their precious candlesticks with which their families had lighted the Sabbath candles for centuries and pried their rings off their fingers. The silver crowns on the Torahs; the rimonim and keters, their bells a soft, silver whisper calling to God; the breastplates pulled off the precious scrolls.

Isaac sat in the synagogue in Seville and appraised the silver and gold as it was collected. His heart felt heavy when he saw the old men kiss the sacred ornaments good-bye, and he wondered how much time this last treasure would buy for the Jews of Spain. He thought about his little Isaac and prayed that he and Moses had made a safe escape. No one, he felt sure, would be looking for Moses. Abraham Senior and his son-in-law Meir Melamed arrived at the synagogue and found Isaac bent over the ledgers. He looked up.

"Abraham! Where have you been?"

"To Toledo and back." He threw two large sacks onto the table in front of Isaac. Isaac opened the sacks and saw more of the beautiful silver and gold.

Abraham sighed. "I'm afraid the world that we know and love is coming to an end, Isaac. These beautiful objects will be melted down, and the record of our existence here in Spain will be erased. The Torahs are naked in their arks, and all that will remain of our culture, our existence, here will be barren synagogues." There were tears in his eyes as he spoke. He quickly looked at Melamed and then said, "Isaac, I must speak with you privately. Meir, pick up here where Isaac has left off. We have no time to waste."

Meir sat down in Isaac's seat and began appraising the silver and gold. Isaac and Abraham walked into the rabbi's study and closed the door.

"Did your grandson escape?" Abraham asked.

"I don't know yet. Judah hasn't returned."

"What diabolical mind would conceive of using an innocent child as a pawn? What mind could scheme against you like that?"

"Need you ask?" Isaac answered, thinking of Torquemada. "And you, Abraham? Have they made any moves against you? I understand they are also pressuring you to convert."

Abraham laughed. "Pressure?" His face inches from Isaac's, he whispered, "I've been threatened with the loss of Jewish lives. Very simple really, I convert or Jews will be killed!"

Isaac sat down and buried his head in his hands.

"Why is God doing this to us? Where is He? Never has there been a more critical time for His coming!"

"By your own estimates, Isaac, He will not come for at least another ten years."

"But we need Him now! We are about to witness the expulsion of three hundred thousand people! Where will they go? How will they survive?"

"There is no future for the Jews in Spain," Abraham said curtly.

"When the tax laws were changed and the king and queen reserved the right to cancel contracts, I began to worry," Isaac continued.

"It was an ominous sign, but what could we have done to counter it? Nothing. We are helpless pawns in a great master plan. We have been here since the destruction of the second temple, and now we are to be cast out as if we had no part in building this great land."

"You cannot convert! Our people will call you a traitor!"

"If they survive!" Abraham retorted angrily. "They can call me what they like! I'm an old man, with a weak heart. I can sacrifice myself and give in to their wishes. God will know what is in my heart, and you, Isaac, you will know."

"Yes, and I shall defend you to my death. But then I will be the only one to lead our people out of Spain?"

"You, the rabbis, other men will surprise you with the strength of their convictions. But Isaac, what about your grandchild? They know you can't leave him behind," Abraham said, and Isaac could see the deep concern on his face.

"My grandchild, my namesake, that sweet little child who threw his chubby arms around me with so much love—I will never abandon him, never!" his soul cried, but quietly he answered, "I pray to God that we will have him with us before too long. He is safe with Moses, and Moses will see to it that they join us in exile."

Abraham stood. "I must go," he said, then placed his hand on Isaac's shoulder. "Perhaps there is still time. Perhaps you and I can still convince the king and queen not to expel the Jews. Perhaps all is not yet lost."

Isaac could not meet his gaze before Abraham left the room.

After a long day of riding, little Isaac began to cry, and Moses was forced to make camp early. The black night drew in around them, but a warm fire glowed between the small clusters of rocks. Huddled close to the fire, Moses held the child to his breast, sang a lullaby, and rocked him to sleep. He gazed at the long brown eyelashes, the high cheekbones and slender red lips and thought, "He will be a handsome lad, someday. He must look much the way Isaac did as a child."

The sun shed little warmth when it rose the next morning. Little Isaac laughed at the puffs of smoke coming from Moses's mouth as he spoke. He reached out but the smoke disappeared as soon as his fingers touched it. Perplexed, he cocked his head to one side, and Moses couldn't restrain his laugh.

"Come, Isaac. Today we will reach Portugal!" he said as he lifted him onto Pegasus.

"Abba?" the little boy asked.

"No, no Abba," Moses answered. He kicked the horse, and they headed for the Guadiana River. The river was low, moving sluggishly in its early winter lethargy. The horse stumbled on the rocks at the water's edge, and then carefully began to swim out into the middle. Had Moses seen the other side a few seconds earlier, he might have been able to turn the horse around. Now that he saw the drawn swords waiting for him, it was impossible, for the child might slip off were he to change direction in midstream. The horse swam with all its strength to the Portuguese shore, and climbed out. Moses shuddered when he saw the nobleman dressed in black with a black patch across his right eye.

"Off your horse!" Málaga commanded.

Moses unstrapped the child.

"Leave the child where he is!"

Moses dismounted and was instantly surrounded by guards.

"What do you want with the child? He is my son. I'm a poor farmer from Castile. What do you want with my boy?"

Little Isaac saw that Moses was in distress, and he began to cry.

"I know who you are. Did you think I would forget, Moses ibn Aknin?" Málaga walked over to the white mare and pulled Isaac off as he kicked, screamed.

"Leave him alone," Moses shouted, trying to break free from the guards. "He has done you no harm!"

Málaga tucked the thrashing child under his arm. Then he and a priest headed for the water.

"Where are you going with him? You have no right, no right to do this!" Moses raged. He broke away from the guards and ran toward the river. He was tackled and pinned to the earth as the priest submerged the child in the water, baptizing and christening him with the name Carlos Málaga.

"No!" Moses cried. "No!" His voice rose into the sky and mingled with the words of the priest.

The baptism was complete. Málaga walked over to Moses and unsheathed his sword.

"How did you know we were crossing into Portugal?" Moses asking, wondering who had betrayed them

"I have been in constant touch with those high in the Inquisition. I know everything about the Abravanels in Spain, about Juan Sanchez de Sevilla, Jonathan Ben Ezra. I've given them all the information they need to connect him to Isaac. Isaac will fall quickly from the queen's grace, and now, I have the child." Then Málaga cried, "Would that this have been Isaac!" and plunged his sword into Moses's heart. Moses stared at the child, crying by the river, reached out to him, then collapsed.

Carlos Málaga grabbed the sobbing child from the priest's arms, strapped him onto his saddle, mounted his horse, grabbed Pegasus's reins, and rode toward what had been Isaac's castle by the sea. As they galloped through the countryside, the child's screams merged with a roaring wind.

The worst that Isaac feared had come to pass. The edict to expel the Jews was going to be issued. He, Abraham Senior, and his son-in-law Meir Melamed rode furiously toward Granada, toward Alhambra. Isaac was unaware of the land as it flashed by, unaware of his own heart beating. The edict had to be rescinded; the Jews of Spain must be saved. Isaac's eyes were riveted to the horizon. Nothing but the mission before him existed. He and Abraham swiftly passed under the sorcerer's arch and made their way up the long winding road to the castle on the hill, to which the king and queen had returned. They dismounted and were granted an immediate audience. Striding into the Hall of the Ambassadors, they were finally forced to come to a halt. Cristóbal stood to one side, and the Count Medina Celi was on his knees before the king and queen.

"I have money for the enterprise. Surely, if this is the only reason for the expulsion, then you must reconsider." He turned to see Isaac, Abraham, and Meir.

Isabella could not raise her eyes to meet Isaac's. She gazed instead at Abraham, who bowed. The Count retreated to where Cristóbal stood.

"Your Majesties," Abraham said. "We have collected three hundred thousand gold ducats." He placed two bags before the king, and Isaac laid another two beside them.

"Three hundred thousand gold ducats!" Ferdinand said and his mouth hung open. Isabella smiled and for the first time turned to Isaac.

"Your Majesties," Isaac said softly. "We came to this land at the time of the destruction of our temple in Jerusalem. We lived here when Christ walked the earth. We have lived by your laws, paid your taxes, and in short have contributed to the health, welfare, beauty, and greatness that is Spain. Do not pass this edict or you will incur the wrath of God in his Heaven." Isaac paused for a moment and then pointed his finger at the king, "Beware, King Ferdinand. Beware Divine destruction which you threaten to bring down upon yourself! Not your mission across the sea, not your penance, or your prayers will deliver you from the wrath of the Almighty if you expel the Jews from this land. In King David's own words, Psalm 11:4-6, he stated, 'The Lord trieth the righteous; But the wicked and him that loveth violence His soul hateth. Upon the wicked He will cause to rain coals; Fire and brimstone and burning wind shall be the portion of their cup.'"

The room was silent as the words from the Bible reverberated off the walls of Moorish design. Isaac fell before Ferdinand and Isabella. He stretched out his arms to them, and pleaded, "Rescind the edict! Accept this gold as our last pitiful cry for mercy. Cast us out, and you sentence us to death as surely as if you were to burn each one of us at the stake. We have nowhere to go! We are a conquered people! Our land, our kingdom was lost to the infidels long ago. We have been loyal, true to you and your cause! Do not turn from us now in our hour of need. Beware the wrath of God! He will turn your victory into defeat and cause your glorious kingdom to crumble."

King Ferdinand's hands shook when he gestured and said, "Rise, Don Isaac Abravanel. You speak words of truth. Your people have paid for their security. They shall be allowed to stay!"

At that moment, a long black shadow was cast across the floor, and all turned to see Tomas Torquemada, standing in the entrance, seeming to blot the radiant sun from the room. He held up a small wooden cross. His frame shook and his voice seemed to crack like lightening as he cried, "Judas Iscariot sold his master for thirty pieces of silver. Your Highnesses would sell him anew for thirty thousand; here he is, take him, and barter him away." With all his might, he threw the cross, hit Isabella in the head, then turned and strode out of the hall.

There was a terrible silence in the room as if two titans had clashed, and the smoke had to rise before the victor could be determined.

Stunned, King Ferdinand stood and cried, "The edict will stand!"

Rubbing her head where she had been struck, Isabella stared at Ferdinand in dismay, then at her hands which had blood from the wound to her forehead. She turned to Isaac and said, "Do you think that this comes from us? The Lord directs the king, as the rivers of water. The Lord turns all as He wills, even the Most Catholic Monarchs." She stood and ran from the room.

CHAPTER 37

As Isaac approached his castle in Alcalá de Henares, several friars of the Dominican Order rode furiously past. Isaac felt relieved at seeing none of his household with them, but then he heard screams coming from the castle's highest tower. As a knot tightened in his stomach, he looked up, alarmed to see Rachel wrestling with someone by the highest turret window. Her head and arms were leaning out the window and, from where he stood, it looked as if someone was pushing her. Isaac watched her disappear back inside the tower. Feeling as if he were caught in a cruel nightmare in which he had no control, he rode into the castle, dismounted and ran toward the high tower. Racing up the steps, he almost collided with Rebecca, who was running down.

"What has happened?" he demanded.

Rebecca had been crying. His stomach churned and his knuckles whitened around her shoulders, "What's wrong? Why were those friars here? What terrible message did they bring? Speak!" he shouted when she still didn't answer but could only weep.

They both sank onto the cold stone floor and after a moment she finally found her voice. "Moses is dead. Little Isaac was kidnapped and baptized when they crossed the border. When Rachel heard the news a few moments ago, she tried to jump from the tower, but Judah held her back."

"Who would do such a thing?" Isaac cried.

Rebecca looked deeply into his eyes, the pain in her own eyes quite clear. "My half-brother," she said as she brushed past him. "Isaac is with Carlos Málaga now."

Isaac rose; his fists clenched and raised above his head, "Why?" he cried. "Why?" He sank back down and began to weep.

Holding tightly onto Rachel, Judah guided her down the stairs. As they passed Isaac, the fury in Judah's eyes seared Isaac to the heart. Rachel was weeping, but her mad abandon seemed to have subsided.

Unaware of time, Isaac sat staring at the stone walls until young Jonathan found him sitting there and took his large hands in his own smaller ones.

"Grandfather," he whispered.

Isaac looked down at the child.

"Rabbi Aboab is here. He says he must speak with you."

Isaac caressed Jonathan's golden hair and patted him on the back. Trying to find his voice, he coughed and said, "Tell the rabbi that I will be there in a moment."

Jonathan scampered down the stairs, and finally, Isaac stood, made his way back into the main hall, and then beckoned the rabbi into his library.

After Isaac closed the door, the rabbi said, "I'm so sorry, Isaac. I just heard about our child, little Isaac . . . . It's a terrible thing that has happened." He shook his head and wiped tears from his eyes.

Isaac sighed, trying to control his voice, he said almost incoherently, "The boy, Moses, my dearest friend . . . . What are we to do rabbi? How can we right this terrible wrong? I must go to Portugal and find the child!"

"Isaac, there are some things that are beyond our power to control. You must not blame yourself for this. And chasing after the child will not bring him home any sooner; you know that deep in your heart."

"But I am to blame! I sent the child to Portugal—can't you see, just now, my own son won't even look at me?"

"Isaac," the rabbi said in a stronger tone, "if it is the will of God,"

"You speak to me of the will of God!" Isaac cried in desperation. "My brother-in-law languishes in the inquisitional dungeons . . . after his beloved was burned at the stake! My closest friend, Fernando Braganza has been murdered and our grandson, my namesake . . . baptized! Tell me, rabbi, tell me that this is how God has planned it all!" he cried, as if the pain in his heart were tearing at the very center of his soul.

In a quiet but very firm voice, the rabbi answered, "Yes, yes, this is part of His plan, and you, Isaac, you are not to question it." He put his hand on Isaac's shoulder. "Isaac, I suffer too . . . we all are suffering. Now that the edict will stand, there is panic everywhere. Our people don't know where to go, what to do. We have had word from Portugal that King João will allow 150,000 Jews to immigrate. We will divide the number evenly allowing 50,000 from each city. What do you think, Isaac? Is Portugal safe for them?"

Shaking the old man, Isaac cried, "Old man, how can you ask me? I can't advise you about Portugal. King João's henchman, Málaga, has just snatched our grandchild, and is responsible for the murder of my friend. Don't ask me about Portugal!" The room began to spin around him, and he put his hands out to stop it. He began to sway, and then the floor seemed to rise up and crack against him.

When he came to, he felt deathly cold, as if a wet shroud were covering him. He was shivering as Judah placed warm shawls around him. Rebecca's head was resting on his chest, adding a little warmth he so desperately needed. The rabbi was leaning over him with a worried expression on his face. Isaac tried to rise, but Judah forcefully held him down.

"Don't move," he said. There was no love in his voice.

Rebecca angrily turned to her son. Isaac closed his eyes, but he could feel her rise away from him, the little bit of extra warmth leaving him, and then he flinched when he heard a hard slap.

"Don't—you—ever use that tone of voice again when speaking to your father!" Isaac heard her say in a cold, hard voice. "Do you blame him for our heartache?"

"Yes, I blame him!" Judah spat.

"Then leave this house. You will not live under my roof in anger and hatred! Your father has done everything, everything in his power to avert these tragedies! My brother rots in prison, and I pray each day that the Lord will take his soul and put an end to his suffering. Do you think I blame your father? Our people are faced with expulsion with no place to go. Do you blame your father for that as well? Do you?" Rebecca's face was red with rage, her words spitting forth.

Rubbing his cheek, tears streaming down, Judah whispered, "No, mother. Forgive me?"

"You ask him for forgiveness, not me," she said and fled from the room.

Judah bent over Isaac, rested his head on his father's chest and wept. Isaac tried to lift his left arm but couldn't. In a muffled voice, coherent to only himself, he whispered, "We will see him again. Listen to me, Judah. Someday we will all be reunited. You must have faith." Isaac looked up at Rabbi Aboab, who was still anxiously hovering over him. He stretched out his right arm to the rabbi. "Tell the people chosen to go to Portugal that they will be safe. King João will not go back on his word. Urge the 150,000 Jews to immigrate to Portugal. I will arrange to set sail with the rest."

"Where will you go, Isaac? Where?" the rabbi asked.

"My own family will go to Naples. I think King Ferrante can be persuaded to let us live in his land. Perhaps we can send some of the others to North Africa."

"We have had word that some Jews would be received in Turkey. What can they do to us that has not already been done?" the rabbi asked.

"I don't know, rabbi. Let us pray that we will all be alive to see the Messiah when he comes," Isaac said, and then closed his eyes, too sad, too weary for more conversation.

Judah stood and said quietly to the rabbi, "We must let him rest. He will come to you in Toledo as soon as he is able."

Isaac had never felt so weak, so vulnerable as he did in those few days he lay in his chambers. He grieved for Moses and for little Isaac, wondering if he would ever see the child again. He had thought that perhaps Elisheba was meant to stay behind in Portugal, protected by her husband, Diego, a Braganza, Fernando's son, that perhaps this was all part of His plan for her to be there when little Isaac needed her. But now, once again, it all fell apart, became too much, too much to bear. He closed his eyes as tears streamed down his face. He knew he had to gather his strength, once more, to face his people, to lead them forth. But he was not Moses. He was not a prophet, and the task before him seemed impossible. How could he arrange the safe exodus of over 300,000 Jews?

A week later, his hands slightly paralyzed, limping badly, Isaac arrived in Toledo to advise the Jews that as many as possible should sail to Turkey. King Ferrante in Naples had heard about the enormous sums of money Isaac had raised for the crusade in Granada, but had not yet issued an invitation. When he met with the elders, Isaac was also confronted with the enormous problem of finding seaworthy vessels to carry the Jews to their various destinations. The captains, whose reputations made Isaac's skin crawl, were asking exorbitant prices for the voyages, and the ships available to them were leaky vessels, barely seaworthy.

Isaac had just met with one of the congregations to inform them of the latest development that ten more ships had been hired, and was passing through the city gates when he saw an auto-de-fé procession. He brought his halted his horse, overwhelmed with grief as he watched ten men and women, wearing the hateful sacks with laughing devils painted on them, sanbenitos, marched to the stakes. Panic stricken, Isaac searched their faces, but none seemed to resemble Jonathan, though there was a tall man dressed like the others in a sanbenito, his skin hanging loose from his bones as he limped along, his shoulders stooped. But his head hung so low that Isaac could not see his face. Shaking, terrified that the man might be Jonathan, Isaac dismounted. "No!" Isaac thought, racing now to keep up with the procession. "Oh, dear Lord, please, please, not him," he mumbled as he tripped and stumbled over people in an effort to get closer to the man. Relatives were hugging the victims, clinging to them as guards pulled them apart. Isaac caught a glimpse of the man's face and, recognizing Jonathan, ran to him, pushing past guards, men, women and children whose faces were distorted with pain, and reached him, grasped him, just before he was led to his stake. Jonathan responded to his grasp with vacant eyes as guards pushed Isaac back.

"Don't you know me?" Isaac said, shaking the guards back. "Jonathan, it's I, Isaac. Jonathan!" Two guards pried him away, shoving him aside, and he fell to the ground.

"Jonathan!" he cried again, but Jonathan did not respond and placidly allowed the guards to tie him to the stake. He raised his eyes to the clear sky and caught sight of a hawk winging high above the white clouds. The fire was lit and began to burn his feet. The searing pain snapped his mind, and staring at Isaac, he suddenly recognized him and struggled to free himself from the flames.

"Isaac!" he screamed. Their eyes locked, as fire crept up his body, but then excruciating, exquisite pain overwhelmed him. He cast his eyes to the sky and cried, "She ma Yisraeil Adonai elo hei nu Adonai echad!" Within seconds the flames devoured his body.

Isaac wrapped his arms around himself, unable to absorb the horror, and fell to the ground. An silvered haired man and his wife pulled Isaac away from the burning inferno, and practically carried him to where the heat was less, smoke still thin. Isaac dropped down to his knees, feeling as if his own body had been consumed, as if his own life had been reduced to ash.

Rebecca couldn't stop her hands from shaking as she tried to tie bundles of Isaac's books. She felt as if the world were indeed coming to an end. Jonathan was gone, her dearly beloved brother, her grandson baptized, living with her half-brother who hated them for no other reason than a difference of religion. She had always harbored the dream that someday Jonathan would be released, that the Inquisition would lose interest in him . . . . But it was not to be.

All their earthly belongings were loaded onto three wagons. Judah and Rachel helped Rebecca onto the first wagon, but when Rachel put her arm protectively around her, she felt no warmth. Jonathan, her golden haired brother, with his carefree laugh and his shining bright eyes, was gone.

With vacant eyes, Rebecca watched as her other children, the boys, Joseph and Samuel, climb into the other wagons along with Isaac's father's chair and desk, her table and chairs, their beds piled high and tied down with cord. Bathsheba, Joseph and young Jonathan had their own wagon. They would all go to Naples together. Queen Isabella had ordered Luís de Santangel to repay Isaac the 1,400,000 maravedis he had contributed to the crusade, and to Colón's expedition.

Handing the iron key of his castle to the stranger who had bought it, Isaac thought of Isabella. He could picture her fine red hair, streaked with grey, her white hands, like marble, her cold blue eyes, eyes that would not meet his on that fateful day in Alhambra. He still could not completely piece together exactly how this exodus had come to pass, and still could not believe that Isabella had, in the end, given in to Torquemada. Too weak to ride his horse all the way to Valencia, Isaac climbed onto the wagon, sat next to Rebecca, and, for the last time, feeling much older than fifty-five, rode away from Alcalá de Henares.

The road was lined with other Jewish families. Some rode on horses and wagons, like the Abravanels, but most walked. Fathers carried what was left of the family's possessions on their backs. Mothers carried their babies in one arm and held onto little ones with the other hand. Children were crying, tired after days of walking. Just in front of the Abravanels, a family walked beside their loaded mule. The grandfather led the mule, and three curly headed children shuffled by his side. The mother sang softly to a little one in her arms, and the father, carrying some books and a few pots and pans, brought up the rear. Suddenly, the grandfather tripped and fell. As the children and mother and father gathered around him, Isaac jumped off the wagon, ran to the man, held his head, while Judah opened his medical bag, but it was too late. The old man's grey eyes stared blindly at the sky, but there seemed to be the slightest smile upon his lips. Isaac and his sons helped to bury him by the side of the road, as the procession of Jews continued. The father looked up at Isaac when they were done and said, "At least he didn't have to leave Spain. Perhaps that's why he was smiling." The father shook his head as the family joined the seemingly never ending procession.

As the darkness crept over them, the Abravanels made camp along the roadside. Before a simple meal of bread and cheese, Isaac led a large congregation of men in prayer. The women and children huddled close to the campfires and whimpered. A pregnant woman screamed out in pain, and her husband and midwives ran to her side. Women wept throughout the service, and the men's voices in the last prayer, were joined by the cry of a new born child.

"Mazel Bueno!" Isaac shouted.

"Don Isaac, how can you say Mazel Bueno when the poor infant is born into such madness?" one young man asked.

Isaac could feel the silence surround him as the men waited for his answer. He closed his eyes and let the words of the prophet Daniel 7:13-14 thunder forth: "'I saw in the night visions, And, behold, there came with the clouds of heaven One like unto a son of man, And he came even to the Ancient of days, And he was brought near before Him. And there was given him dominion, And glory, and a kingdom, That all the peoples, nations, and languages should serve him; His dominion is an everlasting dominion, which shall not pass away . . . . ' The time is near."

Isaac paused for a moment. He looked into the eyes of wise old men, of young men who needed to hear something that would give them the strength to go on, the strength to start new lives in a foreign land. He stared at the women, their heads covered, many with babes at their breasts, waiting to hear words of solace, words of comfort, something to give them the courage to cling to their Judaism even though it meant giving up their homeland. His voice was rich and strong when he said, "We must celebrate His coming for never was there a time when His people needed Him more!" The campfire flickered before him, and he stared into the fire. Isaac paused for a moment and then his voice rose into the black night sky. "We must celebrate! We must rejoice, for the time is at hand! The Messiah will soon come to heal our sorrowful hearts." He began to clap his hands and dance around the campfire. Judah, Joseph, Samuel, young Joseph and young Jonathan joined in the dance. Slowly some of the men joined them until thirty, fifty, a hundred men danced around the campfires singing, crying, praising God and calling for His mercy.

Isaac continued singing to his people as they marched to Valencia, where ships awaited them. They arrived on August 2, 1492, the ninth of Ab in the Jewish calendar, the very date of the destruction of the second temple in Jerusalem, a horrific day to begin a new life. The singing ceased as they saw the ships rocking on their moorings, waiting to take them away across the dark, cold water. A number of women suddenly began to weep, clutching the earth, kissing the ground as if it were sacred. Their husbands had to pick them up and carry them on board like lifeless bodies. The children silently held onto their fathers' hands and like frightened sheep were herded onto the ships as well. Priests were waiting to baptize any who grew fainthearted. A few did indeed bow to the priests' wishes, and were baptized rather than board the dilapidated ships. Most, however, had the courage to sail to another land, once again.

"Have courage!" Isaac called as he handed children to their parents on the ships. "The time is near! The Lord will not forsake us! He will lead us to His everlasting kingdom, and we shall know its peace!"

When the time came for his own family to board, Isaac held Rebecca's hand to help her across the gangplank. He felt distressed as he held her, for she had grown so thin, her face so grey, her eyes so full of pain. He helped her find a comfortable spot to sit down, and the family settled in around her.

Rebecca looked up at Isaac, and for the first time in many weeks, a smile brightened her face.

"What could possibly amuse you?" he asked as he settled in beside her.

"I packed your books instead of the pillows, so I guess we will have to use them now to lay our heads upon."

Isaac held her tightly as he felt the ship list away from the mooring. He kissed the top of her head. "I love you so much." He wept softly, crumbling now that they were really on their way. "I tried so hard to make you happy, to protect you, my family, my people, and I failed." He fell to the deck with Rebecca in his arms.

Though her hands shook badly, she brushed back his tears, "Shush. No, that's not so. How can you talk like that? Look at our beautiful family. Look at how much joy you have brought into my life."

"And those who are not with us?"

"Jonathan," her voice cracked. Then she looked down at him as he sank into her arms and in a stronger voice, rocking him gently in her arms, she continued, "Jonathan chose his path long ago. You are not to blame yourself for his agony. May his soul rest in peace."

"As the rivers of water . . . ."

"What?" Rebecca whispered.

"It's what the queen said to me in the Hall of the Ambassadors. As God controls the rivers of water, so He controls the king in his decision to expel the Jews. I couldn't stop it, waters rushing . . . . Are we damned to wander the earth, like rivers of water, from kingdom to kingdom, never finding a home, a safe haven, always to be invited to live somewhere just at the pleasure of a king until he changes his mind!" Isaac cried.

"Someday, it shall be as it is written in the Bible," Rebecca answered, stroking his fine gray hair. "Someday there will be a Fifth Kingdom, and we shall all live in peace, someday in Jerusalem."

"Yes, but I had hoped to see it in my lifetime, in Spain, where our people have lived for hundreds of years, to see my own family safe and secure from the caprice of kings and queens. It's what my father expected of me."

"Perhaps your father's vision was larger than even he could imagine. After all, Spain is not the Holy Land."

Rebecca cradled him as he wept, but then suddenly, they both looked up as Judah grabbed Rachel, pulling her away from the ship's rail as she shrieked, "My baby! My baby! My baby!"

"Elisheba? Little Isaac?" Isaac choked on the words.

Cristóbal had planned to set sail on the same day the Abravanel's left Spain, but the port in Palos was so crowded with departing Jews that he was forced to put off his departure. Besides, he too knew about the 9th of Ab and did not want to set sail on that date. Before the dawn broke on August 3, 1492, Cristóbal set sail on the *Santa Maria*, accompanied by the *Nina* and the *Pinta*. The square sails of the caravels were raised and billowed out against the blue of the sea and sky.

They had been out at sea for only a day when the crew became terrified. The first mate called to Cristóbal, who hurried up on deck.

"What is the trouble?" he asked.

"The men hear strange noises coming from the horizon. They are afraid of sea serpents."

Cristóbal glared sternly at the sailors. "Nonsense! There are no sea serpents in these waters!" But hearing the wailing sounds which seemed to come from the depths of the water, he studied the horizon half expecting to see dragons breathing fire. Slowly,

a ship appeared on the horizon, then two and three and four. At first Cristóbal's heart pounded against his chest, and he wondered if they were warships, but as they came closer he saw that they were not. The wailing was coming from the ships.

Cristóbal's eyes grew sad; deep furrows formed in his face as he realized that these ships were carrying the Jews into exile. He knew Isaac and his family were on one of the ships. At first, not having the courage, he kept his head down as the ships passed, but then, he did look up and was able to discern the figures of men and women crying and praying. The tear-streaked faces of the children peeked at him as their parents held them in their arms. The ships passed each other on the high seas and continued to sail on in their opposite directions, disappearing over the horizon.

CHAPTER 38

For close to a month the ship the Abravanels and one hundred other Jews were on tossed about the Mediterranean, laboriously making its way toward Naples. Isaac, who had been sitting next to Rebecca, jumped up to chase a rat back into one of the many holes in the deck. He picked his way between the passengers, searching for Judah, whom he had not seen all morning, and found him laying the body of a dead young woman down on the deck and then quickly covering it with cloth.

Isaac sensed his son's distress and whispered, "What is it, son? What's wrong?"

Judah guided Isaac away from the bereaved relatives and whispered, "It's the plague!"

They stared at each other for a long moment before Isaac was able to say, "What must we do to keep this from spreading?"

"We must quickly bury the body at sea, and then we must isolate everyone who has a fever."

"Yes, but how can we do this without creating panic?"

"What do you suggest, father?"

"Shall we just say we don't want sickness to spread?"

Judah nodded.

They went from family to family searching for those with a fever or severe vomiting. They found ten, and quickly isolated them from the rest of the passengers. By the next morning, however, there were twenty with fever, and by that evening it seemed that almost everyone on board was suffering from the plague.

Young Jonathan lay in Bathsheba's arms as she wiped his sweated forehead. His eyes were glassy and his lips parched. Bathsheba was also shaking with a fever.

"Come, Jonathan," Judah said as he lifted the child's head. Young Jonathan grimaced when he tasted the bitter medicine and choked, trying to swallow. Isaac gave him a cup of water, and Jonathan settled back into his mother's lap.

Isaac felt Bathsheba's forehead. "You must take this also," he insisted. Rebecca was sleeping next to them. Isaac bent over and felt her forehead. She too had fever but not as badly as the others. He woke her. "My love, you must take some of this." He and Judah held her as she took the medicine.

It seemed that before their eyes, healthy, pink cheeks faded in color to grey, lips grew parched and sore; eyes that had sparkled grew dull.

The caravel arrived in Naples on August 24. Though other ships carrying Jews were waiting for permission to disembark, King Ferrante had been advised that Isaac was on board and their ship was immediately granted the right to drop anchor. The Abravanels' ship was not the first to have the plague on board so when they disembarked the sailors and laborers who saw the sick and dying being carried off cursed them.

Rebecca and Bathsheba held onto each other as they gingerly made their way down the gangplank. Joseph carried Jonathan in his arms, for the boy's fever still raged. They were escorted to a camp where tents had been erected for the sick, and as they walked past row upon row of Jews suffering from the plague, several held their hands out to them. Only five doctors tended the hundreds of sick, and they were in desperate need of Judah's medical abilities.

The Abravanels had set up a tent on the outskirts of the camp and within their first week, a courier called on them. Isaac was bending over Jonathan, encouraging him to drink some fresh water.

"Don Isaac Abravanel?"

"Yes?" Isaac looked up at the well dressed nobleman.

"King Ferrante wishes a private audience with you."

Isaac and Judah exchanged glances, and Isaac bowed to the courier. "It will be my great honor. If you will kindly give me a moment to change." He excused himself and dressed in his finest black velvet suit, then put on his gold scorpion chain. Fingering it for a moment, tears came to his eyes as he thought of Jonathan, then of Isabella. How she had admired this chain. "Perhaps," he thought, "it will bring us some good luck with this new king." He came out of the tent and was distressed to see a sleek black stallion waiting for him. He didn't know if he was strong enough to mount the stallion nor control him. With Judah's help, trying to hide his weakness, he managed to struggle up onto the horse and follow the courier to the Nuovo Castillo.

Having been raised in the Portuguese court, Isaac was familiar with royal splendor, but the ten years he had spent in the austere court of Spain had left him unprepared for the grandeur before him as he entered Ferrante's court. The ceilings were covered with cherubs gazing upward, and beautiful frescos of birds, flowers, and pastoral scenes circled the room. The checkered marble floors glistened under Isaac's feet as he walked toward Ferrante's throne. Thin and haggard, with dark circles under his eyes, Isaac bowed to King Ferrante and his son, Prince Alfonso.

"Welcome, Don Isaac Abravanel. Your reputation has preceded you, and I hope that you will honor our court with your invaluable service!"

"I am your humble servant, Your Majesty. Sick and homeless, we have landed on your shores. My people will never forget your magnanimity. We will be forever grateful," Isaac answered.

"Don Isaac, let me be brief and to the point. I assure you I will receive you as befits your nobility on another occasion, but now I'm afraid the issues before us are too pressing for such niceties. I also realize you have not yet had time to settle your family, and will assist you as soon as possible. However, the plague is sweeping through the land. Understandably, my subjects have been hostile to the presence of your people, but I am determined not to be swayed. The Jews are welcome. We must immediately enlarge the sick camps so that the plague can be contained. I have arranged for physicians to administer to the sick and ordered my treasurers to pay for medical supplies."

"Your generosity comes at a time when my faith in humanity had ebbed. With proper medical care and supplies we may hope to control the sickness and save hundreds of precious lives."

"I hope so, Don Isaac. King Charles of France has an appetite for conquest, with particular relish for my lands, and I cannot afford to risk arousing the enmity of my own people right now. It is my wish that you will soon find a home and become an integral part of my court."

"It is my honor, Your Majesty, to serve a prince of mercy." Isaac bowed low, overwhelmed by the king's generosity. Ferrante's kindness was in such sharp contrast to Isabella's cruel rejection that Isaac wondered if God had directed him here to this place, this kingdom where he and his people would witness the coming of the Messiah.

It had been a little less than one year since the Abravanels had arrived in Naples. Sitting within a modest but comfortable villa, Judah threw another log on the fire and watched the flames crackle and snap. He took a long taper and lit his mother's fine brass candelabrum, then sat down at his mother's table, running his hands across the smooth wood. He had just returned from the tending to the sick and sat, mystified that his father had accomplished the impossible once again—setting up a comfortable home in a strange land for the third time in his life. Judah marveled at Isaac's resiliency. Isaac was already as powerful in Ferrante's court as he had been in King Afonso's and King Ferdinand's. It seemed Prince Alfonso also held him in high regard, which was comforting, remembering João. A vision of Málaga standing with his fist raised as they crossed into Spain streaked across his mind. He imagined what the moment had been like when Málaga had slain Moses, and had baptized his son. He desperately missed those small, chubby arms slung around his neck, so trusting. "Oh, my child, I was not worthy of that trust," he thought, breaking out in a sweat, trying not to cry, then held his head in his hands for a moment.

"Well, Carlos, you've had your sweet revenge haven't you!" Suddenly afraid that Rachel might be nearby, might have heard him, he glanced over his shoulder, but she was in her upstairs chamber. Too grief-stricken, he had not come to her since they had arrived in Naples. Though his little Isaac had been taken from them, and baptized; he could not say the death prayers, the kaddish, for him. Little Isaac lived in his heart.

For Judah, he was still very much alive, very much part of his family. He was not dead, though the rabbis would tell him so. When he felt as if his heart were bleeding, he turned to pen and paper and under the pen name, Leone Ebro, he wrote:

'O how I long and yearn to see thee . . . .
Darling, fondling loved son . . . .
What villain snatched thee from my bosom?
Who hath made thee a forsaken one?'

Judah threw the pen down and stood. He wanted to scream his pain into the black night. He blew out the candles he had lit, and with a single taper in his hand, he climbed the steps to his chambers. He found Rachel sleeping and gently lay down beside her. He pressed his body close to hers and felt the soft rise and fall of her breath. He was afraid to wake her, afraid of her tears, but he needed her desperately. The world seemed unbearably bleak and cold. He tenderly brushed back her long hair and kissed the nape of her neck. She softly moaned. He slipped his hand inside her satin sleeping gown and found her skin warm and smooth. She woke, and he startled her with a kiss.

"Judah, I can't! My baby! My baby!" she whimpered.

He pressed her tightly against him. "I have suffered too. My heart also is broken . . . ." He cried for a moment. "I've tried so hard to be strong for you . . . . I've tried so hard. I can't anymore. I need you now."

She threw her arms around him as his tears slipped down her breasts. "I love you . . . ."

He dried his eyes and gently pulled off her gown, kissing her neck, her white arms, her breasts. She softly whispered his name, and they united.

Sunbeams, filtering into the bedroom the next morning, woke him. He rose and found scented steaming water waiting for him to wash. He could hear the family downstairs at breakfast and the aroma of fresh bread, eggs sizzling on the grill, drifted up to his chamber. Feeling refreshed for the first time in many weeks, he quickly dressed and went downstairs. With a bounce in his walk, he was about to join the family, when Isaac abruptly stood up to go, a worried look on his face.

"What now?" Judah asked. The sadness he read in his father's face seemed too much to bear.

"King Ferrante is very sick. I must leave at once."

"But why are you so worried? Prince Alfonso holds you in the highest regard. Surely, even if the king, God forbid, should die, we are secure here. There is no need to be so sad."

Isaac sighed. Seeing for the first time in so many months a smile upon Judah's face, he felt pain in destroying his fine spirits. "I'm afraid it is very grave, Judah. King Charles has been planning to invade Naples for some time now."

"But he wouldn't dare! King Ferdinand would stop him before he even set foot in any Italian state."

"That's just the point. King Ferdinand has been looking for an excuse, as well. Both Charles and Ferdinand are waiting for Ferrante's death."

"What does this mean for us?" Judah asked, trying to control his rising feeling of panic. "Rachel can't take any more pain. Our wounds are just beginning to heal! And Mother? What of Mother? Surely you can't put her on another rat-infested ship and expect her to survive a voyage to another, damned kingdom where we can set up house again for a few months before we are forced to flee!"

In a gentle voice, Isaac answered, "If Ferrante dies, and Charles invades, then I will leave you here. I will follow Alfonso into exile, but you and the family will stay. You are right. I cannot move my family again. God will protect you."

He had begun to walk away when Judah grabbed his arms and pulled him around. "Why? Why must you flee? Why can't you stay with us?"

"What choice do I have?" Isaac cried in despair. "I'm one of the king's favorites. How long do you think I would survive in a dungeon?"

"Where will you go this time? Where?" Judah's voice broke.

"I don't know," Isaac answered softly and turned to leave for court.

Judah followed him outside. He watched Isaac's foot slip from the stirrup as he tried to mount his horse, and ran to assist him. Because of his old wounds, Isaac could no longer sit up straight in his saddle, but he turned his horse's head and rode away.

"The king is dead! Long live the king!" was the cry that issued forth from Ferrante's chambers. With the dead king lying between them, Isaac and Alfonso stared grimly at each other. Alfonso dropped his father's hand.

Isaac asked, "How long will it take for Charles to mobilize his forces?"

"A month or two," King Alfonso answered. "We can expect his army by this summer. And if I have to abdicate, Isaac, will you follow me into exile?"

"*Yes,* Your Majesty, I will go with you."

In the summer of 1495, Charles VIII of France invaded Naples.

CHAPTER 39

His sword crossed, ready for a sparring session, the twelve-year-old Carlos Málaga held his left arm back, that hand slightly bent, his face somber. His uncle faced him, intent, with his one good eye.

"Now!" his uncle commanded, and they began to duel. Carlos quickly brought his sword up to meet the oncoming blows. His uncle wielded his sword with quick sharp slashes, sending Carlos back, as with each step, with all his strength, he repelled the repeated blows, forced around the large room, his uncle mercilessly hammering away. He could feel his grip slipping and suddenly the sword flew out of his hand. His uncle laughed, and fear swept through young Carlos as the sword inched closer and closer until it touched his chest.

"If you come any closer, uncle, you'll have my heart," he said, trying to sound unconcerned.

His uncle hesitated a moment as if contemplating driving the sword on through, then pointed it away and said disdainfully, "Pick up the sword, boy." Carlos quickly bent down and while his back was turned his uncle continued, "When I was your age, I could wield a sword with twice your strength."

Carlos turned around to face him.

"But I'm not your son. I imagine I must be more like my father than like you!"

"You mean more like your grandfather." His uncle laughed.

"And who were they, uncle? Why will you never speak of them? Why will you never tell me their names?"

His uncle pointed his sword inches from Carlos' right eye, "Because they were Jews!"

"You lie!" Carlos shouted. "How could they be Jews when you are my uncle? Answer me that!"

"That is my secret, and when I die, the answer will be sealed forever!"

"No!" Carlos said, more calmly now, carefully concealing his real feelings for the man. "I want to know the truth. I have a right to know who I am!" He crossed his uncle's sword, and with all his strength began to fight.

The swords flashed, but even though the twelve-year-old fought furiously, his uncle quickly pinned him back against the wall. With one quick slash, he grazed the boy's hand, his sword clattering to the floor. Holding his bleeding hand under his arm, Carlos bent down, picked up the sword and, catching his uncle off guard slashed his sword from his hand. Now Carlos pointed his sword at his uncle's chest and backed him up against the wall.

"Tell me, uncle, who is my father? He's not a Jew! You lie! Tell me! I have a right to know who he is!"

With an ugly smile upon his lips, Carlos Málaga glared down at his nephew.

"Perhaps you are destined to know the truth. I wanted to save you from the shame that knowledge can bring. Your blood is tainted. You are not pure, just as I am not pure."

"I want the truth!" Carlos said as he jabbed the sword against Málaga's shirt.

"You are Isaac Abravanel, son of Judah Abravanel, grandson of the traitor to King João, and my nephew!"

"King João is dead, and the new King Manuel, the son of the Duke of Viseu, Prince Fernando's brother, had no love for King João."

"What does it matter? Your parents were Jews! Had they come back for you, they would have suffered the fate of all the other Jews who emigrated from Spain in 1492. When King Manuel married Ferdinand and Isabella's daughter, Isabella, the Jews in Portugal were given a choice: baptism or death. I saved you from that fate, you ungrateful bastard!"

"I am not a bastard. Someday I'll find them, my parents. You'll see. I don't know why I was separated from them, but I will find them!" He shouted and dropped his sword.

"Where will you find them? I don't even know where they are? Gone from Spain, that's all I know! If the plague didn't take them, then the pirates did when they slit open the stomachs of Jews to find the gold they had swallowed. They are dead! You can be sure of it. Nothing but bones at the bottom of the sea." Lines of age crease Malaga's once handsome face, eaten away by years of anger, rage, and regrets. He looked up at the very image of Isaac as a young man. Why had he hated him so? Because he was a Jew? Incredulously a relative? No. It was the warm loving family, the beautiful women so in love with their men, the mother he never knew. He met Isaac's eyes and confessed, "You have an aunt, Elisheba Braganza, somewhere here in Portugal. Perhaps she is still alive."

It was seven years since Isaac had seen his family in Naples. King Ferdinand had invaded shortly after King Charles, and war had raged within the kingdom, making it impossible for him to return. He lived alone in a simple waterside cottage on the island of Monopoli, and to pass the long lonely days, Isaac found solace in his writing. Though his fingers were stiff and gnarled, he forced them around his quill and was able to write for an hour at a time.

He had been writing at his desk when he stopped for a moment to listen to the lonely cry of a seagull, reminding him of a child's cry from far, far away. For the first time, he suddenly thought that he might die completely alone, never to see his family and his beloved Rebecca again. To shake off the morbid thought, he stood, taking a moment to straighten his back, and then shuffled outside. He walked along the beach and watched the seagulls dart back and forth as if they were playing with the waves, but today they did not cheer him. A great sadness fell over him as he watched the rhythmic water roll in and out, reminding him of his childhood in Portugal. Then thoughts of the fate of the Spanish and Portuguese Jews who were forced into baptism at the time of King Manuel's marriage to Ferdinand and Isabella's daughter assailed him. He thought of his lost little Isaac, of Carlos Málaga, of his family in Naples under siege until he lifted up his arms as if to push it all away. He looked up at the blue *sky*, and cried, "Why, Papa, why? Didn't I do as you bade me? I tried Papa, I tried so hard but I failed, miserably, you, my people, my family, myself." He fell to his knees and wept. "I did as you bade. You would have me a king's treasurer?"

An old, bitter anger swelled into a rage seizing him. "And so I served my kings! Afonso, Ferdinand and Isabella, Ferrante, Alfonso. I served them, all, down on my knees, sometimes groveling at their feet, sometimes speaking like an equal. And I raised money for them, Papa. Oh yes, I raised money, but it was never enough! They burned us, Papa! They burned us at the stake! Jonathan, Jonathan is dead, long dead . . . ." He fell to the ground, weeping. Finally, after a long while, he drew a deep breath. He was a man alone, living with words, thoughts, ideas. As he slowly stood he thought, "But a man cannot live like this forever, Papa." He needed his wife, his family, desperately missed them. Turning his back on the water, he shuffled back to the cottage.

A few days later on his usual walk along the water's edge, his thoughts, this time, concentrating on a particularly difficult portion of *Deuteronomy, Isaiah*, he looked up to see someone running toward him. As if to shorten the distance between them, the man's arms were stretched out wide. Then suddenly Isaac recognized Joseph, his young son, Joseph, the name felt so sweet on his lips, and he ran. He knew not how, but he ran and they embraced. Having grown painfully thin, he was practically lifted off the ground in Joseph's strong arms.

"Joseph, Joseph!" Isaac cried.

"Father, it's been too long." Joseph relaxed his embrace and gently took his arm and guided him back toward the cottage.

"Your mother?" Isaac stopped to ask.

"She's fine." He hesitated. "Lonely, sad—she misses you terribly."

"Have you wed?"

"Yes."

"And Samuel married?"

"Yes, Samuel too! You should see the children." Joseph laughed.

"Well, let's go in, and you must bring me up to date. The war is not over yet, is it?"

"No, not yet, but I think by the end of this year we can expect peace."

"And King Ferdinand will be victorious?"

"I'm quite sure."

"Then I will never return to Naples."

"I thought as much. That's why Judah and I decided I must come to see you. We are moving the family to Venice."

"Venice?"

"Our papers are all in order, and all we wait for is your approval. I might add that if you don't approve, Judah, Samuel, and I will personally carry you out of here."

They had reached the cottage and went inside.

"Will you have something to eat?" Isaac asked.

"I am starving." Joseph laughed nervously. He was anxious for his father to approve the plan to move the family. Rebecca had grown very weak, and the whole family was anxious to see them together again, before it was too late.

Isaac had hired a woman to take care of his needs, and she had prepared a thick fish stew which was now steaming in a large black kettle on the hearth. Isaac spooned some out for Joseph. Starved for his family, Isaac watched Joseph's every movement and as he took a bite of bread, he felt as if he were the one eating, nourished by the sight.

Joseph laughed. "Someone watching us would think you'd never seen anyone eat before."

Isaac took Joseph's hands into his own. "I remember a day, right after you were born. I was holding you and staring at your tiny hands in my own large ones. And I realized what a miracle a new born life is, so much hope for the future, and look at how much I've missed in your life, in all my children's lives. My life had been impoverished without you. I live like a man imprisoned, with only my books to keep me company."

"We've decided that this has gone on for too long. We are not asking but demanding that you join us in Venice." He looked away, out at the sea. "Mother is getting old. She misses you terribly. I don't know how much longer she has . . . ."

Isaac held tightly onto Joseph's hands. "You don't have to tell me. It's all I've thought about these years . . . waiting for this war to end."

"Judah and I have decided. There is not going to be a debate."

"I had hoped that there would be peace that I would be able to return with King Alfonso."

"And do you really think you still can serve the kings! Look at you, father! Will you give up your life in the service of kings?"

"It was what my father demanded that I do," Isaac said, letting go of his hands.

"And now we, your children, all of us, are demanding that you come home."

"Little Isaac? Any word?" Isaac asked.

"No," was all Joseph was able to manage in reply.

Knowing his father far too well, Joseph decided to change the subject, but he had promised Judah that he would not return without their father; he would not be dissuaded. He also knew how stubborn his father could be, so he said, "Have you done much writing?"

They both looked at the cluttered desk in the far corner of the room. A twinkle appeared in Isaac's eyes. "It has been my sustenance." He got up, shuffled over to his papers and then handed them to Joseph.

Joseph studied the titles: *Days of the World, Passover Sacrifice, Inheritance of the Fathers, Wells of Salvation* and *Deeds of God.* As Joseph glanced at the last title, Isaac said, "This last one is for Judah, and all my sons."

"Me?" Joseph asked incredulously.

"Yes, of course. I read Judah's *Dialogues of Love* and I was truly impressed! So, he has become the poet, Leone Ebreo?"

"But how did you get hold of his work?" Joseph answered, glowing with the knowledge that his father had him in his thoughts.

"Ah, I have ways." They both laughed.

"Well, what do you think of our Leone Ebreo?"

"I thought it so good that I studied Plato again."

"And?"

"My view is a little different from his, but, still, I have been influenced by him."

"I'm sure he'll be very proud."

They enjoyed the simple repast laid before them and then, Joseph sat back and smiled.

"Well, what is your point of view?"

"I agree with Plato that the Earth is destructible; however, I don't think that it will collapse into its original elements."

"No?" Joseph smiled.

Isaac suddenly realized how little time he had given to Joseph and Samuel. It was Judah who had always commanded his attention, and yet here was this charming young man, clearly versed in all that he had taught Judah over the many years. He was proud of him, and his hunger for his family, for Rebecca was now unbearable. He had been in the service of kings long enough. It was time for him to go home and "home" would be wherever his family was. He answered his younger son who was clearly expecting a debate, the kind he had so often engaged in with Judah.

"No. There will be fire and brimstone the likes of which has never been seen before, but from the ashes a new kingdom will be born, as foretold in the Bible. It will be the everlasting kingdom for which we need not our bodies or our world as we know it. It will be a purified world where the love and peace that we seek so vainly today will exist for everyone."

Joseph could not answer him, perhaps the way Judah would have done, but instead, he stood and made his way outside. The time for debates was over. Isaac smiled, following him outside.

As they walked down to the water, Isaac saw that life had sent him much misery and pain, but there had been many blessings too. His sons had made a good decision, without him, better even than the path he had chosen. Venice was the perfect compromise for him. He knew he could not stay here any longer, but he was enjoying Joseph's reversed parental concern.

"But we live in this world now, today, with war and hatred. The Fifth Kingdom will come whether you are living here or in Venice with your family. You must come with me, father. Wherever we wander, let us find our peace in each other. For now, father, it will have to be enough."

Smiling, beaming at his son, Isaac nodded and said, "Somewhere along the way, I must have done something right."

Rebecca was sitting in a chair by a warm fire in their small but elegant villa in Venice. Her head shook noticeably as her fingers worked feverishly on a little shawl for her grandchild who was playing next to her. As the door opened, a cold draft caused the fire on the hearth to blaze, and Rebecca turned to see who had entered. Though Isaac stood beside Joseph, she didn't recognize him. Most of his fine silver hair was gone, and he had become emaciated. She thought to herself, "Who is this stranger with Joseph?" Then, as she stared at the face before her, she began to feel as though she were looking at herself, a part of herself that had been missing for a very long time. She didn't remember standing or walking across the room, all she knew was that she was finally in his arms.

"I can't believe it's you!" she exclaimed.

"How did I survive without you these years? I don't know." His body shook as he wept.

"Don't, my love. You'll make yourself sick, and then what shall we do?" Rebecca said as tears streamed down her cheeks.

"Father!" Bathsheba cried, running to him. Within moments, it seemed the whole family had gathered. Isaac was holding little ones he had never met, hugging Rachel and his sons, Samuel and then Judah. He choked for a moment when a tall golden haired young man walked into the room.

"Jonathan," Isaac said as if he were looking at a ghost.

"Yes," the young man answered, understanding that his grandfather was mistaking him for another.

When Isaac embraced his grandson, he found great solace in the young man's muscular body, his healthy face, his twinkling blue eyes. He was embarrassed that he held him for so long, but for a fleeting moment, he felt as if he were embracing his brother-in-law, his friend. Isaac whispered a prayer for the boy's protection; this Jonathan was a happy, healthy young man, not someone so shackled by past misery that he could not enjoy the life God had given him.

"Isaac, we must speak," his son-in-law, Joseph, said.

"Not now, Joseph!" Judah sternly cut him short.

"What is this?" Isaac asked. "Why are you shouting?"

"It's not important now. It's time to think of your family, nothing else!" Judah answered.

Isaac turned to his son-in-law. "In a little while, my boy, we'll talk," he said and gave him a wink.

The women prepared a wonderful meal of lamb and vegetables. The tomatoes were ripe and the olives slick and black. A thick soup simmering with fish and cabbage, rosemary and thyme bubbled in a huge black kettle, and the children sang as they had never done. Isaac sat mesmerized by these little people, his own flesh and blood, throbbing with life, with love, maybe not exactly understanding who he was, but they seemed to understand that someone important in their lives had come home. As he stood to say the prayer over the wine and the bountiful table, he raised his cup of wine and said, "I have eaten with kings in royal palaces, I have traveled and lived in many lands, but I have never truly appreciated the riches, the beauty that was always mine. My family, though home is now Venice, it is good to be here, finally, with those I love! May we never be parted again!"

"Amen!" the family cried.

"L' Chaim!" they said with one voice. The family's prayers had been answered. All were home now, save one.

As the dishes were cleared, and the men stood up from the table, his son-in-law approached Isaac once again.

"If I may have a word with you?"

"Yes, of course." Judah grabbed Isaac's arm to stop him, and Isaac gave his son a wink. Judah let go. They retired to the small room which had been converted into a library. Isaac ran his hands over his beloved manuscripts.

"You know of course that Vasco da Gama has succeeded in finding an ocean route to India," Joseph said.

"Yes. It's strange that Cristóbal still hasn't found the lands of Khan with his western voyages."

"Very disappointing, I imagine, for the Catholic Monarchs."

Isaac smiled and in a whisper questioned, "Divine retribution?"

Joseph laughed. "I'm afraid I can't answer that. But Isaac, you must realize what Vasca da Gama's success means for Portugal-and for Venice."

"I can imagine the Council of Ten here in Venice must be frantic over the new Portuguese spice trade."

"They're concerned, indeed, concerned, and threatened. One of the members of the Council has approached me and asked if you think we can use your influence with King Manuel to negotiate a fair trade treaty with them."

"Joseph, as his treasurer, you knew King Manuel better than I did when we were in Portugal. What do you think?"

"I did meet the king on several occasions, but that was so long ago with so much tragedy in between. I don't know if he would remember me, but I'm sure he would remember you."

"Yes, of course, the treasurer to the Duke of Braganza, my Prince, Fernando. I loved him well," Isaac said softly, his eyes growing misty.

"Isaac," Joseph said, interrupting his reverie. "May I tell the Venetian Council that you will speak to them?"

"Yes, if you think it will be of some help, I will speak." Joseph gave him a hug then helped him up to his chambers.

Rebecca was waiting for him, having known what was on Joseph's mind. After he had settled into bed next to her, she said with great conviction, "Isaac, I have never asked anything of you. I have followed you from foreign land to land, making a home for you, waiting for you for years on end, but I can't anymore. Don't go to Portugal." When he tried to interrupt, she said, "I know that's what Joseph wants, what the Venetian Council wants, but hear me out! You have dedicated yourself to one ruler after another until there was nothing left for me, for our family. The little ones don't even know who you are. We don't have much time left. Please don't go. If you do, I don't think I will be here when you return."

Isaac held her in his arms and whispered, "And where will you go, my love? How can you speak of leaving me?"

There was that old twinkle in his eye, and she knew that he was making light of this.

"I would never leave you by choice, Isaac, but I've grown so weak that when I lie down at night, I don't think I will rise in the morning. I've only held on this long to see you come home."

Isaac held her tightly and kissed her wrinkled brow. "I will not leave you again. I'm too old to make the trip. I do want Joseph to go, so I will speak to the Council, and they will see the wisdom in sending him instead of me. I'm also hoping that when Joseph is there, he might find out what has happened to our little Isaac," and a great pause, "and to our Elisheba."

"I think of them often," she said softly.

"There is not one day when I don't think of them, of Jonathan, of Fernando. Yes, the Council must be convinced to send Joseph. Besides, I can't even ride a horse anymore. Can you imagine me arriving at the Lisbon Castle in a litter like some old lady?"

They both laughed; it was the first time either had laughed in a very long time.

"Well, for once in your life you are making some sense."

"Yes, you know, I think you're right." He squeezed her and said, "I love you, Rebecca. I was so lost, so alone without you these seven years."

"I was afraid that I might die without seeing you again," she chocked.

"Don't talk that way," he chided; then, lifting up her chin, staring into her thin wrinkled face, he saw only the young girl he had married. "We will not be separated again."

Though Joseph traveled to Portugal and met with King Manuel, he was not able to conclude a treaty concerning the spice trade. Venice lost its monopoly to the countries who ruled the seas. Joseph made several inquiries concerning Carlos Málaga, little Isaac. He couldn't find the great Braganza family and Elisheba. He had hoped that young Isaac might have found his way to her, but it was as if they had all vanished from the face of the earth, as if none of them had ever existed. He did find out that after the death of King João, Málaga had sold Isaac's castle, but he could not even find Carlos Málaga. Devastated more by the loss of family than the failed trade agreement, Joseph was forced to return to his family with the disappointing news that Elisheba and the child were truly lost.

On a bright sunny day in early spring of 1506, just as red roses were budding, Rebecca was tending her bushes when she felt a sharp pain in her heart. She cried out and fell. Isaac was the first to find her on the ground. His arms felt so strong as he lifted her and held her against his breast. She wanted to tell him that she was fine. The pain was gone, and she could feel the warm sun on her face, Isaac's body close to her, but her eyelids were too heavy to lift.

After Rebecca's death, Isaac had no desire to leave his room. He wanted only to be with her, to hear her voice just once more. Though Judah carried him down each evening to sit by the fireside and watch his grandchildren play, he preferred to watch the caravels sail from his upstairs window during the day. Some were outward bound, some coming into port. And with each ship that arrived, Isaac prayed that it carried Elisheba or little Isaac, that he would see them one more time, that the family would finally be whole. On a quiet December afternoon in 1508, as he sat and watched the ships, he felt as though he was the wind that filled the sails.

CHAPTER 40

It was a sultry, peaceful night, but a heaviness filled Judah's heart. He desperately needed some fresh air. He missed his father more than he ever could have imagined. Though they had been constantly separated in life, he never fully realized how very much he loved him until he was really gone. He walked out and let the night air fill his lungs. He stared at the stars circling around, and for a moment, his mind was lost in the heavens. When his gaze focused back on the land before him, far off in the distance, on the top of a gentle rise, Judah saw a small black figure, a man riding a horse, slowly growing larger, as he rode toward him. It took Judah a minute to realize that the rider was heading for his home. Slumped forward in his saddle, a black hood concealing his face, the rider seemed weary, but the horse continued to move forward, lifting one heavy hoof after the other, and then stopped when Judah reached out to touch him. Judah shivered though the air was warm and still.

"Who are you?" he asked the night rider.

"I am seeking Judah and Isaac Abravanel," a young man answered.

"You have found, Judah," he said cautiously. "My father has passed on."

The young man dismounted. He walked over to Judah and threw back the hood. The moon shone brilliantly against his soft olive skin. Judah gazed upon the face of his father as a young man. He thought for a moment that he was dreaming, that the moon had cast a spell upon him, when the young man said, "I am your son, Isaac Abravanel."

Completely overwhelmed, his heart raced as fast as it did on the day he held his son in his arms for the very first time.

"My boy, my boy . . ." he repeated over and over again, unable to fully comprehend that his prayers, the whole family's prayers, had been answered. They held each other for a long while, and then Judah stepped back to stare into the eyes of his son. "So like my father," he whispered. Young Isaac beamed as tears streaked his cheeks. Together, with their arms around each other, neither one willing to let the other go for even one moment, they entered the Abravanel home.

Bibliography

Abrahams, Israel. *Jewish Life in the Middle Ages.* New York:
Meridian, 1958.

Ausubel, Nathan and Maryann. *A Treasury of Jewish Poetry.* New York:
Granger, 1957.

Barreto, Mascarenhas. *The Portuguese Columbus Secret Agent of King John
II.* Trans. Reginald Brown. New York:
Macmillan, 1992

Bear, Yitzak. *History of the Jews in Spain.*

Dos Passos, John. *The Portuguese Story: Three Centuries of Exploration and
Discovery.* New York: Doubleday, 1969.

Encyclopedia Judaica. Vol. 2, 10, 11. New York: Macmillan,
1971.

Graetz, H. *Popular History of the Jews.* Trans. Rabbi A.B. Rhine. New
York: Jordan, 1935.

The Holy Scriptures. Philadelphia: Jewish Publications,
1961.

Irving, Washington. *Tales of the Alhambra.* Ed. Miguel
Sanches. Madrid: Pol. II, La Fuensanta, Mostoles, 1982.

Ivanova, Anna. *The Dance in Spain.* New York: Praeger,
1970.

Kayserling, M. *Christopher Columbus and the Participation of the
Jews in the Spanish Portuguese Discoveries.* New York:
Herman, 1968.

Langer, W.L., ed. *An Encyclopedia of World History.* Boston: Houghton
Mifflin, 1972. 309.

Lea, Charles. *A History of the Inquisition of Spain.* Vol. I. New York:
Macmillan, 1908.

Livermore, H.V. *A New History of Portugal.* New York:
Cambridge UP, 1976.

Lofts, Nora. *Crown of Aloes.* New York: Doubleday, 1968.

Madariaga, Salvodore. *Christopher Columbus.* New York: Macmillan, 1940.

Mariejol. Jean Hippolyte. *The Spain of Ferdinand and Isabella.* New Jersey: Rutgers UP, 1961.

Minkin, Jacob S. *Abarbanel and the Expulsion of the Jews from Spain.* New York: Behrman's, 1938.

Morgenstern, Julian. *Rites of Birth, Marriage, Death and Kindred Occasions Among the Semites.* New York: KTAV, 1973.

Morrison, Samuel Elliot. *Admiral of the Ocean Sea.* Boston: Little Brown, 1942.

Netanyahu, B. *Don Isaac Abravanel: Statesman and Philospher.* Philadelphia: Jewish Publication, 1972.

Nowell, Charles E. *A History of Portugal.* New York: D. Van Nostrand, 1952.

Payne, Stanley, G. *A History of Spain and Portugal.* Madison: UP Wisconsin, 1973.

Prescott, William H. *History of the Reign of Ferdinand and Isabella.* Vol. I. Philadelphia: Lippincott, 1872.

Roth, Cecil. *A History of the Jews of Italy.* Philadelphia: Jewish Publications Society of America, 1946.

—. *A History of the Marranos.* Philadelphia: Jewish Publications, 1932.

—. *Personalities and Events in Jewish History.* Philadelphia: Jewish Publications, 1961.

—. *A Short History of the Jewish People.* London: Horowitz, 1969.

—. *The Jewish People.* London: Horowitz, 1969.

Rubens, Alfred. *A History of Jewish Costume.* New York: Funk, 1967.

Scholem, Gershon. *On the Kabbalah and Its Symbolism.* Trans. Ralph Manheim. New York: Schocken, 1965.

Schwartz, Leo W. ed. *A Golden Treasury of Jewish Literature.* New York: Rinehart, 1937.

Sugar, Robert. *Journey of the Fifteen Centuries, the Story of the Jews of Spain.* New York: Union of American Hebrew Congregations, 1973.

Szule, Tod. *Portrait of Spain.* New York: American Heritage Press, McGraw Hill, 1972.

Walsh, William Thomas. *Isabella of Spain, the Last Crusader.* New York: Robert M. McBride and Co., 1930.

Weinzenthal, Simon. *Sails of Hope.* New York: Macmillan, 1973.

Zinberg, Israel. *A History of Jewish Literature and the Arabic Spanish Period.* Trans. Bernard Martin. Philadelphia: Jewish Publications, 1972.